TOO
WRONG
TO BE
RIGHT

ALSO BY MELONIE JOHNSON

Too Good to Be Real
Getting Hot with the Scot
Smitten by the Brit
Once Upon a Bad Boy

TOO WRONG

TO BE

RIGHT

A Novel

MELONIE JOHNSON

ST. MARTIN'S GRIFFIN
NEW YORK

First published in the United States by St. Martin's Griffin, an imprint of St. Martin's Publishing Group

www.stmartins.com

Designed by Devan Norman

Library of Congress Cataloging-in-Publication Data

Names: Johnson, Melonie, author.
Title: Too wrong to be right : a novel / Melonie Johnson.
Description: First edition. | New York : St. Martin's Griffin, 2023. |
Identifiers: LCCN 2022045422 | ISBN 9781250768827 (trade paperback) |
 ISBN 9781250768834 (ebook)
Classification: LCC PS3610.O366334 T669 2021 | DDC 813/.6—dc23
LC record available at https://lccn.loc.gov/2022045422

Our books may be purchased in bulk for promotional, educational, or business use. Please contact your local bookseller or the Macmillan Corporate and Premium Sales Department at 1-800-221-7945, extension 5442, or by email at MacmillanSpecialMarkets@macmillan.com.

First Edition: 2023

10 9 8 7 6 5 4 3 2 1

Mom.

The love you and Dad shared will always be an inspiration. As a writer of happy endings, I wish I could give you more chapters together. I'm so proud of how you continue on with your story and all the love you continue to give. And I know Dad is proud of you too.

TOO
WRONG
TO BE
RIGHT

CHAPTER I

Kat

"Why is there a crocheted penis lying on the floor?" Kat Kowalski demanded. It was five minutes to five on Friday night, and all Kat wanted to do was close up the flower shop and get on with her evening. She'd been attempting to do just that, briskly sweeping the store's floor, when the broom had abruptly encountered . . . something.

Ronnie, her coworker and second-in-command, leaned over the counter and inspected the object in question. "Yep. That's a dick."

"I know it's a dick," Kat confirmed. "What I don't know is what is it doing here?" She prodded the limp lump of yarn with her broom and it flopped across the shop floor like it absolutely did not give a fuck.

It was a very nice floor too. New. Installed last spring, the gleaming slats looked like hardwood, but they were actually made from repurposed bamboo stalks. Allen, the owner of the flower shop, had always been into conservation, but in the last year or so, he'd taken his green crusade to the next level. He'd installed solar panels and a rain barrel reservoir system and was researching geothermal heating options for a greenhouse.

But as far as Kat knew, her boss hadn't taken up crocheting genitalia.

The wind chimes over the shop's entrance jangled, the up-cycled metal gardening tools hanging from an old terracotta pot clattering against each other in a surprisingly melodic racket. On instinct, Kat dove, broom handle smacking the floor as she snatched up the mystery penis. She straightened and crammed her hands behind her back. "Laura." Kat exhaled, relieved to see it wasn't a customer who had entered, but their delivery driver. "It's just you."

"Hello to you too," Laura said as she flipped the open sign on the door to closed. "Were you expecting someone else?"

"No. But we found a, ah . . ." Kat waved her recent discovery in the air.

"You found my cock!" Laura exclaimed.

"That's *yours*?" Ronnie asked, stooping to pick up the broom.

"Yep." Laura nodded, wiggling her fingers in a *Give me* gesture. "It's my cozy cock."

Kat handed the object over. "It's your what, now?"

"Cozy cock," Laura repeated. "Or cock cozy." She shrugged. "I haven't decided yet." Laura set the cock in question on the counter. Then she reached around and grabbed one of the travel mugs that had collected on the shelf below the register thanks to the employees' caffeine habit. Another Allen rule: all reusable cups, all the time.

"What are you planning to do with that?" Ronnie asked.

Laura flipped the tip open. "Watch." She slid the mug inside the hollow space, then stood the handcrafted organ upright and stepped back with a flourish. "Ta-da!"

Kat's brows rose as she gazed upon the woman's handiwork. Tucked snug inside the, um, shaft, the mug did indeed look cozy. "Okay, that does look nice and warm, but why . . ."

"Why a cock?" Laura grinned. "I'm thinking about starting a side business. I've got ideas for a whole line of products."

"You might be onto something." Kat eyed the yarn penis propped on the counter. "They'd make great favors for bachelorette parties," she snickered. "Speaking of parties," she added, glancing at the clock over the door, "I've gotta finish closing. It's CCC night."

"Ah yes, your weekly movie night." Laura snagged the broom from Ronnie and took over sweeping. "Are you still doing that?"

"Yeah." Kat grabbed the clipboard hanging from a hook by the cooler and began to take inventory of the unsold bouquets. "But we skipped the last few."

"I thought your Friday night tradition was sacred," Ronnie said, removing their name tag and the THEY/THEM pronoun pin they wore and tossing both in a drawer by the register.

"It *is* sacred." Cocktails, carbs, and comedies had been a staple of Kat's life since college. She and her two best friends had been getting together for their Friday night tradition for the better part of a decade. "But lately Julia and Andie have been busy with other plans."

"Things must be getting serious if they're putting dicks before chick flicks." Ronnie tartly observed, counting down the register. "What about your dick, Kat?"

Kat lost her count. "Pardon?"

Ronnie blinked innocently. "How are things going with Chad?"

"Tad," Kat corrected automatically. Ronnie wasn't Tad's biggest fan and always said his name wrong on purpose.

"Any man's name that ends in 'ad' should come with a warning label," Laura said as she emptied the dustpan into the trash.

"I'll keep that in mind," Kat promised. She finished inventorying the bouquets and moved on to the single stems. Knowing Laura's history with her ex-husband Brad, she didn't fault the woman for her obviously biased opinion. "We've been seeing each other for almost half a year now, and things seem to be going well."

"Dating for six months . . ." Laura's nose crinkled in speculation. "I think I was pregnant with my first kid by then. *Not* that I'm suggesting you should follow in my delinquent footsteps."

Kat laughed. Laura was so chill, she often forgot the woman was more than a dozen years her senior, with a minivan and four kids, the oldest of whom was starting high school. "This is the first relationship I've had in ages that lasted longer than a month, but I don't think we're quite ready for that step."

The wind chimes jangled, and everyone's attention jerked to the entrance of the store.

"Speak of the spray-tanned devil," Ronnie muttered.

Kat blinked in surprise as her boyfriend entered the supposedly closed shop.

"Oops." Laura slid them a sheepish look. "I must have forgotten to lock that."

"Probably because you were distracted by your giant yarn wiener."

Smothering a giggle at Ronnie's snarky tone, Kat shifted her gaze back to Tad. "This is unexpected," she said, offering him a warm, albeit confused, smile.

"Sorry about showing up unannounced like this." He propped his elbows on the counter. "But I had to see you."

"That's sweet." Happiness fizzed inside her. Kat hung the clipboard back on the hook and joined him at the counter. "But I'm getting together with my friends tonight, remember?"

"Come on." He reached out and tugged on her braid. "You can ditch 'em."

"I really can't." She bit her lip, torn between appreciation for his apparent enthusiasm to see her and frustration at how easily he dismissed her plans. Her favorite Friday night ritual with her besties had been canceled the last three out of four times, once by Julia and twice by Andie. Kat had given them both a ton of shit about it. Threatened bodily harm if they canceled on her again. There was no way she was going to be the one to bail this time. "This couldn't wait until tomorrow?"

"Actually, no." The sharp edge to Tad's voice made it clear he was put off by the fact she was putting him off. "I really need to talk to you now." He shifted his attention to her coworkers. "Alone."

"We can take a hint." Laura scooped up her cock cozy. "Right, Ronnie?"

"Right." Ronnie held Kat's gaze. "Unless you want us to stay here?"

Appreciating their concern, Kat shook her head. "I'm good, thanks."

They disappeared into the back room and Kat's stomach knotted as she belatedly realized that when somebody said they wanted—no, *needed*—to "talk," it usually wasn't good. But things were good between them . . . at least she'd thought they were. "Is everything okay?"

"Everything is great." Eyes bright, Tad's entire body seemed to radiate an anxious sort of energy. He grabbed her hands and squeezed. "Better than great."

His obvious excitement was infectious, and Kat's initial concern began to ebb. "Tell me already," she encouraged, squeezing back. "What's happening that's so great?"

He beamed at her, flashing his perfect pearly whites. "My flight leaves in a few hours."

Flight? Kat pulled away from him, treading carefully. "You're going somewhere?"

"Canada."

"You're leaving the country?" she asked, voice rising as her heart plummeted. "Tonight?"

"You're upset." Tad sighed.

"I'm not upset," Kat began. "I'm . . . confused. Are you in trouble or something?"

"No." He snorted as if the idea were absurd. "Quite the opposite."

"Oka-a-y," she said slowly. "Then what's going on?"

"My big break!" He threw his arms wide and announced, "*Hot and Single!*"

"*Hot and Single?*" Kat repeated, voice rising once more. Now she *was* getting upset. And she had every right to be. Her boyfriend had just told her he was planning to appear on a reality TV dating show, one known for salacious hookups both on and off the screen. "You're going to be a contestant?"

"No. I'm going to be the new host."

"Oh." Kat paused. That was better, at least. "Wow." Now that the initial shock had passed, her brain tried to catch up. "You already got the job?"

"Not yet," Tad admitted. He turned, pacing around the store's freshly swept floor. "Last month I did a virtual casting call, and yesterday I found out I made the final cut."

"I didn't even know you'd auditioned." Kat tried to brush off the sense of disappointment that he hadn't mentioned anything to her.

"I didn't want to tell you in case nothing came of it. You know how it is."

"Um, yeah. I guess." As an actor, he went on auditions all the time, mostly for commercials. She didn't expect him to tell her about each and every one of those. But not only was hosting *Hot and Single* a much bigger deal than a commercial, it was something they shared, a common interest. They often watched the reality show together and had spent more than one date debating the merits of various contestants and speculating on who was sleeping with whom. "Wow," Kat said again, still trying to process the news. "This is . . . wow."

"I know. It's huge, right?" Tad's perfect lips curved beguilingly. It was that stunning smile that had first caught her attention across a crowded downtown bar, a radiant, rakish grin she was sure would capture the hearts of viewers everywhere. "They're flying me out for a screen test and some interviews with the producers."

"How long is that going to take?"

"A week or two." He reached for her again. "That's why we need to talk. I want to ask you something." He threaded their fingers together and tugged her forward, pulling her through the door of the shop. "I know it might seem like a lot," he said, stopping in front of his car parked along the curb.

"Let me guess," Kat said, tone dry, "you need me to drive you to the airport."

"No," he said, staring at her intently. "This is much more important."

Her pulse began to pound. Did he want her to come with him? She couldn't leave the shop, couldn't drop everything and leave her life here in Chicago . . .

"Will you take care of JoJo?"

"'JoJo'?" Kat echoed, thoughts still swirling, debating, making plans. "JoJo," she repeated as realization dawned. "Your hedgehog?"

Tad nodded, untangling his fingers from hers. "To bring her across the border, I'd need some kind of permit," he explained, opening the passenger door and pulling out a plastic storage tub. "Besides, I'm probably going to be so busy with show stuff, I won't have time to take care of her."

Bemused, Kat peered into the container. When she'd first met Tad's pet, she thought the little critter was charming. She'd never known anyone who owned a hedgehog before. Tad had said he'd only be gone for a few weeks. How hard could it be? "I guess I could," she said.

"I knew I could count on you." He handed her the container and reached back into the car, pulling out bags of supplies. "Thanks for doing this."

"Um, sure." With his flight only hours from now, he wasn't giving her much of a choice. Was it presumptuous of Tad to assume she would agree to watch JoJo? Absolutely. But it's not like she would have said no, and he obviously knew that.

Maybe this was the sign Kat had been waiting for, an indication their relationship was ready for the next level. He was trusting her with something important to him. Asking her to take care of his pet, something he loved. Kat smiled up at Tad. "It will be like we're coparenting."

"Coparenting?" His brow furrowed.

"Well, yeah. I'll be in charge of JoJo while you're gone, and then when you come back . . ."

"I'm not coming back."

Kat blinked. "But you said you would only be gone for a week or two . . ." Her voice faltered as a seed of doubt burrowed between her ribs.

"For the audition." Tad closed his car door and leaned against it. "If I get the job, they'll want me to start right away."

The seed sprouted, tendrils of concern creeping into her heart. "What if you don't get the job?"

"Ouch." Tad clapped a melodramatic hand to his chest. "Wound a man, why don't you."

Kat bit back a snarky reply. He'd told her he was leaving the country. And ditching her with his pet. Yet somehow he had the audacity to make a joke about *his* feelings being hurt.

Oblivious to the direction of her thoughts, Tad continued, "Hopefully, I'll get the hosting gig. I mean, I'm perfect for it. But if not, tons of shows film in Vancouver. Since I'm already out there, why not audition for as many of them as possible?"

Why not indeed. "What does that mean for the two of us?" she asked tightly.

"You and JoJo will get along great," Tad assured her.

He had to be acting purposely obtuse. Nobody could be this clueless. "I was talking about *us*." She gestured between herself and Tad. "You and me." The vines were thick now, apprehension wrapping around her lungs, cutting off her air. She fought for breath and forced the words out. "Are you dumping me?"

"What? No," he stuttered. "I figured you weren't interested in a long-distance relationship," he declared. "You're not . . . Are you?" His sandy brows crept up his perfect forehead, as if the idea were completely absurd.

"I might have been open to discussing the possibility." Kat shifted the tub with the hedgehog to one hip. "But you obviously aren't."

He didn't argue.

Yep, she was being dumped. Fears confirmed, Kat bent, gathering the bags of supplies sitting on the sidewalk with her free hand.

"Here, let me help you." Tad reached for one of the bags, but she jerked away from him.

"I got it," she spat.

"Come on, don't be like that." His tone managed to be both accusatory and aggrieved, implying the current situation was her fault.

Maybe it was. Kat dropped her gaze to the pudgy ball of spikes puttering around in the tub, considering. Not directly, of course, but maybe, if she stopped falling for assholes, she wouldn't find herself standing on the sidewalk, shouting at the jerk who'd told her he was leaving the country, and by the way, here's my pet rodent—or whatever fucking subsection of the animal kingdom a hedgehog was part of—as a parting gift. "I have a fucking right to be mad, don't you think?"

"You're mad?" For a heartbeat, Tad had the decency to look abashed. Some emotion that might not be related to his own feelings flickered across his chiseled features, but it faded as quickly as it surfaced, and he frowned in disapproval. "No need to swear at me."

"When I get mad, I swear. And to answer your question, yes, I'm fucking mad."

Tad let out a heavy sigh and grumbled, "I knew you wouldn't understand."

"Understand what? Why you'd dump me in the middle of the street?" A bubble of laughter escaped Kat. Tad's commitment to placing the blame at her feet was so absolute it was comical. If her hands had been free, she might have poked him in the chest, tried to pop a hole in that inflated ego of his. She settled for glaring daggers at him. "It's because you're a selfish asshole. Thanks for helping me figure that out. Good luck with the audition." She spun on her heel and walked away.

She'd planned to leave it at that. Calmly make her exit before she completely lost her shit. But between the hedgehog container and the bags of supplies, Kat belatedly realized she couldn't open the shop door. Frustration stiffened her spine and she turned to face him once more. "Goodbye, Tad."

The clatter of wind chimes broke the tension as Laura stepped outside. "Everything okay out here?" she asked.

"Yep." Kat slapped a sunny grin on her face. "You see the guy standing on the sidewalk staring at me?"

Laura leaned against the open door and peered over Kat's shoulder. "You mean your boyfriend?"

"Ex-boyfriend," Kat corrected. "Can you do me a favor?"

"You want me to stab him?" Laura wielded her crochet hook like a weapon, a half-finished cock cozy swinging wildly from the end.

"Nah, just flip him the bird. My hands are full." Without waiting to see if Laura would oblige her request, Kat scooted past, dodging the yarn penis and hauling everything into the store.

A moment later, Laura followed her inside, this time remembering to lock the door. "I told ya." Laura clicked her tongue, snarky yet sympathetic. "Gotta watch out for guys with a name that ends in 'ad.'"

"I'll keep that in mind for next time." Did she even want a next time? The longest relationship she'd had, perhaps ever, was over, and Tad had officially joined her hall of former flames. It was getting crowded in there. Kat suddenly felt very tired. Tired of dating jerks. Tired of thinking that this time—this guy—would be different.

Ronnie appeared in the doorway from the back room. "No more Vlad?"

"No more Tad," Kat simultaneously corrected and confirmed.

"What happened?"

"He dumped me," Kat said, dropping the bags Tad had dumped on her while dumping her.

"I offered to stab him," Laura added.

"Which I appreciated." Kat set the plastic tote containing JoJo on the counter. The spiky ball rolled, butting up against the side and coming to a halt. A snub nose appeared, topped by a pair of beady black eyes.

"What the hell is that?" Ronnie asked.

"A hedgehog."

"Oh." Ronnie moved closer and stared down at the creature. "He's a cute little thing."

"It's a she."

"Sorry," Ronnie apologized to the hedgehog with complete sincerity. "We respect each other's pronouns around here."

Laura bent over the makeshift carrier, taking a closer look. "Does this cutie have a name?"

"JoJo." Kat shook her head, recalling the night Tad had introduced her to his pet. Ironically, he'd mentioned he'd named the hedgehog after a contestant who'd appeared on *Hot and Single*. What a twist.

"Nice to meet you, JoJo. I'm Laura."

The hedgehog's nose twitched, and Ronnie reached out a hand, pausing to ask, "Does she bite?"

"I don't think so." Kat shook her head. "I'm not even sure she has teeth."

"Let's see." Ronnie tickled the hedgehog's snout. "Open up, JoJo. Show me your choppers."

Laura snorted. "First, you're afraid of getting bit, and now you want to see her teeth?"

"Sure." Ronnie tapped JoJo's nose again. "That way I know what I'm dealing with."

"Well, appearances can be deceiving." Kat sighed, thinking of all the beautiful men she'd dated who turned out to be ugly on the inside. She ran the tip of her index finger over JoJo's quills. "Like these. They look sharp but actually feel quite soft."

Ronnie squeezed Kat's shoulder. "Are you okay?"

"I don't know." Kat picked at the edge of JoJo's container. "I thought this time was going to be different."

The look Ronnie gave Kat was equal parts sympathetic and exasperated. "You always think that."

"I've gotta be right eventually, don't I?" Kat said. "What's that expression? Even a broken clock is right twice a day . . ."

"We're not talking about clocks," Laura reminded her. "We're talking about cocks. Men are much less reliable."

"Let's avoid the gender generalizations, please." Ronnie turned back to Kat. "What happened?"

"TLDR?" Kat gestured between herself, JoJo, and the bags of supplies on the floor. "Tad got a big break and is flying to an audition in Canada. He asked me to take care of his pet, said it was over between us, and took off."

"What a prick." Ronnie shook their head in disgust.

"Now who's generalizing?" Laura teased.

"Trust me," Ronnie said. "You don't have to own a prick to be one."

"True." Kat nudged the hedgehog onto its back. "Well, I'm done with them," she declared.

"Who?" Ronnie asked. "Pricks?"

"Jerks," Kat clarified. "Hot guys who think they're hot shit. I officially declare, no more."

"Yeah, right," Laura snorted.

"I'm serious!" Kat insisted as Laura and Ronnie both guffawed. "I know my radar is broken. My compass is calibrated to assholes. What if I ignored my instincts and went for the *opposite* of my type? Someone sweet and nice."

"But you're not attracted to someone like that," Ronnie pointed out.

"Exactly," Kat agreed. "If I'm always chasing after Mr. Wrong, how will I ever find Mr. Right?"

JoJo scratched at the side of the container.

"Before we go looking for Mr. Right, how about we find some pet food?" Laura rummaged through the bags of stuff from Tad. "I think the little critter is hungry."

"What do hedgehogs eat, anyway?" Ronnie wondered.

"Ah-ha!" Laura waved a box of kibble in triumph. "Tad might be a narcissistic prick, but at least he left supplies." She sprinkled a few nuggets into the container, and JoJo began to nibble, making soft crunching sounds with the tiny teeth it turned out hedgehogs did indeed have.

"Oh my god, look at her little hands!" Ronnie cooed. "That's adorable."

"Much cuter than my offspring slurping mac and cheese," Laura agreed. "Which reminds me, I need to get going, I have my own hungry brood to feed." Stuffing her cozy cocks and yarn into her crochet bag, Laura prepared to leave. She paused to pat Kat on the back. "Welcome to the single parents club."

"Thanks." Smiling despite herself, Kat waved as Laura exited through the front of the shop.

"Sorry about the breakup," Ronnie said, locking the door again after Laura left. "At least you got this bundle of cuteness out of the deal."

"Did you hear that, JoJo?" Kat rested her elbows on the counter and watched the hedgehog munch away, blissfully unaware of how much her world had changed. "It's you and me now."

"And me," Ronnie noted. "Unless you're planning to take JoJo with you tonight."

Shit. Friday. CCC night. "Are you offering to watch her?" Kat asked. "How much is the average hedgehog sitter charging these days?"

"Depends," Ronnie said, a playful gleam in their eye. "Do you have any of your grandma's cookies upstairs?"

Kat didn't need to be asked twice. She gathered the bags and led the way up to her place. One of the best perks of managing the flower shop for Allen was the apartment that came with the job. "Are you sure all you want is some of Babcia's cookies?" Kat asked once they'd gotten JoJo settled.

"I want *all* of them, thank you." Ronnie popped the lid on

the cookie tin and plopped onto the papasan chair in the corner. "And you'll need to drop off the deposit at the bank."

"Done," Kat agreed. "Anything else?"

"Oh!" Ronnie exclaimed around a mouthful of cookie. "I almost forgot, there is one other thing. A delivery."

Kat blinked. "Tonight?"

Ronnie nodded. "The client specifically requested the drop-off happen at six thirty. Since it was after Laura's shift, I was planning to handle it."

Kat glanced at the clock. It was one of those kitschy cat clocks with the swinging tail and blinking eyes. A gift from her grandmother. Babcia had found it at the thrift store, dusty and broken. She'd tucked it under her arm like a lost kitten and taken it home. Now it perched on Kat's living room wall, as good as new. The tail twitched mischievously as the hands on the clock crept toward six. With all that had happened since closing the shop, Kat thought it would have been later.

But nope. It had taken less than an hour for her life to get upended. "Yeah, okay. I should have time to squeeze it in. Where?"

"O'Sullivan's Funeral Home."

"A funeral?" Kat froze, an unwelcome but familiar ripple of nausea washing over her.

"I know you hate these, but it's a small order," Ronnie assured her. "Everything's packed and ready to go in the delivery cooler. You'll be in and out in no time." Ronnie bit into another cookie, letting the hedgehog nibble crumbs from their finger.

"Fine," Kat grumbled. "I'll do it." She'd been dumped without warning, become the adopted parent of a hedgehog, and now she was headed to a funeral.

Not how she'd expected her evening to go.

CHAPTER 2

Mick

Mick O'Sullivan tugged at the collar of his shirt. It was six minutes after six on Friday night, and he was ready to get the evening
over with. He tugged at his collar again, giving in to the urge to
undo the top button. Across the room, his brother adjusted his
glasses, frowning in disapproval. Mick knew as soon as Joe got the
chance, he was going to give him hell for not wearing a tie. However, Joe was currently occupied comforting a bereaved widow, so
Mick was off the hook for the moment.

Not that a stern talking to, now or later, was going to change
anything. Mick could barely stand the collared dress shirts he'd
agreed to wear during services, he was not going to add a tie. Meanwhile, Joe seemed to enjoy being strangled by his clothes. Tonight,
he was dressed in one of his many impeccable ensembles, complete
not only with a crisp, buttoned shirt and tie, but a jacket and waistcoat too—the whole nine yards.

The suits were all part of Joe's charm. His older brother possessed a quiet sort of competence that clients found reassuring.
With a calm, unassuming demeanor that put them instantly at
ease, Joe's pleasant, polished appearance provided a sense of order
amid the chaos people often experienced following a death. A
useful quality in this business.

Mick glanced around, checking once again to make sure
everything was ready. Water pitcher full? Check. Clean glasses
stacked nearby? Check. Plenty of tissues? Check. The small room
was formal but cozy. One of the private suites the funeral home
reserved for mourning family members, with overstuffed chairs

and large comfortable sofas slipcovered in a tasteful, muted print that hid any manner of stains, from tears and snot to vomit and who knows what else. Grief was messy. This was where those closest to the deceased gathered to collect themselves before, after—and sometimes during—a service.

In one of those chairs sat an elderly woman draped in black lace. The first Mrs. Murphy, ex-wife of the deceased, impatiently tapped a silver-tipped walking stick. The tapping stopped and she pivoted, turning toward Mick.

Before she could ask, he dutifully reported, "Getting closer to six thirty, Mrs. Murphy." She'd been asking him for the time every few minutes since she'd arrived.

Tiny in stature but a giant pain in the ass, the woman had caused trouble from the moment planning for this funeral began. Not that Mick blamed her. If anything, he respected her fervent desire to help with the arrangements for her ex-husband's burial. Unfortunately, the second Mrs. Murphy did not share this sentiment.

Both widows had arrived this evening at six sharp and taken up positions on opposite ends of the family parlor. So far, all they'd done was stare daggers at each other from across the room, but Mick smelled trouble brewing.

"Excellent." The woman turned her attention across the room and smiled.

Mick did not like that smile.

It was a slow, taunting smile. An *I've got you now, bitch* smile. A smile that matched the gleeful victory in her eyes as she stared, unblinking, at her ex-husband's second wife. It was the kind of look that would have prompted ominous music to start playing if this were one of those campy shows his gran liked to watch. Whenever one of those real housewives cracked a smile like the one Mrs. Murphy was sporting, you knew something was about to go down.

God freaking damn it. He didn't need this tonight. Or any night, for that matter.

At first, Mick had assumed the woman was fixated on the time because she was waiting for her sons, who, as immediate family, were also invited to arrive early for a private viewing of the deceased before the service.

Now he wasn't so sure. His Spidey senses told him something was up. Blame it on the blood of generations of superstitious Irish running through his veins, his years studying human behavior while training to be a psychologist, or even his time as a bartender learning to read body language. Bottom line, Mick knew better than to ignore his intuition. With a nod to his brother, he exited the parlor and hurried down the hall. The door to the room where tonight's services were to be held stood open, confirming his fears.

He slipped inside. At the front of the room, someone was hovering over the casket. A woman. Blond. On the taller side. Mick had never seen her before, because there was no way he'd forget those legs. He crept down the aisle, his well-worn dress shoes silent on the padded carpet.

"It's going to be fine," she muttered. "Everything is going to be perfectly fine," she continued, talking to herself. Or maybe she was talking to the dead guy. "Don't think about what you're doing. Hurry up and get it over with."

Mick froze mid-step. *Get what over with?* "Excuse me," he called.

The woman ignored him, still too busy giving herself instructions. "Pretend he's a groom stiff with nerves," she directed as she leaned over the open casket. "And stick it in."

Stick what in where? "Excuse me," he repeated, louder this time.

"Ack!" Her body jerked, and she glanced at him over her shoulder.

Blue eyes met his, and Mick's steps faltered. Whoever she was, she was drop-dead gorgeous. Okay, maybe not the best choice of words, considering their current surroundings, but *damn*. He gathered himself and asked, "What are you doing?"

"What does it look like I'm doing?" One brow arched regally in haughty challenge before she turned her attention back to the casket. "I'm putting a boutonniere on poor Mr. Murphy here."

"Wait," Mick insisted. He wasn't sure what the hell was going on, but he did know that if anything went sideways with this funeral, Joe would blame him. "Stop!" Sprinting the last few steps to the platform, Mick reached for her arm.

The woman twisted, evading his grip. "Oh god, I think I touched him." She recoiled in horror, stumbling on the platform.

In a morbid instant of clarity, Mick realized if she continued on her current trajectory, she'd face-plant into the casket. Instinctively, he wrapped his arms around her middle and yanked backward. The momentum sent both of them toppling to the ground.

"*Oof*," Mick grunted, the air rushing out of him in a painful *whoosh*. Her ass had landed squarely on his breadbasket. It was a very nice ass, he couldn't help noticing, even if it was cutting off his oxygen supply. The thick braid of her hair was in his face, golden silk tickling his nose, smelling of wildflowers, like some fairy princess escaped from a tower.

She untangled her legs from his and scrambled to her feet. "What is your problem?" she demanded.

"*My* problem?" he repeated, blinking up at her. "You were the one playing pin the boutonniere on the body." Mick stood gingerly and gestured at the casket. "Listen, princess, you're lucky you didn't end up in there with him."

Her face flushed, blue eyes blazing with a fire so icy Mick swore he was getting a brain freeze. But whatever furious response was forming on her lips got lost in the cacophony of noise that erupted as the two widows burst into the room. They were shouting—at him and the woman by the casket or at each other, Mick couldn't tell—probably both.

Calm as ever, Joe trailed behind the melee. Slowly, Mick noted. At a safe distance. Which was unfortunate, because if his brother had been moving faster, he might have been able to prevent what happened next.

Mrs. Murphy Number Two marched up to the coffin and reached inside. But before she could snatch the flower that had so recently been pinned to her dead husband's lapel, Mrs. Murphy Number One stepped in to block her with her cane. A scuffle ensued, the two elderly ladies still yelling, now hurling insults. This time, Mick had no doubt they were directing the shouts at each other.

"Ladies, please," Joe implored the women, "there's no need for such boisterous antics."

Mick doubted either of the warring widows could hear his brother. They were "boisterous" enough to wake the dead. His mouth twitched at his own rather terrible choice of words. He shifted his gaze to the woman responsible for this chaos, surprised to find her watching him.

The icy look she was giving him was full of accusation, as if she blamed *him* for the current debacle. The noise continued, increasingly nasty insults coloring the air, the tussle threatening to turn into a brawl. She glanced at the fray, then turned her attention back to him.

Again, one golden eyebrow arched in challenge, like she was wondering if he was going to do anything. She had a point. Someone needed to put a stop to this nonsense.

Shaking his head, Mick sucked in a breath and bellowed, "LADIES." In contrast to his brother's placid tone, Mick's voice was loud and sharp, cutting through the bickering. "I think we've had enough of that."

Unfortunately, the Mrs. Murphys didn't agree. His order only seemed to rile them up more, spurring the argument from verbal to physical. He should have known better. They'd passed the point when talking could have defused the situation. It was time for action.

Mick stepped between the women, wrapping an arm around each of their waists. Then he hoisted them both off the floor and swung around, one cantankerous old lady braced against each hip. He nodded to his brother, the two women in his arms still hollering at each other. Before he headed down the aisle, Mick glanced over his shoulder and gave the ice princess a wink. She bristled, and he chuckled, hustling the bickering biddies out of the room.

He set them down in the foyer. Like windup dolls let off their strings, as soon as their feet hit the floor, they both immediately attempted to return to the funeral parlor. Mick planted himself in front of the entrance, blocking their way. He crossed his arms. "Now then," he began conversationally, his training in psychology kicking in. "What's this all about?"

The first Mrs. Murphy pointed a gnarled finger. "She wouldn't let me choose any of the flowers."

"Because it's not your place," the second Mrs. Murphy countered. "*I* was his wife when he died. *I'm* his widow."

The ex–Mrs. Murphy made a screech like a banshee and went on the attack. Mick stuck out his arm, halting the cane mid-swing. He shot a warning glance at the "official" widow Murphy. If she didn't tone down the haughtiness, she was likely to get bludgeoned.

From behind him, a throat cleared. Mick shifted his stance in the doorway, letting his brother pass through. The blond boutonniere bandit followed close behind. Unable to help himself, his gaze traveled down her long, lithe legs, remembering how they'd felt tangled with his.

"Now then," Joe said, interrupting Mick's impromptu and admittedly inappropriate perusal. "Miss Kowalski here has been kind enough to shed some light on the situation." Straightening his tie and glasses, Joe addressed the ex-wife. "Mrs. Murphy, did you place an order for a floral delivery?"

"I did. A bouquet with asters. And a buttonhole for Frank."

The feisty old woman notched her chin. "It's what he would have wanted."

"How would you know anything about his wants?" The other woman scoffed. "Frank was *my* husband."

"He was my husband first," the older Mrs. Murphy countered, pounding the floor with her cane. "How dare you refuse to let me, or any of my children—*his* children—help plan his funeral? Things may not have worked out between us, but Frank was always a good father to our boys and remained a good friend to me." Her eyes narrowed shrewdly. "That's what this is about, isn't it? You're jealous."

"Of *you*?" The second Mrs. Murphy huffed out a breath so hard it ruffled the other Mrs. Murphy's silver bangs. "Hardly."

"Yes, you are. That's why you refused to include asters in any of the arrangements, even though you knew they were his favorite flower. You've always hated how he sent me a bouquet of them every year on my birthday. Frank was a class act." The woman clicked her tongue. "Can't say the same for you."

And the claws were back out. The second Mrs. Murphy howled in outrage and lunged.

"Ladies! Ladies, please. Remember why you're both here." Mick placed a soothing hand on the second Mrs. Murphy's shoulder. "To honor your dearly departed husband." He rested his other hand on the first Mrs. Murphy's shoulder. "And ex-husband." He kept his voice free of censure. "It's obvious you're feeling emotional because you both cared for the man very much, and he cared for you."

"Exactly," Joe added. Either his brother sensed an impending injury claim or Joe had finally had enough because he joined Mick, moving to stand between the two women and patting them both on the back gently. "How would Frank feel to see the two women he loved most in his life come to blows?"

"The old guy would have loved it," Mick muttered under his breath. He fought the grin threatening to spread across his face and schooled his features into something more appropriately solemn.

He shifted his gaze and caught the florist watching him again. Was it his imagination, or were her lips twitching too?

"Now then." Joe tactfully eyed the grandfather clock on the other side of the foyer, the one next to the stand with the guest book. "The service will be starting soon. If you wish to have a private moment with the deceased before the other mourners begin to arrive, we best be about it." Joe offered an arm to each widow. "But you have to promise to behave yourselves," he warned before escorting them through the doors and back down the aisle to the casket.

"Do you think they'll be okay in there?" the florist asked. "Together, I mean."

"Probably." Mick nodded. "Now that they got it out of their system. It's an emotional day." He slapped his hands together. "Well, I suppose that settles that."

She stared at him, blue eyes still holding a lingering chill. "You're not going to apologize?"

He stared back. "Apologize for what?"

"For accosting me over a . . . a . . ."

"Corpse?" he offered helpfully.

She winced. "Coffin," she corrected.

"With a corpse in it," he couldn't help adding.

"Stop saying that word," she hissed, glancing in the direction of the subject in question.

Mick lowered his voice. "I don't think Mr. Murphy can hear you."

"No, but his wives can."

"I'm pretty sure they know he's dead." Still, he shut the parlor doors, allowing the women some privacy. As Joe had said, other guests would be arriving soon.

"That's not what I mean." She shook her head in frustration. "Isn't it disrespectful to call a dead body a . . ."

"Corpse?"

She glared at him as if she knew he kept repeating that word on purpose to annoy her.

Which was fair. Because that's exactly what he was doing—and enjoying it immensely. He studied her for a moment. Not a hardship, as she was absolutely gorgeous. Stunning, really. The kind of pretty he usually avoided. The kind of pretty that usually spelled trouble. But there was something about her that pulled at Mick, and he couldn't help being curious. "It's rather strange," he mused.

"What is?"

"For someone who delivers flowers to funerals, you're pretty squeamish about dead people."

"Weddings are more my thing." She sniffed. "I don't usually handle funerals, and I certainly don't usually get attacked for doing my job," she added accusingly.

"How was I supposed to know who you were?" he protested. "Or what you were doing?"

She tilted her head, golden braid falling over one shoulder. "Is that supposed to be an apology?"

"Look, I walked in and saw somebody messing with the corp—" He stopped himself. "With Mr. Murphy, and I reacted. You could have been desecrating the poor man."

"With a boutonniere?" Her blue eyes widened, emphasizing the doubt in her voice. "I was simply following the delivery instructions. I had no clue a flower was a point of contention that would lead to . . ." She waved a hand toward the doors.

"Yes, well, Mrs. Murphy does have a flair for the dramatic." His mouth quirked. "Both of them."

"I picked up on that myself," she said, a reluctant grin tugging at her lips "Who knew funeral homes needed bouncers."

"You'd be surprised," Mick snorted. He could recall several occasions when a scuffle had threatened to turn a service into a boxing match. "You think it's easy hauling off two squabbling biddies with your bare hands?"

"I suppose instead of asking for an apology, I should be thanking you, Mr. . . . ?"

"O'Sullivan. And you're welcome."

"O'Sullivan?" Her brow arched.

"It's a family business. The stiff in the suit is my brother, Joe. The one with the glasses, not the one in the coffin," he added with a wink.

"I gathered that," she replied dryly. "Nice to meet you, Mr. O'Sullivan."

"Call me Mick," he said, offering her his hand. "Miss Kowalski, was it?"

"Kat Kowalski, from Allen's Arrangements." She took his hand, wincing when he shook it.

"Shit." Mick frowned at their joined hands. "You're bleeding." He pulled a pack of tissues from his pocket and dabbed at the cut. "Did one of the Golden Girls scratch you? I didn't realize you'd gotten caught in the crossfire."

"I didn't." She took over, holding the tissue in place and piercing him with a frosty glare. "I must have stabbed myself when some jerk walked in and scared the pants off me."

Her words immediately conjured images of those long legs, bared to his gaze. Mick swallowed. "Sorry about that," he said, pushing the thoughts away. Jesus, he was an idiot. He reached for her uninjured hand. "Come with me."

"Where are we going?" she asked.

"This jerk is going to get you patched up."

"I'm fine," she protested.

"You will be," Mick agreed, tugging her down the hall and not letting go until he reached the office. She hovered in the doorway, her curious gaze a tangible weight as she watched him rummage in the desk. He opened a drawer and pulled out a Band-Aid. "Will this do?"

"I told you, I'm fine," she said, still dabbing at the cut.

From the other side of the room came a long, flirtatious whistle.

Kat jerked her head in the direction of the noise. "What was that?" she demanded.

"What was what?" Mick asked, feigning ignorance.

Across the room a voice called out, "Hell-o-o-o-o, gorgeous!"

Her brilliant blue eyes narrowed. "Are you a ventriloquist or something?"

He laughed. "Nope." He tore the Band-Aid open and gestured for her to come closer.

Gaze still suspicious, she inched into the office, searching the room for the source of the sound.

Mick waited, wondering what she would do when she found it.

After a moment, she halted, eyeballing the large cage that had initially been hidden from view on the other side of the door. "There's a bird in here."

"There is," he confirmed, but refrained from offering anything further.

She stared at him, obviously waiting for an explanation. When none was forthcoming, she turned her attention back to the cage. "It's true that funerals aren't usually my thing, and maybe you do need bouncers, but I'm pretty sure large exotic birds aren't a standard feature." She paused, then added, "Or birds of any size or kind for that matter."

"They probably aren't," he agreed, watching as she moved closer to the cage. In response, the bird moved closer too, hopping along its perch until its beady black eyes were inches from hers.

"Hello." She smiled at the bird.

"Hello," the bird echoed, cocking its red-and-yellow-crested head to the side and studying her.

"I'm Kat," she said, pointing to herself. Then she pointed to the bird. "What's your name?"

"Seamus," the bird chirped.

"Seamus," Kat repeated. She turned to look at Mick. "Is that Irish?"

"Well, he is an O'Sullivan. My grandfather named him." Mick gazed fondly at the old bird. "How you doin', Seamus?"

"Fine, fucker."

She blinked. "Did he just call you . . ."

"Yep." Mick bit back a grin. "Granda taught him most of his vocabulary too."

"I see."

"He's a naughty boy," Mick said fondly, turning the criticism into a compliment. "Aren't you, Seamus?"

"Naughty boy, naughty boy," the bird sang, whipping its head from side to side in a comical dance move.

Kat giggled, and Mick could tell she was charmed by the bird's antics. Everyone was. Well, mostly everyone. His brother couldn't stand being around him. The feeling was mutual, as Seamus didn't care much for Joe either.

"What kind of bird is he?" Kat asked, reaching a hand toward the cage.

"A cockatoo."

"I've never seen a pink one like this," Kat said, stroking the plump fluff of salmon-colored feathers on Seamus's chest.

"Careful," Mick warned, moving around the desk to join her. "He bites."

Kat froze.

"I'm kidding." He chuckled softly. "Though I think this is my last Band-Aid, so better safe than sorry."

She relaxed, but Mick noted how she still pulled her hand back slowly.

"Don't worry. He's never bitten anyone. Well, except my brother, Joe."

"The 'stiff with the glasses'?"

"That's the one." Mick reached for her hand. "Here, let me check the damage." He gently peeled away the tissue covering the cut and examined the thin red line running across the heel of her palm. She was right, it wasn't serious, but he bet it stung like a bitch. "I'm sorry you got hurt," he said. "This probably wasn't how you expected to spend your Friday evening, huh?"

"You have no idea," she admitted dryly.

Mick felt a pang of disappointment. He focused on peeling off the protective backing on the bandage. "Hot date with the boyfriend?"

"Not tonight." Her voice shifted, grew caustic.

Mick knew he should leave it at that, but he couldn't. Keeping his attention on her hand, he positioned the Band-Aid over the scratch. "But there *is* a boyfriend?" he asked, smoothing his fingers over her bandaged palm.

"There *was*," she corrected, tilting her face to meet his gaze.

A fissure of awareness sparked through him and his hand tightened in reflex, closing around hers.

"However," she added, slipping out of his grip, "that's none of your business."

"None of your business!" Seamus echoed. The bird hopped toward Mick, squawking aggressively. "Eejit!"

A snort of laughter escaped Kat. "Your grandfather again?" she asked, turning to Mick for confirmation.

He nodded, chuckling. "If I had a dollar for every time Granda called someone an eejit . . . hell, for every time he called *me* that . . ."

Her lips pursed in a mischievous twist of a smile. "I think I'd like him."

"I think he would have liked you too," Mick said, meaning it. "If he was still around."

"Oh." Her face fell, a note of genuine sympathy in her voice. "I'm sorry."

"Don't be. Granda led a good life," Mick assured her. "Besides," he added, tapping the cage. "A bit of him is still with us in Seamus here."

The cockatoo whistled a few notes of an Irish tune.

"More than a bit," Mick amended.

Kat laughed again. "It was nice to meet you, Seamus." She braved reaching her finger into the cage once more and stroked the crest of feathers on his head. She shifted her gaze to Mick, blue eyes twinkling as she eyed him up and down. "Not sure if I can say the same for you."

"Hey," Mick blustered, making a show of being offended while inside he was reeling, skin tingling every place her gaze had landed. He opened his mouth to return fire with a sarcastic comeback, but his mind suddenly went blank. She was so damn gorgeous. And funny. And fun to talk to. "Well, it was very nice to meet you," he said, the honest admission slipping out before he could stop it.

"Is that so?" she asked.

He nodded, and the teasing grin playing about her lips unfurled into a wide sweet smile, so warm and bright Mick wanted to bask in it. Stand there and soak it up like sunshine.

"Mick?" His brother's voice carried down the hall like a roll of thunder. "Where are you?"

Mick blinked. He'd completely lost track of the time. "Shit."

"Naughty, naughty," Seamus chided.

"If that isn't the pot calling the kettle black," Mick grumbled.

Sure enough, a moment later, his brother appeared in the doorway and Seamus greeted Joe the way he always did: "Hey, asshole!"

Joe shot the foulmouthed bird a dark look before turning to Mick. "The guests are starting to arrive for the service."

"Oh." Kat's face paled. "I better get going," she stammered, backing out of the office like the place had caught fire.

Immediately, Joe offered Kat his arm. "Allow me to walk you out."

"I can do that," Mick insisted, rushing forward.

"You need to get the slideshow started," Joe said in a tone that brooked no arguments. "I'll escort Ms. Kowalski."

Ever the gentleman, Joe tucked *Ms. Kowalski's* hand into the crook of his elbow. Mick scowled. He'd like to escort his brother off a bridge.

"Um, thanks," Kat said to Joe. She paused to glance in his direction. "I guess this is goodbye."

Mick didn't want it to be goodbye, not yet, but his bossy brother's interference really didn't leave him much of a choice. Swallowing his frustration, he pasted a casual smile on his face and waved. "Bye."

"Bye-bye, gorgeous!" Seamus let out another long, low whistle.

"You got that right, buddy," Mick agreed fervently. He shook his head. A few minutes ago, he'd been tussling with her over a coffin, wondering who the hell she was. Now he was wondering if he'd ever see Kat again.

Not how he'd expected his evening to go.

CHAPTER 3

Kat

Head down, heart racing, Kat allowed Joe to guide her through the halls of the funeral home. As he'd said, guests were starting to arrive. The quiet voices and solemn murmurs triggered a nervous sort of nausea. Her stomach churned, and she gripped Joe's arm tighter while he maneuvered them through the growing crowd in the foyer.

When they reached the exit, Joe offered to walk Kat to her car.

"That's not necessary," she said. Any other time, Kat would have eaten up his gentlemanly manners with a spoon and licked the bowl clean for good measure. "But thanks."

"No, thank *you* for your help this evening," he said, holding the door open. "And for your patience."

Kat appreciated his kindness, but the last thing she felt right now was patient. All she wanted to do was get the hell away from that building. "No problem!" she chirped.

Once outside, she forced herself to turn and wave farewell. Then she booked it to the parking lot. She reached the delivery van and paused to catch her breath, filling her lungs with brisk evening air until her pulse slowed and the panic that had begun to build subsided.

The hybrid engine was nearly silent as it hummed to life. Kat frowned at the clock glowing on the dashboard. So much for "in and out in no time." She'd expected the delivery to be quick. Drop and dash. She didn't think she'd actually have to go anywhere near a . . . a corpse. With the way her day was going, if she didn't show up soon, CCC night would be canceled again. Kat sent Julia and Andie a quick text through their group chat, letting them know that she was on her way.

Less than twenty minutes later, she headed up the stairs to Andie's place, each step a familiar groove in her memory. She'd lived here in college, sharing the space with both Andie and Julia, and had been the first to leave after graduation, taking the apartment above the flower shop. Not long after, Julia had moved to a matchbox-sized studio downtown. Andie's parents owned this condo, so she'd stayed, and their Friday night cocktails, carbs, and comedy tradition had continued on. For how much longer, she wasn't sure.

Kat pushed away the sad thoughts as she pushed open the door. "I'm here," she announced, setting her purse on the kitchen counter and perusing the snacks arranged on the island. Her stomach began yowling the way it always did when she was hungry.

"Finally!" Andie declared. She and Julia were sprawled on the couch, drinks in hand.

"I see you started without me," Kat observed.

"One cocktail," Julia promised. "As a test run."

"What does our resident mixologist have on the menu for tonight?" Kat asked, more than ready for a drink.

"A mango daiquiri." Andie bustled into the kitchen and set about making a fresh round.

"That sounds promising." Kat watched her friend roll the rim of a glass in what looked like sugar but was speckled with a red substance. "How is it?"

"Fantastic!" Andie crowed.

"It's great," Julia confirmed, sliding off the couch and joining them in the kitchen.

Kat kept her eye on Julia, watching for any hints to the contrary. Andie liked to experiment. Sometimes the drinks she came up with were good, and sometimes they were . . . not so good. Julia gave her a subtle thumbs-up and Kat relaxed.

"Do you two really think I don't know you're passing secret messages to each other?" Andie demanded. Her dark eyes flashed, more amused than offended. "Trust me. It's good. I tried this recipe out on Curt last week and he loved it."

"Well, if Curt loves it, then it has to be good, right?" Julia teased, her voice managing to be affectionate and sarcastic at the same time.

"Jules has a point." Kat watched as Andie measured shots from several different bottles. "Curt loves everything you make. Even that drink with Malört. Which we can all agree was objectively awful."

"It was disgusting," Andie admitted. She brushed the fringe of bangs out of her face and added, "But I think he might have actually liked that one for real."

"No," Kat said, accepting the finished cocktail Andie offered her. "He likes *you* for real." More than liked, Kat thought, staring into the contents of her drink and wondering how it would feel to have that kind of unconditional support. Someone who loved everything about you—flaws and god-awful cocktails and all.

Kat traced a wistful finger along the sugared rim of her glass. She'd never had that kind of support from a romantic partner. That's what she wanted. What she was wishing for. Someone who would put her first in a way nobody else ever could. She licked the sugar from her finger. "Whoo, that's got a kick," she said, surprised at the spicy burst of flavor on her tongue.

"Serrano chile," Andie explained.

Curious, Kat took a sip of her cocktail. "Ooh, this *is* good." She sighed with pleasure, savoring the first sweet hum of alcohol in her veins. "I forgive you for not waiting for me."

"Why were you late, anyway?" Andie asked, stacking several pieces of cheese on one cracker. "After all the shit you gave us for missing the last few Fridays, I'm surprised you weren't camped out on my couch at six fifty-nine."

"I probably would have been," Kat admitted, "but Tad stopped by the shop when we were closing."

"Oh?" Andie arched one dark brow. "What did Mr. Aquafresh want?"

Despite herself, Kat smirked at her friend's nickname for Tad, which had stuck ever since Andie saw him in a toothpaste commercial. "To tell me he's leaving the country."

"What?" Julia cocked her head in surprise. "When? Why?"

"Tonight." Kat took a fortifying gulp of her cocktail. "He's auditioning for *Hot and Single*."

Julia gasped in outrage. "But Tad is *not* single!"

"He is hot, though," Andie said pragmatically. Julia elbowed her in the ribs. "Ow!" Andie scowled at Julia. "Well, he is."

"He *is* hot," Kat agreed. "And single," she added. "He broke up with me."

"Oh no." Julia set her glass down and wrapped her arms around Kat. "I'm so sorry."

The sympathy was almost Kat's undoing. She'd been too mad to be sad, but now the reality of her situation was setting in. She'd been dumped. Again. She was single. Again. The pattern was so consistent, Kat was starting to think that this was who she was. How she was wired. Something in her id or whatever was in control of her sense of attraction seemed to prefer guys that tended to be assholes.

"What an asshole," Andie growled, echoing Kat's thoughts. "I'm sorry, Kitty Kat, that sucks."

"It does suck." Kat sighed and stared into her glass. "I thought things were going so well. We'd been together for six months. *Six months!* I know it might not seem like a lot to either of you, since you've both been in relationships for over a year now, but it was a big deal to me."

"Six months *is* a big deal, Kat," Julia assured her.

"Don't forget we were in the same boat as you not that long ago," Andie added.

Her friend meant well, but the reminder stung. "Well, since my boat seems to be sinking, bottoms up." Kat raised her glass, swallowing past the burn in her throat. "The worst part is, I didn't see it coming. It was like a giant iceberg appeared out of nowhere and I sailed right into it—*pshew!*" She blew out her lips, making crashing noises. "He showed up unannounced, told me he was flying to Canada for an audition," she paused to gulp down more daquiri, "and oh, by the way, could I adopt JoJo?"

"Hold up." Julia the journalist wasn't going to let that pass without a fact-check. "JoJo is Tad's pet hedgehog, right?"

"*Was*," Kat corrected. "She's my pet hedgehog now."

Andie glanced toward the kitchen counter, as if checking to see if Kat had tucked the critter into her purse.

"I didn't bring JoJo with me," Kat assured her. "Ronnie is babysitting."

"Kat . . . ," Andie began, "if you needed to ditch us tonight, we would have understood."

"It's not like we haven't done the same to you a bunch of times lately," Julia added. "Thanks for being understanding about that, by the way."

"Look, I get it." Kat struggled to keep the hurt from her voice. "I won't say I *like* it, but I get it." She waved a hand, dismissing the last few weeks. "It was silly of me to think we could keep our weekly tradition going forever."

"You're not suggesting we shut CCC Fridays down, are you?" Julia asked, concern furrowing her brow.

Now Jules and Andie were exchanging looks. Kat bit her lip. She wasn't oblivious to when they did that either. The three of them had been best friends for too long to miss even the most subtle of cues between each other. Despite their closeness, lately it had started to feel like the lines of their friendship were being redrawn.

"No, nothing like that." If Kat wanted to be a part of mapping this new landscape, she better take some control while she still could. "But maybe we switch to making this a monthly thing instead of a weekly thing."

"I've been thinking of suggesting that myself," Andie admitted.

"Honestly, I have too," Julia chimed in, a little sheepishly.

Kat glanced between her friends. Andie and Julia may have been thinking about suggesting it, but they hadn't. Part of Kat had held out hope that they would tell her she was being ridiculous. That of course they would continue their weekly tradition forever. Obviously, that's not what either of them wanted, but they hadn't said anything because they didn't want to hurt her feelings.

"Then it's settled. From now on, CCC will only be once a month." It wasn't as good as weekly, but better than not at all. Kat had been right to speak up. The last thing she wanted was to force her friends to keep doing something when they didn't want to. She refused to turn her favorite thing into a pity party. "Neither of you will feel bad for having to cancel because you'll have time to make plans with your significant others, and I won't feel like a loser for being the only one in the group who isn't in a serious relationship."

"You're not a loser," Andie said firmly, her coach's voice brooking no argument. "And you never will be. No matter what your relationship status is."

"Andie's right. But if a serious relationship is what you want, it's going to happen for you, Kat," Julia insisted, her hazel eyes bright with passion. "The right one for you is out there somewhere. I know it."

"When did you become such a romantic, Jules?" Kat had always been the softie of the group, the dreamer who believed in finding your one true love and firework kisses and happily ever after. Whereas Andie had always been agnostic at best, and Julia was the skeptic.

"What can I say." Julia blushed. "Love has made me a changed woman."

"Things must be good between you and Luke," Kat said.

"Very good." Julia's blush deepened. "We're thinking of getting a place together."

"Wow." Kat comforted herself with more carbs. "Moving in together, huh? That's a big step, Jules. Exciting."

"It is. And scary as hell." Julia laughed.

Kat smiled. Her friend had a bright, bubbly laugh that made it impossible not to want to laugh too. "I'm happy for you." She raised her glass. "A toast to exciting, scary things." Kat clinked glasses with her friends and downed the rest of her cocktail.

Andie cleared her throat awkwardly. "I also have news."

"Oh god." Julia dropped the quiche she'd been about to eat. "You're pregnant."

"What?" Andie wheezed. "No! Curt asked me to move in with him. The house he's building is almost finished."

Kat wilted. "Isn't that all the way up in Milwaukee?"

"It is." Andie dropped her gaze, fiddling with her glass. "Which is why I haven't said yes yet."

"But you're going to," Kat concluded. She'd said things couldn't stay the same forever, but it was one thing to discuss change in theory and another to experience it in practice. "And then there was one," she declared, trying to quell the hint of jealousy creeping into her voice. It wasn't that she was jealous of her friends' happiness, or even envious of their current relationship status . . . except she kind of was. Not an angry kind of envy in which she wanted to take what they had, but more wistful. Wishing that she could have it too.

"I'm sorry things didn't work out with Tad," Andie said. "But . . . maybe it's a good thing," she suggested cautiously.

"Andie!" Julia chided.

"What? Like you weren't thinking the same thing," Andie shot back.

"You're right. Both of you," Kat said, cutting in before the two of them started bickering. "Breaking up with Tad was for the best," she admitted. "I've decided I'm done."

"Done dating?" Andie blinked. "Forever?"

"I hope not." Kat laughed. "I'm done dating assholes."

"Seriously?"

"Yep." Kat nodded. She didn't think it was possible, but Andie sounded even more incredulous than before. "The two of you give me hope," she confessed. "Like Julia said, the right one for me is out there somewhere. But I'll never find him if I keep chasing after the wrong ones."

"Exactly," Julia said. "Your problem is groundhogging."

"Tad left her a hedgehog, not a groundhog," Andie tsked. "Pay attention, Jules."

"Like you pay attention to my articles." Julia rolled her eyes. "I wrote about groundhogging for *TrendList*. It's a dating syndrome where you have a type of person you're drawn to and end up repeating the same mistakes over and over. In relationship after relationship."

"Well, that sounds familiar," Kat grumbled. "So how do I break the cycle?"

"Isn't it obvious?" Julia nudged her. "Go after someone different."

For one incongruous moment, an image of the dark teasing eyes of the guy from the funeral home flickered in Kat's mind. She shook her head and finished off her cocktail. "Easier said than done."

"What you need is a plan." Andie stood and gathered up the empty glasses. "And another drink."

"A plan . . . ," Kat mused. "A plan to stop dating assholes."

"How about starting with a list," Julia suggested.

"Sure." Kat smirked. Julia was known for her love of lists. "We can call it 'Top Ten Qualities Making Up My Mr. Right.'"

"Why not?" Andie glanced up from mixing drinks. "Do you have your notepad?" she asked Julia.

"Always." Julia pulled her ever-present notepad out of her purse. She ripped off a sheet and handed it to Kat.

"But I don't have a—"

Julia held up a pen.

"Thanks." Kat clicked the pen for a few seconds, thinking. Finally, she scrawled across the top of the page, "Recipe for Mr. Right."

"Recipe, huh?" Julia asked, sneaking a glance over Kat's shoulder.

"Mm-hmm." Kat winked. "I gotta come up with the right ingredients."

"Do you want a date or a drink?" Andie teased, rejoining them on the couch and handing Kat a fresh cocktail.

"First things first." Julia stole her pen back and wrote a number one on the paper. "What are the top qualities this supposed Mr. Right needs to have?"

"Um . . . he should be loyal." Kat set her glass down, gathering her thoughts. "Dependable."

Julia scribbled on her notepad, murmuring, "Not likely to take off for Canada. Got it." She glanced up. "What else?"

"He should polite, respectful, and very affectionate," Kat said. "Someone who enjoys cuddling."

"What about sex?" Andie prodded.

Kat shook her head. "Not important."

Her friends gasped their disbelief in stereo.

"I'm serious," Kat insisted.

Julia stared at her, eyes wide. "You don't think good sex is important to a relationship?"

"Not *most* important," Kat admitted. "No. How many times have I dated a guy simply because I thought he was hot?"

"Do you really want me to answer that?" Julia asked.

Kat shook her head. Knowing Julia, she'd have the exact number. "Let me rephrase that; how many times have those relationships worked out?" Kat made a circle with her fingers. "Zero. The point is, I've always let attraction guide my dating choices and they never last because intercourse is not a shortcut to intimacy."

Andie wrinkled her nose. "So your plan is to date guys you're *not* attracted to?"

"My plan is to do things differently. Like Julia said. Ignore my instincts and find someone who matches the qualities on my list."

"Loyal. Dependable. Affectionate. Likes to cuddle," Andie read from the paper. "You don't want a date. You want a pet."

"Well, then lucky me," Kat said dryly. "Thanks to Tad, I already have one of those." A breakup, a new pet, and a funeral. It had been a strange evening. Though it did give her an idea.

Kat grabbed the remote and did a quick search for the movie she wanted to watch. "But enough about that. It's CCC night. Andie made the cocktails. Julia provided the carbs, and I've got the comedy."

"*Four Weddings and a Funeral*?" Andie asked, reading the title as it popped up on the streaming service home screen.

"In honor of the delivery that made me late," Kat explained. "To a funeral home."

"I thought Tad made you late." Julia eyed Kat over the rim of her cocktail glass.

"I thought you hated funerals," Andie added.

"He did and I do," Kat agreed. Ever since her grandfather died, funerals gave her major anxiety. "But I promised Ronnie I'd handle it while they watched JoJo tonight."

"You could have canceled," Andie said again.

"Yeah," Julia chimed in. "You know we'd have understood."

"No way." Kat shook her head. "I needed this tonight. Especially after everything that happened. The breakup was the tip of the iceberg." She gave her friends a rundown of the rest of her evening's escapades, starting with almost taking a nosedive into a casket and ending with the strangely charming encounter with a foulmouthed cockatoo.

"A bird that swears in an Irish accent?" Andie snorted. "Sounds like you stumbled into a rom-com to me."

"Maybe she did." Julia nudged Kat with her elbow. "Tell us more about the guy you had a meet-cute with."

"We met over a dead body, it was definitely *not* a meet-cute," she protested. "Besides, I literally broke up with Tad less than an hour before meeting Mick." Kat ignored the tickle in her belly when she said his name. "That would be, like, textbook rebound. The definition of a very bad idea."

"A bad idea you're considering?" Andie pressed.

Kat's gaze caught on the Band-Aid stretched across her palm and a sudden rush of heat bloomed in her cheeks. Maybe she shouldn't have offered up quite so many details. Her friends were too intuitive. Tonight's encounter with Mick had been bizarre, but there had been something about him.

Her mind replayed how he'd picked up the bickering widows and carried them out the door, still hurling insults at each other. Before he'd hauled them away, he'd stopped and looked back at Kat, giving her a wink. Kat was a sucker for a wink. Even though she knew from experience what a wink meant. Guys who winked tended to be confident, cocky assholes. In other words—exactly her type.

The type she needed to avoid.

Which is why it was a good thing she was unlikely to ever see Mick O'Sullivan again.

CHAPTER 4

Kat

Kat scrubbed a hand over her face. It was Saturday, the shop's busiest day, and she was running late. Punching in the security code, she slipped through the back door and navigated the shadowed space by memory. The low rumble of generators from the various coolers filled the still air with a quiet hum, like monks gathering for morning prayer. After the night she'd had, the near silence was a welcome respite.

She flicked on the lights and set JoJo's cage on the break room table. She probably could have left her new pet upstairs, but she'd been worried about leaving the animal all alone in an unfamiliar space. In less than twenty-four hours, the recently adopted hedgehog was already taking over her life. She sighed and eyed the spiky ball tucked into one corner of the cage Tad had packed, a pink plastic hut shaped like a castle. "Finally tired yourself out, huh?" Kat whispered groggily.

For a moment, Kat contemplated going back upstairs and tucking herself into bed and curling into a similar ball. At least for a few more hours. She yawned. Caffeine. She needed caffeine. If she'd been smart, she would have taken the extra sixty seconds to brew a quick cup of coffee at her place before coming down. But her sleep-deprived brain hadn't been firing on all cylinders.

Allen refused to allow one of those single-cup machines into his business, not even after Kat explained they made reusable pods that you didn't have to throw out. Which meant they were forced to wrestle with an ancient coffee maker they'd nicknamed

"Mr. Pokey." The prehistoric machine was sluggish as fuck, but it did brew adequate, if not excellent coffee.

With Mr. Pokey sputtering and grunting away, Kat reviewed her schedule for the day. There was the Shaughnessy wedding, two quinceañeras, and a bat mitzvah. Thinking through the arrangements she had planned, Kat smiled. She loved her job. Truly loved it. Getting to be a part of the most important celebrations in people's lives, using her imagination to design and create the beautiful backdrop for their memories . . . it was the best.

"What are you grinning at?" Ronnie asked.

"Ack!" Kat jumped, glancing up to see Ronnie standing only a few feet away. "I didn't hear you come in."

"No shit." Ronnie chucked a thumb toward the coffee maker. "You can't hear anything while that beast is doing its thing."

As if on cue, Mr. Pokey let out a loud belch, announcing it had finished percolating. From experience, Kat knew to wait until the coffee maker let out a few more sputters before attempting to lift the antiquated carafe.

"Hook me up too, please," Ronnie said, hanging their jacket on a peg.

"Already on it." Kat handed Ronnie a mug then held her own cup up to her nose. "I don't think I've been this tired since college," she admitted, breathing in the heady scent of freshly brewed coffee, trying to wake up her brain.

"You didn't get home very late last night," Ronnie observed. "Did something happen after I left?"

"JoJo happened." Kat sipped her coffee and smothered another yawn. She really did feel like she'd become a single parent overnight. "Did you know hedgehogs are nocturnal?"

"No. But I do now."

"Did you also know hedgehogs run an average of twelve miles at night?"

"On that squeaky-ass wheel?" Ronnie eyed Kat over the rim of their mug. "No wonder you look like shit."

"Thanks." Kat made a face. The sound of JoJo's exercise wheel spinning endlessly was going to haunt her nightmares. If she ever fell asleep again. "I cannot tell you how close I came to chucking that 'squeaky-ass wheel' out the window." She didn't, but she wanted to.

"How is our little running rodent doing today?" Ronnie asked, clearly finding the situation amusing.

"See for yourself." Kat nodded toward the cage. "Sleeping Beauty finally tuckered herself out."

"Aw, look at you all snug and cozy in your pink palace," Ronnie cooed, taking out their phone and snapping a few pics of the napping hedgehog. "I'll say this about Tad, he treated his pet like a queen."

Kat nodded. "Yeah. It would be sweet, except for the fact that as soon as it was inconvenient, he ditched her royal highness's spiky ass."

"At least Tad made an effort to make sure she was cared for before he left," Ronnie pointed out, tilting the phone for a close-up of JoJo's little sleeping face. "You gotta give him props for that."

"Do I?" Kat set her mug down. "Why do we have to give men—"

Ronnie cleared their throat.

Kat paused. "*People*," she corrected. "Why do we have to give people credit simply for being basic decent human beings?" She crossed her arms. "Though let's be honest, it's usually men," she added.

"Usually," Ronnie agreed. "But not always."

"Is the bar really so low?" Kat sighed and topped off her mug. She was going to need the extra buzz to keep going today.

"Unfortunately, yes." Ronnie chuckled ruefully. "Yes, it usually is."

A sudden loud rapping on the front door of the shop startled them both.

Ronnie glanced at their phone screen and cringed. "It's almost five minutes past opening."

The brisk, impatient tapping grew louder.

It was Saturday. Which meant . . .

"Mr. Schwartz!" Kat yelped and rushed out of the break room, scrambling to the front entrance. She flipped the sign to open and unlocked the door, putting on her best smile for one of the shop's best customers. "Good morning, Mr. Schwartz."

"You're late," the elderly gentleman grunted. He shook out his umbrella and strode past her, muttering under his breath as he headed for the display of single stems.

His gruff attitude didn't faze Kat in the slightest. That's how he always was. She knew underneath that grumpy-old-man exterior beat the heart of a true romantic. Rain or shine, every Saturday morning like clockwork, Mr. Schwartz was the first customer of the day. He always got a fresh bouquet of flowers for his wife, and he always insisted on picking each stem himself. No premade bouquets for Mrs. Schwartz.

While he inspected the stock, Kat gave Ronnie a pointed look. They both adored the crabby codger and appreciated his steady business, but he was a pain in the ass to wait on. Long ago, they'd agreed to take turns. This morning, it was Ronnie's turn.

Message received, Ronnie took one more sip of coffee, then set the mug behind the counter, put on their name tag and pin, and went to assist Mr. Schwartz.

Kat turned her attention to the Shaughnessy wedding arrangements. She'd finished with the bridesmaids' flowers and was starting on the bridal bouquet when the wind chimes jangled over the shop's front door. She glanced up to see Laura strolling in. "Why don't you ever come in through the back like a normal employee?" Kat grumbled.

"Because I hate parking my minivan in that alley," Laura said. "It's bad enough I have to maneuver a delivery van in and out of that sadistic death trap. Good morning to you too, by the way."

"Sorry," Kat mumbled.

"Ignore her," Ronnie warned as they walked past, arms loaded with Mr. Schwartz's selections. "She's tired. And hangry."

"Hangry?" Mr. Schwartz repeated, shuffling up to the counter. "What is that?"

"When you're so hungry, you're angry," Laura explained. "My ten-year-old son is in this state constantly. I think he was born hangry."

"Hmpf." Mr. Schwartz sniffed. "You probably aren't feeding the boy enough."

Laura laughed, unoffended by the criticism. "He's a bottomless pit. I don't think there is such a thing as enough."

"Next Saturday, I'll bring you some of my wife's knishes. That'll fill him up."

"Wow, that's very nice of you Mr. S. Thank you." Laura beamed, her smile sincere. "And nice work today," she added, glancing at the flowers Ronnie was wrapping.

"Mr. S has impeccable taste," Ronnie agreed, handing the man his bouquet before ringing up the sale.

Kat nodded. "Mrs. S is a lucky lady."

"I'm the lucky one," Mr. Schwartz said as he inspected the gift he'd created for his wife. For an instant, the sweetheart hiding inside the grouch peeked out. The love and adoration shining in the old man's face was so bright and pure Kat wanted to burst.

But the moment was gone as quickly as it came. "Hangry," he harrumphed, giving Kat a solid dose of skeptical side-eye. "Nonsense," he muttered to himself as he shuffled toward the exit.

He paused to fumble with his umbrella, and Kat scurried to help. "I'll bring you a knish too," he told her, then glanced back at Laura and Ronnie. "Knishes for everyone." He shook his head, jowls quivering with disapproval. "But make sure you open on time next week."

"Yes, Mr. Schwartz," Kat promised, holding the door for him

as he passed through. Then she waved goodbye, even though she knew he wouldn't wave back. God love him.

Laura set her crochet bag on the counter, shaking her head. "It never ceases to amaze me how happy it makes that grumpy-ass man to buy flowers for his wife."

"Flowers can do that." Grinning, Kat got back to work on the bridal arrangement. A riot of ivory roses and trails of bells of Ireland, the color palette was simple, but the effect was stunning.

"I guess." Laura shrugged, crochet hook looping rhythmically. "I've never been much for a bunch of dying plants myself. I prefer my gifts to last longer than a week." She held up the new cock cozy she was working on. "Like this."

"Um, Laura," Ronnie muttered as the chimes rang over the door, "I don't think now is a good time to whip out your cock again."

Kat bit back a laugh and turned to greet the customer, but their attention was focused on Laura, who was busy stretching a rainbow-striped crocheted penis over her travel mug. Kat was about to apologize when the woman asked, "How much does that thing cost?"

"How much would you pay for it?" Laura asked, surprising Kat with her immediate and savvy response.

Ten minutes later, Laura was one cozy cock lighter and fifty bucks richer. She cackled gleefully. "I'm telling you, we should sell these here."

"If it was up to me, I'd let you set up a whole display rack of dicks," Kat assured her. "But you know Allen would FTFO."

"What doesn't make that man freak the fuck out?" Ronnie shook their head. "I've never known anyone who could be so chill and such a hardass at the same time."

"Careful," Laura warned. "He's probably spying on us right now." Laura shifted her gaze to the security camera mounted in the corner. "Hi, Allen!" She waved her crochet hook in the air.

"Do you think he actually watches us?" Ronnie asked.

"No." Kat hesitated. "Maybe." She thought for a moment, recalling all the times over the years Allen happened to appear whenever a minor crisis erupted in the shop. "Yes."

"You'd think he could trust us enough to handle things on our own," Ronnie grumbled.

"I don't think it's trust Allen has issues with," Kat said. "It's control."

"You mean like the way he tallies how much toilet paper the shop uses every week?" Laura snorted.

"Or how he weighs our non-compostable waste?" Ronnie crossed their arms. "He needs better hobbies."

"I know Allen can be a bit much," Kat admitted. "But he's passionate about the environment. And conservation is a big deal to him."

"You can be green without being mean," Ronnie said.

Kat frowned. "I wouldn't say he's mean. Difficult and demanding, yes. But not mean."

"Too bad you're not the owner," Laura said. "You'd make a great boss."

"I am your boss," Kat reminded her dryly.

"And you're doing a great job." Laura patted Kat's cheek and resumed her crocheting.

Was she? Kat had been working at Allen's Arrangements for half a dozen years now. Getting hired here was one of the first steps of her detailed business plan that stretched across the next decade. It allowed plenty of time to gain experience, build a reputation, pay off her school loans, and grow her savings so she could buy her own shop.

In the beginning, she'd checked off a lot of things on the list. Graduating college. Getting a business degree. Paying down her student loans. But after a few years, her progress had stagnated. Having a plan that was perfect on paper didn't guarantee it would be perfect in reality. Because sometimes, reality sucked. There were egregiously expensive unexpected visits to the dentist and tanking economies that flushed your interest rates down the toilet and all manner of unpleasant detours and roadblocks that could derail even the most steadfast of goals.

Now Kat was more than halfway through her ten-year plan, and unless she started taking the necessary steps to make her dreams come true, they would never be anything more than wishes. Even the list she'd made to help find her Mr. Right was a useless collection of adjectives until she actually got out there and started looking.

Like loose topsoil, Kat didn't have to dig far beneath the surface to reveal the root of her problem. She couldn't blame external obstacles. Those could be overcome. The reason she hadn't made more progress on her plans was simple. She was afraid. Afraid to take risks. Afraid to fail.

CHAPTER 5

Mick

Mick adjusted the strange material of the suit his sister had asked him to try on. "Asked" was a relative term. More like demanded. "Suit" was generous as well. Bodysuit maybe. Like scuba gear or some kind of skintight onesie. "Do I wanna know how much this thing cost?"

"You sound like Joe," Mary-Kate accused. Mick could hear her rolling her eyes at him through the bathroom door. "Do you have it on yet?"

"Yes."

"Can I see it?"

"No."

"*Mick.*" Mary-Kate's tone held a note of warning.

Face peeking out from a narrow oval in the hood of the suit, Mick stared at himself in the mirror. "I look absurd. Like something from the superhero reject pile," he grumbled. "Like I got my powers from falling in radioactive garbage."

"Open the door."

He ignored her, studying the strange material stretched over his torso. "Is that what this thing is made of?" He lifted an arm, sniffing the fabric. "Garbage?"

"Michael Colin Patrick O'Sullivan," his sister snapped, a perfect imitation of their grandmother when she'd had her fill of his shenanigans. "Open this door *now.*"

"Fine." He exhaled like the dramatic six-year-old he was being and flipped the lock.

His sister yanked the door open. She glared at him, dark eyes sparking with impatience. Mary-Kate was a redhead, but like Mick and Joe, she'd inherited the O'Sullivan eyes, a deep rich brown so dark they appeared almost black. She gestured for him to come out of the bathroom.

"Tell me the truth, MK." Mick shuffled into the hallway. "Is this thing made of garbage?"

"Organic materials," she replied, walking around him slowly, carefully examining the suit from all angles.

"That's just a fancy word for 'trash,'" he said, turning in a circle with her.

"Stop moving," she ordered. "It's not made of trash." She ran a hand over his arm, pinching the fabric between her fingers. "It's mushroom."

"I'm wearing a mushroom suit?"

"Well, fungi spores," she clarified. "They'll sprout into mushrooms later, once the decomposition process begins."

"That's it," Mick said, marching back into the bathroom. "I'm taking this off. Now."

"Not yet," she protested. "Joe hasn't seen it yet."

"What haven't I seen?"

At the sound of his brother's voice, Mick peered into the hall. Joe stopped dead in his tracks. "What on earth are you wearing?"

"Isn't it obvious?" Mick replied with as much dignity as one could muster while encased in fungi spores. "It's a mushroom suit."

"Look," his brother eyed him with befuddled amusement, "if this is about me wanting you to wear a tie . . ."

"It's not about the tie," Mary-Kate snapped. She pushed Joe out of her way and continued her examination. "How does it feel? Is it itchy?"

"Does it matter?" Mick grimaced. "Isn't the person wearing this going to be dead?"

"Good point." His sister's expression turned thoughtful as her gaze traveled over Mick from head to toe.

"What's this all about, Mary-Kate?" Joe asked, the brief moment of humor replaced with what Mick liked to call his brother's "Sam the Eagle face." As the oldest sibling, ever since their parents had retired and handed over the business to the three of them, Joe had taken his role as head of the family seriously. Very seriously. He reminded Mick of the eagle from *The Muppets*. The one who would occasionally emerge from his dressing room to declare, "You are all weirdos!"

Which, to be fair, they kind of were.

"The mushroom suit is part of the green burial initiative I want to launch," Mary-Kate explained.

"I don't know about this." Joe's brow furrowed, Sam the Eagle frown firmly in place. "It sounds very New Agey to me."

"Listen to my presentation before making up your mind."

"Can't this wait until our family business meeting on Monday?" Joe glanced at his watch. "I've got a client coming at ten."

"I'll make it quick, I promise," Mary-Kate begged.

"Fine." Joe sighed. He shifted past them, heading down the hall. "We can finish this conversation in the conference room."

"Um, can I take this off now?" Mick asked.

"But you're my visual aid," his sister protested.

"You've seen it. Joe's seen it. I've seen more than enough of it, and it's my meat suit rubbing up against fungi spores or whatever the hell is in this mushroom suit, so I'm changing." Mick slammed the bathroom door and stripped. He cringed at the thought of some stray fungi finding a dark crevice to cling to. It would have been great if he could have jumped in the shower, but he settled for splashing off in the sink. He tugged on his jeans and T-shirt and hurried to join his siblings.

They were seated in leather chairs at one end of a long, polished table. Most of the time, Joe used this space to meet with clients and review details for funeral and burial arrangements. But at least once a month, the three of them gathered in here for a business meeting.

Mick dropped into the chair closest to his sister and handed her the suit.

"Um, thanks." She accepted the wadded ball of fabric. "You could have folded it."

"I could have left it on the bathroom floor too," he shot back.

"This cost fifteen hundred dollars," Mary-Kate chided.

"How much?" Joe asked, eyebrows leaping over the wire rims of his glasses.

Uh-oh. Nothing got their big brother's attention faster than money. Cautious and steadfast, Joe considered it his duty to keep the family business afloat. Anything that threatened to rock the boat was cause for alarm. He didn't like change and balked at anything new, different, or expensive. Mary-Kate's mushroom suit was all three.

"Don't worry," she assured Joe. "This is a sample the company sent me."

"See, Joey? It's a free sample. You can close your mental checkbook." As the middle child, Mick often found himself playing mediator between his siblings.

"It's on loan, though, and I need to return it by tomorrow," she added. "That's why I didn't want to wait until our meeting to show you."

The family mortician, Mary-Kate was on a mission to start offering customers alternatives to traditional funeral practices by providing ways they could honor their loved ones and respect the earth at the same time. Mick agreed with his sister's ideas and shared her goal of modernizing the family business, but he also knew convincing their brother to make any changes would take some finessing.

While his sister waxed poetic on the benefits of burial by mushroom, Mick's thoughts strayed to the florist from last night. The way she'd watched him, a soft smile playing about her lips, as if she'd heard a joke and was about to share it with him. Mick realized he might be the punch line of that joke, but that was fine by him. If she found him amusing, he could work with that.

"Mick!" Mary-Kate shouted, poking him with her pencil.

"Hey, ow." Mick turned his attention to his sister. "What was that for?" he asked, rubbing his arm.

"You were tuning me out," she accused.

"Was not," he lied.

"Really." She leaned back in her chair, crossing her arms and staring him down, eyes narrowed with doubt. "What was I talking about?"

"The mushroom suit." He waved a hand toward the pile of material on the table.

"And?" Mary-Kate pressed.

"And . . . stuff."

"Ugh." His sister grunted in disgust. "I was explaining my plan for O'Sullivan's to start offering green burials. The mushroom suit is one option, but I also think we should sell tree pods."

"You mean those things where a tree grows from human re- mains?" Mick asked.

"If you were listening, you would know that yes, that's exactly what I mean." Mary-Kate breathed in slowly, and he could tell she was fighting for patience. "You would also know they are legal here and available for both standard burials and cremations."

Joe coughed. A polite little sound that still managed to be dismissive. "And I was explaining to our sister that offering these 'green alternatives' will cost us a lot of green." Joe grinned at his little pun, sobering as he added, "We're barely in the black as it is."

Mick tapped his fingers against the polished surface of the tabletop. "I know it feels crass, MK, but Joe has a point. O'Sulli-van's makes the bulk of its income on coffin and urn sales."

"It's not crass, it's business," Joe declared haughtily.

Mick was about to point out that the two were not mutually exclusive when Mary-Kate stepped in.

"I am aware this is a business. Correct me if I'm wrong, but in a business, people pay for services that they want." She paused, and when Joe didn't contradict her, she continued, "And that's what we will be offering them. I'm not saying we take away the options we already have available. Instead, I want to add some new alternatives for those who might want them."

Joe leaned back in his chair, tapping his pencil against the edge of the table. Mick knew his brother was balancing the razor-sharp edge of their profit margins in his head, assessing risk versus return. Numbers were Joe's game and Mick was glad to leave that part of the business to him.

"What do you think, Mick?" Joe asked.

"Huh?" Mick blinked.

"Since it's her proposal, Mary-Kate is obviously a yes. I'm leaning more toward no. What about you?" Joe tapped his pencil again. "What do you say?"

Shit. With ownership of O'Sullivan's split three ways, decisions were made by vote. If two of the siblings agreed, the motion passed . . . which meant, as was often the case, Mick was the deciding factor.

"Well, you're both right," he hedged. "This is a business. Granda always said the most important thing was to give the customer what they want. If they want to help the earth by turning their loved one into a tree or a pile of mushrooms or whatever, then why not. If that's what makes them happy, if that's what brings them peace—then it's our job to make sure that's what they get."

"Exactly," Mary-Kate said. "And if O'Sullivan's doesn't offer these options, people who want them will go to a funeral home who does."

"That's a good point," Mick said, turning to look at Joe. "We'd be ahead of the competition."

Joe narrowed his eyes, considering.

"Mick's right," Mary-Kate spoke quickly, "and he has a great plan to lure in new clients too."

"What's this about?" Joe demanded. "What plans?"

Mick winced. Mary-Kate had sensed their brother was wavering, and out of excitement or desperation or both had dragged Mick into the discussion to tip the scales . . . the only problem was, her stunt could push Joe in the opposite direction.

"Um, don't you have a meeting in here at ten?" Mick asked weakly.

"We've got time," Joe said, not even glancing at his watch. "What plans?" he repeated.

"They're not plans . . . exactly."

"Then what are they, *exactly*?" Joe pressed.

"They're more like ideas," Mick hedged. While Joe and Mary-Kate had stepped into their roles with confidence, their positions clear-cut, Mick's duties were vague. Mostly, he saw to it that his siblings had what they needed to do their jobs and kept them from killing each other. Over time, he'd become a jack-of-all-trades. Tackling whatever tasks needed doing and filling in the cracks.

Logically, he knew what he did was essential to keeping the business running smoothly, but it didn't seem like it. In his heart it didn't feel like enough. He wanted to do more. He'd spent a lot of time thinking about ways he could help make the business better and had recently started talking his ideas over with Mary-Kate. Which—Mick now realized—might have been a mistake.

"Go on," MK said. "Tell Joe about the bar."

"Bar?" Joe asked, voice rising in concern.

Yep. Confiding in her had definitely been a mistake. "Like I said, it's more of an idea than an actual plan." Mick swallowed. Guess he was doing this now. "But I've been thinking that what O'Sullivan's needs is a bar."

"O'Sullivan's has a bar," Joe reminded him. "Uncle Mike's."

"I'm not talking about that kind of bar," Mick snapped, temper stretching. Obviously, he was aware the O'Sullivan family had a bar. He'd worked at their uncle's pub all through college. Some-times, Mick swore his brother thought he was an idiot. "I'm talking about a bar here."

"Here," Joe repeated. "In a funeral parlor."

"It wouldn't be in the *actual* funeral parlor," Mick said.

"But it would be an actual bar?" Joe stared at him, and yep, his brother was looking at him like he had a screw loose.

"Yeah." He shrugged. "Well, sort of."

"Where would this 'sort of' actual bar go?"

His brother's skepticism made it clear Mick wasn't selling this well. He pulled his thoughts together and tried again. "The gathering room in the basement. We already host wakes down there. With some upgrades, we could turn it into a decent event space. A place for people to celebrate."

"Are you out of your mind?" The glare Joe was giving him indicated he certainly thought so.

"I'm serious," Mick insisted. If his brother already thought he'd walked off the deep end, he might as well keep going. "It's a growing trend. People want to remember their loved ones in a more positive way. Send them out with a party."

"He's right," Mary-Kate said.

Joe turned to her, eyes skeptical behind his glasses.

"I've heard buzz around this concept at some of the mortuary conferences I've been to. There's a few doing it on the East Coast, but I don't think anyone's tried it around here yet." She crossed her arms. "We could be the first."

"Come on, Joey," Mick pressed. "How different would this be from the wakes we already do? There's food and booze and music. Only now we'd offer it on a formal level." He scrambled for something Joe would understand, something that would make sense to his brother. "And we can charge for it."

"How much?" Joe asked.

Mick grinned, a spark of optimism flickering to life. Mary-Kate might have been onto something after all. They'd hooked his brother, all they needed to do now was reel him in. "Once we spruce up the space and make it a little fancier, we can start charging higher room-rental fees. Offer food and drink packages at different price points."

"I don't know," Joe said, shaking his head. "Sounds like a lot of work."

"I'll handle it," Mick assured him.

Joe eyed him skeptically. "Do you really think you can, little brother?"

Mick paled, the excitement that had been building fizzling out.

"Joseph Patrick Sean O'Sullivan," Mary-Kate snapped, sharp enough to cut week-old soda bread.

"I'm sorry," Joe said, not sounding sorry at all, "but we're barely clearing expenses as it is." He waved his pencil between Mick and Mary-Kate, pointing at each of them in turn. "And now you want to shrink our already miniscule profit margin with New Age burial alternatives, while you want to spend money on fancy up-grades for *parties*."

Mick smothered the flare of anger at the way his brother had sneered while saying that last part. "You gotta spend money to make money. Isn't that what they say in business?"

"Business, huh?" Joe eyed him shrewdly.

Mick didn't like the way his brother was looking at him. As if he was being weighed and measured and coming up short. "This is a business, isn't it? A family business." He crossed his arms and met Joe's gaze across the table. "And I'm part of this family."

"Fine," Joe said curtly. "You put together an official business proposal for this funeral bar, and I'll consider it."

"But . . . ," Mary-Kate protested, "What about *my* plans?"

"Include it in the proposal and bring it to the meeting on Monday," Joe instructed. "If the two of you can show me how you intend to make both of these ideas work, *without* blowing our budget, I'll consider it." As if that settled the matter, Joe raised his hand. "All in favor?"

Knowing he was going to get hell from his sister but hoping she'd forgive him once they figured this out, Mick raised his hand.

"Mick," Mary-Kate objected. "Why are you siding with him? I'm part of this family too. We could team up, two to one."

"Yeah, but if anything went wrong, Joey would say I told you so." Mick leaned closer to his sister. "I don't know about you, but I can't stomach the idea of having our brother lord this over us for the next decade."

"You're right." She frowned, considering. "We'd never hear the end of it."

"And then we'd have to look at that smirk he makes." Mick contorted his face into an impression of Joe at his smuggest.

Mary-Kate snorted. "What do you suggest we do?"

"We'll play Joey's game his way, and we'll win."

"I'm right here, you know," Joe reminded them from across the table. "I can hear you. And see you," he added, frowning at Mick.

"Good." Mary-Kate shot their brother an aggressively sweet and very toothy smile as she raised her hand in the air. "Then you'll be pleased to hear your motion has carried."

"Done." Joe tapped his pencil like it was a gavel. "I expect to see that proposal on Monday."

"No problem," Mary-Kate declared. She dropped her arm and reached for Mick's hand, squeezing it tight. "Right, Mick?"

"Right," he agreed, palms starting to sweat. He'd pushed for this, and if he couldn't deliver, it would only confirm Joe's doubts in him. "No problem."

Actually, there was one problem. One big problem. Mick had never written a business proposal before. And now he had two days to put one together.

CHAPTER 6

Kat

For the past several months, Kat had spent most of her Sundays with Tad. They'd grab brunch somewhere, then have sex, shower, nap, binge on reality TV, order food, and do it all over again. In stark contrast, this Sunday she'd gotten up alone, eaten a granola bar alone, showered alone, and tried to nap . . . alone. However, she wasn't actually alone, as one very noisy hedgehog with one very squeaky wheel was her constant companion.

That afternoon, around the time she and Tad would have been getting their second wind, Kat found herself pushing a loaded shopping cart down an aisle of the pet supercenter. And she wasn't alone. Kat nudged the flap of her purse open and checked on JoJo. Nestled inside a dish towel, the hedgehog's little brown snout twitched. Kat tapped it affectionately before tucking the flap closed again. Yes, she'd been that weirdo on the L with an animal in her purse.

Smuggling JoJo onto the train might have been against the rules, but she doubted it would be a problem here. A lot of people were shopping with their pets. A lady with a bunny on a leash strolled past and Kat considered whether she should get something like that for JoJo. She decided against the leash, though. Today's shopping spree had already gotten out of hand.

Kat eyed the loot in her overstuffed cart. She should probably put some of this back. After all, did a hedgehog really need a bed that looked like a donut? But it was so soft and squishy, and JoJo would look so cute snuggled in it.

Kat realized what she was doing. Between Tad dumping her

and her friends announcing they were about to cohabitate with their significant others, the hole she'd carried in her heart since she was a kid had started to grow. She could feel the dark hollow stretching and expanding, a gnawing emptiness fed by fear. Fear of being left behind. Of being alone. And now she was trying to fill the hole with stuff.

But buying shit wasn't going to solve her problems.

Mind preoccupied, Kat absently steered her heavy cart around the corner . . . and crashed straight into another customer. "Oops!"

There was a *whoosh* followed by a waterfall of tiny pings. Kat watched in dismay as hundreds of seeds spilled onto the store's tile. "Oops," she said again. She bit her lip and forced herself to look up, blinking in surprise. "It's you!"

Kat stared into the sable eyes of the dark-haired man she'd plowed into. "*It's you*," she repeated. "Mick." His name came out sounding like an accusation.

"That's me." He winked. "Kat, right?"

She nodded, pulse skittering. "I didn't expect to um . . ." Her voice faltered as she tried to gather her bearings. She didn't expect to what? See him again so soon? See him again ever? All of the above, frankly. "What are you doing here?"

"Buying dinner for Seamus." He held up the bag of birdseed. A few stragglers sprinkled out, ending with a pathetic final ping as the last seed landed on the floor. "At least, I was."

Her cart must have ripped the plastic open in the collision. Kat winced. "Sorry about that."

"You should be apologizing to Seamus, not me." The corner of his mouth kicked up in an amused smirk. "It's his dinner you've ruined."

A flirty grin tickled her lips in response and Kat clamped down, struggling to keep from smiling. She was not doing this. She was not falling for the first guy she met after her last breakup. That was the old Kat. The new Kat had a plan. A checklist. Maybe in addition to her Mr. Right checklist, she needed to make a second list, detailing all the reasons she was not falling for Mr. Wrong.

Kat gathered herself, grateful for her height that allowed her to meet Mick's gaze directly. There was something about him . . . something that pulled at Kat despite herself. She was a sucker for a smirk or a wink, and he wielded both with heart-fluttering ease. He may not sport the killer bad-boy appeal that had gotten Kat into trouble more often than she cared to admit, but there was a vibe about him. An energy beneath the careless exterior that spoke to her on a cellular level.

He was dressed in faded jeans and a sweater, cheeks shadowed with stubble, and dark hair mussed in a way that looked like actual bedhead as opposed to the artfully coiffured mess she'd watched Tad create. He was the epitome of *just woke up like this*. An image of Mick sleeping flashed in Kat's mind. Tangled in his sheets. He didn't seem to be a pajama guy, but she wasn't sure he was an in-the-buff type either. A fact that was irrelevant since she'd vowed to stop falling for guys simply because she wanted to fall into bed with them.

"Do I have birdseed in my hair or something?" Mick asked, running a hand over his head.

Kat blinked. "Um, no."

"Then why are you staring at me?"

Because I'm picturing you in bed and debating if you'd be naked. "I'm not staring. I'm uh, looking for Seamus. Where is he, any-way?" She glanced around the aisle, seeking a distraction. "Is he with you?"

"Seamus?" Mick choked back a laugh. "God, no."

"Oh," Kat said, disappointment coloring her voice. "It would have been fun to chat with him again. He's so spunky."

"Exactly my problem," Mick explained. "His vocabulary is a little too salty for public consumption. Also, I refuse to be one of those people who totes their pets around like children."

"What's wrong with that?" Kat asked, self-consciously tugging on the flap of her purse.

"Nothing," he admitted. "But that spoiled ball of feathers doesn't need another level of pampering to feed his ego. He thinks he walks on water as it is."

"He's a bird." Kat wrinkled her nose. "Doesn't he fly?"

"You're not appreciating my metaphor." Mick shook his head, attention shifting to the seed scattered at his feet. "I suppose I better get this mess cleaned up."

"Here, let me help," Kat offered. She knelt, scooping up seeds and pouring them into the bag—where they promptly spilled out the hole at the bottom again. "So much for that."

"Don't worry about it." He tied the ripped ends of the plastic bag into a makeshift knot and dumped a handful of seeds into the bag. Some stayed in this time—most did not. "That didn't work as well as I expected," he admitted.

"Should we call for someone?" Kat suggested. "You know, 'clean up in aisle seven' or whatever?" She stood and turned back to her cart, heart freezing when she noticed her purse was open. "Uh-oh."

"It's fine," Mick insisted, attention focused on the knot he'd made.

"It's not fine," Kat snapped, unable to quell the panic rising in her voice as she groped around in her purse. "I lost JoJo."

His brow rippled in confusion. "Who's JoJo?"

"My hedgehog." Kat dropped to her hands and knees. "JoJo!" she called, crawling down the aisle, frantically scanning the shelves for any sign of her spiky companion. How could the little critter have disappeared so fast? Must be all the hours spent running on that damn wheel. Kat cursed, furious with herself for being so careless. Why did she have to bring JoJo with her? Because she was lonely? It had been selfish.

"What does JoJo look like?" Mick asked.

"What do you mean, 'what does she look like?' She's a hedgehog." Kat's voice was sharp and condescending, fear making her testy. "She looks like a hedgehog."

"With honey-colored quills and a chocolate-tipped nose?"

"Yes," Kat said, running a hand along the baseboard of one of the shelves. "How did you . . ." She paused, glancing over her shoulder.

Mick was standing next to her cart. In his hands was the donut bed. And perched on top of the fluffy fake pink frosting was one very naughty hedgehog.

"JoJo!" A wave of relief washed over Kat, stronger than she could have anticipated. Slowly, Kat got to her feet. She felt wrung out, like she'd aged a year in the past minute. If this was what being a parent was like, she wanted nothing to do with it. "You gave me quite the scare, you little stinker."

"Aw, she only wanted to test out her new bed," Mick said. "I'd say she approves."

"And I was about to put that thing back on the shelf," Kat admitted. JoJo nestled deeper into the hole of the donut, whiskers twitching, perfectly content and absolutely unrepentant. Kat groaned. How was she supposed to resist such cuteness? "Fine, we'll keep the bed."

Mick chuckled and eyed the pile of stuff in Kat's shopping cart. "I think Seamus isn't the only spoiled pet."

"Hey." Kat bristled. "I'm still new at this." She rummaged in the cart for the fancy new pet carrier she'd picked out. "Ah-ha!" She held up the carrier in triumph. Unzipping it, she gestured at Mick to pass the recent escapee over. "JoJo was an unexpected acquisition," she explained.

"How does one accidentally acquire a hedgehog?" Mick asked.

With JoJo settled safely inside the carrier, Kat zipped it up and set it in the front of the cart, next to her purse. "It's a long story."

"Oh?" Mick's dark brows arched with curiosity. He leaned against a shelf, crossing his arms, and offering her a lazy smile. "I've got time."

Her insides fizzed and Kat struggled to repress the flirty grin tugging at her lips. She dropped her gaze, fiddling with the zipper on JoJo's carrier. What was wrong with her? She was desperate for connection, that's what. The second a guy paid her the slightest bit of attention she was ready to set out the welcome mat. Nope. No can do. Not this time. Her groundhogging days were over.

She was breaking the cycle. This time, she was going to be careful. This time, she was going to be smart. This time, she was going to be patient and wait for Mr. Right . . . and Mick O'Sullivan, with his mischievous grins and playful teasing, was not him. Been there, done that, burned the T-shirts.

From behind her, a throat cleared. Kat turned and was confronted with the angry glare of a teenager in a tie-dyed PET-A-PALOOZA smock.

The employee gestured at the pile of birdseed scattered across the floor. "Does this belong to either of you?"

"Um, no." Mick's eyes were wide and innocent as he lied his ass off. "Someone made quite a mess, though, huh?"

With an aggrieved sigh, the teen yanked a walkie-talkie from the pocket of their smock and grumbled into it, "Clean up in aisle seven."

Kat smothered a giggle. "I should probably get out of the way." She gripped the handle of her shopping cart and retreated back down the aisle, refusing to meet Mick's gaze, even though she could feel the tickle of his amused stare as he followed her.

The second she turned the corner, Kat lost it and snorted with laughter. She paused, punching Mick in the arm. "You're terrible."

"What?" Mick rubbed his arm, looking as unrepentant as JoJo had been while lounging in the donut. "It was the truth. That bag didn't belong to me."

"Only because you hadn't had a chance to buy it yet."

"I would have, but some wild customer rammed me with her shopping cart before I could." His face scrunched in consideration.

"Maybe I should report the incident." He moved to head back to the other aisle.

Kat whipped her cart to the side, blocking his path. "I don't think you need to trouble them with that."

"I don't know." Mick pointedly eyed her cart, which had been inches away from striking him again. "I'm afraid she might still be on the loose."

"No, she is not still on the loose," Kat hissed.

"Are you sure?" he pressed, lips twitching.

"Yes, I'm sure." She took a breath. "And I'm sorry for hitting you with my cart."

"Apology accepted." He grinned.

"You don't have to be so gloaty about it," she grumbled.

"Is 'gloaty' a word?"

"Did you understand what I meant?"

"Yes."

"Then it's a word." Determined to make it her last word, Kat pushed the cart down the next aisle.

To her chagrin, Mick continued to shadow her.

"Why are you following me?"

"I'm not following you."

She jerked her cart to a stop, causing him to almost bump into her.

"I think you need a license to drive that thing," he said, side-stepping her to avoid another collision.

"And I think you need to stop following me."

"I'm not following you," Mick insisted. He reached past her and pulled a new bag from the shelf. "I needed to get more bird-seed."

"Oh." Kat stared at the bag, identical to the one her cart had demolished a few minutes ago. "Right." She was an idiot.

"Seamus would go berserk if I came home empty-handed."

"He gets hangry, huh?"

"You have no idea. He makes this god-awful noise." Mick shivered. "Someone called the cops once."

"Really?"

"Uh-huh." Mick nodded, voice grave. "I mean, the sound is unsettling enough, but to have it coming from a funeral home . . ."

Kat's eyes widened in horror. "Oh no."

"Yep." He winced. "I think our neighbors are still convinced we had an exorcism that night. Or maybe a zombie attack."

Despite herself, Kat laughed.

"It's not funny." Mick paused. "Actually, yeah, it is." Humor brimmed in his rich coffee eyes. "But not something I ever want to repeat."

"Understood." Kat laughed again. "Here." She nudged the cart toward him. "Toss your bag in. I'm buying."

"I can't let you do that."

"I insist," Kat said. "It's the least I can do for destroying the first one."

"Well, if you insist on buying Seamus his dinner, I insist on buying you yours."

"That's not necessary." She maneuvered the cart into a checkout line.

"Please," he said. "It's the least *I* can do for making you almost lose your hedgehog."

Kat started guiltily. In the last few minutes, she'd completely forgotten about JoJo. She peeked through the mesh screen of the carrier, relieved to see the nocturnal nugget snoozing peacefully. "Thanks for finding her, by the way. And I appreciate the offer of dinner, but I've got to get her home." Kat glanced over the pile in her cart. "Frankly, I don't know how I'm going to fit all this on the train."

"You're going to try and ride the L hauling all of this?" Mick's eyebrows rose. "*And* a hedgehog?"

"I underestimated the size of my shopping list," she admitted. "New-pet-owner problems."

"I still want to hear that story," Mick reminded her. He cocked his head. "Here's an idea. Why don't I drive you home?"

"I couldn't ask you to do that."

"You're not asking, I'm offering." Mick waved a hand over the cart. "You can drop off all this stuff, get JoJo settled, and then we can grab something to eat. Unless . . ." He hesitated. "You have other plans tonight?"

Kat shook her head. No, she did not have other plans. The reminder stung. She swallowed, considering. It was sweet of him to offer to drive her home, and it really would help her out. The line inched forward, and Kat made up her mind. "Okay, sure."

"Great." Mick beamed at her.

The delight radiating from his smile caught Kat off guard. Warmth spread through her, quickly followed by a twinge of wariness. Maybe she shouldn't have agreed to his offer. But really, what harm was there in saying yes? And since she wasn't trying to date him, this couldn't count as groundhogging. It was only dinner. A casual meal between two casual acquaintances.

Kat realized she'd enjoyed talking to Mick and wouldn't mind getting to know him a little better. As a friend. With Andie moving to Milwaukee and Julia moving in with her boyfriend, she could really use a new friend. As long as she established clear boundaries and stuck to them—as long as they became friends and nothing more—everything would be fine.

CHAPTER 7

Mick

Mick trailed behind Kat as she pushed the cart toward the exit of the pet supply supercenter. The automatic doors whooshed open and he scooted ahead of her, leading the way through the parking lot toward his car. "That's me," he said, pointing his key fob and popping the lock on his hatchback.

"Hmm." Kat pulled the shopping cart up to the trunk. "Not what I expected."

"Let me guess." Mick began loading her bags of supplies into the back of his car. "You thought I drove a hearse?"

She evaded answering him by grabbing the empty cart and returning it to a nearby corral.

"You did, didn't you?" he pressed, opening the passenger door for her.

"No," Kat said defensively, rolling her eyes and shaking her head as she dropped into the seat. She settled the tote with the hedgehog inside on her lap and yanked the car door out of his grip, shutting it with a petulant *click*.

Chuckling, he made his way around to the other side of the car. After he slid into the driver's seat, Mick couldn't resist razzing her a little bit. He cocked a brow and stared at her.

"Okay, fine," she grumbled, avoiding his gaze as she pulled her seatbelt into place. "I *might* have been expecting a hearse. It's like a company car, right? People drive company cars all the time."

"Not quite the same." He smirked. "I wouldn't be caught dead driving one of those things unless I absolutely had to."

Her eyes narrowed to azure slits. "Is that supposed to be some kind of funeral home humor?"

"No. I'm dead serious."

Her lips pursed and Mick couldn't tell if she was appalled by his jokes or trying not to laugh. He recalled how agitated she'd been near the Murphy coffin. How she'd reacted to the word "corpse." He didn't need his psychology degree to know something more was at play here. Much as he wanted to dig deeper, instinct told him to back away from what was obviously a sore subject for her. Besides, there was another mystery he could assuage his curiosity with.

"You mentioned a story." He buckled his seatbelt. "About how you ended up with a hedgehog?" he prompted.

"I did," Kat said, a strange note creeping into her voice.

Mick started the car and backed out of the space, hoping she'd take the cue and start talking. But as he wound his way through the parking lot and eased onto the street, she remained silent.

They hit a red light and he took advantage of the moment to glance over at Kat. "Well?"

"It's a long story."

The light turned green. "Then I guess you better get started," Mick said and hit the gas.

By the time he took the last turn on her directions, he knew all about JoJo the adopted hedgehog and the wannabe-reality-show-host boyfriend who'd been current as of Friday but was now an ex. An ex who'd moved to Canada. "Is his name really Tad?"

A glimmer of a smile broke through her dour expression. "I've already been lectured on the pitfalls of dating men whose names end in 'ad.'"

Mick chuckled. "I've never met a Chad who wasn't a total dou—" He stopped himself and focused on finding the address she'd given him. Swallowing, he added, "Maybe I'm stereotyping here, but Tad sounds even worse."

"The worst," Kat confirmed, voice tinged with bitterness.

The guy sounded like an absolute prick, pawning off his pet on her and then leaving the country. Definitely not good enough for the woman seated next to him. Not that Mick thought he was good enough either, but at least he'd never dump her without warning. He knew how that felt all too well and carried the scars as a reminder.

He parked in front of the building she indicated and cut the engine. "Wait a minute," Mick said, noting the sign above the striped awning. "This is the flower shop."

"It is." She pointed to a window on the upper floor of the building. "It's also my home."

"Makes sense." Mick unloaded Kat's stuff from the trunk and hurried to follow her around to the back of the building. "My family lives above a funeral home."

She paused in the process of typing a code into the keypad and looked over her shoulder at him. "And you wondered why I thought you drove a hearse?" A teasing grin flickered across her face.

"I actually live in the building across the street now," he admitted. "But my gran and sis still live in an apartment above O'Sullivan's. The upper floors of the building are zoned for residential use . . . it helps with taxes."

Kat nodded and led the way inside. "Yeah, I think that's why Allen—he's my boss—lets me stay here so cheap." She eyed the heavy shopping bags he was carrying. "Wow. I really did buy too much stuff."

There was a sheepish note to her voice that Mick found charming. It was cute how she couldn't resist pampering her pet.

Her brow pinched in concern. "Are you okay with lugging all that upstairs?"

"I'm fine," Mick assured her and adjusted his grip so the handles didn't cut into his wrists. "Lead me to the elevator."

"About that." A smile tugged at the corner of her mouth. "The elevator is for special use only." Kat held the door to the stairwell open for Mick and motioned for him to go ahead of her. "I hardly ever use it. My boss gets super pissy when I do."

"Why?" Mick clomped up the steps. "Another way to save money?"

"No, to save energy. Allen's big into conservation efforts." Kat slipped past him and led the way up the next flight of stairs. "Almost there."

"Your boss should meet my sister." Mick paused on the landing to catch his breath. "She's into that stuff too. Save the earth, live green, and all that."

"Really?" She waited for him to catch up. "What kind of conservation efforts does a funeral home have?"

"I'm not sure you want to know." He shuddered, skin growing clammy with the memory of the mushroom suit.

Her laughter was a ray of sunshine in the dim hallway. She unlocked the door and stepped inside, leaning against it and waving him in.

Mick hesitated. The other night at the funeral home, he'd wondered if he'd ever see her again. And now he was standing at the threshold of her apartment. He forced his feet to move, a wave of nervous tension rolling over him as he followed her into the living room.

"You can set those down there." She gestured toward a coffee table. "Thanks."

"No problem." The space was cute, with furniture in bold pops of color and bright paintings on the walls.

"Sorry about the mess," she apologized, attention on the pet carrier she was unzipping.

"You call this a mess?" Mick scoffed, maneuvering around a pile of boxes. It was cluttered but not dirty, and most of the stuff scattered about appeared to be hedgehog paraphernalia. He thought of the gobshite ex that had dumped all this on her so carelessly and jetted off to Canada. Tad. He hoped the jerk got picked for a random cavity search at the border. Did they do that kind of thing for real, or was that only in the movies?

"What's wrong?" Kat demanded, lifting the hedgehog out of the carrier.

Mick blinked. "Huh?"

"The face you were making." She stared up at him, blue eyes wide. Resting on her chest, the hedgehog stared too, beady black eyes peering at Mick from beneath its spiky brow. "What were you thinking about?"

Mick floundered. What was he supposed to say? *I was imagining your butthole ex-boyfriend getting served a bit of poetic albeit unpleasant justice?*

A strange noise broke the awkward silence.

"I think your pet might be dying," Mick said, eyeing the creature she was holding.

"Um . . . ," she bit her lip, "that was me."

"That sound came from you?" Mick couldn't hide the surprise in his voice.

She nodded sheepishly. "Normal people have a stomach that growls like a grumpy dog. Mine yowls . . . apparently like a dying hedgehog."

"Sorry, I didn't mean to embarrass you." Mick shook his head. "I really thought JoJo there was giving up the ghost." He grinned. "This is a much easier problem to solve."

Another of those odd sounds emanated from her midsection.

"We better get some food inside you before whatever creature is making that noise tries to eat you instead."

"Very funny," she grumbled.

"I'm not sure I'm joking." He nodded toward the door. "Come on. I promised you dinner, remember?"

"Fine. There's a little French bistro around the corner from here." Kat moved to set the hedgehog inside a pink plastic monstrosity. "We can go there. But this isn't a date. I'll buy my own dinner."

......

There was a moment, as Mick followed Kat through the pair of gilded French doors, that he hesitated. Who the hell did he think he was? He wasn't the guy gorgeous blondes went to dinner with at fancy bistros, that's for sure. But this wasn't a date. A fact she'd been sure to remind him of. A fact he needed to remember.

Kat led the way to a table in the corner. "Isn't this place the cutest?" she warbled.

Warbled. All gushy and excited, like his sister had been about that mushroom suit.

"Sure." Mick looked around at the little crystal chandeliers dotting the ceiling, the glass shelves filled with a pastel rainbow of cloudlike cookies, and the frail, teensy tables that looked like they'd collapse if you put a real plate on top of them. "So cute."

He had the urge to tiptoe as they crossed the room. What did Gran always call him when he used to run circles around her dining room table? A bull in a china shop. Knowing his luck, he'd try and sit on one of those chairs that looked like they were made of matchsticks and end up breaking it to pieces, like Goldilocks on her crime spree in the three bears' house.

He eased onto a chair slowly. Luckily, the thing was sturdier than it appeared.

A man with the kind of IDGAF attitude that turned passive-aggressiveness into an art form drifted over. "Are we ready to order?"

"Uh, *we* just sat down," Mick said. "We didn't even have a chance to look at the menu yet."

The server pointed one pale bony finger at the wall over the counter.

Mick squinted at the menu board. "Everything is in French."

"Oui," the man said in an exaggerated accent. "This bistro is French."

Mick suspected the dude was about as French as Seamus, but for Kat's sake, he kept his mouth shut.

"I'll have a café au lait to start, please," Kat said.

"And for monsieur?"

"Coffee. Black," he said, feeling like one of those grumpy old men who wanted to know what the hell was a "venti" and why couldn't he simply order a "large" dagnabbit.

After Mr. Faux François walked away, Kat leaned forward and whispered, "I don't think he's actually from France."

Mick chuckled, some of the tension easing out of him.

"I know this place is a bit much, but I love it," she confessed. "I like to come here and pretend I'm living in Paris, doing fancy French-lady things."

"What kinds of things?"

"Mostly gobbling up croissants," she revealed with a sheepish giggle. "They're really good. You have to try some. My treat."

Mick grinned. She was almost too adorable. He decided not to burst her bubble by telling her that date or not, there was no way he was letting her pay for croissants or dinner.

"You wanna know a secret?" Kat asked, leaning closer, blue eyes sparkling. She pointed at the tiny bouquet sitting on the table between them. The little array of flowers was nestled in a vase the shape and size of a perfume bottle. "This is mine. My design I mean."

"You made this?" he asked.

"I made the bouquet." She waved a hand and pointed out similar arrangements decorating the other tables. "I made all of them." She tucked her hand to the side of her mouth and whispered conspiratorially, "We have a deal worked out."

"Oh really?" Mick decided to live dangerously and leaned an elbow on the wafer-thin table.

"Mm-hmm." Still talking behind her hand, she said, "They get their flowers for wholesale, and I get free croissants."

"You eat here for free, huh?" Mick nodded sagely. "That's why you offered to treat me."

"Perhaps." With a self-satisfied grin, she dropped her hand into her lap as the server returned.

Mick frowned at the coffee cup placed in front of him. It was the size of a thimble, like something from a fairy-princess tea set. Free or not, he hoped the croissants were human-sized. He snagged some sugar from the condiment caddy and shook them into his coffee. He noticed Kat watching him. "What?"

"Nothing." She shrugged and reached for the same number of packets. "I didn't take you for a sugar-in-your-coffee kind of guy."

"Why?" Mick couldn't resist teasing her. "Think I'm already sweet enough?"

"Hardly." She snorted, unfolding her linen napkin and placing it on her lap.

A lopsided grin curved his mouth. If he didn't know better, he'd think she was—not flirting with him, exactly—but enjoying teasing him too.

The server waltzed by again, dropping a cloth-covered basket on the table.

Kat rubbed her hands together in anticipation before lifting the cloth. Warm steam rose along with the rich aroma of buttery, fresh-baked croissants. She rotated the basket, turning it to offer him first pick. Unlike the fairy coffee, the croissants were made for giants, huge, flaky pillows the size of his hand. He selected one and then nudged the basket back toward her.

"Thanks," Kat said, wasting no time in choosing one for herself. She bit into the croissant, moaning in ecstasy as she chewed.

Mick downed his thimble of coffee in one gulp. He cleared his throat.

"Sorry." She blinked, setting the pastry down. "I tend to get a little Meg Ryan when I eat these."

"Who?" He cocked his head.

"You know," Kat prompted. "'I'll have what she's having' from *When Harry Met Sally.*"

"Oh. The movie where the lady fakes an orgasm while eating a sandwich." Mick shuddered. "I saw that movie with my mom."

Kat snorted. "How old were you?"

"Old enough to be traumatized by delis forever." He gazed into his empty thimble thoughtfully. "Maybe that's why I don't really watch rom-coms."

"What?" she gasped. Her half-eaten croissant slipped from her fingers and landed on the table with a *thunk*. "You don't like rom-coms?" It sounded more like an accusation than a question.

"Now hold on. I said I don't really watch them, I never said I didn't like them." At first, Mick thought she was teasing him back. But when her aghast expression didn't change, he realized she was serious. "If I made a random Tolkien reference, I wouldn't expect you to get it."

"Maybe I would."

"You would?"

"Okay, probably not," she conceded, poking at what was left of her croissant. "But my friend Andie would. She loves all that stuff about elves and orcas."

He winced. "*Orcs.*"

"Oh my god, she makes that same face when I get one of her nerdy details wrong." Kat shook her head, smiling indulgently. "You two should meet. I think she'd like you."

"Um," Mick drummed his fingers on the table, suddenly uncomfortable, "maybe I'm getting the wrong idea here, but . . ."

"Do you think I'm playing matchmaker?" she asked, then burst out laughing.

"I'm going to do my best not to take your reaction personally," Mick grumbled, taking it very personally. He shoved the rest of the croissant in his mouth.

"No, it's not that." Kat shook her head. "Andie has a boyfriend. A serious boyfriend. They met last summer." A soft smile played about her lips. "Curt is her perfect match. She's getting ready to go live with him in the house he's almost done building. And Julia, my other bestie, recently announced she's moving in with the guy she also met last summer."

"Whoa," Mick said around a mouthful of flaky pastry. "That must have been some summer."

"I know." Kat laughed again, but this time the humor seemed forced. "And it even happened in the same week. Wild, huh?"

"Unbelievable," Mick agreed.

"You have no idea." She dropped her gaze, brushing crumbs from her fingers. Her lips quirked. "It's strange."

Mick studied Kat. There was something in the way her mouth twisted, something melancholy, that tugged at his heart. "What is?"

"I never thought I'd be the last of my best friends to be single." She fiddled with her napkin, folding it into smaller and smaller squares. "Not that there's anything wrong with that. Plenty of people like being single and that's cool. But of the three of us, I was always the most romantic one. In fact, until Julia met Luke, she didn't even believe in true love."

"But you do?" he prodded.

"Believe in true love?" Kat asked.

Mick nodded, wanting to know the answer more than he cared to admit.

"I do." A golden eyebrow rose in self-mockery. "Not that I've ever found someone to give me a reason to."

"Nobody?"

She shook her head.

"Now, that really is unbelievable." Mick hadn't been able to stop thinking about Kat ever since the first night they met. He'd have bet men fell at her feet, offering eternal devotion on a daily basis. "Nobody. Really?"

"Really. Well, nobody worth mentioning."

Her voice was flippant, but Mick caught how Kat twisted the napkin in her fingers. He watched her for a moment, debating whether or not to ask any of the questions that were bobbing on the surface of his mind. Personal questions that weren't really any of his business. He took another croissant from the basket. "But there was somebody," he remarked, biting off the end and hoping he sounded casual. "The hedgehog guy."

"Tad." She released her death grip on the napkin, mouth pinching, like she'd tasted something sour.

"He was a jerk who didn't deserve you." Mick couldn't understand how anyone could ever walk away from someone like Kat. "It's not my place to say this, but you're better off without him."

"I know that, in theory. But it's hard to remember in practice. And that's my problem."

"That you're attracted to jerks?" Mick surmised.

She paused mid-sip, eyes flicking to his over the rim of her cup.

"Sorry," Mick winced. "Too harsh?"

"No, you're right." She set her cup back in its saucer. "I recently came to the same conclusion myself." Her lips twitched. "But the real problem was that I wanted what my friends have so badly, I was willing to try and make things work with the wrong guy." Kat shook her head. "Obviously, the solution is to find the right guy."

Mick wanted to argue, suggest maybe the solution was she stop trying to rush into a serious relationship, but he'd overstepped enough already. Fortunately, at that moment, their server deigned to grace them with his presence once more, refilling Mick's coffee and begrudgingly asking for their dinner order. Thank god. Mick had started to worry the basket of croissants *was* their dinner.

Kat rattled off something in what Mick assumed was French. He blinked and glanced at the menu board again, searching for any words that looked familiar. If he wasn't careful, he'd end up ordering snails or frog legs or something that belonged at the Shedd Aquarium, not on his dinner plate.

The waiter tapped his pencil against his notepad impatiently. More like stabbed, Mick thought, watching as the guy jabbed the point into the paper over and over again. Not wanting to know which of his body parts the server was imagining driving the tip of that pencil into, Mick made an executive decision to hurry the fuck up. "I'll have what she's having," he announced.

Kat snickered.

Heat crept up the back of Mick's neck as he belatedly recalled their earlier exchange. Once the waiter had walked away, Mick turned to Kat, desperate to steer the conversation away from orgasms, fake or otherwise. "What *are* we having?"

"A croque monsieur and pommes frites," Kat said. "Didn't you hear me order?"

"Oh, I heard you," Mick said, "I just didn't understand you."

"Don't worry," Kat assured him. "You'll like it."

Mick glanced over his shoulder and whispered, "I don't think he likes me."

"Who?" Kat followed his gaze to where the server stood glowering behind the counter. "Oh." She grinned. "I don't think he likes anyone." She leaned toward him, whispering too. "But I like you."

"You do?" Mick's heart ping-ponged between his lungs and bounced off the pile of croissants in his gut before settling somewhere in the vicinity of his belly button.

"Mm-hmm." She nodded. "And I like this. It's been nice. Sitting here talking to you." She studied his face, blue eyes soft and curious. "I was wondering . . . how would you like to be friends?"

"'Friends,'" he repeated. Jesus, he sounded like an idiot. Mick wished the table wasn't so freaking tiny, then maybe he could crawl under it and disappear. But even in the midst of his embarrassment, he realized he liked the sound of that. He wasn't going to lie to himself and say he wasn't interested in being more than friends, but she was right. Talking to her was nice. Better than nice. Their conversation had been relaxed, her companionship natural and easy. He had to stop reading more into it when she clearly wasn't feeling the same. "Um, yeah," he said, finally pulling himself together. "I'd like that too."

Grouchypants returned, and Mick was actually grateful for

the server's interruption, and not only because he brought food. Mick studied his plate for a moment, bemused.

"What do you think?" Kat asked.

"I think my fancy French dinner is a grilled cheese," Mick said.

"A grilled cheese with ham," Kat corrected. "That's what makes it a croque monsieur."

"Well, well. Bonjour, monsieur." Mick glanced down, greeting his sandwich. "And I'm guessing 'pommes frites' means French fries?"

"Oui." Kat picked up a fry and popped it in her mouth. "Usually, I order the soup du jour, but sometimes a girl's just gotta have fries."

Mick grinned. "My sister would appreciate that sentiment."

"Is this the sister interested in the environmental stuff?"

"Mary-Kate, yes. She's my only sister, and the youngest." For some reason Mick found himself wondering what MK would think of Kat. He bit into his sandwich. The bread was crispy, and the tangy melted cheese was decadently ooey-gooey. "Mmmph," he groaned.

"Good, huh?"

Mouth still full, Mick nodded. He swallowed. "Very good, but I'm not going to, uh, you know . . ."

"Go all Meg Ryan on me?" she prompted, lips twitching.

"That." He nodded. "Not doing that, but damn, the French know how to work some magic with cheese and bread."

Kat beamed at him. "I'm glad you like it."

They sat in companiable silence for a few minutes, both focused on their food. Finally, Mick brought himself to set the remainder of his sandwich down. "Okay," he declared, waving a fry in her direction. "I've told you about me, now it's your turn."

She blinked. "The guys I usually have dinner with are perfectly happy to talk about themselves all the time."

"You really are attracted to assholes." Mick clamped his jaw shut. That had slipped out before he could stop it. To his relief, Kat laughed. A sharp bark of sound that was both shocked and amused and . . . something else.

He liked that about her. Appreciated how she could laugh at herself, even though he could tell the truth hurt her too. The trained psychologist in him itched to unpack the layers of emotion in that laugh, sift through the mix of feelings flitting across her face. But more than that, he wanted to get to know her.

"I can keep rambling about myself, if you want," Mick suggested.

"No, no." Kat waved her hand. "Too late. It's my turn now." She straightened in her seat. "Let's see. I have two older brothers."

"Any other siblings?"

"Nope, I'm the youngest." Kat toyed with the fries left on her plate. "I always thought it would be cool to have a little sister, but it's probably better for everyone my parents stopped procreating." She dropped the fry she'd been twirling and glanced up. "Um. Sorry for the overshare."

"No such thing," Mick assured her. "We're friends now, remember?" Like a dentist approaching a sore tooth, he debated whether to prod what was obviously a tender subject. He didn't want to press too hard and cause her more pain, but he couldn't help wanting to locate the source of the ache. "I'm guessing your parents don't get along?"

"Depends on the day." She leaned back in her chair, wariness in the stiff set of her shoulders. "Their relationship is . . . volatile."

Mick proceeded with caution. "Divorced?"

"It would be easier if they were." Her mouth drew into a tight line.

"I didn't mean to bring up a difficult subject."

"No, it's fine." Kat shook her head. "It's strange, but all their toxic bullshit is part of why I wanted to become a florist."

Before he could attempt to unravel that statement, she continued.

"My mother isn't a nice person. She isn't a happy person either. Growing up, the only time I could ever recall seeing her smile, and I mean really truly smile, was when she got flowers." Her expression softened, turned almost wistful. "It was like this secret door opened in her heart, and flowers were the key."

"Does she have a favorite?" Mick asked

"That's a good question." Kat tilted her head, looking at him. "I'm not sure, but if I had to guess, I'd say zinnias. They come in all the bold bright colors. Like candy."

"They sound pretty."

"They are. She got them a lot."

"So did you always know you wanted to be a florist?"

"It might sound odd, but yeah."

"That's not odd." Mick shook his head. "I think it's cool you knew what you wanted to do."

"What I really want to do is have my own shop," she admitted, brushing crumbs from the napkin on her lap. "Ever since I was little, I had this picture in my head of a cute little flower shop. In grade school, while my friends doodled pictures of ponies and mermaids, I made sketches of my store. And in middle school, while other girls were pinning up posters of boy bands, I was putting together collages of window displays and wedding bouquets."

"Not even one boy band poster?" Mick teased.

"Maybe one." She grinned. "I even brought it to college with me."

"Did you go somewhere around here?"

"In the city, yeah." She nodded. "Undergrad in horticulture and then a business degree."

Mick lurched in his seat. "You went to business school?"

Her eyes narrowed. "Do you find that surprising?"

"No," he said, realizing how his reaction must have come across. "It's exciting." I'm starting to think our running into each other at the pet store today was rather serendipitous." Mick set his hands on the table, steepling his fingers the way Joe always did, hoping he looked professional.

Kat eyeballed him warily. "What are you doing?"

"Trying to show you I take you seriously."

"You look like a Bond villain."

Heat crept up the back of Mick's neck. So much for looking professional. "Sorry. Um, let's try this again. I'm guessing you know something about writing business proposals?"

"It's like the first thing I learned in business school," Kat said. "I've written dozens." She shrugged. "All of them hypothetical, of course. For assignments and projects."

"Do you think you could write a real one?"

"Probably."

"Do you think you could help *me* write one?"

"Why?" She cocked her head, studying him. "Are you starting a new business?"

"In a manner of speaking, yes," Mick managed. "I want to offer some new services, and since O'Sullivan's is a family business, before moving forward, I need to come up with a proposal for how the new stuff would, well . . ."

"Impact the old stuff?" Kat supplied.

"More like fit in with the old stuff." Mick sighed, hoping she understood what he was doing a piss-poor job of explaining. This is why he desperately needed help. "You know how you said weddings are more your thing than funerals?" He fiddled with the handle on his cup. "What if I wanted to make funerals more like a wedding?"

She was silent, but the look she was giving him basically said, *What kind of creepy ass shit is this?*

"It's not as weird as it sounds," Mick hurried to explain. "I'm not talking about the wedding part. Just the reception."

"You mean like a party?" Kat asked.

"Right." Mick nodded. "A celebration of life."

"I'm not Irish, but isn't that what a wake is?"

Mick bit back a growl of frustration. "My brother said basically the same thing."

"He's the one you referred to as 'the stiff in glasses'?"

"That's him."

"He was very nice." Kat's smile was soft and sweet. "Walked me to the door and even offered to accompany me to my car."

"Sounds like my brother," Mick said, unable to wipe the bitterness from his voice completely. "Gentleman Joe." His brother. So polished. So polite. So perfect. So much better than him. Mick's chest tightened, the dull ache between his ribs like the twinge of an old injury. *Elsi.*

It had been almost a decade since that summer of betrayal and heartbreak. The first time Mick had ever really been in love. The first time he'd been serious about someone. Serious enough to invite Elsi to spend break with him and his family. Mick had thought she felt the same way for him. And maybe she had. But as soon as she'd met Joe, it was all over.

Those old wounds had nothing to do with this moment or Kat. Mick shook off the memories and forced himself to relax, to focus on the here and now. "Joe's the one who demanded to see a proposal before agreeing to move forward with making any changes." He straightened in his chair. "Maybe you could help me hash out the details. What do you think?"

"I don't know . . ." Kat stroked her chin and now she was the one looking like a Bond villain. "What's in it for me?"

Mick squirmed beneath the scrutiny. What could he offer her? He glanced around, seeking inspiration. "How about an agreement like you worked out with the café?" He suggested. "But instead of free meals in exchange for bouquets, you can trade business advice for . . ."

"For what?" A golden brow arched. "A free casket?" She shivered in obvious revulsion. "No thank you."

"What about more business?" Mick offered, grasping at straws. "I can recommend you to our clients." He leaned forward, warming to the idea. "And I can honestly say I'm giving a good recommendation. You do great work."

"And you know this after only one delivery from me, hm?"

"One was all it took." He grinned.

"Aw, I'm flattered," she said. Her lips curved, mirroring his grin.

Mick was about to pat himself on the back when he noticed that Kat's smile seemed forced. In fact, she looked annoyed. His grin slid sideways. "Did I say something wrong?"

"A recommendation? Really?" She huffed. "Exposure. That's what you're offering me?"

"Um . . ." Mick hesitated. This felt like a trap. Like when his sister asked his opinion on a new outfit.

"Here's something else I learned in business school," Kat said, not waiting for him to muster a reply. "If you want customers to appreciate your worth and acknowledge the value of your work, you can't sell yourself short."

She had a point—she deserved to be compensated for her time. "Fair enough," Mick agreed. "What would you suggest, then?"

Kat tapped her index finger against her lips, considering. "Rather than simply recommending me as a florist to clients, would O'Sullivan's be willing to consider an exclusive contract?"

"Ah . . ." Gaze still snagged on her mouth, Mick struggled to organize his thoughts. Business. Not pleasure. Contracts. Not kissing. "You mean like a partnership?"

"Mm-hmm."

Did her lips have to press together so lushly when she said that? He glanced at the tiny vase of flowers on their table, the bouquet Kat had arranged, like she'd arranged an agreement with this café. She was talented and savvy, and her suggestion was a good one. "I think we could make that happen, but I'd have to run it by my siblings first. Our business meeting is tomorrow night, why don't you stop by?"

"It just so happens I'm free tomorrow night." She flashed him a brilliant smile. "I'll be there."

"Good." The warmth of her smile settled into his skin. For a heartbeat, the old wound throbbed again, reminding Mick there was a strong chance he was going to regret this, but even if that were true, he knew he'd probably do it anyway.

CHAPTER 8

Kat

Every Monday afternoon, Kat rode the train up to take her grand-mother out for lunch. Well, Babcia usually treated Kat to lunch. Even after Kat had graduated and was making a decent salary, Babcia insisted lunch was on her. Kat had given up arguing a long time ago. She'd never known anyone as stubborn and set in her ways as her grandmother.

She'd also never known anyone as loyal and loving. Babcia was her most favorite person in the world. Kat had grown up in a volatile household, with parents who weren't all that great at being parents. Babcia was her safe harbor. She'd cared for Kat like no one else had. And now that she was older, Kat was happy to reciprocate.

At eighty-seven, her grandmother refused to admit she might be slowing down. Babcia was old-school. She came from hearty, hardworking Polish stock and was as proud as she was stubborn. She would never show weakness or admit she needed assistance, no matter how badly she could use it. Over the years, Kat found ways to offer help without being asked. Sneaky things that Babcia could pretend she didn't notice.

After getting ready and checking on JoJo—who was fast asleep after another midnight marathon, the little stinker—Kat headed downstairs. As was her habit, she popped into the shop for a minute, picking out one of the premade bouquets still left in the cooler. She always brought flowers for her grandmother. Kat did it even though she knew that when she showed up at the retirement complex today, bouquet in hand, Babcia would tell her she shouldn't have. It was a dance they did every week.

It wasn't just about being frugal. Nothing made Babcia happier than taking something that would have been thrown away or over-looked and giving it some love and attention. Her favorite hobby was spending an hour or two in her church's secondhand shop. Babcia liked to say they should call it a "second-life shop" because every-thing that comes in goes on to start a new life with a new owner.

It was a lovely thought. Kat appreciated the sentiment, but she did wonder about the stuff that sat in the shop for years. She asked her grandmother about that once, about the things that nobody seemed to want and never sold. Babcia's answer was heartfelt and immediate. She believed all the items would find a new home eventually, it was simply a matter of time. The right person hadn't come along yet.

Kat had grown up holding that hope inside her. The belief that if she waited long enough, the right person would come along. The problem was, she was impatient. She didn't want to sit on a shelf waiting to be found. She wanted to find her person now. And she'd tried, oh how she'd tried. Maybe she hadn't been trying hard enough.

No. She'd been trying too hard, wasting her efforts on the wrong ones. Her decision to stop chasing after the kind of guys she was usually attracted to made sense. After all, wasn't the defi-nition of madness doing the same thing over and over again and hoping for a different result?

But she was done with that. The list she'd made with Andie and Julia was the first step. It was good to have a plan. Her boss, Allen, liked to say that those who fail to plan, plan to fail. And Kat was done failing. The train pulled into the station, and she gathered up her things, suddenly feeling optimistic.

Of her siblings, Kat was the only one still in Chicago. Both of her brothers had hightailed it out of Chicago as soon as it was possible. Kat didn't blame either of them, not really. Sometimes it was hard not to feel like they'd abandoned her; but Babcia had always been there for her, and Kat would always be there for her grandmother.

In a few short minutes, Kat was ringing the bell to Babcia's place. Her grandmother buzzed her in. By the time Kat reached Babcia's floor, her grandmother was standing outside the door to her apartment, waving, face wreathed in smiles.

Kat's heart lifted at the sight. "Cześć," she called as she hurried down the hall and into her grandmother's arms. The familiar scents of bergamot and honey enveloped her, and she inhaled deeply, breathing in warmth and comfort. Babcia always made her feel welcome. Wanted. Loved. They kissed cheeks, right, left, right, and Kat handed her grandmother the bouquet.

"Ah, you shouldn't have." Babcia clicked her tongue, inspecting the flowers. "Really," she said again and turned to head into the apartment, "it's too much."

"*Drobiazg,*" Kat replied automatically, following her grandmother inside. "It's nothing. Another day at the shop and I wouldn't be able to sell them. Too pretty to waste, don't you think?"

"I think you spoil me is what I think." Babcia blew out a dramatic sigh. "*Dzięki.*"

"You're welcome." As usual, Babcia put on a big show, but Kat wasn't fooled. She'd caught the bright burst of joy lighting up her grandmother's eyes. Kat had never known anyone who didn't appreciate getting flowers, whether they admitted it or not.

While Babcia went through the motions of clearing out last week's bouquet, rinsing the vase, and arranging the new one, Kat slipped into her grandmother's bedroom and changed the sheets. It was one of the little routines they had. Babcia refused to let Kat hire a cleaning lady, even on a monthly basis. And while her grandmother could handle most of the basic chores involved in keeping her place tidy, some of the bigger things were too much for her.

Kat popped the pillows into fresh cases and lined them up

neatly against the headboard. She smoothed the bedspread over the fresh sheets, smiling to herself. Her grandmother had brought this quilt with her from Poland. It had been part of her hope chest, something she'd made as a young girl in anticipation of her wedding day.

A collection of framed photographs lined the bedside table. Kat gazed at them, a familiar twinge of sadness tugging at her heart. Her grandfather had been gone for more than twenty years now, but Kat knew Babcia still kissed him good night, even if only in her dreams.

"Kasia?"

"Coming!" Kat hurried to gather up the used bed linens. Only her grandmother called her that, a nickname based on the Polish version of her name. She stopped in the bathroom to rinse her hands and Babcia appeared in the doorway.

"There you are, Kotku."

Kitty cat. Her heart squeezed with affection at the endearment. "Here I am." Kat smiled. "Ready for lunch?"

"Let me add a little bit of color first." Babcia rummaged in a drawer. She pulled out a tube of lipstick and dabbed her lips. Standing beside Kat at the sink, Babcia gazed in the mirror. "So beautiful."

"Are you talking about you or me?" Kat asked, putting on a bit of lipstick too and grinning at her grandmother's reflection.

Babcia huffed out a laugh. "You, of course."

"Well, everyone knows I get my good looks from you." Kat bent and pressed a kiss to the top of her grandmother's head. Over the years, Babcia's blond hair, once the same color as Kat's, had faded to a lovely shade of ash white. Kat hoped hers would do the same when she was older.

"Who is this 'everyone'?" Her grandmother snorted dismissively, but her eyes sparkled with pleasure.

Flowers and compliments. Two things Kat believed could make anyone happy . . . as long as they were given honestly. From the heart. That was the key. "Come on, gorgeous," she said, shooing her grandmother out of the bathroom. "Let's go eat."

Hugging the northern outskirts of Chicago, the neighborhood her grandmother had retired to had many perks, one of which was the collection of restaurants. With an eclectic variety of family-owned establishments, there was pretty much something to satisfy whatever food mood you might be in. Today, Babcia decided she had a craving for curry.

Her grandmother spent the meal regaling Kat with tales of the other residents in her retirement community. A natural-born storyteller and a busybody, Babcia could turn even the most mundane bits of gossip into something intriguing. Despite the entertaining stories, by the time the check was paid, Kat found herself fighting off a yawn.

Babcia fell silent and sipped her tea, watching Kat over the rim of her enameled cup. "Are you feeling well, Kotku?"

"Fine." Kat pushed her empty plate away and picked up her own cup. "Why?"

"You look tired."

"I thought I looked beautiful," Kat reminded her, voice teasing.

"Beautiful but tired," Babcia amended, undeterred. "Is that man working you too hard?"

"Who, my boss?" Kat laughed. "No." For some reason, her grandmother was convinced Allen was a tyrant. "Honestly, he hardly comes to the shop anymore."

"Why should he?" Babcia huffed. "You do all the work for him."

"That's my job. I'm the manager."

"You work so much, Kotku." Babcia shook her head.

"And I love my work, you know that."

"I know you should have your own place. Your own shop. That's what I know."

"I will," Kat promised. She debated telling Babcia about her meeting tonight at O'Sullivan's, but she didn't want to jinx it in case nothing came of it. Building her client list and establishing partnerships was a start, but that's all it was. A start. So instead, she said, "I have a plan. It's going to happen. In my own time. My own way. One day."

"So stubborn." Babcia clucked her tongue. "Your own time. Your own way. You sound like your dziadek." She set her tea down and reached for Kat's hand. "One day could be now if you'd let me help you."

Kat sighed. This was an old argument with her grandmother. Babcia had been the first person to know about Kat's dream to own a flower shop. For years, she'd tried to convince Kat to let her pitch in.

But while Babcia's heart was big, her bank account was small. She lived on a fixed income that luckily provided for a comfortable existence, but there wasn't a lot of wiggle room. An occasional meal out or splurge on a high-end lipstick was one thing, helping Kat buy a business was another.

It was scary enough contemplating risking her own savings, there was no way Kat would ever consider risking her grandmother's. She squeezed Babcia's hand. "I appreciate the offer, but we've talked about this. It's my dream, and I'll make it happen on my own. I need to do this by myself."

"It's not a sin to accept help, you know," Baba chided.

Kat snorted. This coming from the woman who had to be coerced into letting someone do her laundry. Rather than try and argue further, Kat decided to change the subject. "Come on." She gathered her things and stood, helping her grandmother out of her chair. "Let's go shopping."

At the secondhand store, Kat took her time browsing the aisles, knowing where she'd find her grandmother. It was part of their routine. Babcia liked to end her weekly trip to the thrift store with a peek at the used-book section.

Sure enough, her grandmother was tucked away at the back

of the store, in a cluttered corner called the Book Nook. "Find anything good?"

Babcia nodded and held up a paperback. "Look at this one."

On the glossy cover, a woman with flowing red hair was on her knees, an old-timey dress in an inexplicable shade of fuchsia barely clinging to her heaving bosom. A dark-haired man stood behind her, buck naked. Kat leaned closer, studying the couple on the cover. "Is he . . ."

"Schtupping her in the back?" Babcia supplied. "Looks like it."

Kat snickered, amused by Babcia's use of the word "schtupping" almost as much as by how it did indeed look like the hero was banging the heroine between the shoulder blades. She tugged the book from her grandmother's grip and read the summary on the back.

While Kat shared a love of romantic comedies with her friends, she shared a love of romance novels with her grandmother. Babcia had always encouraged her to read whatever she wanted, granting a young Kat the freedom to pick any book she liked from her collection.

Turning the book back over, Kat studied the cover again. "Whatever he's doing to her, she really seems to be enjoying it."

Her grandmother's gaze turned sly. "Maybe that's what's been keeping you up late."

"Babcia!"

The finely drawn lines of her grandmother's penciled-in eyebrows danced mischievously. "What's the name of the young man you've been seeing? Thad?"

"Tad." Kat paused, tracing the gold-foil lettering of the book's title. "But we're not seeing each other anymore."

"When did this happen?"

There wasn't judgment in her grandmother's voice, but sympathy. And either Kat was imagining it or projecting her own feelings, but she thought she also sensed a hint of disappointment. She squirmed under her grandmother's scrutiny. "We ended things Friday . . . *he* ended things."

Babcia sighed. "I thought things were going well this time."

This time. The weight of those words hung between them.

How often had Kat told Babcia about a guy one week only to have to tell her it was over the next? More times than she cared to think about. Too many times. "I thought so too," Kat finally admitted. "But I was wrong." She was always wrong. But not anymore. Kat had a plan. A list. And this time, she would pick right.

"My poor Kasia." Babcia reached up, brushing a strand of hair out of Kat's face. "Tell me you didn't spend the night weeping over this dupek."

"Oh no," Kat assured her. "Absolutely not. That jerk isn't worth my time."

"That's my girl." Babcia patted Kat's cheek. "Then why . . ." She gently rubbed her thumb under one eye.

"Why do I have bags under my eyes big enough to pack for a trip to Paris?" Kat shook her head. "Because of a hedgehog."

Babcia's hand dropped. "A what?"

"A hedgehog. It's a . . ." Kat stopped, suddenly feeling every bit as tired as she apparently looked. "It's a long story." She held up the book. "Speaking of stories, why don't you let me buy this for you?"

"Only if you promise to read it first," Babcia insisted. "You could use a happy ending."

"Thanks," Kat said dryly, ignoring the not-so-subtle observation about her love life. Sometimes, her grandmother could use a filter.

"Romance, that's what you need," Babcia said. She tapped the cover, that sly look back in her blue eyes. "Some romance, and some schtupping."

Case in point. Kat laughed, pressing a kiss to her incorrigible grandmother's cheek. If only the happy endings in books were as easy to come by in real life. Kat used to believe they were. And somewhere deep down, she still did.

CHAPTER 9

Kat

That night, after stopping at home to feed JoJo and change clothes, Kat pulled into the parking lot of O'Sullivan's funeral home for the second time in three days. Strange to think that less than seventy-two hours ago, fresh off her breakup with Tad, she'd arrived for what should have been a quick delivery but had ended up nearly joining the guest of honor in his coffin.

Thankfully, there wouldn't be any encounters with dead bodies today. At least she didn't think so. Still, as she approached the entrance, Kat couldn't help the sudden chill of apprehension freezing her in place. Adjusting the strap of her laptop bag, she muttered, "You have got to move past this fear. It's affecting your life. Your career." It had been years since the incident at her grandfather's funeral and well past time Kat worked through her issues. "Get your shit together."

A tapping sound broke through her thoughts. She glanced up, startled. Someone was waving at her through one of the windows. Mick. Even from this distance, she could see his dark brows quirking in teasing curiosity. Of course, he would spot her standing out here, talking to herself like a fool. Straightening her shoulders and summoning a smile full of confidence that she didn't feel, Kat opened the door.

Mick met her in the foyer. "Wow." Admiration flickered in Mick's dark eyes. "Pink is your color."

"Thanks." Kat glanced down, glad she'd taken the time to change. She'd figured something a little more professional was required and had chosen a pant suit in a deep rose. It was her favorite outfit to wear for wedding consultations. "You did say this was a business meeting, right?" she asked, giving Mick the once-over as well.

He was wearing jeans with a ripped knee she'd bet wasn't a stylistic choice, paired with a concert tee so faded she could barely make out the band name. Mick wasn't a slob, exactly, but there was something about him that was undeniably . . . *scruffy*. That's the word that came to mind when looking at him.

"Yeah, but this is a family business." He grinned. "I'm sure my brother would love to enforce a dress code at all times, but I prefer to keep things casual." He turned, gesturing for Kat to follow him. "Joe went to round up our sister. They'll join us in the conference room in a few minutes."

Kat tightened her hold on her laptop bag and forced her wobbly legs to move. Cold sweat tickled the back of her neck. With every room they passed, she held her breath, some illogical part of her waiting for the doors to swing open and dead bodies to spill out, their limp, cold hands reaching for her.

Mick came to a stop in front of a door at the end of the hall. When he turned back to face her, his brow pinched with concern. "Are you feeling all right?"

"I'm fine," she lied. It's not like she could tell him the truth. He'd think she was nuttier than Babcia's fruitcake.

"Okay." He yanked on the handle and held the door open for her. "After you."

Kat was relieved to see no evidence of coffins or urns or other obvious reminders that this was a funeral home. Some of the nervous tension coiled inside her unwound. She placed her laptop bag on the table and settled into the chair he offered her. "Thanks."

"Would you like some water?" he asked, gesturing to the pitcher at one end of the table.

"Sure." She glanced around. He'd called it a conference room, and that's what the space felt like. In fact, with its large, polished table and comfy leather swivel chairs, it wasn't very different from the hotel business rooms she often met in for wedding consults, water pitcher and all.

"They shouldn't be long now." Mick handed her a glass, then poured one for himself. He took the seat next to her, watching as she chugged her water. "Are you sure you're feeling okay?"

Kat was about to assure him she was fine when she met his eyes. His gaze was curious, maybe even a tad worried, but not judgmental. "Funeral homes make me nervous," she admitted. There. That was the truth. Part of it, anyway.

"Ah." He nodded, as if she'd confirmed his own suspicions. He took a sip of water and paused, eyeing her over the rim.

"What?" she demanded.

Mick set his glass on the table. "Maybe this wasn't such a good idea."

She frowned and set her own glass down. "Are you backing out of our deal?"

"No," he hurried to say. "But I am wondering why you want to work with a funeral home if they make you so uncomfortable."

"When we were talking in the café, I realized the arrangements I do for them are small potatoes. If I want to open my own shop one day, I need to branch out and start cultivating more partnerships. Funeral homes are one of the most lucrative markets for florists."

"But is it worth causing you anxiety?"

"I do have some hang-ups when it comes to coffins and . . . dead people inside of them." Kat licked her lips, which had suddenly gone dry. "I read somewhere that prolonged exposure can help cure a phobia. Do you think that's true?"

"Yes, it can help, but there's a process." Mick studied her. "Part of that is talking about what happened to cause the trauma in the first place."

"Oh." Kat jiggled her foot, nervous tension vibrating through her.

"Not now," Mick said, voice soft. "When you're ready."

In that moment, wrapped in the unexpected warmth of his sable eyes, so steady and patient, Kat felt like she could tell Mick anything.

The door to the conference room swung open. "Mickey!" Joe called. "Ready to do this?"

"We're both ready." Mick nodded and then gestured to Kat. "You remember the florist from the other night?"

"Katy, right?"

Still off-kilter, Kat pulled herself together and plastered on her most professional smile, the cool, serene one that had seen her through countless stressful weddings. "It's Kat, actually," she corrected.

"Nice to see you again, *Kat*," Joe corrected himself, voice polished and polite. He settled himself at the head of the table. "I hope we didn't keep you waiting too long."

"It's my fault," a young red-haired woman gushed, hurrying past Joe and plopping into the seat next to Kat. "I was dropping Gran off at Monday night bingo and got sucked in."

"I know what you mean," Kat's mouth curved in another smile, this one genuine. "My grandmother plays bingo too."

"I'm Mary Katherine," the woman beamed. "But you can call me Mary-Kate. Or MK works too." Her lips quirked with exasperated affection as she flicked a hand toward each of the men. "And yes, I have the dubious honor of being related to these two."

Kat grinned. Now that she looked closer, she could see that despite the striking difference in hair color, all three siblings shared the same eyes, a rich shade of brown so dark as to be almost black. "Nice to meet you."

"Same." Mary-Kate said. She reached out, clasping one of Kat's hands in both of hers. "I'm O'Sullivan's resident mortician."

"Ah, Mick mentioned that." Kat fought the instinct to yank

her hand back when she realized the hands touching her hand had touched dead people—a lot of dead people. *Keep your shit together.* "I hear you're interested in green burials."

"Obsessed, really." Mary-Kate smiled brightly. Her disposition was so sunny and sweet, the juxtaposition to the subject matter was rather jarring. "My brother says you're going to help us put together the proposal?"

"Pardon?" Joe shifted his gaze to Mick. "What's this about?"

"You told me you wanted a business proposal. Since I don't know how to write one, I found someone who did." Mick gestured at Kat.

"Forgive me." Joe cleared his throat and glanced her way. "But you're a florist."

"A florist with a business degree," Kat elaborated, keeping her tone neutral. It was obvious Joe had no idea what his brother had been cooking up. She could understand his frustration.

Joe closed his eyes, pinching the bridge of his nose between two fingers. "So what you're telling me is not only is the business proposal not ready, but someone else is writing it?"

"I'm not writing it for him," Kat explained. "But I did agree to offer guidance on how to write it."

"Yeah." Mick nodded. "What she said."

"Fine." Joe steepled his fingers. "Let's get this meeting started, shall we?"

Kat liked Joe's brisk way of handling things. It was obvious he was someone who took charge and got things done. Someone you could count on. She pulled out her laptop and settled in. For the next hour, she took copious notes, asked questions, and made suggestions as Mick and his brother debated the logistics of opening a bar in a funeral home and his sister explained the benefits of eco-burials.

"Well?" Mick asked once Mary-Kate had finished delivering a moving appeal for tree pods. "What do you think?"

Kat turned her attention to all three siblings. "First of all, both

Mick and Mary-Kate's visions have merit. I can see the value their ingenuity and passion could bring the business and the community O'Sullivan's serves." She paused and clicked on her laptop, pulling up the expense sheet she'd cobbled together during their discussion. "But implementing their ideas will take time and money."

"That's exactly what I'm worried about." Joe adjusted his glasses, addressing Kat with a new level of respect. Not that he hadn't always been respectful, but Kat could sense something had changed. Before this meeting, she'd simply been the blond woman who delivered flowers that caused riots among his elderly clients. "There's a lot of up-front costs to consider."

"Agreed." Kat flashed Joe a confident smile. He'd heard his brother's and his sister's pitches, now it was her turn. "That's why it makes sense to move forward on forming a partnership with me. O'Sullivan's will receive a commission on all sales, of course."

"We will?" Mick asked.

"Mm-hmm." Kat nodded. "It's customary."

"I didn't know that," Mick said. "Joey, did you know that?"

"Yes, *Mickey*, I knew that." Joe kept his gaze on Kat. "Twenty percent."

Kat shook her head. The amount he was asking wasn't absurd, but it was on the high end of average. And they both knew it. "Ten."

"Fifteen," he countered.

"Twelve," Kat said.

"Done," he agreed.

"And I'd like to set up a showroom here," Kat added.

Joe hesitated.

"A small space, to highlight some special options," she clarified.

He frowned. "Expensive options, you mean."

"More money for you as well."

"Not if the client ends up spending more of their budget on your flowers and less on our services," Joe volleyed.

"Fair point," Kat said, gaining new respect for Joe as well. Beneath that pleasant demeanor was a shrewd businessman.

"What if we added floral options to the reception packages?" Mick suggested.

Kat cocked her head, "Now there's an idea."

"Mick is good at figuring out compromises." Mary-Kate grinned. "He plays mediator between me and Joe all the time."

Mick shrugged. "Middle-child syndrome."

Kat had a feeling it had less to do with birth order and was more about Mick himself.

"I figure we'll be putting together a showroom for the reception decorations," Mick added, "it would make sense to include floral arrangements too."

"It would make sense," Joe agreed. "*If* we move forward on your plan to host receptions." He tapped his pen on the top of his notepad. "I want to see some actual numbers before making a final decision."

"Come on, Joe," Mary-Kate groaned. "Why are you always such a stick-in-the-mud?"

"Someone needs to be."

Kat caught the strain in the oldest O'Sullivan's voice, but there was pride as well. It was obvious Joe liked being in charge. Liked taking care of things. He was such an *adult*. It was appealing. Unlike the boys she'd dated, Joe was a grown-ass man. But she wasn't here for that, Kat reminded herself. She was here for business. "It's good to be cautious," Kat said. "Rushing into things always leads to trouble."

She certainly knew that well enough.

"Don't worry," Mick assured her. "Joe never rushes into anything." The way he said it didn't make it sound like a compliment.

Mary-Kate rolled her eyes and swiveled to face Kat. "If you give me a minute, I can give you the price lists you asked for."

"That'd be great, thanks."

"Actually, Mick can you grab those?" Mary-Kate asked, sliding out of her chair. "They're in a folder on the desk in my office."

"Why can't you get it?"

"Because I need to pick up Gran from bingo." Mary-Kate paused, a spark of mischief in her eyes. "Unless you want to."

"No, no. It's fine," Mick said quickly.

Mary-Kate leaned toward Kat conspiratorially. "The bingo babes are always trying to hook Mick up with one of their grand-daughters."

"Ugh." He groaned and stood. "They see me as a project. A mess in need of fixing."

"Someone they can iron all the wrinkles out of?" Kat glanced down at his rumpled shirt. "Figuratively and literally?"

"Exactly." Mick nodded. "I'll be right back with those lists."

"It's not fair." Mary-Kate sighed. "Here I am, a perfectly eligible bachelorette. I wish they'd spend more time helping *me* find a date." She let out a beleaguered sigh. "Anyway, it was nice meeting you, Kat."

"Same." Kat grinned.

Alone with Joe in the conference room, Kat turned to face him across the table. "The proposal is going to take some time to pull together, but there's no reason why we can't draw up the partnership agreement now," she pressed, holding his gaze. "What do you say?"

"Excellent plan, *Kat*." He smiled as he emphasized her name again.

Kat returned the smile, noting his effort to make sure he got her name right this time. Was she imagining it, or was there a hint of something more than professional courtesy beneath his veneer of politeness?

Joe led Kat back to the funeral home's main office. He opened the door and gestured for her to go ahead of him. The moment she crossed the threshold, a familiar whistle pierced the air. "Hello, gorgeous."

"Hello, Seamus," she said, grinning at the bird.

"I see you two have met," Joe observed.

"Hey, asshole," Seamus barked at Joseph.

Kat stifled a snort. This salty cockatoo was fast becoming one of her favorite nonhumans.

"My apologies," Joe said. Above the starched white of his crisp collar, his neck flushed red. He frowned at the bird. "That's not the kind of language we use in front of a lady, Seamus."

"This lady doesn't mind," Kat assured him. "Is that what he always calls you?"

"Unfortunately, yes." Joe heaved out an aggrieved sigh.

"Pretty lady. Pretty lady." The bird repeated the phrase over and over, turning it into a little song.

Joe shook his head. "He's incorrigible, I'm afraid."

Kat settled into the chair Joe offered. "I think he's adorable."

"That's debatable." Joe grunted and took a seat behind the desk. "Now then, about the contract for the commission fee." He opened a drawer and pulled out ledger. "What percent did we say?"

"You know perfectly well it was twelve, Joey."

Kat jumped. Mick was standing in the doorway to the office.

"Excuse me, *Mickey*." Joe glowered at his brother. "I was merely confirming the details with our new business partner."

The level of testosterone shot up in the room and Kat wanted to roll her eyes like Mary-Kate had done minutes before. As much as she missed her own brothers, she didn't miss this bullshit. Were all brothers like this?

Once Kat had signed the agreement, Joe snapped the ledger shut. He stood and reached for her hand, and for a moment, Kat thought he might be planning to kiss it, like one of those chivalry-isn't-dead kind of guys who only exist in books and movies. Instead, he politely shook it. "I believe we're all set here?" His tone was still friendly, but there was a briskness now.

Kat nodded, taken aback by the sudden shift.

"I look forward to working with you." With a quick jerk of his head, he excused himself, brushing past his brother who still lingered in the doorway.

Kat pursed her lips. She tried not to feel offended by the brusque dismissal. That was ridiculous. This was business.

"Goodbye, fucker!" Seamus screeched.

"You said it, pal." Mick crossed his arms and leaned against the doorframe. "Don't take my brother's stick-up-the-ass routine personally." Mick handed her a folder. "Here's the info you needed from my sister."

"Thanks." She tucked the papers into her laptop bag and got to her feet. "See you later, Seamus."

"Later, gator," the bird squawked.

Kat turned to Mick. "That's a new one."

"You were expecting him to say something more colorful weren't you?" Mick asked.

"Guilty," Kat admitted. "But that was cute too."

"Don't tell Seamus you think he's cute," Mick warned. "That bird is enough of a narcissist as it is."

"I've sworn off narcissists, but I suppose I can make an exception."

Mick laughed and followed her out of the office. "Thanks for coming today. I appreciate the help."

"It was my pleasure," she said. "Really." They reached the foyer and Kat turned to face him. "Besides, it's not like I didn't benefit from this meeting too."

"I know. You're quite the negotiator."

Kat warmed in the glow of his praise. "You weren't so bad yourself," she said. "The idea to add floral options to the reception packages was a good one."

"I have my moments." The corner of his mouth lifted.

Kat's lips twitched as her gaze met Mick's. She should leave now, but she couldn't seem to bring herself to walk out the door. Something about that cocky little quirk of a smile made her legs wobbly. Kat cleared her throat. "I'll send you an email with some tasks you can get started on for your proposal," she said, hitching her laptop bag higher on her shoulder. "At some point we should probably set up another in-person meeting. Maybe over lunch?"

"Sounds great," Mick agreed. "But I'll pick the place this time."

CHAPTER 10

Mick

Mick leaned against a lamppost, watching Kat scan the row of storefronts lining the sidewalk. Over the past few weeks, he'd gotten to know Kat better through their almost daily texts and emails. Their communication was lighthearted and casual, and Mick had come to look forward to her messages. He was excited about the proposal coming together, of course, but he also simply enjoyed chatting with her. With every exchange, he seemed to learn something new about her.

He hadn't seen her since the business meeting at the funeral home, but within seconds of seeing her in person again, he knew.

He was fucked.

They'd finally set a date for lunch, and as promised, Mick picked the place. Only, he hadn't given Kat an address, just directions to the corner where to meet. When she'd arrived, he'd told her to guess which restaurant on the block was his favorite. It was interesting to see what she chose. It gave him a peek inside her mind, an idea of how she might perceive him. So far, she'd guessed three. And had been wrong every time.

"I'm too hungry to play this game anymore," she finally said. "I give up. Which of these establishments holds the dubious honor of being your favorite?"

He smirked at the mocking note in Kat's voice. She had a penchant for sarcasm that amped up when she was impatient, which he'd noticed was often. It made it a little too easy to push her buttons and a whole lot of fun. Taking pity on her, Mick pointed at an unassuming diner entrance. It looked like any one of dozens of other diners scattered through the city like sprinkles on a donut. "I know what you're thinking," he said, guiding her toward the door. "But trust me. This is no average diner."

The aroma of bacon frying and coffee brewing wafted up to greet them as he escorted Kat inside. One of those odd yowling sounds emanated from her midsection, loud enough to be heard over the clatter of silverware and chatter of diners. "Come on." He tugged her toward the counter.

They'd barely settled onto a pair of stools when a familiar face appeared in the window of the kitchen. "Hey, Mikey!"

Mick waved at his friend, middle finger extended. Fidel knew how much he hated that nickname.

Kat tipped her chin toward him. "'Mikey'?"

"Yes." Mick grunted in disgust. "But nobody calls me that. Except for Fidel here, because I let him get away with it."

"Yeah, you do," Fidel chimed in. With a sly smile, the chef leaned through the window and addressed Kat. "He'll let me call him anything I want as long I let him keep eating here."

"It's true." Mick sighed. "I have no shame when it comes to Fidel's cooking." He held up two fingers. "Two of my usual, please." He paused, tuning to Kat. "Wait, you're not a vegetarian, are you?"

"Nope."

"Any food allergies or sensitivities?"

"None that I know of."

"Perfect." He wiggled his eyebrows. "Do you trust me?"

Kat held his gaze, wary humor matching the soft tilt of her lips. "I don't *mistrust* you."

"Good enough." He held up his fingers again. "Two. The works."

"You got it, *Mikey*." Fidel whistled and disappeared from view.

"That was nice of you," she said.

"What was?"

"Asking about my food preferences." Kat looked at him,

expression thoughtful. "And you weren't being sarcastic or mocking either."

"Why would I do that?" He wondered what kind of assholes she'd been hanging around. Self-absorbed dicks who ditched her with their pet hedgehogs, obviously. Before she could answer, a server swung by with the coffeepot. Mick flipped over the soup bowl–sized mug sitting on a coaster in front of him and the waitress filled his cup with the dark, steaming brew. "Now *this* is a coffee cup," he said, lifting it with both hands and sighing in pleasure.

Kat flipped her own mug over. "It's a swimming pool."

"Order up!" Fidel called, slapping two platters in the kitchen window and ringing a bell

"That's us," Mick said.

"So fast?" Kat blinked as the server set the food down on the counter in front of them. She studied her plate. "It's an omelet."

"Oh, this is more than an omelet, sweetheart."

Her blue eyes frosted over, icy enough to turn the swimming pool in his coffee mug into a skating rink.

"I'm guessing you don't like being called 'sweetheart.'"

"You guessed right."

"Noted." He cleared his throat. "I suppose this means 'princess' is off the menu, too."

"Actually . . . ," her lips quirked playfully to the side, "I kinda like that one," she confessed. "I call JoJo a princess all the time."

In wordless agreement, they both unrolled their silverware and dug in.

"Oh my god," Kat groaned.

"Good, right?" Mick asked.

"'Good' doesn't cover it." Kat took another bite and chewed slowly, groaning again. "This is incredible."

"I know." Mick managed to avoid saying he told her so but couldn't help the note of pride in his voice, and yes, a bit of smugness too. Packed with creamy melted cheese and spiked with spicy

crumbly sausage, the omelet was a symphony of textures and flavors. And colors too, dotted with diced red, green, yellow, and
orange peppers and adorned with avocado.

After they finished their meal, Kat pulled out her laptop and
got down to business. "I think your next step should be making
final selections for vendors."

"Then I'm ahead of schedule."

She eyed him over the rim of her giant coffee mug. "Really?"

"Yep." Mick winked. "Because I already got my florist locked in."

"True." One corner of her mouth hitched. "Lucky you."

"I am lucky," Mick said. "I really don't know how I would have
pulled this all together without you."

"Thank you. It's been fun. Working with O'Sullivan's has
motivated me to start thinking more actively about starting my
own business."

"Planning on partnering with other funeral homes?"

"One is enough for now," Kat assured him. "More than
enough," she added, drumming her fingers on the counter.

The nervous gesture told Mick something was on her mind.
Recalling her admission that funerals made her anxious, he eased
back on his stool and sipped his coffee quietly, giving her space to
talk when she was ready. *If* she was ready.

His cup was almost empty when she tilted her face toward
him. "I've been thinking a lot about what you said." Her fingers continued their brisk tap. "About needing to be able to talk
through a traumatic experience before you can get over it."

"The only way past is through." Mick hazarded a glance
her way, careful to keep his voice neutral. "Do you think you're
ready?"

His question was met with silence, a quiet void filled by her
drumming fingers. Kat was silent for so long that Mick was sure
she wasn't going to answer him. Finally, she shifted on her stool,
hands quiet as she swiveled toward him, and Mick knew she was
ready to talk. Reluctant, but ready.

"Dziadek—that's my grandpa—died when I was seven." Her words were soft, nearly blending in with the noise around them. "My grandmother, Babcia, still keeps a picture of him on her nightstand."

He smiled, a bittersweet ache cramping in his gut. "My gran has the same of Granda."

His admission seemed to loosen the knot holding her pain so tight. A ghost of a smile crossed her face before she continued. "His funeral was open-casket. I didn't want to go up there to see him, but my parents insisted." She shook her head. "My mother was so angry that day. To be honest, she was always angry. But on that day in particular, she was furious. Not sad. Enraged."

"Death brings out all kinds of emotions in people," Mick said. He kept his tone free of judgment, but inside he wanted to throttle Kat's mother for the rough edges she'd given her daughter. Kat's pain in those few short sentences was so sharp, it cut him too.

"Something happened that day. More than my grandfather's death. Something that made my mom so angry she and my grandmother had a terrible fight. They haven't really spoken since." Kat paused, fiddling with the handle of her mug. "My mother wanted to leave. She screamed at me to hurry up and say goodbye to my grandfather. But when I told her I was too scared, she dragged me over to the coffin, lifted me up, and forced me to look at him."

Mick bit his cheek and willed himself to remain silent, to hold back a rebuke of her mother's atrocious behavior.

"For a moment, I thought she was going to throw me inside the coffin with him." Kat's voice was trembling now. "And then I felt bad because I didn't want to go with Dziadek to wherever he was going, even though I knew he'd be all alone." A tight little laugh rattled in her chest, the sound like a dried-out husk scraping against stone.

"But you don't say no to my mother, so I did what I was told. I looked at him . . . I don't know if it was blood or something else, but a dark liquid was seeping from his nose and mouth." She broke off, shuddering. "Sorry, I know this isn't something you want to hear about right after you ate."

Mick wanted to reach out to her. But he remained still, giving her space. "I've been around dead bodies all my life, Kat," he assured her. "Trust me, I'm fine."

"I wish I'd been fine." Kat laughed, but the sound fell flat. "I had nightmares for years after. Even in college, after a particularly stressful week, I'd wake up screaming, the image of my grandfather's rotting corpse etched in my brain." She let out another laugh, still shaky, but not quite so devastated. "So that's why I get freaked out at funerals." She placed her palms on the counter, fingers splayed wide. "I can't believe I'm still not over it after all these years."

"It's not uncommon at all." Mick placed a hand over hers. "Those kinds of traumatic moments can leave a lasting mark." He squeezed her fingers gently. "And thank you for telling me." He hoped she knew how much it meant to him that she'd shared this piece of herself. "I know that couldn't have been easy."

"It wasn't as hard as I expected," she admitted, sounding surprised. "Thank you for listening." Her shoulders lifted. "You're an easy person to talk to."

"Any time." Mick gave her hand a final squeeze.

Kat cleared her throat and slid her laptop back into her bag. It was clear she wanted to move on.

Following her lead, Mick asked, "So what's the next step for the proposal?"

"You've made a lot of progress." She zipped the bag and slid off her stool. "If you keep this up, I think we can have everything done by the end of the month."

"By Halloween, huh?" Mick asked, dropping some cash on the counter and standing up. "That's great."

"Do you have plans for Halloween?" she asked, following him out of the diner.

Mick shook his head as he held the door for her. "Not really."

"How do you feel about mixing business and pleasure?"

He nearly tripped but forced his feet to continue moving alongside Kat, matching his pace to hers. "Meaning?"

"I was hoping you'd come to a party."

"With you?" They paused to wait for a traffic light.

"No, with my hedgehog," Kat snarked. "Yes, with me. My best friends will be there with their boyfriends, and I really don't want to spend the night alone."

He raised his eyebrows.

"That sounded bad, didn't it?" A pretty flush crept up her cheeks and she quickly added, "I mean, I don't want to spend the evening alone. At the party. And you'd be coming with me as a boy. Not a boyfriend. A person. A nice person who's my friend. Oh god, I'm babbling."

She was adorable when flustered. The light changed, and as they crossed the street, Mick had to cram his hands in his pockets, fighting what seemed to be a near-constant urge to touch her. "I haven't been to a Halloween party in years."

"Then you have to come," Kat insisted. "Also," she paused as they stepped onto the curb. "I do have one more thing to ask."

"Only one more?" he teased.

"Would you be my wingman?"

Mick's brow furrowed. "You mean like someone to steer assholes away from you?"

"Or steer me away from the assholes," she snorted. "To be honest, I really could use some help with that."

He chuckled. "Happy to be of service."

"You're the best, thanks."

"Hey," Mick said, "that's what friends are for."

"You're right. And you are turning out to be a great friend." She surprised him then, leaning closer and pressing her lips to his cheek.

The kiss was quick. Pure and platonic and nothing to get excited about. But as Kat continued walking down the block, Mick trailed behind, unable to resist pressing a hand to his face, palm over the lingering tingle where her lips had been. He hurried to catch up with her. "Anything else I can help you with?"

"Well, since you asked . . ." She flashed him a smile that was remarkably angelic despite the wicked gleam in her eye.

Oh, shit. Mick had a bad feeling about this.

CHAPTER II

Mick

Only a few days remained until Halloween, and Mother Nature had finally gotten the memo that it was fall. Mick pulled up to the flower shop and parked. A chill wind blew through the trees planted in a neat row all along the block, shaking leaves loose and scattering them across the sidewalk. It had been over a month since he and Kat had walked to that snooty French café around the corner and first discussed the idea of working together.

He cut the engine and debated what to do next. Did he wait for Kat here? Knock on the shop door? Go around back? Mick didn't even know what they were doing today, only that Kat had asked him to pick her up so he could perform his first official duty as her wingman, whatever the hell that meant.

Trouble. That's what it meant.

As if on cue, Kat rounded the corner of her building. She was wearing her hair in the same style as the night they'd first met, her long golden braid trailing over one shoulder like a fairy princess in the tower. A bright pink scarf was looped around her neck in thick fluffy folds, the ends flapping in the autumn breeze. She waved, blue eyes brightening when she caught sight of him. "Hi."

"Hi," he said, trying to go for casual. Not an easy feat considering his heart was currently tapping out an Irish step dance in his chest. Mick wanted to tug on that scarf, pull her close, and see if her lips felt as soft as they looked. Instead, he got out of the car, hurried to the passenger side, and opened the door for her.

"Thanks." Kat dropped onto the seat, smiling up at him. "Such a gentleman."

"That's me," Mick said, keeping his smile frozen in place while he waited for her to get settled. Then he shut the door, cringing as he walked around to the driver's side. A gentleman. Right. When he was standing there imagining what it would be like to kiss her.

After their last in-person encounter, Mick knew he had to get a handle on himself around Kat. If they were going to continue spending more time together, as friends, he was going to have to start doing a better job of controlling his feelings of attraction to her. She'd joked about mixing business and pleasure, but the reality was the potential for things to get awkward and messy was definitely a factor he needed to keep in mind.

"What's the plan today?" Mick asked as he started the car.

"Well, as my official wingman, you're going to help me find a costume guaranteed to grab the attention of the right guy."

"I don't think that's going to be a problem," he muttered.

She swatted his arm playfully and gave him directions to the costume shop. Once there, Mick had to fight the urge to hold her hand as they crossed the parking lot. Seeking a distraction, he glanced up at the banner haphazardly covering whatever store had once occupied this space. "Do you ever think about what happens to these places when it's not Halloween?"

"Not really." Kat followed him through the entrance. "Why?"

"They seem to appear and disappear. Sometime in September they start popping up out of nowhere. Only to vanish almost overnight on November first." Mick gestured at the wall of monster masks that seemed a mile long. "What happens to all the stuff that doesn't sell?"

"They bury it in an unmarked grave," she suggested.

"Ha." He eyed the unholy variety of plastic weapons on display.

"They burn it as a sacrifice to Beelzebub, their lord and master."

"Ha. Ha."

"How should I know?" Kat shrugged as they passed by a large

assortment of wigs. "They probably have a giant central warehouse it all gets sent back to."

"Maybe," Mick said, not convinced. "Seems very shady to me."

"Wait." She turned to look at him, lips twitching. "Do you have some kind of conspiracy theory involving a chain of Halloween stores?"

"All I'm saying is—" They rounded a corner and Mick screamed. Not just any scream, but a high-pitched undulating shriek.

"What's wrong?" Kat asked, eyes wide as she whirled around to see what had spooked him.

Mick clapped a hand over his mouth and tried to keep further humiliating noises from escaping.

She glanced at the animatronic display looming over them. "Mick," she pressed, her voice full of suspicion. "Are you afraid of clowns?"

"No," he mumbled, refusing to make eye contact with the gigantic creepy-ass circus demon sent from hell to drain his happiness and eat his soul.

"Are you sure?" Kat nudged him closer to the display.

"Why do his teeth look like needles? Why? Do clowns not have good dental plans?" The evil thing shifted, rotating in his direction, one robotic hand lifting a massive bloodstained mallet. "Aaah!" he shrieked again, squeezing his eyes shut so he didn't have to see the menacing painted face leering down at him.

She giggled.

"Fine." His eyes snapped open, and he glared at her. "Yes. I'm scared of clowns." Mick backed away from the sinister Bozo. "I fucking hate clowns."

"There's nothing to be ashamed of," she assured him. "Lots of people are scared of clowns."

"Then why are you laughing?"

"I'm not laughing at you," she protested.

He raised a skeptical brow.

"Okay, maybe I am. A little." Her lips twitched. "That was some scream. The sorority girls running haphazardly through the woods have nothing on you." Her blue eyes twinkled with humor, but the look she gave him wasn't mocking. Kat grabbed his arm again. "Don't worry, I'll protect you," she said and pulled him along, giving the animatronic homicidal clown wide berth as she headed toward a rack of frilly dresses.

"How about this?" she asked, holding up an outfit.

"What's it supposed to be?"

"A French maid."

Mick narrowed his gaze. "Where's the rest of it?"

"Hilarious." Kat's tone was dry, but she put the dress back on the rack. "They've got all the usual suspects," she said, sorting through the hangers. "Sexy cop, sexy devil, sexy angel, sexy nun . . ."

"Sexy nun?" He repeated in disbelief.

She tossed him a skimpy black-and-white costume.

"I'll be damned." He probably would be too, after seeing that atrocity. Mick squeezed his eyes shut and frantically shoved the costume back on the rack, a dozen years of parochial school making him desperate to dislodge that image as quickly as possible. "What you're saying is, basically, take anything you can think of and make it sexy," he surmised.

"Basically."

"Sexy chicken?" Mick suggested.

She paused and glanced at him across the top of the clothing rack. "Are guys into that?"

"If I said yes, would you believe me?"

Her lips twitched, caught between a smile and a smirk. "You're picturing it, aren't you?"

She shook her head in denial, but her mouth gave her away.

Mick felt his own mouth quiver with repressed amusement because now he was picturing it too. Well. Sort of. "Please tell me you're not imagining the same thing I am," he begged.

"Don't worry, I couldn't possibly fathom what is happening inside that strange brain of yours," she said, smirk winning for a moment.

"Big Bird in a bikini," he admitted.

And then the smile was back in full force, lighting up her entire face as she burst out laughing.

Mick sucked in a breath, fighting against the sudden sharp, sweet sting piercing his lungs. Or maybe it was his heart. Damn it, he knew this had been a bad idea. He turned his attention back to the costumes. The best thing for him to do was to stay in his lane and keep his promise to be her wingman. And maybe steer her toward an outfit that wouldn't make him lose his mind.

"Bingo," Mick said, pulling a box off a shelf. "This is the one."

Kat squinted. "What even is that?"

He held up the box, showing her the picture of the costume plastered to the front. "An inflatable T. rex."

"Absolutely not." She snorted. "How would I even do shots in that thing?"

Mick laughed. "I appreciate the fact this was your first concern." He put the box back on the shelf and turned his attention to a wall of onesies. "How about this?"

"Uh-uh, I'm not going dressed as a furry." She shook her head. "I mean, everyone has a right to their kink, but that's not my scene."

"Right. Totally." Mick dropped the costume as if it burned him. And here he'd thought it was the Easter Bunny.

"Here we go." She pulled a costume off a rack and held it up.

"A cheerleader uniform?" *Oh sweet Sister Michael on a pogo stick.*

"A Chicago Bears cheerleader uniform," she corrected.

He eyeballed the outfit skeptically. "Isn't a cheerleader outfit a little cliché?"

"It's classic."

"I thought you didn't want to dress too sexy."

"Please." She scoffed. "It's a sweater. Which means my cleavage won't be falling out of some skimpy top. Plus, I can wear sneakers instead of heels." She held the costume up to herself. "Okay, so the skirt might be a little short . . ."

"A little," Mick grunted. He doubted it would cover London, much less France.

"Come on." She grabbed his hand and dragged him toward the dressing rooms. "I'm going to try it on and see how it fits."

Mick slumped against the wall next to Kat's stall in defeat, waiting for her to change and trying not to think about the fact she was changing. After a few minutes, when she still hadn't come out, he straightened and asked, "Everything okay in there?"

"Everything's fine," she mumbled.

Thanks to his sister, mother, and grandmother, Mick was already a firm believer of the universal truth that when a woman said everything was fine, it meant the exact opposite. But even without that, he still would have known by Kat's tone that everything was *not* fine. "Is there something wrong with the costume?"

"I don't know."

"Are you decent?"

"That's debatable." More mumbling.

He knocked on the stall door. "Can I see it?"

Silence. Then a heavy sigh. Followed by the bolt on the changing room door sliding open.

Mick almost swallowed his tongue. He knew he was staring but couldn't seem to stop.

"The sweater is a little tighter than I expected," she said, crossing her arms over her chest in a self-conscious move that made Mick want to kick himself in the nuts.

He was a tool. He cleared his throat but before he could say anything, Kat was twirling in a circle.

"At least the skirt isn't too short," she said, checking her backside in the mirror. "What do you think?"

I think I just got a peek at cheek. He averted his gaze and decided it was best if he stared at the floor. Yeah. The floor was good. "Hey, there's a stain on the carpet," he said.

"Mick."

"It kind of looks like Florida, doesn't it?"

"*Mick.*"

"Do you think the stain is coffee? I hope it's coffee."

"Will you stop talking about the carpet and pay attention to me!" She yanked him into the dressing room and slammed the door shut behind them. "Now look at me and tell me what you think."

He snapped his chin up and looked her in the eyes. Right in the eyes and nowhere else. "It's, ah . . . nice," he managed to choke out. "Very nice."

A flurry of emotions swirled in her blue gaze, amusement and frustration and . . . doubt.

"I'm sorry." The apology spilled from his lips, bumbling but sincere. "For, um, ogling."

"I know you are." Kat collapsed on to the little bench in the corner of the room. She tugged at the pleats of the miniskirt. "This is going to sound obnoxious, but I'm aware of the fact I have the kind of body that gets a lot of attention."

"That's not obnoxious, that's a fact," Mick agreed. "And I say that with respect," he added.

She laughed, a small, dry sound that crackled with bitterness. "Well, not everyone does," Kat said. "Respect me, I mean."

His gut twisted. There were layers of hurt here, pain in the tight lines furrowing her brow and bracketing her mouth. A hot burst of anger roiled through him. *Fuck them*, he wanted to say. Fuck everyone who had ever made her feel this way.

Fuck himself too. What she needed was a friend, not another hornball trying to get under her skirt. He'd be a liar if he said he wasn't attracted to her. But being her friend wasn't some consolation prize to sleeping with her. It's what mattered the most. He needed to make sure she knew that.

"I'm sorry," he said again. "And I do respect you." Cautiously, Mick eased onto the bench next to her. "I think you're smart and funny and I can't imagine anyone meeting you and not seeing those things."

"You know what really sucks?"

Mick didn't answer. His training to be a therapist had taught him it was better to wait and let her tell him rather than guess.

"It sucks how much time and energy people waste analyzing women's bodies." Kat tapped her toe. An angry staccato beat thumping against the fitting room's stained and faded carpet. "Constantly criticizing what we wear or don't wear. If we're over-dressed or underdressed. Are we too much or not enough, too sexy or too boring . . . it's bullshit."

"It is," he agreed.

She was silent, eyes narrowed, as if studying him for any sign he was patronizing her.

He wasn't. But the fact that she seemed to expect him to struck Mick deeply. He hated that she felt this way. Hated that her ex-periences in life had taught her to assume the worst. Caused her to form a defensive shield to protect against the poisoned barbs of judgment.

"It took me a while to get the negative voices out of my head, but after the bullshit I put up with in high school, I decided I was done trying to conform to someone else's standards. I'd dress the way I liked, to please one person. Me." She picked at edge of the sweater. "This might sound silly, but it felt like a victory. To wear whatever I wanted because of how it made *me* feel, regardless of what anybody else thought."

"That doesn't sound silly at all," Mick said. "I've fought a life-long battle with my brother against wearing ties and fancy suits. Though that's more about indulging my general laziness than making a statement." He leaned toward her and whispered. "I don't like shirts with collars."

A sliver of a smile tickled her lips. "I noticed." Kat stood, moving to examine herself in the full-length mirror. "I think I look hot." She turned to face him, hands on her hips. "Though maybe not as hot as Big Bird in a bikini. What do you think?"

"As your official wingman, I think I'm going to need to carry a stick." He heaved a sigh. "Are you sure you don't want to wear the T. rex costume? It would make my job a lot easier."

"Not a chance," she laughed. A mischievous glint lit her eyes. "Though I did see a clown costume I'd be willing to try on . . ."

"Nope. We're good. This is good." Mick got to his feet. "Go Bears!" he cheered.

She burst into giggles.

Oh holy Mary, the things that were happening in that sweater as she laughed. Mick flicked his gaze to the ceiling and willed himself to be a better man.

"Um, I changed my mind. You should wear the clown outfit instead."

"Too late." The smile she gave him was wicked. "I only hope the reaction I get to this costume at the Halloween party is half as good as yours."

Mick winced. "Was I that obvious?"

"The look on your face when I opened the door was pretty priceless," she admitted.

"Then I guess you've found your costume."

"Now it's your turn," Kat said.

"Um, no thanks," Mick hedged, escaping her dressing room while he still had a shred of dignity left. "I'm sure I can find something to wear at home."

"Oh!" Kat peered at him over the top of her stall. "You should invite your brother and sister to the party. It'll be fun."

"Fun," Mick echoed weakly. He almost wished she'd suggested they go to the circus.

CHAPTER 12

Kat

A waitress in a sexy pirate costume scooted past, carrying a treasure chest packed with candy corn–colored Jell-O shots. Kat wished she'd been fast enough to snag one; she could use the double-barreled jolt of sugar and alcohol. She felt on edge, like a rubber band stretched taut, ready to snap. Ever since she'd decided to find Mr. Right, the prospect of dating had felt more stressful than ever.

When she'd made that checklist with her friends, it was like a stopwatch had been clicked. Now the race was on, and with the clock ticking, every second she floundered, the farther she fell behind. Andie and Julia were moving in with their guys, and it stung that her friends were taking this step together without her. She might have been able to handle things better if it was only one of them . . . but both?

Kat forced herself to step away from those thoughts before she descended into an anxiety spiral. She had a plan. She would follow that plan. She scanned the pop-up pavilion and immediately recognized a mop of sandy blond hair hovering above the crowd. Bingo. At six foot four, Julia's boyfriend Luke was conveniently easy to spot in a crowd.

Maneuvering through the throngs of costumed partygoers, Kat made her way toward the group. They were gathered around a reserved table near the front of the karaoke stage. She eyed the rope marking off the area. "VIP, huh?"

"Perk of the job," Julia said, giving her a hug.

"I thought you didn't like to accept work perks," Kat said,

grabbing the empty seat next to Julia. "Something about journalistic integrity?"

"There are times when I can make an exception," Julia said with a grin. "This happens to be one of them."

"Besides," Andie chimed in, "depending on who's singing up there, it's more of a curse than a perk."

As if to make her point, someone in a sparkly rhinestone Elvis costume reached the chorus of "Viva Las Vegas" with a voice that likely had the real king of rock and roll rolling in his grave.

Kat winced and settled back in her seat. Thankfully, Elvis soon left the building, replaced with a mermaid in a bright red wig whose rendition of "Part of Your World" wasn't half bad. The crowd seemed to be into it, though that might have had more to do with the starfish pasties the singer was sporting. "Didn't Ariel wear a clamshell bra?"

"I don't think Prince Eric will be complaining," Julia snarked. She adjusted the crown over the long blond wig covering her own auburn waves, the movement revealing a pair of pointy elf ears.

Kat glanced around the table, heart sinking as she took in everyone's costumes. They were all wearing pointy ears. "I thought you were doing couple costumes, not a foursome."

"What about a foursome?" Curt asked.

"In your dreams, butter bean," Andie said. "Wait. Never mind. You better not dream about that."

Despite the hurt squeezing her chest, Kat couldn't help laughing.

"We're not a foursome," Luke piped up. "I'm Link and Julia is Princess Zelda."

"Oh," Kat said. "Um, that's a video game, right?"

"Yes." Luke flinched. "It's a video game." He looked as pained as Curt had when he saw Kat's Bears' uniform. Or Mick when she'd gotten a detail wrong about that *Lord of the Elves* movie.

Thinking of Mick eased the sting she'd felt upon seeing all her friends in matching costumes. Kat hoped he'd show up soon.

Julia had Luke and Andie had Curt and it would be nice if she had someone that was here just for her too, even if he was only a friend.

"Then what are you two supposed to be?" she asked, turning to Andie and Curt. "Because I gotta say, you all look like elves to me."

"We are not elves, we're hobbits," Andie declared. "Curt is Samwise and I'm Frodo." Andie held up her hand, pointing to a gold band on her finger.

Kat gasped. "Is that . . ."

"No!" Andie exclaimed, chuckling. "It's part of the costume." She pet the ring, crooning in a raspy, high-pitched voice, "My precious."

"You're all a bunch of weirdos," Kat said, laughing too, relieved to know her friends hadn't banded together and left her completely out. Maybe it was childish and petty, but she felt like an outlier enough as it was.

"My brother says the same thing about me all the time," a familiar voice observed from behind her.

Kat jumped, glancing over her shoulder to see Mick standing on the other side of the velvet VIP rope. Joe and Mary-Kate stood next to him.

"You're here!" she said brightly. A little too brightly. Kat tried to rein herself in. She took it down a notch and waved a hand, inviting them over. "I'm glad you could make it." She gestured at the empty spots at their table, which conveniently sat eight. "Grab a chair."

"That's very kind of you," Joe said, the epitome of a gentleman as he held a seat out for his sister.

"Of course." Kat nodded, tempted to curtsy in response to his impeccable manners. Instead, she made the rounds of introductions with her friends. "We were just talking about our costumes," she explained.

"Ooh, fun." Mary-Kate clapped her hands. "Can you guess what mine is?"

Kat noticed the small, single-serve boxes of cereal stuck to the front of Mary-Kate's dress. A plastic butcher knife protruded from one of them. "You're a cereal killer, right?"

"Correct!" Mary-Kate declared.

Next to Kat, Joe surreptitiously reached up and tugged at something on his shoulder. She turned and realized it was a snack-sized bag of potato chips.

"He's the guy with a chip on his shoulder," Andie guessed.

"Correct again!" Mary-Kate said brightly, voice booming like a game show announcer.

Julia turned and looked at Mick. "Are those candy wrappers on your shirt?"

"They are," Mick said.

"Hmm . . . ," Julia mused, gaze narrowing thoughtfully.

"Here's a hint," Mick offered, pulling a knit beanie out of his back pocket and putting it on.

"A diabetic hipster?" Julia guessed, tone only half joking.

"Um, no." Mick pulled the hood of his sweatshirt up over the beanie and crossed his arms. "How about now?"

Kat smirked. She'd already figured out his costume but decided to let Julia have this one.

"Oh, I get it," Julia declared, eyes lighting up. "Eminem. But, like M&M's."

"Actually, I was going for candy *rapper*," Mick admitted "But I like your idea even better."

The entire table laughed. Kat met Mick's eyes and grinned. This was fun. It was nice having them there. And so much better than being the odd one out at the couples' table. She was glad he was here and glad he'd brought Joe and Mary-Kate too. Kat leaned toward Mick and asked, "Whose idea was it to go with the punny costumes?"

"That would be me." Mary-Kate waved her hand.

"Well done," Kat said.

"Very clever," Julia agreed. "I'm feeling inspired to write a new article. Something like 'Top Ten Halloween Costumes You Can Make Using Stuff from Your Pantry.'"

"Personally, I like breadwinner." Andie grinned. "Grab a trophy or a medal and a loaf of bread, and you're good to go."

"Nice one, babe." Curt gave Andie a high-five. "I got one," he said. "An avocado with a halo."

Mary-Kate smacked the table like she was buzzing in with the winning answer on a game show. "Holy guacamole!"

"Ding-ding!" Curt said, giving her a high-five.

Everyone at the table laughed.

Kat sobered and realized if she wanted to set her plan in motion, she needed to grease the wheels. "I'm hitting the bar to grab a drink," she announced. "Anyone want anything?"

"This is VIP," Julia reminded her. "We get table service."

"Oh. Um. Cool." Kat glanced around the venue, considering her options. "Well, next time a server comes by, order me something good." She slid out of her chair. "I'm going to check out the song list."

"I'll join you," Mick said quickly and accompanied her to the DJ stand. He sidled up next to her as she opened one of the song books. "See anything you like?"

"Not yet," she said, flipping through the pages.

He leaned closer, the wrappers stuck to his clothes crinkling. "I was talking about dudes, not tunes," he said, loud enough to catch the attention of the DJ.

Kat snorted. "Smooth."

"I'm sorry, I'm being a terrible wingman." Mick glanced around the crowd. "But you gotta admit, I don't have a lot to work with here."

"Is that so?"

He gestured toward the stage, where a guy in a mullet that may or may not have been fake was butchering "Old Town Road."

"You think you could do better?" Kat teased.

"Oh, I know it."

"Then prove it." A wicked smile tugged at her mouth. "Mister candy wrapper."

"Fine." Mick crossed his arms. "But only if you agree to do the same."

"Fine." Kat nodded. "As long as you go first."

Mick tugged his hoodie into place. "Challenge accepted."

While Mick waited his turn to go onstage, Kat rejoined the others at the table.

"Where's my brother?" Joe asked.

"He's going to sing."

"He's going to what?" Mary-Kate asked, voice rising with incredulity.

"Sing." Kat's wicked grin returned. "Rap, actually."

Mary-Kate snorted with laughter. "What did you do, bribe him?"

"I promised to go next," she admitted.

"Good thing I ordered you a cocktail," Andie said and pushed a glass toward Kat. "You're going to need it."

Kat eyed the bluish-purple liquid suspiciously. "What's in it?"

"Not Malört, if that's what you're worried about," Andie assured her.

Kat took a tentative sip, discovering nothing more outrageous than a very strong, very fruity martini. "Is that blueberry I'm tasting?"

"Boo Berry," Andie said, grinning.

The flavor still fresh on her tongue, Kat forgot all about what she was drinking when the DJ announced Mick's name. Mic in hand, M&M took the stage. Pounding bass notes throbbed through the speakers and the crowd cheered, keyed up as he began to chant the opening lyrics to one of Eminem's most popular songs.

"He's really doing it," Joe said, eyes wide with shock as he watched his brother.

"And he's not bad," Mary-Kate added, equally shocked.

As Kat watched Mick close out the song, she had to agree. The crowd belted out the final words with him before erupting in applause while he returned the mic to the DJ and bounded off the stage. He strolled over to their table, knocking back his hoodie and taking off his beanie. His dark hair was damp with sweat, curling against the flushed skin of his neck.

Mouth suddenly dry, Kat sucked down the rest of her martini.

"How was that?" he asked.

"You know the words, at least," she said, setting her empty glass on the table and doing her best to act unimpressed.

"Don't listen to her, you were amazing," Andie said.

"Epic," Julia agreed.

"Hey!" Kat nudged her friends. "A little loyalty, please."

Andie patted her. "I'm sure you'll be great too, Kitty Kat."

"What song are you going to sing for us?" Julia asked.

"Yeah, Kat." Mick dropped into his chair with a casualness so studied it came across as antagonistic. "What are you going to sing for us?" He was baiting her, just like she'd baited him.

When she'd put Mick up to the test, she'd expected him to bail. But he'd knocked it out of the park. And now Kat felt like she had to at least step up to the plate. "I'm not sure," Kat admitted.

"I could help you pick a song," Joe offered.

"She doesn't need your help, Joey," Mick snapped.

"I say it's up to the lady to decide, *Mickey*." Joe turned his attention to Kat. Behind the lenses of his glasses, his rich brown eyes were identical to his brother's, minus the teasing glint. "May I be of service?"

"Sure." Kat smiled. "Why not." She glanced back at Mick, noting his scowl. It was obvious he didn't like the possibility of Joe taking over his role of wingman. Or maybe it was typical sibling rivalry. Like the way the brothers were constantly giving each other shit over their nicknames.

That gave Kat an idea. Her mouth twisted with mischievous glee. "You know, I think I might have a song in mind, after all."

She stood and grabbed Joe's hand. "Come on, you can tell me what you think."

Kat retraced her steps to the DJ stand, the weight of Mick's gaze glued to the back of her cheerleader sweater. Joe dutifully waited as she thumbed through the pages in the binder. "J, K, L . . . ," Kat read aloud under her breath. She paused when she got to M, scrolling her finger down the list of songs. "This one." She tapped the page, holding up the binder so Joe could read it. "What do you think?"

Joe primly adjusted his glasses exactly as Kat imagined Clark Kent would do. She contemplated the possibility that a superhero could be hiding beneath his calm, polite exterior. Wouldn't that be nice. She wasn't asking for much. He didn't need to fly or have X-ray vision.

In fact, forget the "super" and focus on the "hero." A kind, caring man who put her needs first. All qualities at the top of her list. She studied Mick's brother with new interest.

"That one?" Joe asked, underlining the title she'd indicated with his index finger.

"That's the one." Kat glanced up, meeting his eyes. "Should I go for it?"

"He's going to be mad," Joe warned her.

"I know," she said. "That's kind of the point."

"He'll blame me."

"This was my idea," Kat assured him. "I promise to take full responsibility."

"I can't let that happen." Joe set the binder down. "We'll do this together."

"You're going to get up there and sing with me?" she asked. He didn't seem the type. But then again, she hadn't expected Mick to turn into the real Slim Shady either.

"I'll be your backup singer, at least." A gentle smile curved Joe's mouth. "I can't promise much," he admitted, reaching for her hand, "but at least you won't be alone."

"Thanks." When it came down to it, that's all Kat wanted, really. Her fingers gripped firmly in his, she held her breath, hoping for some tingles. Despite what she'd said about physical attraction not being important, Kat couldn't help wishing for a spark. Joe's touch was pleasant, but nothing more. Not even the faintest crackle of electricity.

So what? When had sparks ever been a sign of something good? She was supposed to be doing things differently. Forget fireworks. They burn out in a flash. Focus on the bigger picture. Solid. Steadfast. Secure.

Joe was sweet, and it was rather heroic of him to offer to join her onstage. Although, from what Kat knew about brothers, this probably wasn't a completely altruistic move on Joe's part. He was going to enjoy razzing Mick too. And that's exactly what Kat planned to do—give Mick some shit and have fun while doing it.

The DJ announced their names and they walked onstage together. Kat squinted against the glare of the spotlight, waiting for the blurry sea of people to come into focus. She'd just managed to locate her friends' table when an iconic drumbeat blasted through the speakers. The audience cheered, obviously recognizing her song choice. By the irritated look on Mick's face, he recognized it too. He was close enough to the stage that Kat swore she could see a muscle ripple in his jaw.

Joe raised his hands in the air, clapping along with the beat. It wasn't long before the crowd joined in. Aiming a teasing smile in Mick's direction, Kat launched into the opening lines of "Mickey."

At first, she'd stared straight at Mick to let him know she'd picked this song specifically to provoke him. But as Kat continued to sing, eyes locked on his, the dynamic shifted. A ripple of awareness washed over her, as invisible yet tangible as gravity. Suddenly, she realized she couldn't look away, even if she tried.

As for Mick, well . . . he didn't seem able to look away either. His jaw was still set, his mouth a hard line, but he didn't look so annoyed anymore. Something had changed. Something in his eyes. The way they held hers. He was motionless, attention fixed on the stage. On her. Surrounded by throngs of dancing, singing people, his stillness made him stand out even more.

The crowd blurred, became a mass of colors and movement swirling in her peripheral vision. Her world narrowed to the man in front of her, the eye of the storm. And in this little bubble, holding only the two of them, Kat didn't feel like she was singing *at* Mick, but almost like she was singing *to* him.

The last verse began, and Kat finally managed to tear her gaze away. Heart racing, she jogged over to Joe, repeating the chorus again. She wasn't much of a singer herself, but the lyrics weren't exactly challenging. And the audience was helping a lot. She finished the song standing next to Joe and together they took a bow before exiting the stage.

"That was fun," Joe said, offering her his hand as they stepped off the stage.

"Yeah." Kat tugged a smile into place, still distracted by the pulsing throb of blood in her veins. It was definitely something. What, she wasn't sure. And she wasn't sure she wanted to find out.

When they got back to the table, everyone burst into another round of applause.

"Great work, you two," Julia said.

"The cheerleader uniform was a nice touch," Luke noted with approval.

"Huh?" Kat cocked her head.

"It was a great nod to the video."

"Oh, right." Julia's boyfriend was a game geek obsessed with all things retro. If anyone would have the details of the music videos from the eighties memorized, it would be Luke.

"Isn't that why you chose the song?" Luke asked.

"I know why she chose it," Mick said, his voice laced with sardonic acknowledgment.

Between the crowded bar and her dance under the stage

lights, Kat was already uncomfortably warm, but she still felt a flush of heat at Mick's words. The challenge in his voice.

"I bet you do, *Mickey*." Joe shot his brother a taunting glance as he pulled out a chair for Kat.

"Thanks." Kat hesitated. She appreciated the gesture but was too keyed up to sit down yet. "Um, if you'll excuse me, I need to run to the restroom," she announced, needing a minute alone to gather her thoughts. To process. To pull the pieces of herself that had scattered onstage back together.

"We'll come with you," Julia said.

"Field trip!" Andie announced.

"Count me in." Mary-Kate stood as well. "I really need to pee." She glanced at her brothers, still seated at the table. "Behave yourselves while we're gone, boys."

In the bathroom, Mary-Kate made a beeline for a stall while Kat crossed to a sink and splashed cold water on her face.

Her friends crowded around her, not wasting any time.

"What the hell was that?" Julia demanded under her breath.

"*That* was a whole lot of eye fucking between you and the candy wrapper, was what that was," Andie said in a snarky whisper. "No wonder you need to cool off."

"I don't know what you're talking about," Kat protested, grabbing a paper towel and blotting her flushed face. "Mick and I are friends."

Andie's brows lifted, a dark slash of doubt. "Friends with benefits?"

"Definitely not." Kat glanced up and met the shrewd gazes of her friends in the mirror. She couldn't prove them right so quickly. Was she really that predictable? She turned around to face them. "Mick and I are just friends, period."

Julia stared at her, face screwed up in concentration, as if Kat were a puzzle she was trying to solve.

Her friends knew her too well. Something had happened

between her and Mick out there, something that went beyond their blossoming friendship . . . but Kat was not about to admit it. Doing that would give it weight. Make it real. And she was having a hard enough time ignoring her attraction to Mick as it was. Giving in to that attraction was sure to spell disaster for their friendship, and Kat refused to let that happen.

"Fine. If you say you and Mick are just friends, I believe you." Julia crossed her arms. "But what about Joe?"

"Joe is nice," Kat said.

"Yeah, but do you think he could be your Mr. Right?" Andie mused.

"He appears to meet a lot of the requirements on your list and is quite the gentleman, but . . ." Julia paused, biting her lip as if considering how she wanted to phrase what she was thinking.

"But what?" Kat pressed. A toilet flushed and she glanced nervously at the line of stalls.

"But he's not the kind of guy you usually date," Julia finished.

"Not the same level of hotness," Andie clarified. "A panty-dropper, Joe is not." She glanced up, eyes growing wide as Mary-Kate joined them at the sink. "Um, sorry."

"No worries," Mary-Kate said, scrubbing her hands. "Though I'd rather not think of either of my brothers and the phrase 'panty-dropper' in the same sentence ever again."

"Understandable," Julia agreed, laughing.

Kat wanted to wash herself down the drain. Thankfully, the youngest O'Sullivan seemed amused rather than offended.

"Don't worry," Mary-Kate said, catching Kat's eye. "What happens in the bathroom stays in the bathroom." She wrinkled her nose again. "That didn't come out quite right. What I mean is that whatever you wanna say about my brothers won't get back to them. They won't hear it from me." She paused. "Unless you want them to."

"Ooh, a spy on the inside," Andie said, rubbing her hands together.

"I don't want a spy," Kat protested. "But some inside information might be helpful," she admitted.

"What would you like to know?" Mary-Kate asked.

"Well, I've got this plan . . . sort of like a business proposal, actually, but personal, with the goal of finding my Mr. Right."

"Ah, the list I heard mentioned." Mary-Kate blinked in understanding. "I was wondering about that." She propped her hip against the bathroom counter. "Is Mick aware of this plan?"

"He agreed to help me." Kat nodded. "He's here tonight as my wingman." She glanced at her friends. "And yes, I'm starting to think Joe might be a good candidate."

"Oh, this is fantastic." Mary-Kate tilted her head back and laughed again. A big, bold laugh, almost evil in its rich amusement.

People standing at the other sinks eyed their group warily. Kat was feeling a bit wary herself. "What's so funny?"

"Let's just say there's a complicated history between my brothers when it comes to dating." Placing a hand on Kat's shoulder, Mary-Kate squeezed gently. "Whatever happens, I think you're good for both Mick and Joe. If you need help—with either of them—let me know."

"Thanks." Kat smiled, and something tickled inside her. Something sweet and hopeful. She'd been grateful to find a new friend in Mick, and now it seemed she'd made another friend in his sister. As to what his brother might be remained to be seen. But her friends had a point. Joe checked several boxes on her list. Could she be friends with Mick and date his brother? Or would that screw things up in a completely different way?

The bathroom door banged open, startling Kat out of her thoughts. A woman in a Harley Quinn outfit stormed in and yelled, "Is there a Julia in here?"

Julia raised her hand. "Um, my name is Julia."

Harley pointed her baseball bat toward the exit. "There's a giant elf looking for you."

"That must be Luke," Julia muttered.

"Obviously," Andie snorted, tailing after her. "But what does he want?"

Kat mirrored Mary-Kate's bewildered expression and they hurried to catch up.

"There you all are," a testy voice declared as they spilled out of the bathroom.

"Luke?" Julia stared up at her boyfriend, hands fisted at her hips. "What's going on?"

He pressed a finger to his lips and nodded toward the stage.

It didn't take long for their curiosity to be appeased. The DJ's voice crackled through the speakers, announcing the next performer. "Next up we have Curt, with a message for someone special—Andie this one's for you."

Another eighties song began to play, a familiar Madonna tune—familiar because Kat had heard it last summer—when Curt had performed it once before. Kat reached for Andie's hand. "Did you know Curt was going to . . ."

"No." Andie shook her head, eyes wide in a rare moment of surprise.

Julia straightened her wig. "Should we get back to our—"

"Yes." Andie nodded, springing into action and lurching through the crowd, knocking a gaggle of girls dressed as the Kardashian sisters out of the way like bowling pins.

By the time they reached their table, Curt was well into the second verse. He'd added a bridal veil to his hobbit costume and was rolling around the stage doing a bizarre reenactment of his previous performance in a wedding party flash-mob dance to "Like a Virgin."

But unlike last summer, the show wasn't over when the song ended. As the final notes faded, Curt stood and moved to the front of the stage. He gave the DJ a thumbs-up and another song started playing. Flipping the veil out of his face and pinning his gaze on Andie, Curt began to sing a passionate, if off-key, rendition of Bruno Mars's "Marry You."

The crowd cheered and Andie froze like a deer in headlights.

Kat exchanged glances with Julia. "Do you think he's actually . . . ," she mouthed.

Julia shrugged and lifted her eyebrows in a silent, *No idea.*

On instinct, they both moved closer to their friend, each grabbing one of her hands. A fissure of excitement jolted through Kat, an electric hum of anticipation that seemed to zing back and forth between all three of them.

Once the song ended and the applause had died down, Curt tugged on the end of the wedding veil and wiped his sweaty face with it. Breathing heavily into the microphone, he invited Andie to join him on the stage.

"Andie?" Kat asked gently. Her friend was gripping her hand so tightly Kat's knuckles were grinding together. "Are you okay?"

"Fine," Andie squeaked.

Andie never squeaked.

"You don't have to go up there if you don't want to," Julia whispered.

"No, I wanna go," Andie said.

Onstage, Curt dropped to one knee.

Andie squeaked again.

"Are you sure?" Kat asked, wincing as Andie squeezed even tighter.

"Definitely." Andie nodded. "Maybe."

"Well, you better make up your mind." Julia wiggled her fingers free and glanced over her shoulder. "Soon," she added, eyes darting around the crowded room as if planning an escape route.

"Definitely," Andie repeated, more firmly this time. More like her old self. She released Kat's hand and jogged forward. Rather than bother with the stairs, she vaulted onto the stage, furry hobbit feet sliding.

Kat reached for Julia, and they clung to each other as they watched their best friend get engaged. It seemed to happen so fast, one second Curt was on bended knee, and the next he was replacing the costume ring on Andie's finger with a real one. In a blink they were kissing, and the crowd was going wild, while the DJ shouted congratulations and encouraged the audience to raise their glasses in a toast.

The couple returned to their seats in a flurry of well-wishes. The guys clapped Curt on the back and shook his hand while the girls ensconced Andie in excited hugs and closed in for a better look at the ring. Kat squeezed her friend tightly. "Not that I'm not super thrilled for you—because I am—but what happened to not being sure if you ever wanted to get married?"

"To tell you the truth, five minutes ago, I still wasn't sure," Andie admitted. "But then he asked, and in that moment, I knew." Her normally droll face split into a radiant smile. "Something inside me told me it was right."

The pop of a champagne cork burst into their conversation. "Here, trade you," Curt said, handing Kat the bottle before sweeping Andie onto the dance floor.

Kat gripped the bottle, watching as Julia and Luke joined Andie and Curt, the four of them grooving to the music with terrible rhythm but wonderful enthusiasm. She dropped her gaze, picking at the bits of foil stuck to the top of the glass.

Mick moved to her side. "Why the long face?"

"Tonight isn't going the way I'd planned." Kat took a sip of champagne. "I'm happy for Andie, of course, but I dunno." She took another sip and waved a hand at herself, standing on the sidelines. "I feel like I wore this outfit for nothing."

"Trust me," Mick said, heat flaring in his gaze, a pair of lit coals scorching a path from pom-pom sneakers to pigtails and back down again. "It wasn't for nothing."

"Okay, okay." Kat gave him a playful push. "Put your eyeballs back in your head." She told herself her skin suddenly felt warm and rosy because of the champagne, or the crowded room, the stage lights, anything except for the lingering heat of Mick's gaze. She took another swig from the bottle.

"Can I get you a glass?" Joe offered, coming to stand at Kat's other side.

"That's very thoughtful," Kat said, "but I'm good, thanks." She lifted the bottle in salute before chugging it, bubbles tickling her nose.

Amusement curved Joe's mouth as he watched her.

"Want a sip?" she offered, tilting the bottle toward him.

"No thank you." He shook his head. "But I would like a dance?"

"Oh." Kat grinned. "Okay." She turned to Mick, offering him the bottle. "Would you mind holding this for me?"

"Sure." Taking the bottle from her, Mick tossed his head back and took a long pull, Adam's apple working above the loose collar of his hoodie. Then he wiped his mouth, shadowed gaze holding hers. "But I can't promise it won't be empty when you get back."

"Oh." An echo of what had passed between them during her performance fizzed through her and she shivered. "Okay."

And then Joe was taking her hand and leading her toward the dance floor.

As Kat followed Joe through the crowd of people, her fingers clasped in his, she tried to listen for that inner voice. The one Andie had heard. The one that in a moment of clarity would tell her she'd found her Mr. Right. That Joe was what she'd been looking for.

If only her inner voice didn't suck at giving advice.

CHAPTER 13

Mick

It was the day after Halloween. The Day of the Dead. Appropriate, since Mick felt like death warmed over. It had been a long time since he'd nursed a hangover. Those candy corn Jell-O shots had been a terrible idea. The half bottle of champagne even worse.

Mick closed his eyes and inhaled slowly. Something was seriously wrong with him. The thought floated through his alcohol-logged brain like soggy cereal at the bottom of the bowl. He shook his head, trying to clear his thoughts, and immediately regretted it. What the hell had he been thinking?

And while he was at it, what the hell had happened with Kat last night? He wasn't sure what had passed between them, but he knew it was something. When she'd sang that stupid song—the one she'd picked to taunt him—they'd had a moment. That was a moment, right? She might have been onstage with Joe, but her attention had been laser focused on him. Mick hadn't imagined it.

Or maybe he had, since Kat spent most of the rest of the night dancing with Joe. His chest tightened. Why had Mick thought this time would be different? Why had he thought Kat would be different? He'd agreed to be her wingman, knowing how challenging that was going to be. And now, as he was a glutton for punishment, it looked like she'd pinned her sights on his brother.

A surge of bitterness pulsed through him. He'd been trying so hard to be the friend he knew Kat needed. The friend he'd promised to be. Mick had convinced himself he could show up at that party last night as her wingman, ready to help Kat find her Mr. Right. But not Joe. It could have been anyone but Joe.

The universe was such a fucker.

The first thing Mick needed to do was wash the memories of last night away. He felt a little better after a shower, but as he made the short walk from his apartment to the funeral home, he decided he wasn't quite ready to head to the office. He'd planned to tackle the last of the paperwork for the proposal, but the idea of reading through contract agreements made his head spin. Instead, he went around back, sucking in a bracing lungful of chilly November air as he crossed the funeral home's parking lot and headed for the mortuary.

He was still several feet away from his sister's domain when the pounding bass of a dubstep song throbbed in his eardrums. He cringed. Mick could barely stomach his sister's taste in music on a good day. Right now, he thought it might actually kill him.

Steeling himself, he punched in the key code to the building at the back of the O'Sullivan property and slipped inside. As expected, the music was so loud his sister didn't even realize he was in the room, so it was easy enough to walk over to the speaker docked on her desk and shut it off.

"Hey!" Mary-Kate yelled. She glared at him over her shoulder. "I was listening to that."

"It's a wonder you have any hearing left," Mick said. "That shit is loud enough to wake the dead."

"Obviously not," Mary-Kate huffed, indicating the motionless form on the gurney. "Though I do think Mrs. Kelly here would enjoy today's playlist."

"What the heck was that crap anyway?"

"Ashnikko." Mary-Kate gave Mick a scathing glance over the top of her surgical mask. "You look like you crawled out of a crypt."

"I feel like it," Mick mumbled. He slumped onto the swivel chair and rummaged around in his sister's desk.

"Excuse me," Mary-Kate chided. "But may I ask what you are doing?"

"Trying to find some aspirin."

"Ibuprofen. Left middle drawer."

Mick located the bottle of pills and gratefully popped two, washing them down with a sip from the coffee mug his sister had left on her desk. "Ugh, this is cold."

"Seriously?" she scolded from behind her mask. "You're going to steal my coffee and then complain about it?"

"Thanks. I owe you one." He swiveled around on the chair to face her. "How come you don't look like hell? You had at least as many of those candy corn shots as I did, if not more."

"For every shot I did, I drank an entire glass of water."

Mick snorted. "No wonder you were in the bathroom so long last night."

"That's not why." Mary-Kate glanced at Mick through the clear plastic screen of her protective eyewear. "I had quite the interesting conversation in there."

His sister's mouth might be hidden by a mask, but Mick still sensed the teasing smirk he knew was stamped on her face. "Did you," he said, forcing his voice to sound as bored as possible even though his heart had tripped at her words. His pulse picked up, thumping in a rhythmic tempo, pounding in his ears like the iconic beat of the song Kat had performed last night.

She'd fled to the bathroom right after singing that song . . . right after their moment. Like a line of ducklings, all the women at the table had promptly followed, including his sister. Mary-Kate had been in the bathroom with Kat. Had she talked to her? What did Kat say? Did it have anything to do with what happened between them when she'd been onstage?

Because something had happened. He was sure of it.

But when Kat had come back from the bathroom, she'd been different. Though Mick supposed witnessing one of her best friends accept a marriage proposal might have something to do with her sudden shift in mood.

Mick swallowed his questions. Hopefully, if his sister wanted him to know something, she'd tell him. Instead, he leaned back, elbows resting on the desk behind him, and asked, "What do you think of her?"

"Kat?" Mary-Kate gently shook a bottle of pigment before attaching it to a small airbrushing gun. "I like her. A lot, actually." The quiet thrum of the air compressor kicked on, followed by a soft hiss as his sister began to apply a delicate coating of foundation to Mrs. Kelly's face. "What do *you* think of her?"

Mick blinked. He should have seen that question coming. What did he think of Kat? He spent so much time thinking about her, the answer should be easy. But it wasn't. He thought she was gorgeous. And smart. Good-natured and sweet but also snarky and unexpectedly funny as hell.

"Never mind," Mary-Kate said, airbrush gun poised midair as she eyed him knowingly. "The answer is stamped all over your face."

Whatever his sister thought she saw there, Mick wasn't going to bother trying to protest or deny it. Instead, he asked, "What do you think Kat thinks of me?"

Mary-Kate chuckled. "Oh no," she replied, shaking her head. "I'm not playing that game with you." She turned her attention back to her work. "Next you'll want to know what she thinks of Joe."

"Why?" Mick swiveled again on the chair, turning sharply toward his sister. "Did Kat say anything about him?"

Humming something that sounded suspiciously like the song she'd been blasting earlier, Mary-Kate ignored him and focused on her work.

"MK, come on," Mick wheedled, rolling the chair closer to the gurney. Not too close, but close enough he knew he was in her line of sight. He'd told himself he wasn't going to pump his sister for information, but it was obvious she was holding out on him "You were all in the bathroom a long time. What did you talk about?"

Mary-Kate shrugged. "Lots of stuff."

Her words were flippant, but Mick caught the thread of

something beneath her casual demeanor. "Stuff about me?" he pressed. "Or maybe Joe?"

"I can't say."

"Can't or won't?" Mick challenged, unable to suppress the gruff note of frustration in his voice.

"Sorry, I'm sworn to secrecy." His sister set the airbrush aside. "Bathrooms are like confessionals."

"Is there anything you *can* say?"

She switched off the compressor. The sudden silence seemed heavy, almost oppressive.

The coffee and pills he'd downed sloshed uneasily in the pit of his stomach and Mick swallowed, acid stinging the back of his throat. "She likes Joe, doesn't she?"

Rather than answer, Mary-Kate fussed with the collection of makeup brushes assembled on her tray. "What do you think, Mrs. Kelly?" she asked, directing her question to the lifeless form on the gurney. "Should we go with Dusty Rose or Autumn Sunset?"

Mick bit his lip in frustration, watching as his sister held up two pots of blush, head tilted inquisitively, as if she expected an answer to be forthcoming.

"Autumn Sunset, good call. Perfect for the season." Mary-Kate began to apply the color to the dead woman's cheeks. "I wouldn't say Kat likes Joe," she said conversationally, her attention still focused on Mrs. Kelly's face. "But she is interested in him."

Mick sucked in a breath, realizing what his sister was playing at. She might not be willing to spill the beans to him directly, but if he happened to overhear her conversation with someone else—even if that someone else was no longer among the living—apparently that wouldn't break the holy covenant of the bathroom. He watched as Mary-Kate put the finishing touches on Mrs. Kelly.

It was true, then. Kat was interested in his brother. Mick shouldn't be surprised. How did that saying go? Those that don't learn from history are doomed to repeat it. Mick had been down this road before. The one time he thought he'd found someone special. The only time he'd ever been serious about a girl, serious enough to bring her home to meet his family, and she'd taken one look at Joe and decided to trade up.

Compared side by side, Joe was serious-relationship material and Mick was a fun friend. And that's exactly what he and Kat were. Friends. At least this time, he'd known up front where he stood. Clearly, that's where he was going to stay. Whatever he'd imagined had passed between them last night . . . these fantasies he was spinning about there being something more between them—that was on him.

"See, Mrs. Kelly?" Mary-Kate sighed and placed a clear plastic sheet over the woman's face. "This is why I didn't want to say anything." She gently tucked the ends of the plastic into place, securing them like she was covering a freshly iced cake with cling wrap. "I knew it would upset my brother."

"I'm not upset. Really," Mick insisted, not sure who he was trying to convince. "Kat and I are just friends."

Mary-Kate didn't answer him, but the side-eye she aimed in his direction let Mick know she wasn't buying it.

"Fine," he admitted. "I might have *considered* the possibility we could be more than friends, but if she doesn't feel the same then it's not a possibility worth pursuing. Besides, now that she's in a partnership with O'Sullivan's, it's probably best we keep things platonic."

"Is that so?" Mary-Kate drawled, and Mick scooted out of her way as she carried a tray of brushes over to the sink. "The looks you two were shooting each other last night could hardly be categorized as platonic."

The stool lurched to a stop and Mick almost slid right off it. Again, his heart picked up the pace. "It *was* real," he said, voice low and quiet, speaking mostly to himself. "I thought maybe only I'd felt it. That I'd imagined it."

"What?" Mary-Kate asked over the rush of water.

"The vibe between me and Kat." Mick stood and pushed the stool back to its spot at the desk.

"Vibe?" Mary-Kate laughed, obviously enjoying his suffering. "Oh, someone has it bad."

"It's not funny." Mick scrubbed a hand over his face. "I'm supposed to be her wingman."

"I heard about that."

"You did?" He dropped his hand in surprise. "The bathroom really is a confessional, isn't it?"

Another gleeful chuckle was his sister's only answer.

Mick sighed. "Kat's got this plan—"

"To find Mr. Right?" Mary-Kate's lips twitched. "Yeah, I heard about that too."

"Holy shit." Mick stared at his sister. "Is there anything you *don't* know?"

"Well, I wasn't sure how you felt about Kat . . ."

Mick snorted. He wasn't sure about that either.

". . . or how Joe feels about her."

"Right." His stomach dropped as he recalled his sister's words from earlier. "You said Kat was interested in him."

Mary-Kate nodded. "She thinks he might be a good fit."

"Of course." Now it was Mick's turn to chuckle, though his laugh was devoid of mirth. Of course, Kat would see his brother as a potential Mr. Right. Perfect, polished Gentleman Joe.

The security monitor to the mortuary beeped. Mick glanced up to see his brother standing in the doorway. "I'd say speak of the devil, but I doubt he dresses as boring as you."

Joe ran a hand over the front of his beige shirt, smoothing the already pristine, smooth fabric and making sure it was neatly tucked into his equally pristine beige slacks. "Funny you mention the devil." He gave Mick a scathing a glance. "Because you look like hell."

"That's what I said," Mary-Kate chimed in.

"We have a service this afternoon," Joe said primly. "I hope the guest of honor is looking more presentable than our brother."

"Of course." Mary-Kate nodded toward the gurney. "Mrs. Kelly is pickled and primped."

"Excellent." Joe dipped his chin in a quick, sharp nod, as if scratching off a task on his mental to-do list. Then he turned his attention to Mick. "What are you doing out here anyway?"

"Helping Mary-Kate," Mick said. It wasn't exactly true, but it didn't matter, because any answer he gave that wasn't the one Joe wanted wouldn't be good enough anyway.

"Bothering her is more like it," Joe groused.

And there it was. His brother always managed to make Mick feel like an incompetent third wheel.

"Actually, I could use Mick's help transferring Mrs. K into her casket," Mary-Kate said.

"Fine." Joe waved a hand and then pinned Mick with a stare. "When you're done here, meet me in the office. There's a pile of paperwork waiting for you."

Mick didn't bother explaining he'd already been planning to deal with the paperwork. Instead, he forced his lips into a facsimile of a cheerful grin. He probably looked like one of those creepy clowns he hated. "Great. Looking forward to it."

Completely missing the sarcasm dripping from Mick's words, Joe nodded again and turned to leave, attention already on the next task.

The door clicked shut and Mick swore he could hear the echo of a tick mark as Joe mentally checked off another item on his list. "How does he do it?"

"Do what?" Mary-Kate asked. She'd reclaimed the stool and was at her desk, entering data on her computer.

"Walk with that pole jammed up his ass."

Mary-Kate choked, sputtering into her coffee mug. "You're extra testy this morning because of what I said about Kat being interested in him."

"No, I'm testy because I'm hungover."

"That," Mary-Kate agreed. "And because of Kat."

Mick didn't respond. Arguing with his sister was as pointless as reasoning with his brother. Besides, she was right. Hearing that Kat was interested in Joe did bother him. But what was he supposed to do about it? Oh god. What if she wanted his help somehow? He'd signed up to play wingman, not matchmaker. Especially not with his brother.

An image floated through his mind, like a snapshot from their future wedding album. Mick, the best man and brother of the groom, watching Kat walk down the aisle, dressed like a fairy princess, ready to marry his prince of a brother. *No fucking way.*

"Stop brooding and go get Mrs. K's casket."

"I'm not brooding." Mick scowled. "I'm thinking."

"Thinking while scowling. That's brooding. Now go." Mary-Kate nudged him with the toe of her work clogs. "Bin six."

······

Inside the funeral home it was quiet as a tomb. Unlike their sister, Joe liked to work in absolute silence. Of the two options, Mick decided he preferred the noise pollution Mary-Kate listened to. He rounded the corner to the office and found his brother seated at the desk, sifting through the stack of documents Mick had printed out, organizing them into smaller, individual piles.

Mick leaned against the doorframe and crossed his arms. "I said I was going to handle that."

Not bothering to glance up, Joe continued to inspect the papers. "I'm simply facilitating the process. Consider it a head start."

The complete absence of sound in the room unnerved Mick. Belatedly, he realized why it was bothering him. He straightened, shifting his gaze to the cage in the corner. "You didn't uncover Seamus?"

"An extra hour or two of sleep isn't going to kill him," Joe scoffed, his attitude clearly indicating he found this fact disappointing.

The second Mick tugged the dark wool blanket off the cage, the bird stirred to life. "Good morning, fucker," he squawked.

"Morning." Mick grinned, hanging the blanket on a hook that had been installed precisely for that purpose.

Seamus stared through the bars and pinned a baleful black eye on Joe. "Asshole."

Mick snorted. Those extra hours under the blanket might not harm the bird, but they definitely pissed him off. Joe wasn't the only one who liked to stick to a schedule. Mick started guiltily and hurried to scoop some birdseed into the feeder. Usually, he was the one to tend to Seamus in the morning, but today he'd been busy tending to a hangover.

Joe placed the last paper on one of the piles he'd arranged and proceeded to straighten each stack.

Since Mick was about to sort through those papers himself, those stacks weren't going to remain neat for long, but he refrained from reminding his brother of this fact. Joe was the kind of person who made the bed right before he slept in it.

"Everything in order?" Mick asked, wincing internally at the note of nervous tension in his voice. Despite himself, he still craved his older brother's stamp of approval.

"Actually, yes."

"You don't need to sound so surprised," Mick grumbled.

"I'm impressed," Joe admitted. "What you've put together looks pretty good."

Coming from Joe O'Sullivan, "pretty good," was high praise. Mick sent up a silent prayer of thanks for Kat's brilliance. Her guidance had made the process so much smoother. "Does that mean you're ready to sign off?"

"I didn't say that." Joe shook his head. "Not yet."

Mick heaved a frustrated sigh and dropped into one of the chairs facing the desk. "What else do you need?"

"It's a solid business plan, and the projections outlined in the proposal look promising . . ." Joe paused, adding, "But before we dive into the deep end on this and start applying for permits, I'm thinking we should dip our toes in first."

"Meaning?"

"We do a test run. Offer some of these services on a trial basis. See how clients respond." Joe folded his hands and rested them on top of the desk. "Gather some concrete data and get some customer feedback before we commit to taking the next step."

"The next step or the right step?" Mick challenged.

Wary confusion flickered across his brother's face. "I'd like to think it would be both."

"Yeah, so would I. But I can't help wondering if that's what is holding you back. You're stalling on giving this the green light because you don't think it's the right move for the business."

Joe bristled. "I've been up front about my reservations concerning this plan from the beginning."

"Because it's *my* plan." Mick jabbed his thumb into his chest. "My idea. And you don't believe anything I come up with could possibly work."

"I'm not your enemy, Mickey."

"Are you sure, Joey?" Mick shot back. "Because you fight me at every turn."

"I'm not fighting against you. I'm fighting for you, for us . . . for our family. For the business. The next generation of O'Sullivans."

"Ha." A hoarse chuckle interrupted them. "And where is this next generation you mention, eh?"

Both men startled, turning in unison to see their grandmother in the doorway of the office.

"Hello, gorgeous," Seamus cooed, adding an appreciative whistle.

Gran's face split into a wide smile. "Hello, you," she said with deep affection, reaching a bony finger through the bars to stroke the bird's crest.

Mick always got the feeling that whenever Gran talked to Seamus, she was also talking to her husband. And in a way, he supposed she was. He stood and enveloped her in a hug. "How are you this morning?"

"Better than you, I'm guessing," Gran said with an impish grin. "Had fun last night, did we?" She patted his scruffy cheek.

The gesture reminded Mick of his disheveled state. Which was worse than usual. He'd showered but realized he must have forgotten to shave. And while the candy corn Jell-O shots were no longer performing an encore from *Riverdance* inside his skull, his head still throbbed with the lingering vestiges of a hangover. "Um, yes. We all had fun," Mick clarified. "Mary-Kate came with me." He nodded toward his brother. "Joe was there too."

"Is that so?" Gran swiveled her head in Joe's direction. "Well, Joseph, how was it? Did you meet anyone special?" Her snowy eyebrows waggled. "Maybe someone to help you get started on this next generation of O'Sullivans I heard mentioned?"

"Geez, Gran. Boundaries." Joe flushed.

Mick bit back a snort of laughter. When it came to the subject of potential grandchildren, Gran knew no shame. As the oldest, Joe bore the brunt of their grandmother's wish for progeny, but Mick wasn't sure why her comments got under Joe's skin so bad. It was no secret that his brother wanted kids, hell, starting a family was probably on Joe's master list of tasks. Another box to check off.

The thought stopped Mick in his tracks. Maybe Kat and his brother were more alike than he realized. Could Joe really be the Mr. Right she was looking for? The two of them had spent a lot of time on the dance floor together last night. Mick knew because he'd watched them, downing Jell-O shots and chasing them with champagne whenever a new song came on. His stomach somersaulted at the memory.

Mary-Kate had said Kat was interested in their brother, but was Joe interested in her? Mick couldn't imagine how anyone wouldn't be. On one hand, Mick hoped his brother didn't like Kat, but on the other hand, he'd made a deal to help her. Mick might be conflicted about his feelings for Kat, but one thing he knew for sure—he wanted her to be happy.

CHAPTER 14

Kat

On Saturday morning, a week after Halloween, Kat went through the motions of opening the shop on autopilot, a sense of ennui shadowing her steps. She'd been moping around like a sluggish snail for days. Trudging to the front of the shop, she flipped the sign and unlocked the front door.

"Opening a whole three minutes before we're supposed to," Ronnie said, appearing from the back room with two cups of coffee. "Mr. Schwartz won't know what to do with himself."

Kat glanced out the window. "No sign of him yet."

"Watch this be the day he finally sleeps in."

"First time for everything, I suppose." Kat yawned.

"JoJo still keeping you up at night?"

"Unfortunately." Kat shuffled over to join Ronnie at the counter and accepted one of the mugs. Gripping it in both hands, she let the heat seep into her fingers.

"Well, your nocturnal pincushion is currently zonked out in the back." Ronnie took out their phone and showed Kat a series of pictures on their camera roll. "I snapped these while the coffee was brewing. She even slept through Mr. Pokey."

"I'm jealous of her ability to sleep through anything . . . except the night." Kat took a long, slow sip of her coffee. While waiting for the much-needed caffeine to trickle into her bloodstream, she admired the photo montage of JoJo snoozing, a prickly puffball of contentment. Kat had to admit, the nocturnal nuisance looked freaking adorable. "These are darling."

Ronnie zoomed in on a particularly precious one of JoJo on

her back, soft belly exposed and little feet dangling in the air, and Kat almost died from the cuteness. "Aw," she cooed. "I love it."

"It's nice to see you smile," Ronnie said. "I fully support RBF and would happily cut the tongue out of anyone who suggested you should smile more, but I gotta say, it was getting pretty grim around here."

"Sorry about that." Kat stared into her coffee. "I've had some stuff on my mind."

Ronnie picked up their mug and studied Kat over the rim. "Do you want to talk about it?" they finally asked, breaking the silence. It was a silence they'd kept all week, leaving Kat alone to stew in the juices of her bad mood. It wasn't that Ronnie didn't care. Quite the opposite. Ronnie was a good friend. The kind who took boundaries very seriously.

Kat knew if she told Ronnie she wasn't ready to talk then that would be that. "I don't want to talk about it," she began.

"All right." Ronnie nodded and took another sip.

"But I probably should."

"All right," they said again in the same even tone, setting their mug down and meeting Kat's eyes. "Then talk. What's bothering you?"

"A lot of stuff." Kat ground out a laugh. "The easier question might be what isn't bothering me."

"How about you start at the top. What's bothering you the most right now?"

"This is going to sound terrible . . ."

Ronnie held up a hand. "No judgment on feelings."

No judgment on feelings. The words echoed in Kat's mind. It was comforting, the freedom that statement seemed to give her. Because while it was true a variety of things were bothering her, she knew exactly what had specifically triggered her bad mood. Knowing didn't help. In fact, the knowledge only made her feel worse. Guilty for being so self-centered.

Fortifying herself with another gulp of coffee, Kat dove in

before she changed her mind. "On Halloween, one of my best friends got engaged."

"Julia?" Ronnie asked.

Kat shook her head. "Andie."

Ronnie blinked. "Really?"

"Yeah, the proposal took us all by surprise—Andie most of all." A grin flickered to life as Kat replayed the moment. "She said yes and I'm so happy for her—I really am—but I can't seem to *be* happy for her. Does that make sense?"

Ronnie nodded but didn't say anything.

Their silence encouraged Kat to continue. "Of course, I immediately offered to do the wedding flowers. Insisted, actually. But whenever I try to start planning the designs for Andie's arrangements, I end up holding my own little pity party." Kat gulped down some more coffee. "I've arranged flowers for weddings for years, designed countless bridal bouquets, and it's always been a joy. But now, when it's one of my best friends, one of my favorite people in the world, I'm miserable. And I feel like such a shit for being so petty."

"It's not petty," Ronnie said, "it's human."

"I keep picturing the moment at the wedding when the bridal bouquet gets tossed." Kat could see it so clearly: Andie standing on the church steps, veil snapping in the breeze as she tossed the gorgeous blooms like the athlete she was. The flowers would soar through the air, landing decisively in Julia's outstretched hands as if the Fates themselves had pinned a target on her that said, "You're next."

"Let me guess." Ronnie's voice was dry but not unkind. "You never catch the bouquet."

"Nope." Kat shook her head. "Julia does. Every time." She shrugged. "I know what's going on . . . my fears are manifesting themselves in these visions. But that's just it. I'm scared."

"Of being alone?"

"Yeah, but more than that, I'm scared of being left behind." Kat brushed her thumb over a chipped edge on the handle of her mug. "You know those little cars in the game of Life?"

"You mean the ones with gendered pink and blue pegs?"

"They updated that. There's a nonbinary peg now."

"For real?" Ronnie paused mid-sip. "What color?"

"Purple."

Ronnie set their mug on the counter and grabbed their phone. "Are you googling this?"

"Maybe," they said, fingers flying over the screen. "Okay, yes. I was. And you're right. There's even pegs for pets now."

"Fabulous," Kat snarked. "My two best friends have both found their pegs . . . er, person. And now they're getting ready to zoom ahead to the next level. Meanwhile, my car is stalled out in the single lane . . . but at least I can take my hedgehog with me."

"First of all," Ronnie said, setting their phone down. "The single lane rocks. Second of all, that's not how life works. This isn't a race. Life isn't a game."

"I know that. But good luck telling my brain." Kat stared into her coffee, as if waiting for the solution to her problems to bubble up from the depths like some caffeinated Magic 8 Ball. Andie's surprise engagement had thrown Kat's sense of purpose off-kilter. Not to mention whatever the hell had happened between her and Mick when she'd been onstage.

Kat didn't know what to think about Mick. She knew what her friends thought. But Julia and Andie were wrong. They had to be. Kat was *not* developing feelings for Mick. Not beyond those of a friend. And she really wanted to keep him as a friend. She liked having him as a friend. She needed him as a friend.

Her throat tightened as the word "need" sunk in. It was strange, how fast she'd come to rely on their budding friendship. Part of her worried that she was setting Mick up as her bestie backup plan. Someone to fill the void she dreaded was coming once Andie and Julia moved on with the next phase of their lives. Ronnie had said it wasn't a game, and they were right, but that didn't mean Kat didn't fear losing.

She needed to stick to her plan. Mick might be all wrong for her Mr. Right list, but his brother on the other hand . . .

Joe was completely different from the kind of guys Kat usually dated. Julia and Andie were right about that. But like she'd told them, those differences were kind of the point. Exactly what she was looking for. After the Halloween party, Kat had hoped Joe might follow up with a call this week. She even would have been okay if he'd used the partnership as a pretense. But nope. Nothing.

Kat frowned, sour feelings rising up like heartburn. She shoved thoughts of Joe and her list aside for now. Thinking about all of this was putting her in a bad mood again. She needed cheering up, stat. "Hey, Ronnie?" Kat asked. "Do you have any more pics of JoJo?"

"Maybe a few." Ronnie beamed, proudly scrolling through their gallery of JoJo images. "I hope you don't mind, but I posted a few on my Insta."

"Doesn't bother me," Kat said. "It'd be a crime not to share all this adorableness with the world."

"Right?" Ronnie grinned. "This one seems to be the favorite," they said, pulling up a photo of JoJo nestled in a pot of marigolds. "Check out all those likes! Pretty cool, huh?"

"My JoJo is a little celebrity!" As Kat scrolled through Ronnie's feed, she noted how many posts featured JoJo posing with flowers from the store. Her brain began to whir with inspiration. "And every celebrity needs an endorsement deal, right?"

"Why?" Ronnie's eyes widened with excitement. "Do you know someone who'd be interested?"

"Sort of." Kat leaned closer. "How would you feel about helping me make JoJo the official spokesperson for the shop? Well, spokeshedgehog."

"For *this* shop?" Ronnie wrinkled their nose. "I'm not sure Allen would go for it."

"What wouldn't I go for?" a droll voice asked over the sound of the wind chimes.

Kat jumped, narrowly missing splashing coffee on Ronnie's phone. "Allen!" she chirped. "This is a surprise." Her boss rarely stopped by the shop these days, and never on a Saturday. She thought about what Laura had said. Had Allen been spying on them? Was he mad about JoJo? "What brings you in today?"

"Alaska," Allen said.

Ronnie and Kat exchanged glances. Their boss had always been on the eccentric side, but this was a new brand of odd.

A moment later the doorway chimes clattered again.

"Mr. Schwartz, hey!" Ronnie shot the old man a teasing grin. "You're late."

"Hmph." The old man joined them at the counter, and Kat noticed he seemed to be moving a little slower than usual. "I didn't want to risk having to wait outside again."

Allen cocked his head. "What's that?"

"You mentioned something about Alaska?" Kat prompted, eager to shift the conversation away from the fact they'd opened late a few weeks ago.

"Alaska?" Mr. S echoed. "Me and the missus took a cruise there for our sixtieth wedding anniversary."

Sixty years of marriage. Kat sighed. Now, that was a happily ever after.

"Beautiful country." The old man's gruff voice softened with wonder. "Majestic."

"My husband and I have always dreamed of retiring there," Allen explained, "and we recently learned about this new set of condos opening in a place called Moose Springs. It's exactly what we're looking for."

"Lucky bastard," Mr. Schwartz chuckled. "Good for you." He

paused, one grizzled eyebrow raised. "What's going to happen to this place?"

Kat's heart flip-flopped. She met Ronnie's eyes, wondering if her own face looked as shellshocked as theirs. "That's a good question." She turned to her boss. "Allen?"

"I'm going to sell, of course," he said, meandering around the store, inspecting the arrangements on display. "Much as it pains me to give this place up, it doesn't make sense to keep it when I'll be living three thousand miles away."

"When?" Kat asked, heart in her throat.

"Soon," Allen said, crossing to the back of the shop and poking through the coolers. "The mister and I have socked away a decent amount for retirement, but those mountaintop condos aren't cheap."

Allen was selling the store. Soon. Whatever the hell that meant. Kat's brain was whirring so fast she felt dizzy. She'd always planned to branch out on her own eventually, but she still had years left on her plan, a plan she was already running behind on.

The store's favorite grumpy old man set a tin on the counter, where it landed with a heavy *thunk*, yanking Kat out her mental tornado.

"What did Mrs. S make this time?" Ever since that rainy Saturday about a month ago, Mr. Schwartz had been dropping off a batch of something tasty every week.

"Latkes." He nodded toward the tin. "I like them with a bit of sour cream, but the missus prefers applesauce."

"We'll be sure to try them both ways," Ronnie promised, taking the tin to the back room.

"Please tell your wife thank you," Kat added.

Mr. S nodded. "I wanted to talk to you. About my wife."

Kat frowned. Something in his tone made her skin prickle "Is everything okay?"

"With my wife? Yes. With me?" He shrugged. "Eh."

"Eh?" What the hell was that supposed to mean? "What's wrong?"

"Other than the fact I'm probably not going to see my next birthday?" He shrugged again. "Nothing."

Kat frowned. "That's not funny, Mr. S."

"Who said I was making jokes? I'm dead serious." His wrinkled face creased in a flash of amusement. "Excuse the pun." Sobering, he dug around in the pocket of his jacket and pulled out a thick envelope. "After I'm gone, I want you to make sure my wife still gets her weekly flower delivery."

"Mr. Schwartz . . ." Kat's lip trembled.

"I've been a loyal customer here for more than twenty years, I don't think I'm asking too much." He slid the envelope across the counter toward Kat. "Every Saturday," he insisted, wagging a finger. "Promise me."

Kat nodded, fighting the prickly sting of tears. "I promise."

"Thank you." Mr. Schwartz patted her hand. "You're a good girl."

The tears spilled over, and Kat turned away, wiping at her face. This was all too much. Too much change happening too fast. She glanced Allen's way, considering. She'd always thought owning her own shop meant starting over somewhere new, by herself, from scratch. But what if she could buy the shop from Allen and make it hers? The more she thought about it, the more the idea appealed to her. She could keep working with Laura and Ronnie. Keep her apartment. Juggling the expenses would be tricky, but she wouldn't know how tricky until she talked to Allen.

After she finished helping Mr. S pick his flowers and sent him on his way with a hug he grudgingly allowed, Kat tracked down her boss. "Allen? Can I talk to you for a minute?"

"About?" He was at the trimming station, working on corsages for a quinceañera. He may not stop in often, but when he did, he always dove in and helped, still loving the work.

Kat joined him. "You mentioned you plan on selling soon . . ." She bent down and pulled out some of the postconsumer-waste boxes from a stack under the counter. "How soon were you thinking?"

"Probably early next year."

"Oh." Kat swallowed. "That soon?"

"Why the long face?"

"Because . . ." Kat hesitated. "I'm worried about what will happen to the shop."

"I already have a buyer in mind." Allen peered at her. "I think you know who I mean."

Stewing in her own misery, it took Kat a moment to process the words coming out of her boss's mouth. She cocked her head. "What are you saying?"

"I thought it was obvious." Allen peered down at her. "I'm saying I'd like to sell the business to you."

"Really?" Hope flickered to life. Ever since Kat had started working for Allen, she'd set aside a bit of each paycheck—seed money to buy her own place one day. Over time, she'd watched her savings slowly grow, but her little nest egg was still years away from being ready to hatch. Her heart sank as reality set in. She could apply for a business loan, but the approval process would likely take longer than she had. Besides, having made a decent dent in her student loans, she wasn't eager to sink into the deep end of debt again.

"I admit, I thought you'd be more excited." Allen crossed his arms. "It's a great opportunity for you."

"It *is* a great opportunity," she agreed.

"Then what's the problem?"

"January is right around the corner. I'll never be able to get enough money together in time to make you a reasonable offer," she admitted.

"You don't know what might be reasonable to me," Allen

countered. "Besides, there are other factors to consider besides money."

"Like what?" Kat couldn't help asking.

"Like the fact it's important to me to leave my business in the hands of someone I trust." He set aside a finished corsage and started on another. "Someone who I know will care for this place as much as I do and carry on my vision."

Kat watched Allen's deft fingers turn a collection of flowers into a work of art. He still had the magic touch. He'd taught her almost everything she knew about the business. He was a demanding employer and a mentor with high expectations, but he was generous too. As much as she wanted this, Kat couldn't take advantage of that generosity. "I couldn't let you do that," she said. "Owning a flower shop is my dream. And I do care for this place very much. But I have my own plans. My own vision. And if you give me your flower shop, I'd feel obligated to give those dreams up."

"*Give* you?" Allen blinked owlishly. "Who said anything about giving it to you?"

Kat bit her lip. "Isn't that what we're talking about?"

"Goodness, no." Allen shook his head, a bemused expression crossing his handsome, distinguished face.

"Oh." Kat wanted to slip between the cracks of the upcycled bamboo floorboards beneath her feet and disappear.

"I told you I wanted to sell the shop," Allen continued.

"And I told you, I don't have nearly enough money saved." She squeezed her hands into fists, embarrassed and confused. "I don't see how I can possibly buy . . ."

Allen held up the corsage he was working on and shushed her. "I meant what I said. It's worth a lot to me to pass this place on to someone I know will care for it. And while I can't afford to give you the shop—like I said, those Alaskan condos aren't cheap—I have an idea that might work for both of us." He snipped off several lengths of ribbon and laid them across the counter. "What if we set up a payment plan?"

"What kind of payment plan?"

"One that you could afford." Allen spread out the pieces of ribbon. "We take the down payment needed to buy the mortgage on the building and divide it up in a monthly amount you feel comfortable with."

Kat fiddled with the end of a satin ribbon, twirling it around the spool. "So, like a layaway situation?"

He nodded. "Precisely. I'd remain owner until you finish paying off the down payment, and then the lease is yours."

Kat juggled the numbers in her head. Even with Allen's offer, it would still be tricky. And there was something about the way he'd harped on continuing his vision that bothered her. She didn't want to carry on Allen's legacy. Honor it, sure. But she also wanted to create her own. That had always been the dream. If she said yes, she'd be giving up that dream.

But Kat couldn't say no either . . . couldn't walk away from this store and the people she'd come to love: Ronnie and Laura and even crabby old Mr. Schwartz. If she turned Allen down, he'd have no choice but to sell the store to someone else. What if the new owner wanted to hire a new staff? What if the new owner didn't even want to keep the place as a flower shop. What then?

She felt her resolve slipping, reasons to say no falling like petals. This wasn't how she'd imagined things happening, but the important thing was the shop would be hers. That goal would be met. She'd have what she'd always wanted . . . sort of. And something was better than nothing, right? A bird in the hand is worth two in the bush, or whatever Babcia would say.

"It's an incredibly generous offer," Kat said, turning to face her boss and her future. "But it's also a big decision. Can I have some time to think about it?"

"Sure." Allen nodded. "My partner and I are going up to Alaska around Thanksgiving to check out the condos and make plans for the move. I can give you until the end of the year, but I'll need an answer by New Year's."

It was already the beginning of November. Which meant she basically had two months to get her shit figured out and decide what she wanted her future to look like.

The rest of the day passed in a blur as Kat contemplated the possibilities. She'd finished counting down the register when Laura charged through the entrance, a large cardboard box in her hand. "By day she delivers flowers, by night she delivers pizza!"

The holy trinity of basil, rosemary, and oregano permeated the shop and Kat's stomach made one of its terrible yowling noises. Suddenly ravenous, Kat realized she'd been so distracted she never ate lunch.

Laura set the box on the counter. "I was starving after my last round of deliveries. You want a slice?"

"Yes, please." No need to ask her twice. Kat dove into the box. She sunk her teeth into the cloud of gooey cheese and tomato sauce and groaned in pleasure at the first, perfect bite.

"There's wine too," Laura said, pulling a bottle out of her crochet bag. "Screw top."

Kat smirked. It was nestled inside one of Laura's cock creations. "Classy."

"That's me." Laura reached under the counter for some coffee mugs and served them both a healthy pour.

"Cheers." Kat clinked her mug against Laura's.

Ronnie poked their head in from the back room. "Are you folks having a party without me?"

"An impromptu get-together," Laura said.

"Consider this your invite." Kat slid the pizza box toward Ronnie. "Where'd you go, anyway?"

"Don't get mad," Ronnie warned. "I know I should have asked you first, but when Allen showed up unannounced, I thought it might be a good idea to take JoJo out for a little field trip."

"Field trip?" Kat blinked. "Where?" she demanded, more

surprised than anything. She'd been so distracted, she hadn't even noticed her pet was gone.

"To a friend's place," Ronnie explained. "Are you mad?" Their face scrunched guiltily. "Please don't be mad."

"I'm not mad, but I wish you would have said something to me first."

"I know, and I'm sorry," Ronnie apologized in a rush. "Bertie—that's my friend—is an amazing designer and makes the cutest little outfits for his hamster. I thought, if we're going to make JoJo the store's mascot, like you suggested, we should take it up a notch. I asked Bertie if he could whip up a few things and we got carried away."

"Where is JoJo now?"

"Still at Bertie's. The fitting is taking longer than we expected—those spikes are tricky to work around—so I was hoping maybe JoJo could have a little sleepover with me tonight—oh my heavens you should see the pj's Bertie is making—and I'll bring her home safe and sound tomorrow?" Ronnie stopped rambling long enough to suck in a quick breath. "Please," they begged earnestly, hands clasped together. "You're always telling me how she never lets you sleep at night. This way you could get a break."

"Say yes," Laura said in a stage whisper. She nudged Kat with her shoulder. "Take it from someone who hasn't had a decent night's sleep since her first kid was born fourteen years ago."

A night free from JoJo's midnight marathons would be welcome. And Kat trusted Ronnie completely. Honestly, they took better care of JoJo than she did. After all, Kat reminded herself, she hadn't even known JoJo was missing.

"Okay," Kat said, the mix of concern for JoJo's safety and the anticipation of a night free making her wonder again if this was what it felt like to be a parent. "Yes, JoJo can have a sleepover with you."

CHAPTER 15

Kat

About an hour later, Kat, Laura, and Ronnie had finished off the pizza and wine together. Laura headed home to her kids, Ronnie headed back to Bertie's with a promise to send pics from the slumber party, and Kat headed upstairs to her empty apartment. She kicked off her shoes, set the tin of latkes from Mr. Schwartz on her coffee table, and collapsed onto her couch. It had felt good to laugh. To eat pizza and drink wine and shoot the shit. She'd been too serious lately, obsessed with her need to catch up to her friends. Friends who she didn't even get to see much lately.

It had only been about a month since they'd decided to pull back on CCC nights and Kat missed that time with her besties desperately. This evening was the closest thing she'd had to it in weeks. All that had been missing was a movie.

And that was easily fixed.

Kat reached for the crocheted blanket draped over one arm of the couch. Clicking the remote, she scrolled through her streaming options, looking for a good rom-com. Nothing new, though. She was in the mood for something she'd seen before. Something she loved. A comfort watch.

She made her choice and was about to hit Play when her phone buzzed. Kat glanced down, expecting to see a text from Ronnie featuring JoJo all dolled up in an evening gown or something equally outrageously glamorous, but instead, Mick's number flashed across the screen. Curious, she answered the call. "Hello?"

"Hey. Kat?"

"That's me." A little blip of joy skipped across her heart at the sound of his voice. The kind of feeling she got when she opened her mailbox and discovered a surprise card or letter. It was nice to hear from him. Beyond some email threads about the business proposal and a few work-related texts, they hadn't spoken since last weekend.

"It's Mick."

"I know." Kat fiddled with the edge of her blanket, a gift from Laura last Christmas, before she'd shifted into her new phallic phase of crocheting.

"Right." He cleared his throat.

In the awkward pause that followed, Kat thought this call must feel weird because of what happened on Halloween—which was impossible because nothing had happened.

Keep telling yourself that, Kitty Kat, Andie's voice chided in her head.

"I was calling to see if you were available to come by O'Sullivan's tomorrow night."

"Why?" Her voice turned suspicious. "You don't have another widow looking to order a boutonniere out of spite, do you?"

Mick chuckled. "No. Though I gotta say, I kind of like the idea of revenge flowers."

"As long as they don't lead to a fistfight over the corpse."

"You said the c-word," Mick said.

"I did, didn't I? Huh." Kat waited for the apprehension to creep over her, but nothing happened. "Just because I can say the word without freaking out doesn't mean I want anything to do with them. I'm not touching any dead bodies."

"Don't worry," Mick assured her. "Mr. Donnelly's body has already been taken care of. The funeral service will be in the afternoon, but we're going to do a trial run of the new party format after."

"That's not a bad idea," Kat mused.

"Joe suggested it," Mick admitted. "Demanded, actually. Rattled off stuff about concrete data and customer feedback."

"And you need me there to do what? Observe? Take notes?"

"That would be helpful, sure. But to be honest, I could really use another pair of hands." Mick paused for a moment, then added, "How do you feel about serving drinks?"

......

On Sunday evening, as Kat made what was now becoming the familiar drive to O'Sullivan's, she realized she was looking forward to it—she was actually looking forward to spending time in a funeral home—a place that had always struck her with a deep sense of dread. Who would have thought it was possible? Maybe there was something to that exposure therapy theory. She hoped so. If the plan for a partnership worked out, she'd be making this drive a lot more often.

The parking lot was so full Kat had to wedge the delivery van into a spot way in the back. Dearly departed Mr. Donnelly must have been very popular. As she made her way toward the entrance, she tensed, half expecting the usual panic to settle in. But nothing happened. Not even when she opened the door and entered the lobby. Her lungs didn't feel like they were shriveling up and her pulse remained steady.

Kat stood in the foyer and inhaled deeply, confidence growing with each breath. Her bravado faltered when she realized how quiet it was. The eerie silence broken only by the ticking of the grandfather clock. Considering how many cars were parked outside, the place should be packed.

All those people had to be here somewhere. Mick had to be somewhere. Kat made her way down the hall, pausing at the main office. The door was ajar, so she pushed it open and stepped inside.

A shrill whistle greeted her. "Hello, gorgeous!"

Kat grinned. "Hey, handsome." She moved closer to the cage. "Where's Mick?"

"Downstairs."

"Ack!" Kat hopped back from the cage, belatedly realizing the reply hadn't come from the bird. She jerked her attention to the door. "Joe. You startled me."

"My apologies." Joe raised his hands, dark brown eyes contrite. "I wasn't expecting to find anyone in here."

"Mick asked me to come," Kat said. Her gaze traveled over Joe's neatly combed hair and immaculate suit and she wished she'd have thought to change before heading over. Or at least put on some lipstick. She wasn't expecting to see Joe here tonight, but she shouldn't have been surprised. This was his business too. He was the one who wanted this test run. Of course he would be here. "When I got here, nobody was around." She gestured to the cockatoo. "Except Seamus here."

"And you thought what . . . ?" Joe's eyebrows lifted gently. "You'd ask the bird for help?"

Kat's lips quirked, but she bit back the sarcastic retort that hovered on the tip of her tongue. She couldn't be sure if he was simply stating a fact or teasing her. If it was Mick, there'd be no question he was giving her shit and she wouldn't have hesitated to dish it right back. But Joe was so nice. She didn't want to risk offending him. "I mean, it couldn't hurt right?" she finally asked. "He's pretty smart."

"Pretty smart. Pretty smart." Seamus echoed, and Kat swore the bird was prancing on his little platform.

"Actually," Joe said "Seamus is the reason I came up here. His presence has been requested."

Requested? Kat blinked. *For what?*

Joe draped a linen napkin over his arm and opened the cage. He bent his elbow, drawing it parallel to the cage door. At first Seamus didn't move. Joe nudged his arm closer, and in a flurry of feathers the bird surged forward, wings outstretched. Startled by the sudden movement, Joe jerked back, taking Seamus with him.

Seamus squawked. His crest spiked in indignation, claws clutching at the cloth. "Careful, gobshite."

Kat giggled. "He really has a way with words."

"Thanks to my granda," Joe muttered and steadied his hand.

"Mick mentioned something about that too." Kat smothered

another laugh, feeling a little guilty about how entertained she was watching Joe struggle to get Seamus situated. It was obvious the man was not comfortable dealing with the bird. Frankly, neither party seemed very happy with the current arrangement.

"That's why he has the accent, right?" she asked. "He's mimicking your grandfather?"

Joe nodded. "Sometimes it's like hearing a ghost."

Kat tried to imagine owning a bird that talked like Babcia. She wasn't sure if she would find it creepy or comforting. "Cockatoos can live up to eighty years."

"That's true." Joe shifted his arm. "With any luck, this old bird here will be an octogenarian soon."

Again, Kat wasn't sure if he was joking or not.

Seamus, however, swiveled his head and turned a baleful eye on Joe. As if he fully understood the insinuation.

"Do you know how old he is now?"

Joe shook his head. "Granda sort of inherited him from a client."

"Inherited him from a . . . Oh." Kat swallowed, putting two and two together. She glanced at the cockatoo, curious as to how many owners the "old bird" had gone through. "Does Seamus live in the office full time?"

"Pretty much. We've tried to relocate his cage upstairs, but he throws such a tantrum that we always bring him back here." He shrugged. "This is where he wants to be."

"Doesn't he get lonely?"

"One of us is almost always around, and our gran and my sister still live in the apartment upstairs, so if he needs anything, they'll know." Joe pointed to a device in the corner by the cage.

Kat squinted. "Is that a baby monitor?"

He nodded.

"For a bird?"

"If you think that's strange, just wait." Joe motioned with his free hand for Kat to join him at the door.

"I thought you said Seamus doesn't like to leave this room. Isn't he going to freak out if you take him out of here?"

"Seamus doesn't mind field trips," Joe assured her. "Especially when he gets to be the center of attention."

"What's that supposed to mean?"

"You'll see," Joe said cryptically and turned to head down the hall, leaving Kat no choice but to follow.

He led her around the corner, past the conference room where they'd had the business meeting, and out through a set of French doors that Kat assumed would lead to a gathering room similar to the one at the front of the building—the one where she'd had her first encounter with Mick. Instead, she found herself in another foyer.

"Wait a minute." She glanced outside and sure enough, there was her delivery van. "I could have come in this way?"

"Mick didn't tell you?"

Kat shook her head.

Joe heaved an exacerbated sigh, as if his brother couldn't be trusted with the smallest of tasks. "Sorry, yes. We use this entrance for wakes." He indicated a stairwell. "It leads straight down to the lower level. My brother should have explained this."

While she agreed that this information would have come in handy, Kat felt a sudden rush of protectiveness for her friend. "It's not a big deal," she assured Joe, offering him a bright smile. "It probably slipped his mind."

Joe huffed but didn't say anything else.

She understood his frustration. Joe was competent and controlled and expected the same level of attention to detail from others. Responsible, respectful . . . in so many ways he was exactly what she was looking for. Her ideal Mr. Right.

So far, the only thing Kat had noticed that didn't fit her list was his attitude toward Mick. Joe had a major chip on his shoulder when it came to his sibling, but Kat decided to give her potential Mr. Right the benefit of the doubt. He was a well-intentioned but overbearing older brother, that's all. It was a trait she could appreciate. A flaw she could definitely live with.

"I know how much it means to Mick to get this test run right. That's why I'm here. To help make sure everything goes well."

"Is that so?" Joe paused at the bottom of the stairs and glanced back at her, a glint of admiration in his eyes. "Well, with you here to help, I'm sure tonight will be a success."

Kat basked in the warm glow of his compliment and hoped his prediction proved true. But as she followed Joe down another corridor, she had to admit she had her doubts. She still didn't hear the slightest peep that would indicate a single soul was down here, let alone an entire party. She'd always thought wakes were supposed to be big boisterous affairs.

As if reading her mind, Joe pointed and said, "Everyone is right through here."

"There?" Kat eyed the paneled wall doubtfully.

"The paneling hides a pocket door built into the wall. It's a bit hard to see at first, but that's the point. Joe chuckled. "According to my granda, this room was once used as a speakeasy."

"Like, from the prohibition?"

"Exactly. If you believe the stories, all the legendary Chicago mobsters have been here. John Dillinger. Baby Face Nelson."

"Al Capone?" Kat asked. It was the only old-timey gangster name she knew.

"Of course." Steadying his arm to keep Seamus balanced, Joe reached out his free hand and slid the heavy door open.

A blast of sound hit Kat, almost knocking her over. She blinked in surprise. That was some impressive soundproofing. From the other side of the door, you never would have guessed anything was happening in here. The place was packed to the gills. People of all ages, dressed in various shades of funeral black, were clustered in groups like magpies, laughing and talking.

Kat glanced around, taking stock. The banquet tables covered in vinyl cloths and metal folding chairs gave off a distinct church basement vibe, but the room itself was nicer looking than she'd imagined. Elegant, even. With a coffered ceiling and walls lined in walnut wainscoting that made it easy to picture what it must have been like back in its heyday. She'd been expecting something that would require a lot more work to elevate to a formal event space. In reality, all that was necessary were a few strategic upgrades.

Running numbers in her head, Kat began adjusting the expense sheet she'd worked on with Mick. Completely absorbed in drafting a mental list of suggestions, it took her a moment to realize the room had grown quiet. She glanced up and noticed a crowd had begun to gather in the middle of the room. Kat inched closer, craning her neck to see around the people in front of her. To her surprise, she discovered Seamus sat in the center of the circle.

The center of attention. Kat recalled Joe's words and had a feeling she was about to find out what he'd meant.

Seamus had abandoned Joe's arm for a perch on a stool. Next to the bird stood a man with a violin—or maybe it was a fiddle— was there a difference? Kat didn't know. The musician lifted his bow and began to play. As the first notes of a mournful melody filled the room, Seamus swayed from side to side, his head bobbing back and forth. Then the bird's crest rose, spiking to its full glory, and he began to sing.

"Sing" wasn't quite right. It was more like warbling, but that word didn't give justice to the sweet clear notes coming from the cockatoo.

"What do you think?"

A shiver passed down Kat's spine as Mick slipped through the crowd to stand beside her. "It's beautiful," she said, her words coming out in a soft sigh. "Seamus sounds like an Irish tin whistle."

"You recognize it?" The corner of Mick's mouth lifted. "I'm impressed."

"Don't be too impressed," she warned. "I'm not sure if the man with him is playing a violin or fiddle."

A soft snort of laughter escaped him. He leaned closer and whispered, "They're the same thing."

"Oh. Okay." Kat nodded, refusing to acknowledge how the warm tickle of his breath against her ear sent a delicious tingle down the column of her neck. "Well, you learn something new every day. As for the tin whistle, I knew about that thanks to my grandma. And *Titanic*."

Mick's brow furrowed. "The boat?"

"The movie. It's my babcia's favorite."

"I see," Mick said, but he still looked confused.

"I've seen it so many times, I have the soundtrack memorized. Trust me, there's a *lot* of tin whistle."

The song drew to a close and the crowd burst into applause, showering the cockatoo with praise and shouting out requests.

Kat joined in, clapping her hands enthusiastically. "I had no idea Seamus was such a star."

"I told you the bird has a big ego." Mick's smirk was indulgent, as if he couldn't fault the bird's pride.

After that performance, Kat rather agreed. "I'd say he's entitled," she said, watching as guests began to line up and feed Seamus treats, sharing bits of cracker and cake. Kat frowned. "Can he have that stuff?"

Mick shrugged. "Crackers are fine. And as long as they're not giving him the frosted bits, the cake is fine too, but no whiskey."

Kat gasped. "Who would try giving alcohol to a bird?"

"With this crowd, I think the easier question is who wouldn't." Mick clapped his hands together. "Are you ready to serve some drinks and see this wee plan of ours in action?"

"*Our* plan?"

His dark eyes held hers. "None of this would have happened without your help, Kat."

Pleasure bloomed at his compliment. It was nice to feel appreciated. To have her efforts acknowledged.

Mick guided her over to a corner of the room where a makeshift bar had been set up. Very makeshift. In contrast to the surprisingly elegant walls and ceiling, the bar consisted of a few sawhorses topped by planks of plywood. A broad-shouldered man with a snowy white mullet was filling pint glasses from one of three kegs stacked on a trolley. Beside him, a red-haired woman poured out shots of the aforementioned whiskey.

"I know it's a bit . . . rustic," Mick admitted, "but I've already got some quotes on installing a real bar."

"I'm surprised there isn't a bar already," Kat said. "Your brother mentioned this place used to be a speakeasy."

"Precisely. What happened if the cops showed up? Can't have the evidence in plain sight." He winked.

The mention of cops made Kat pause as a thought struck her. "Um, Mick . . ." She hesitated. Kat knew how much getting this idea up and running meant to him, and she didn't want to criticize his efforts . . . she had a feeling he got enough of that from his brother. At the same time, she'd noticed he sometimes rushed through the details . . . which is why she was concerned he might have skipped some crucial steps, especially in his eagerness to win Joe over. "I should have asked before. How did you get the liquor license approved so quickly?"

"I didn't," he admitted. "But don't worry," he added. "I've got a workaround." He gestured at the man behind the bar. "That's Big Mike, my uncle. Great-uncle, actually."

"Great-uncle," Kat repeated. "Your grandfather's brother?"

"Mm-hmm. He owns O'Sullivan's Pub."

"I thought the funeral home was the family business."

"It is, but Uncle Mike decided he preferred serving stiff drinks to dealing with stiffs."

"Never going to give up trying to make that joke land, eh, Mickey?" Still pouring out beers, the older man tipped his head in greeting. "Wanna introduce me?"

"Uncle Mike, this is my friend Kat."

"Girlfriend, is it?" he asked, a glint in his dark eyes that Kat was beginning to think must be a trademark in the O'Sullivan genetic code.

"*Friend*," Mick said firmly. "Though don't get any ideas."

The older man chuckled. "Wouldn't dream of it."

"And Gran would kill you dead," the red-haired woman with the whiskey bottle added. "Hi." She flashed Kat a smile. "I'm Kathleen. My cousin Mick has told us all about you."

"He has indeed." Big Mike winked. His voice held the Irish lilt, but only the slightest hint of an accent. "Will you be helping us serve up these drinks then, darlin'?"

"That's the plan," she said, matching his wide grin. He may not have much of an accent, but the charm was definitely there. "So, how does this work exactly?"

"First, you grab a tray," Mick said, handing her one from the stack at the end of the makeshift bar. "Second, you load it up with glasses and hand them out to the crowd," he explained. "Third, you come back for more."

"I understand that part, smart-ass." Kat glowered. "What I mean is how does it work that you're selling booze without a license."

"I'm not selling it . . . Uncle Mike is." Mick crossed his arms. "His pub is supplying all the alcohol this evening and the client's family paid him ahead of time. Directly."

"Hmm," Kat mused. She wasn't sure if this was technically legal but decided it wasn't her problem. "Are you monitoring how much the guests drink?"

"As if that were bloody possible," the older man guffawed. He slapped the makeshift bar top, rattling glasses.

"What my granda means to say is we can't control what they've got in their flasks," Kathleen said. "But each guest is limited to three drink tickets." The redhead's eyebrows rose in warning. " As long as we remember to collect them."

"Gotcha." Kat nodded and began filling her tray with drinks. After more return trips than she could count, Kat set her empty tray on the bar and stretched. She was used to being on her feet all day at the flower shop, but this was different. Balancing a heavy tray of drinks while navigating a crowd of people—a crowd growing increasingly tipsy—was taking its toll.

"Hey there," Kathleen said. "You look like you need a break."

"I am pretty tired," Kat admitted.

"Here." The woman set a tumbler in front of Kat and poured a bit of whiskey in it. "This will perk you right up." Then she poured herself a shot as well and clinked her glass against Kat's.

"Thanks." Kat tipped the drink back and let out a strangled gasp as the intensity of the alcohol made her throat close up. She forced herself to swallow and almost gagged while the whiskey burned a path to her belly.

"Okay?" Kathleen asked, auburn eyebrows raised in concern.

Kat nodded. "Yeah," she wheezed. "But this stuff doesn't mess around."

"O'Sullivans never skimp on the booze," Big Mike said, sliding a pint glass toward her. "Chase it down with this."

With a bit more care than she'd downed the shot, Kat sipped the dark beer. The stout was rich and thick. Malty chocolate and sharp bitter notes of coffee slid over her tongue and went down smooth. "Guinness?" she asked.

"Nah." He shook his head and whispered, "My own special blend."

"My grandfather is rather infamous for his experiments," Kathleen explained. Her lips quirked in an affectionate teasing smile. "Sometimes, he's even good at it."

"I know someone like that." Kat grinned, thinking of Andie.

"You rest here a bit," Kathleen instructed, topping off Kat's whiskey glass and surveying the room. "We'll be cutting off this crowd soon, anyway."

"Thanks." This time Kat sipped the whiskey slowly, letting it fill her mouth and ease its way down. It helped that the first shot, as well as the beer, had taken the edge off. She leaned back against makeshift bar, enjoying the languor stealing over her limbs, easing the ache in her sore muscles.

Across the room, Joe mingled with guests. Kat took another sip of her drink, attention trained on Mick's older brother. He wasn't the tallest in the crowd, but his impeccable posture made him easy to spot, the set of his shoulders and straight line of his back unmistakable. She considered walking over and striking up a conversation. Ask Joe how he thought things were going this evening. Maybe see if he wanted to grab a drink together later.

Her head swam, and the lights in the room went fuzzy for a moment. Kat set her glass down and waited for the wave of wooziness to pass. Okay, so maybe no drinks. But she could ask him out for coffee. He probably liked coffee.

Kat tilted her head, studying Joe. She bet he drank his coffee black. A man like that, all business and no nonsense. Nothing froufrou. She giggled, imagining Joe rolling up to a Starbucks drive-through and ordering some caramel mocha choco latte sugar bomb.

She could ask him. What harm was there in that? Ever since Halloween, Kat had been waiting for Joe to make a move. But so far there'd been crickets. Which meant it was up to her. If she thought there was a chance he could be her Mr. Right, she needed to find out. Maybe it was the whiskey talking, but now seemed like as good a time as ever.

At that moment Joe reached out and placed a hand on the shoulder of the woman standing next to him, a comforting earnest expression on his face. Kat's gaze drifted to the spray of flowers pinned to the woman's dress. She sputtered, recognizing the corsage. She'd made it herself. For the mother of the deceased.

Yep. She'd been about to flirt . . . at a wake.

Oh, Kitty Kat, this is a new low, even for you.

CHAPTER 16

Mick

"Drinking on the job, huh?" Mick teased, easing up beside Kat. "Better not let the boss catch you."

"Don't worry." Kat waved a hand. "I'm friends with the boss."

"Is that so?" Mick narrowed his eyes. Something was off with her. He'd gone upstairs to settle Seamus back in his cage for the night, and when he'd come back down, he'd found Kat standing at the bar, staring forlornly into the crowd of mourners.

"Join me in another?" He motioned for his cousin to pass the whiskey and poured himself a healthy dollop.

"I'm not sure," she began, but he'd already tilted the bottle and was replenishing her tumbler. "Okay, then."

"To Mr. William Donnelly." Mick raised his glass. "May joy and peace surround you."

Kat touched her glass to his. "That's a nice sentiment."

"It's part of an old Irish blessing." Mick sipped his drink. "Now, this is the good stuff." He sighed reverently, the smoky flavors of oak and barley lingering on his tongue.

"O'Sullivan's don't skimp on the booze," Kat said. "Or so I've heard."

Mick grinned. "You've been talking to Uncle Mike."

Her lips curved in response, but he noticed the smile didn't reach her eyes. Something was definitely bothering her. And she still hadn't touched her drink. "Do you not like it?"

"Like what?"

"The whiskey." He gestured at the glass she was fidgeting with. "You're nursing it."

"Actually, I think I like it too much." She leaned closer and confessed in an exaggerated whisper, "This is my third one."

Well, this was an unexpected development. Mick propped his elbows on the bar and leaned back, eyeing her. He'd been worried Kat was upset about something, but perhaps she was tipsy. "I do believe you're drunk."

A hoarse giggle erupted from Kat. "I do believe you're right." She copied his position. Or attempted to. But one of her elbows slipped and she tilted sideways.

"Easy there." He scooted closer so she could lean on him for support. "Someone can't handle their Irish whiskey."

"Someone has never had Irish whiskey," Kat corrected primly. "Before today, that is."

Mick took on a thick Irish brogue and teased, "If I'd known that darlin', I'd have never poured you a third."

"Did you say 'turd'?" she asked. Kat studied him over the rim of her glass. "Why are you talking like a leprechaun?"

"That's enough for you, lass." Mick snaked the whiskey out of her grip. He'd finish it off himself, but he had a feeling he was going to need his wits about him, so he passed the glass to his uncle to empty and rinse.

"Fine," Kat murmured. "I didn't want it anyway."

Beside him, she was making weird faces, moving her mouth all around, and he had a feeling he knew why. "You can't feel your lips right now, can you?"

"Of course I can," she insisted. She reached a hand up as if to touch her mouth . . . and missed.

Mick swallowed a laugh. He had to at least try and be serious. He shifted, catching the eye of his uncle. "I might have to duck out early. Can you and Kathleen wrap things up here without me?"

"In our sleep, lad," Uncle Mike snorted. "This is nothing compared to what the pub looks like on any given game day."

"True enough," Mick agreed. He'd worked his fair share of

shifts at the pub, too, and knew they were more than capable of closing this party down. "Thanks. I owe you one."

"Nothing doing. It was my pleasure." Uncle Mike slapped the towel over his shoulder. "The two O'Sullivan businesses working together like this. I wish your granda could have lived to see it."

"Me too." Mick swallowed. He didn't want to ask, but he couldn't help himself. "Do you think he would have been proud?"

"He *is* proud." Uncle Mike leaned across the plywood and wrapped one burly forearm around Mick. "I know it."

A burn that had nothing to do with whiskey stung the back of Mick's throat. He gave his uncle an appreciative slap on the back then turned back to keep an eye on Kat, but she wasn't where he'd left her.

Damn. He did a quick survey of the room. Joe was deep in conversation with the Donnelly family, which was great, since his brother would be preoccupied and hopefully wouldn't notice one very tipsy blonde on the loose somewhere in the crowd of mourners. It was also not so great, because Mick had spotted his quarry, and she was making a beeline for his brother. *What the hell was Kat planning?*

Mick preferred not to find out. He circled the perimeter of the room, looking for an opening in the crowd that would allow him to cut Kat off before she reached Joe. He'd finally picked a spot on her trajectory and was about to head her way when Kat abruptly stopped. Her eyes widened in horror, and she clutched her stomach.

Oh no. Oh no, no, no.

A second later she'd spun on her heel and was running for the entrance to the restroom.

Seems his Polish barmaid couldn't stomach Irish whiskey. Literally.

Mick glanced at his brother. Joe was still talking to the family, oblivious to the drama unfolding around him. Good. Oblivious

Joe was good. Much better than Angry Joe or his personal favorite, Mick-What-Did-You-Do-Wrong-Now Joe.

Slipping through the crowd, Mick hurried to the restroom. He tapped his knuckles on the door. "Kat?"

"Go away." The order came out in a low moan.

"Is anyone else in there with you?" He waited a beat. "Hello?"

Mick took the silence as his answer and entered, wincing in sympathy at the sound of retching. He stepped into the stall with Kat, crowding behind her, making sure her hair was out of the line of fire, and rubbing a palm over her back in slow, soothing circles.

Once the heaving stopped, he wet some paper towels with cold water. "Here," he said, crouching down and passing her the towels. "Wipe your face and put one on the back of your neck, it will help."

Kat propped herself against the wall and did as he instructed.

"Feeling better, princess?"

She nodded.

"Good." He stood. "I'll be back in a minute."

"Don't leave me," she croaked. "Please."

Mick's heart lurched. "I'll be right back." A few golden strands clung to her clammy cheeks, and he brushed them back. "I promise. And then I'll take you home."

"But the wake isn't over . . . ," she mumbled. "What about your test run?"

Mick didn't answer her, because he didn't have an answer. He pushed through the restroom door and bumped smack into his brother.

"Mick," Joe's voice was pleasant and conversational, at odds with his rigid spine. "What were you doing in there?"

"Ah . . . helping someone?"

"Helping who with what?" Joe pressed.

Mick's jaw clenched. He needed to explain the situation in a way that didn't make Joe think he was being a complete fuckup—and not only him, but Kat too. She was counting on establishing a partnership with O'Sullivan's.

Control. With Joe, it was always about control. Mick had to convince his brother that everything was under control. Situation normal.

"It's Kat. She's sick." *Not a lie.*

"I'm sorry to hear that."

Mick thought he saw a hint of real concern flash across his brother's face. For Kat or the inconvenience their absence might cause, he wasn't sure. "I'm going to take her home."

"Take her home?" Joe frowned. "Now? Didn't she drive here?"

"Yeah, she did but . . . she's in no condition to drive." *Also not a lie.*

"Uncle Mike and Kathleen said they'd handle closing up the bar. And don't worry about Seamus, I've already taken him back to his cage."

"Sounds like you have everything under control," Joe said.

Yep. That's me. Totally in control. Mick did not miss the hefty note of surprise in his brother's voice. "I'll check in with you when I get back and we can debrief on how the event went." *See Joe? I can use big words like "debrief."* "Sound good?"

"Sounds great, actually." Again, Joe's tone held a note of surprise. "See her home safe."

"Will do," Mick said.

"Oh, and Mick?" Joe called.

Shit. Mick froze. *Shit. Shit. Shit.* Mick pulled himself together. He was almost off the hook. Calm. In control. Fly casual. He turned back toward his brother. "Yeah?"

"It's nice to see you be so responsible."

Mick's instinct was to respond with something snarky. He would love to say his big brother's stamp of approval didn't matter to him. But that would be an even bigger lie than his current charade. So instead, he simply nodded. "Thanks."

As he led Kat out of the building and toward her van, Mick

began to wonder if leaving had been necessary, she seemed to be doing much better now. But the moment he climbed into the seat next to her, Mick knew he'd made the right decision. Kat was fumbling with her seatbelt and missed the lock mechanism twice before he finally took it from her and clicked it into place himself. His hand snagged on something jammed between the seats.

It was a piece of string or something. Mick wriggled his fingers, trying to untangle himself, and whatever was attached to the string sprung free, smacking him in the face. "What the . . . ?" He held up what looked like a ball of yarn—correction—balls. As in, two of them. "Um, Kat. Why is there a giant penis in your van?"

"The van's not mine."

"And the yarn penis?" he asked.

Kat glanced at the object dangling from his fingers and snorted with laughter. And this wasn't any snort. It was a real, full-on, barnyard-pigs-snuffling-in-the-mud snort. She clapped a hand over her mouth, stifling the sound as she shook her head.

"Not yours either, huh?" Mick eyed her, feeling like a cop on a drug bust. "Next you're going to tell me you were holding this for a friend."

"Well, yes, actually. I mean, no. Not exactly." She paused, brow furrowing.

Mick swore he could see the wheels of her whiskey-soaked brain spinning haphazardly. "What does that mean?"

"It means the van belongs to Allen. Laura drives the delivery van during the day, and she must have dropped a cozy cock."

"'Cozy . . . cock'?" he repeated.

Kat nodded. "It's a drink holder." She reached over, demonstrating how the top opened. "You put your cup of coffee or tea or whatever tickles your fancy inside here and it stays all warm and toasty. Cozy."

Mick eyed the hollow space dubiously. "And it looks like a wiener because . . ."

"Because it's fun." She beamed at him. Her cheeks were still flushed, the tip of her nose was now a matching pink in the cold night air. "Laura crochets all kinds of stuff. Wine bottle holders, lip balm cases . . ."

He handed the yarn back to her. "And everything is shaped like dicks?"

"Yep." She bounced the cozy cock on her knee "People love 'em. I helped set up her online shop and we're working on a marketing plan."

Once again, Mick was impressed with Kat's creativity and gumption. "That's one of the many things I admire about you, Kat. You're always thinking outside the box."

Kat gave him a tipsy sidelong glance. "I'm always thinking about cocks?"

"That too." Mick bit the inside of his cheek, holding in a laugh. He buckled his seatbelt and prepared for a bumpy ride. When he was with Kat, things were never boring.

CHAPTER 17

Mick

Sometime during Kat's explanation regarding the handmade cock merchandise in her delivery van, it had started to snow. A lot. Mick gripped the steering wheel and forced himself to concentrate. He needed his full attention to navigate a vehicle he was unfamiliar with through streets quickly disappearing beneath a slick layer of fluff. Thankfully, the flower shop wasn't too far. Even going well below the speed limit, they made it to Kat's place in about half an hour.

Not long, but still enough time for Kat to nod off. Mick grinned, watching her out of the corner of his eye as he pulled the van into a spot in front of the shop. Her head lolled back, mouth agape, little snores ruffling the wisps of blond hair framing her face. He half expected to see drool. But no. Not yet anyway.

Even if Kat did drool, he wouldn't care. She snorted. She snored. She got drunk off her ass on three shots of whiskey. And he was charmed by all of it. Mick cut the engine and banged his head on the steering wheel. He was in so much fucking trouble.

Kat stirred, a snort-snore combo escaping as she jerked awake. She blinked, staring groggily through the windshield. "Is it snowing?"

"First snowfall of the year."

"Nooo," Kat moaned. "It's too soon. It's not even Thanksgiving yet."

"We've had blizzards on Halloween."

"I know." Kat pouted. "And I don't like it." She slouched in her seat. "It should only snow on Christmas."

"Only Christmas?"

She nodded. "From Christmas Eve to New Year's Eve. It can snow all that week. Then I want it to go away."

Mick smirked. "Good luck with that, princess."

He was about to get out and come around to open her door when she grabbed his arm and said, "You shouldn't be here."

Her words stopped him cold. An icicle might as well have dropped off the side of the building and pierced him in the chest. "Geez, Kat. It's not like I'm planning to spend the night."

She shook her head. "No. You can't park here." She pointed at a sign on the curb. "Allen would kill me if his van got towed."

"Oops." He started the car again, covering his embarrassment with a laugh. Chicago had some bonkers parking regulations, especially when it came to snow.

"Go around back," Kat instructed. "You can park in the alley."

Mick followed her directions and guided the van into a narrow parking spot behind the building. "Jesus," he muttered under his breath.

"Something wrong?"

"I'm wondering what sadist designed this," he grumbled. "The space is freaking tight."

She snickered.

Mick glanced over at her. "What's so funny?"

"Laura complains about this spot too. And there are definitely some euphemisms involved." Kat made an obscene gesture with the cock cozy.

"I can only imagine." Satisfied with his parking job, Mick pulled the key from the ignition. "You know, between the parking innuendos and all the yarn peen in this company vehicle, HR would have a field day with your friend Laura."

"Good thing we don't have HR, then. Only Allen." Kat opened her door and squeezed out. "For now."

Mick would have come around to help her, but he could barely fit out his own side. It was like prying yourself from a sardine can.

He wiggled free and joined Kat. "'For now'?" he echoed. "What does that mean?"

She gave him a shy smile. "It means he's retiring, and I'm planning to buy him out."

"Whoa. That's your dream, right? To have your own shop. That's amazing."

Her mouth tightened. She was still smiling, but it was strained. "It is amazing," he faltered. "Isn't it?"

"Yeah, it is . . ."

"But?"

"Was my 'but' that obvious?"

He chuckled. "Oh, yeah. Your 'but' was hanging way out there."

Apparently, she'd sobered up enough to be more annoyed than amused by his cheap joke. She rolled her eyes and grabbed her keys out of his hand, then turned and started walking toward her building.

Mick trailed behind Kat, waiting for her to explain. When she didn't, he finally said, "Are you going to leave your 'but' hanging?"

"If I answer that, will you drop the ridiculous metaphor?"

"I'm not sure it's a metaphor."

"Whatever," she said, punching a code into the keypad and opening the door. "I was a business major, not English, remember?"

Mick followed her into the building. They paused in the foyer and stomped their feet on the doormat, shaking snow from their shoes and coats before heading upstairs. "Is it money?" he asked.

"Huh?"

"Your 'but.'"

"Stop calling it that." She glanced over her shoulder. "And no. Not exactly." They reached the second floor and headed down the hall. "I've been saving for my own shop for years, but it's not nearly enough to buy the place outright. Allen said he's willing to work with me on figuring out a layaway plan."

"Then what's the problem?" Mick pressed.

"The problem is my boss has a hard time letting go of control."

"I know someone like that." Mick leaned against the wall outside her apartment.

"Ha. You mean your brother?"

"Got it in one."

"Don't get me wrong, Allen's been a great boss, but he likes things done a certain way. Owning my own shop is my chance to do things *my* way. I'm worried that if I accept his offer, and he's still owner or partial owner or whatever, there will be issues when it comes to making changes . . ." She paused, turning the key in her lock. "As long as it's his name on the deed, I'll never be able to feel like it's really my store."

"And that's important to you?" he asked.

"It's everything to me," Kat said bluntly. She pushed her door open. "Do you wanna come in?"

Hell, yes, he wanted to come in. Mick hesitated. "I dunno, it's getting kind of late."

"Geez, Mick, I'm not asking you to sleep over."

Heat stung the back of his neck. Why did he have to say that before?

"I'm teasing." She grabbed his arm and dragged him inside her apartment. "Get in here." Kat kicked off her shoes and hung her damp coat on the rack by the door. "How 'bout a drink?" she asked.

Mick cocked his head at her, one shoe still on. He raised his eyebrows.

"Tea," she clarified.

"I'd love some." He finished removing his other shoe.

Kat broke into giggles.

He stared at her. He thought she'd mostly sobered up, but maybe he was wrong. "What's so funny?"

"Your socks."

"What's wrong with my socks?" Mick glanced down, worried his big toe was sticking out or something.

"They don't match," she explained. "At all."

"Kat, my socks haven't matched since I could put them on my own feet." It was true. He could never be bothered. "As long as I have one sock on each foot, I'm good."

She giggled again and hung his coat on the rack next to hers. "Now, what was that about tea?"

"Yes. Wholesome, hot, booze-free tea coming up." Kat scuttled off to her little kitchen area and began clattering about. "Make yourself at home," she called.

He stepped into her living area and eyed the pink plastic castle in the corner by the papasan chair. Nothing stirred inside. Mick moved closer, searching the wood shavings for signs of life. "Uh, Kat?"

"Yeah?"

"Where's JoJo?"

She came around the corner, two steaming mugs in hand. "At a slumber party."

"Pardon?"

Kat handed him one of the mugs. "JoJo is at a sleepover."

Okay, so he had heard her correctly. "What, with other hedgehogs?"

"No. With a hamster."

"Is that a thing?" Mick asked. "Do people organize slumber parties for their little critters?"

"I've heard of birthday parties for dogs, so why not?" Kat laughed and settled onto the couch. "My coworker Ronnie has a friend, Bertie, who is a costume designer and also makes outfits for his hamster."

"Let me guess," Mick said, joining her on the couch. "Now Bertie is making some costumes for JoJo."

"Apparently, an entire wardrobe." Kat shook her head. "She

was only supposed to spend one night, but when you asked me to help out tonight I called Ronnie to see if JoJo could stay an extra day, so it's become a whole weekend extravaganza with Ronnie and JoJo and Bertie."

"Don't forget Bertie's hamster," Mick added.

"And Bertie's hamster." Kat giggled, blowing bubbles into her tea. "Oh! Ronnie sent pics." Kat set her mug down and pulled out her phone. "Wanna see?"

"Why not." Mick leaned closer to look over her shoulder. On Kat's screen was a photo montage featuring JoJo in various outfits. "Wow," he chuckled. "It's an entire fashion show."

Kat kept scrolling, stopping to coo at various images. Mick tried to focus on the photos, murmuring his agreement on how adorable the hedgehog looked in everything from a tutu to a tuque, but his attention kept straying to Kat. Like always, she smelled of wildflowers. The fresh scent drifted across his senses, sweet and warm and earthy.

"JoJo looks like she's having fun, doesn't she?"

"Um . . . I guess," Mick agreed, happy to humor her.

She turned, meeting his gaze. Her mouth tilted in a self-conscious smile. "It's silly, but I was nervous about letting JoJo spend the night somewhere else. And now she's away for the whole weekend."

"We are discussing a hedgehog-hamster-wardrobe-fitting-slash-slumber party," Mick said, deadpan. "Silly has left the building." He set his mug down next to hers. "But I can totally understand why you'd be nervous. You're a new parent."

"Exactly." Kat sighed and leaned back against the couch cushions. "I really feel like one too. I've been so exhausted. Last night was the first decent night's sleep I've had in over a month. JoJo keeps me up all night."

Mick shook his head in sympathy. "If we forget to cover Seamus's cage, that turkey can keep the whole neighborhood awake."

"JoJo's not that bad, it's her wheel." She pointed toward the castle. "That darn exercise wheel is so freaking squeaky. I've tried fixing it. I've oiled it and greased it and tightened it and loosened it and . . ." She shrugged. "Nothing."

"You could throw it away," Mick suggested.

Kat shook her head. "JoJo loves it too much. I tried switching it out with a different wheel and she went on a hunger strike."

She smothered a yawn, and Mick fell a little bit harder. The fact that Kat hadn't gotten rid of the thing made him want to pull her into his arms and cuddle her close. Instead, he tugged at the blanket draped over the back of the couch and covered her.

"You're so nicesh," she cooed in a sleepy tipsy mumble.

"I'm 'nish,' huh?" Mick snickered at her mushy pronunciation. "Are you saying I'm nice?"

"Mm-hmm." Kat hummed, a blissful grin dancing on her lips. "I learned something tonight," she added, closing her eyes and snuggling deeper into the cushions.

"What's that?"

"I can't handle Irish whiskey."

"No shit." She looked so sweet and cozy wrapped in that big, fluffy blanket. Mick leaned forward, the urge to get under there with her and kiss her so strong it was a physical tug, a cord wrapping around his heart, pulling him closer.

"Can you believe I almost tried flirting with your brother tonight?"

The cord snapped. Mick's chin jerked up. "What?"

"At the wake." Kat opened her eyes and looked at him. She pinched her thumb and forefinger together. "I came this close to walking up to your brother and asking him out on a date."

"What stopped you?" he asked. "Oh, wait, I know. You had to puke." He slumped back against the arm on his side of the couch. "Maybe you should take that as a sign."

Kat nudged his leg. "Do you think it would be a bad idea to ask your brother out?"

Absolutely. Terrible. He tuned out the answers shouting in his brain. "Maybe. You know, that whole thing about mixing business and pleasure. If you're worried about things getting personal . . ."

"Things already are kind of personal, aren't they?" Kat crossed her arms. "I mean, we're friends."

"We are friends," Mick agreed. *Just* friends. He reached for his tea. It had gone cold, but he gulped it down anyway.

"And you'd never let our personal relationship interfere with the business relationship, right?"

Mick stared into his mug. "I'd try not to."

"I'm sure the same could be said for your brother," Kat insisted. "Joe is so professional."

"He is." Mick couldn't deny that.

"Now that I think about it, Joe is *too* professional," Kat mused. "He probably would have turned me down if I had asked him on a date."

"Not necessarily."

"Really?" Kat perked up. "You think there's a chance he'd say yes?"

"Probably," Mick said, wanting to bite off his own tongue. But if Kat truly was interested in Joe, then he wasn't going to get in the way by lying. He should have seen this coming. His sister had warned him. Mary-Kate had told him that Kat was interested in Joe. "Only one way to find out."

"I haven't had the best of luck in that area," Kat admitted. "And I haven't been on a date since my breakup with Tad." She fiddled with the TV remote. "I spent last night and most of today on the couch, buried under a blanket and watching movies all by myself."

"Sounds pretty awesome to me." Mick leaned back into the cushions. He had the distinct impression that Kat didn't like being alone. He itched with curiosity, but he repressed his natural instinct to dig deeper and instead asked, "What movies?"

"I had a whole theme going with rom-coms set in Chicago.

While You Were Sleeping, My Big Fat Greek Wedding, My Best Friend's Wedding . . ."

"That's a lot of weddings. Anything filmed *after* we went through puberty?"

Kat laughed. "There's a Christmas one that came out on Netflix not too long ago. I believe it's set in Logan Square." She paused, mouth twisting in a grin. "Come to think of it, that movie is about two people who agree to be each other's plus-one for holidays and stuff."

"Is that so?" Mick asked.

"Yeah. It's fine, but nothing beats the movies from the nineties. That was the golden age."

"Why do I get the feeling I'm in the presence of a rom-com expert?"

"I guess you could say that. I've certainly watched enough of them." She smiled, her face lighting up with a warm happy glow. "My friends and I had this whole thing where we'd get together every Friday night and watch romantic comedies."

"Every Friday night?"

Kat laughed. "Pretty much. We started doing it in college and kept it going every week for years. Until recently, that is." The light dimmed, her face sobering. "I knew we couldn't keep it going forever, but I wasn't prepared for things to change so fast. I barely see my best friends anymore. And now Julia is living with Luke. And Andie is moving to Milwaukee and getting married." Kat groaned and pulled the blanket over her head.

"Do you think I have issues?" she asked, the question muffled by the blanket.

"Everyone has issues," Mick said. He certainly did. Plenty of them. A bundle of them was sitting next to him on the couch right now. "Are you upset your friend got engaged?"

"No." She shook her head. "I'm happy for her . . ." Kat hesitated, sighing.

"I'm sensing another 'but.'"

"But I'm sad for me," Kat declared. She sat up straighter and tugged the blanket off her head. "There. I said it. My best friends are strapped in, ready for the roller coaster to start. Meanwhile, I'm waiting in the single-rider line."

"Um, if it's any consolation, the single-rider line moves faster," Mick said. The look she cut him made him want to hide under the coffee table. Not a joking matter. Message received. "Serious question," he ventured, careful to keep his tone neutral. "Why does it matter so much if your friends are dating someone and you're not?"

"It's not about dating someone. It's about finding someone. *The one.* It's about knowing who your person is. At Andie's wedding, all I'm going to have is a meaningless 'plus-one.'"

"I can be your plus-one," Mick offered.

She shook her head. "That's sweet of you, but I'm hoping by the time invites are sent out, I'll have found my person too."

"You mean your Mr. Right?" The words left a bitter taste in his mouth. God, he was getting tired of hearing that phrase.

She nodded.

"Keep me as a backup option, then," he suggested. "If your plan doesn't work out the way you hope and you end up flying solo to the wedding, let me be your copilot." He cringed. "Okay, that sounded really schmaltzy."

"I like schmaltzy." She grinned at him, her mood seeming to lighten. "You'll really be my backup plus-one?"

"I promise. Consider it part of my duties as your wingman." Mick's promise was in earnest. He wanted to help Kat. To be there for her as a friend. But inside a dark corner of his heart lurked a possessive hunger, and Mick knew his offer wasn't completely altruistic. They'd agreed to be just friends. She'd declared her interest in his brother. Despite this, some selfish and perhaps deluded part of him held on to the hope there might be something more between them. "Maybe they'll have karaoke at the reception," he suggested. "Since Curt used it to propose."

"He surprised us all with that proposal."

"Strange things can happen during karaoke," Mick said. "Emotions come out that you don't expect."

She stiffened.

Mick held his breath, wondering if she'd pick up on his meaning.

But after a moment, Kat relaxed. "That reminds me," she said, turning her attention toward the TV. "I never got around to watching *My Best Friend's Wedding*. There's a karaoke scene. Do you wanna watch it with me?"

Either she'd missed his signal completely or was choosing to ignore it. Or maybe there was nothing to ignore. Maybe the connection he'd felt between them that night was all in his head. Mick shoved those thoughts away. "Um, sure."

"Great." She clicked through the menus on her streaming service and started the movie. Then she grabbed a tin from the coffee table.

"Are there cookies in there?" Mick asked hopefully. He'd been so nervous about making sure everything was ready for the Donnelly event tonight, he hadn't eaten dinner and suddenly realized he was starving.

She shook her head. "Latkes. One of the customers at the flower shop brought them in." She popped off the lid and held out the tin. "Here. Try one."

"I dunno." Mick peered at the food. "This isn't a customer you pissed off, is it?"

"Just eat one already," Kat ordered, handing him the tin and standing up. "I'm going to get us some napkins."

"Yes, your highness," Mick said and shoved a bite in his mouth. Her bossiness should annoy him, but the embarrassing truth was, he rather enjoyed it when Kat ordered him around.

"What do you think?" she asked, offering him a napkin.

"Not bad. Reminds me of a boxty."

"Boxty," she repeated slowly, as if tasting the word on her tongue. "Is that Irish?"

Mick nodded. "It's basically a potato pancake." He swallowed the last bite and wiped his hands. "My uncle's pub serves them."

"Big Mike?" She took a latke from the tin and set it on her napkin.

"Yep. Big Mike." Mick helped himself to another, smiling at the memories flitting through his mind. "I worked in his pub. First as a busboy in high school and then as a bartender in college."

"Ah, so you have the skills to back up your idea for the bar in a funeral home. Now it's all making sense." Kat nibbled on the edge of her pancake. "Can I ask you a question? And this isn't a judgment or anything, I'm just curious."

"Okay," he said carefully.

"Did you want to work in the funeral home?"

He shrugged. "It's the family business."

"But did you ever want to do something else?"

"When my parents announced their retirement and handed control over to us . . . it was a natural transition for my siblings."

"Well, sure. That's what they always planned to do." Kat said. "More importantly, that's what they wanted to do. Right?"

Mick nodded

"But not you."

"Not me," he echoed, shaking his head. "It was clear what Joe and Mary-Kate could offer the business, where their skills fit. But me?" He shrugged. "I tried to fill in the gaps."

"Be the glue, huh?" Kat studied him. "You've been so busy trying to wedge yourself into the spaces in between your siblings, that you forgot something very important." Her lips quirked in a bemused half smile.

Feeling bemused himself, Mick asked, "What did I forget?"

"You can create your own space. You said it was clear what skills your brother and sister had to offer the business. The same is true for you."

"That's what I'm doing by opening the bar."

Kat shook her head. "That's still you trying to find a way to fit in instead of figuring out where you fit."

"But I don't fit. That's the problem."

"Sure you do." Kat rested her palm against his cheek. "Think about what skills you have to offer. What you're good at doing. What you want to do."

"What I want to do is be a therapist," he admitted.

"Then be a therapist." She tilted her head, gaze steady on his. "O'Sullivan's should offer grief counseling services . . . well, you should, specifically."

Her suggestion landed in Mick's brain like a tree falling across the highway. He sat in stunned silence. What Kat said was so simple, yet so absurdly profound.

"You hate the idea," Kat said.

"No . . . ," Mick said slowly, " I just can't believe I've never thought about it before."

"Really?" Kat's voice was thick with doubt. "Never?"

He stared at his half-eaten pancake. "Maybe a few times, in an abstract sort of way. Like when those two old ladies were fighting, remember?"

"Oh god," Kat snorted. "The Murphy widows?"

He nodded. "If they'd had some time to sit down and work through their feelings, they might not have tried to claw each other's eyes out."

"See?" She grinned at him. Her expression wasn't smug, exactly, but satisfied. Like she'd found the last piece of a puzzle, the one that had gotten lost under the table or behind a chair and finally made the picture complete. "That's your space."

Her observation made him feel seen in a way he wasn't sure he'd ever felt before. A way he wasn't sure he'd ever seen himself.

He wanted to tell Kat how much her insight meant to him. How fucking brilliant she was. He wanted to pull her into his arms and kiss her.

But he couldn't, so he swallowed it down with the last of his latke and turned his attention back to the movie. "Hey, it's the karaoke scene you mentioned."

The distraction worked. Kat glanced at the screen, wincing at Cameron Diaz's terrible singing. "Do you think he loves her because or in spite of how awful she is?"

"Both." Mick turned to face Kat. "I think when you love someone, you love them in spite of their flaws, but at the same time, it's their flaws that make you love them even more. It makes them real. Makes them yours."

"Oh," Kat breathed. "That's a good answer." She licked her lips, and for a moment, Mick had the sense she was going to say something else, but then she yawned. Her head drooped, and she listed toward him.

He shifted on the couch so that she rested against his chest, cheek pressed to his heart. It wasn't long before she drifted off. He gazed down at her, grinning as the soft buzzing sound of her snores filled the room. He tucked the blanket around her a little tighter, pulled the tin of latkes closer, and settled in.

When the movie ended, Kat was still fast asleep. Like, dead to the world, out like a light, asleep. Careful not to wake her, he gently rotated Kat so she was resting on the arm of the couch instead of him. Then he got to his feet and crept toward the sliding glass door leading to Kat's balcony.

Nudging the drapes aside, Mick swallowed a gasp at the sight that greeted him. *Holy fuck.* A full-on blizzard was in progress. A thick layer of freshly fallen snow blanketed the balcony railing. Below, the alley between the buildings was a sea of swirling white, parked cars rising up like snowy islands.

Well, it looked like he would be staying here for the night. He doubted Kat would be waking up anytime soon, and that big round chair in the corner looked comfortable enough. The problem was, he still felt wide awake. Wired.

Mick glanced across the room, attention snagging on JoJo's cage. Inside the pink palace, the wheel sat motionless. Silent and still. For now, anyway. Feeling like Santa Claus—or that other story with elves, the one with the shoemaker—he quietly extracted the hedgehog's exercise wheel from the cage and got to work.

CHAPTER 18

Kat

A bright white light pierced the inside of Kat's eyelids. She stirred and fluttered her lashes as the light shone brighter, nearly blinding her with its epic force. She winced and squeezed her eyes shut. After a moment, she tried again, opening only one eye. Slowly.

The light was coming from her living room window. The room itself was still mostly dark, filled with gray shadows save for the spot where the drapes were askew, allowing for a single beam of light to hit her full in the face with the power of a supernova.

Kat groaned and rolled over. She must have crashed on the couch while watching the movie. Brain still fuzzy with sleep, her head ached with the dull but familiar throb of a hangover. She groaned again, the sequence of events from last night slowly sliding into place. Whiskey. She'd had whiskey last night. Too much whiskey.

Then Mick had driven her home.

Mick!

She torpedoed into a sitting position and immediately regretted it. Her brain swished inside her skull, bobbing back and forth like one of those bubbles in a construction level. Like in a game of connect the dots, Kat tried to piece together the sequence of events that had led to this moment. Mick had driven her home. Walked her up to her apartment. Come inside for tea . . .

Kat glanced at the tin of latkes on the table. They'd eaten and talked, and she'd put the movie on and . . . she touched the side of her face, remembering the feel of his shirt, his warmth, the gentle rise and fall of his chest, the soothing, rhythmic beat of his heart beneath her cheek.

"You're awake."

The sound of Mick's voice surprised Kat. She whirled around, and in her haste to try and pinpoint his location toppled sideways and fell off the couch.

"Ow," she moaned into the carpet. Julia Roberts made falling off furniture appear much more graceful.

"You okay?" he asked.

"Peachy."

"I'd get up and help you, but I think I'm stuck."

"What?" Kat braced her hands on the coffee table and managed to pull herself off the floor. Impressed with her own fortitude, she peered into the shadows of her apartment, now a lighter gray, and caught sight of Mick nestled in her papasan.

His eyes met hers from across the room and he gave her an awkward wave. "Morning."

"What are you doing here?"

"Do you mean in your apartment or in this torture device disguised as a chair?"

"Both, I suppose."

"Well, you were hogging all the space on the couch, and while you did tell me to make myself at home, I figured you didn't want me sleeping in your bed so . . ."

"I was not hogging the couch."

"Um, yes. You were. And snoring."

"I don't snore."

"Yeah, you do."

"Fine. I snore." With another impressive show of strength and agility, Kat got to her feet. Look at her go. She should be in the hangover Olympics. "But only when I'm drunk."

"If you say so, princess." She could hear more than see Mick's smirk.

"Fine," Kat said. "I'm a drunk, snoring couch hog."

"But at least you're a cute, drunk, snoring couch hog."

Ignoring that, Kat shuffled to the sliding glass door. She tugged the drapes open wider and gaped at her snow-covered balcony. "Holy shit."

"My sentiments exactly." Mick gestured at the winter wonderland outside. "That's why I ended up staying here last night."

"For the record, you could have taken the bed."

"Good to know for next time." Mick flailed around in the papasan. "If I ever get out of this chair."

Next time? Kat did not plan to make the events of last night a habit. Though she did appreciate that Mick had been there to look out for her. It was embarrassing but also sweet, and it made her feel cared for. Like when Babcia pinched her cheek. Her insides squished in a soft happy way. "Thanks for everything."

"I should be thanking you," Mick said, grunting as he tried to eject himself from the papasan. "I was the one that called you to help me, remember?"

"Right." Kat came to his rescue and offered him a hand. "Do you think it worked?"

"If you mean do I think we convinced my brother to agree to my plan for the event space, I don't know." Mick clasped her fingers, using the leverage she provided to wiggle forward. "We were supposed to have a talk last night after the wake but . . ."

"But you were here babysitting me," Kat surmised. She braced her feet and pulled. With a final tug, Mick sprung free from the chair, skyrocketing to his feet and landing pressed against her. Their bodies smashed together, face-to-face, both of them breathing hard from the exertion . . .

A bolt of desire surged through Kat. Her insides squished in a completely different way. Mick was always so goofy and awkward, he continually caught her off guard. The heat between them kept sneaking up and ambushing her. Like now. Her defenses had been down and *bam*—lust punch to the vagina.

Kat took a step backward, tripping over her own feet.

"What's wrong?"

"Nothing," she said quickly. Too quickly.

"Are you sure?" he asked, the husky edge of his morning voice rasping in his throat.

Kat shivered. He was looking at her, midnight eyes heavy lidded, his chin dusted with the most deliciously sinful shadow beard. "Yes, I'm sure," she croaked. What the hell was happening? How did Mick suddenly get extra sexy?

"I uh . . . need to go brush my teeth," Kat announced, and made a beeline for her bathroom.

Mick followed her. "Do you mind if I join you?"

Kat paused in washing her face. "You can go first, but you'll have to use your finger," she said, handing him the tube of toothpaste. "I don't share my toothbrush."

"That's fine." Mick spread some toothpaste on his index finger and scrubbed. He spit into the sink, turning on the water to rinse out the basin. "I'm not a barbarian."

She laughed and opened the medicine cabinet. "There's mouthwash if you want it."

"Is that a hint?"

"That you have bad breath?" Kat asked, pulling out the bottle of mouthwash and uncapping it. "Not that I noticed." She handed it to him, stepping back from the sink to let him swish and spit again.

After he'd finished, she took a minute to rinse out the basin, then wiped the counter and faucet off.

Mick watched her. "Um, don't take this the wrong way but . . . aren't you going to brush your teeth too?"

"Of course. I'm not a barbarian," she parroted.

"Then why are you cleaning everything up now? It's only going to get messy again."

"Habit," Kat admitted, squeezing a glob of toothpaste onto her toothbrush. "I can't stand the sight of a dirty sink. It's one of my pet peeves."

"You remind me of my gran," Mick said, a warm smile curving one scruffy cheek. "Granda used to say the house could be on fire, but she'd still stop to wash the dishes if there were any in the sink."

Kat laughed, almost choking on a mouthful of toothpaste. She bent to spit, and he moved out of the way, giving her more space. It should feel strange, sharing such a personal routine together like this. But it was easy. Natural. Not awkward at all. Like good friends the morning after a sleepover. Finishing up with the mouthwash, Kat put the bottle back in the cabinet and debated the floss but decided against it. She might be feeling surprisingly comfortable around Mick, but running a string through her teeth crevices inches away from him would be going a little too far.

As she closed the cabinet, her eyes caught Mick's in the mirror. Kat studied his reflection, wondering what he was thinking. He'd brushed his teeth but obviously hadn't been able to shave, and the dark shadow of his jaw gave him an almost dangerous edge.

There was something about him that reminded her of an ad with cowboys for cologne or rugged outerwear. And *then* there were his eyes, those deep, dark eyes, now pools of liquid heat she could easily imagine sinking into, drifting deeper into their depths, losing herself . . .

Behind her, Mick leaned against the bathroom doorframe and crossed his arms. The move accented the broad curve of his shoulders. He had a nicely defined chest. Not chiseled, not even sculpted, but not bad. Not bad at all.

"Are you checking me out?" he asked.

"What?" Kat's eyes met his in the mirror's reflection. "No," she said quickly, but her protest sounded weak even to her ears.

"Yes, you were." He pushed away from the doorframe and moved to stand next to her, self-satisfied grin creeping across his face. "You think I'm hot."

"Do not," she snorted.

"You think I'm sex-ay," Mick sang the words. Badly.

"Shut up," Kat said, a smile tugging at her mouth.

"You want to hug me." Mick started to dance. Also badly. "You want to kiss me."

"You do know that's from a rom-com," Kat said, snickering.

"Nah." Mick shook his head.

"It totally is," she insisted, thinking back to the last time she caught *Miss Congeniality* on one of the zillion cable stations.

"Quit trying to change the subject," Mick said. "The truth is, there's a vibe between us."

Kat swallowed and dropped her gaze to her stockinged feet. "I don't know what you're talking about."

"I think you do." Mick crossed his arms again. "I thought I felt something the first time we met, but I wasn't sure. Then, on Halloween, I knew I felt a spark between us."

The memory of that night crept over her. The intensity of the moment of connection they'd shared. Stupid karaoke. He'd tried to bring it up last night, and Kat realized this might be why.

"We could test my theory," Mick suggested.

Her head snapped up. Kat leaned back and gripped the edge of her sink. "How?"

He shrugged. "Kiss me."

Should have seen that one coming, Kitty Kat, Andie's voice snarked in Kat's head. Awesome how her friends could give her shit when they weren't even there. Andie and Julia would be eating this up with a spoon. Savoring the irony. Was this irony? It was a sticky situation, is what it was, and Kat needed to figure out how to get unstuck.

"I don't see how that will prove anything," she hedged.

"On the contrary," Mick took a step closer to her. "It'll prove whether this thing I think we're feeling is real or not."

"Fine," Kat said. She squeezed her eyes shut. "One kiss." She puckered her lips, her entire body going rigid as she braced herself to fight off whatever hint of attraction she might feel. Not that she was going to feel anything. But even if she did, it wasn't going to change anything. Kat's eyes flew open. "Wait!" She pressed her palms to his chest, halting his progress. "Before we do this, I want you to promise me something."

He quirked a brow.

"I want you to promise me we'll still be friends."

"Kat—"

She pressed a finger to his lips. "Whatever happens next—not that anything is going to happen, but if something does—do you think you can still be my friend?"

Mick hesitated. "If you're worried this will mess things up between us . . ."

"That's exactly what I'm worried about."

"I promise you I can handle it." He stared at her a moment longer, considering. "But your friendship is too important to me to risk losing." Mick stepped back. "We don't have to do this."

If he'd answered immediately, she might have called the whole thing off. But Kat sensed the weight of honesty in his words and decided to be honest with herself. Yes, she felt a zing of attraction to Mick, but she'd often felt that zing. And it never led to what she really wanted.

This was an opportunity to prove to herself—to both of them— that there was nothing more between them. Certainly nothing to cause a problem with their friendship. Or interfere with her plans for his brother. "No," Kat said, tugging him back. "I want to."

"Are you sure?" Mick asked again. His words held none of the cocky challenge from before. He was checking in with her. Exactly the way a true friend should.

"Yeah." She nodded. The issue of their "vibe" needed to be addressed or it would always be hanging over them. His confession had cracked open a door. If they didn't do something now, that door would remain open, and who knows what other trouble could slip through. This was the only way to kick that door closed.

"I'm sure." Kat shut her eyes once more, tilted her face toward his, and waited.

Tension crept up her spine as awareness settled over her and the playful mood between them shifted. The change was subtle but tangible, a perceptible thrum of energy that made the tiny hairs on her arms and the back of her neck stand on end, like the air before a storm. She was being ridiculous. Kat cracked one eye open. This was Mick. Scared-of-clowns, socks-never-matched Mick. She cleared her throat. "For the good of our friendship," she said, pasting on a brave face. "Let's do this."

"Geez, Kat, you don't have to look like you're going off to war," Mick grumbled. He stepped closer. "It's just a kiss."

"I know," she said, retreating and abruptly bumping into the sink.

"Comfortable?"

"Not really."

"We could move somewhere else . . . The bedroom?"

"This is fine," she said quickly. No way did she want to do this anywhere near a place they could get horizontal. Not that there weren't plenty of surfaces that would serve that purpose in her bathroom. An image of Mick pressing her up against the wall of her shower slid into Kat's head and she slid it right back out. Nope. Not happening. "Can we get this over with already?"

"Why are you in such a hurry?" Mick bent toward her and whispered, "Are you afraid you're going to fall madly in love with me?"

"Ha." Kat snorted. "This isn't some fairy tale." She'd given up on those. She wasn't looking for her prince, or even a knight in shining armor. She was done with the fantasy. She wanted someone down to earth. Sensible. Responsible. Someone who might not sweep her off her feet (or fuck her in the shower), but at least he'd stay grounded. Someone like Joe. Kissing Mick wasn't going to change that, and she was about to prove it. Kat threw her head back, looked him straight in the eye and ordered, "Now shut up and kiss me."

"Okay, princess."

As he bent his head toward her, Kat's eyes drifted closed once more. She tilted her face, and something hard cracked her in the forehead. "Ow!" Her eyes snapped open. "What did you do?"

"You coldcocked me!" Mick rubbed his jaw. "Do you have a steel plate in your skull or something?"

"No." Kat glared at him. "Let's try this again."

"Fine," Mick snapped. He puckered his lips and approached slowly, mouth hovering above hers.

Kat giggled.

He pulled back. "I haven't even kissed you yet and you're laughing?"

"Sorry." Still giggling, she released her death grip on the counter. "You look like one of those duck-lip selfies."

"Way to mess with a man's confidence," Mick grumbled.

"I'm sorry." Kat schooled her features. "I'm ready now."

"You sure?"

"Absolutely."

"Okay." He cleared his throat. "I'm going in."

The snicker died in her throat as Mick snatched her around the waist and pulled her against him. Then his lips were brushing hers and holy heliotropes, did Kat feel it. The sweetness and heat and tingling promise of so much more. She whimpered in surprise.

He pulled back, breaking the tender contact. "Something wrong?"

She shook her head. Maybe she'd imagined how good that was. Maybe it was like when you were really hungry, crappy food tasted really amazing. It wasn't that Mick was a great kisser, it was that Kat hadn't kissed anyone in a while. It had been more than a month since her breakup with Tad. Maybe when Mick kissed her again, he would be a slobberer, or use too much tongue. Only one way to find out. "Is that all you got?"

Mick's dark eyes narrowed in speculation. Then he bent his head, flashing her a roguish smirk full of devilry.

And in the millisecond before his mouth was on hers again, Kat knew she was in deep shit.

This time, when Mick wrapped his arms around Kat, he lifted her, setting her on the edge of the sink. They were at eye level now. Nose to nose. He leaned closer, brushing his cheek against hers. The scrape of his shadow beard against her skin sent sensation skittering through her entire body.

Holy fuck. What was happening right now? The audacity of this man. To be so good at this. He traced his tongue over the curve of her upper lip, and Kat repressed another shiver. She couldn't let him see how affected she was. Rather than overpower her with a show of force, he'd launched a covert operation. A sneak attack meant to weaken her defenses. And it was working.

Kat resisted the urge to return the kiss, but then he bit her bottom lip, sucking it the tiniest bit. A throaty groan escaped her. She opened her mouth and he accepted the invitation immediately, thrusting his tongue inside. *Yes.* That was what she wanted. She needed him invading her body, craved to have him inside her someway, somehow. Aching to bring him closer, Kat wrapped her legs around Mick's hips, ankles locked against his back.

Things were getting really good when he suddenly stopped. "Well?" he asked, his voice low and ragged. "What do you think?" He leaned into her, the hard edge of his erection pressing against the heat between her thighs. "Is there a vibe?"

A vibe? Um, no. That word was too small for the need filling her right now, too casual to describe the desire flooding her senses. Kat was *burning* for him, lust threatening to turn her into a pile of ash. She answered him silently, wordlessly pulling his mouth back to hers, threading her fingers through his hair and kissing him. She answered him with her body, squeezing her thighs and tightening her grip around his hips.

He groaned and she swallowed the sound, wanting to devour him, the need to have any part of him she could get inside of her escalating. She began to rub herself against him, brain switching to a new word. *NOW.*

It was the force of that word, and the intensity of the feeling behind it, that finally infiltrated the sexual fog steaming up her thoughts like a hot shower. What in the actual fuck was she doing? Mick was her friend. A real friend. And she didn't want to lose that. She wasn't about to screw it up by casually screwing him.

Kat pulled away, breaking the kiss. But as she loosened her legs and scooted back, her butt slid into the sink, tailbone smacking into the metal knob covering the drain. She grunted in pain. That was going to leave a bruise.

To add insult to injury, as she floundered and tried to shimmy her backside out of the sink, her elbow knocked into the faucet. "Ouch!" she yelped as a jolt of pain vibrated through her funny bone and up her arm. "Aah!" she screamed as cold water filled the basin and drenched her entire bottom half.

Well, that was one way to cool off her overheated bits.

"Shit." Mick scrambled to shut off the water. "Are you . . . um . . . okay?" His gaze drifted lower, and Kat could tell he was trying very hard not to laugh.

Trying and failing.

"Go ahead and laugh," she growled, "but help me out of here while you do it. My ass feels like it's sitting in an ice bucket."

As uncomfortable as a cold soggy butt was, Kat decided it was probably for the best. If her plan was going to work, she couldn't fall into old habits. She didn't need this complication. This was how she got herself into trouble. The Kat that relied on physical attraction and sexual intimacy was gone. The new Kat didn't do that.

Mick wrapped an arm around her waist and hauled her out of the sink. As he set her on the ground, cold water from her soaked pants sluiced down her legs, pooling on the tile floor. Kat slipped on the puddle quickly forming at her feet. Mick reached out to steady her and ended up slipping too.

A yelp escaped him as he tumbled backward, feet flying up in a move that would have been hilarious if it wasn't horrifying. He tripped over the lip of her tub, landing in it with a sickening thud.

"Mick?" Kat scrambled toward him, heart pounding in her chest. "Are you okay?"

"*Argghhuhhhh.*" The sound floated up from the tub, a noise somewhere between a wheeze and a groan.

He was alive. Relief washed over Kat, and her heart slowed the tiniest bit, only to kick into overdrive when she saw the blood smeared on his head. More blood trickled down the white porcelain. Kat sat on the edge of the tub and willed herself not to pass out. Mick needed her.

"Kat?" Mick's voice was rough around the edges, and fuzzy, like he was drifting off to sleep.

Sleep. No. That was bad. Kat wasn't a doctor, but she knew that falling asleep after a head injury was not good. "I'm here." She gave his shoulder a careful squeeze and contemplated what to do next.

His sooty lashes lifted slowly, dark gaze dreamy as he looked up at her. A silly grin slid across his face. "That was some kiss."

CHAPTER 19

Mick

Mick's eyelids fluttered. Twitched, really. He attempted to open his eyes, but they were too heavy. His lashes felt like they'd been caked in cement. Darkness crept around the edges of his consciousness. He was about to slip back into the welcoming oblivion when someone squeezed the fingers of his right hand.

He frowned. Or at least he thought he was frowning. It was hard to tell what exactly his face was doing.

The finger squeeze came again. More insistent this time. *All right, all right. Give me a minute.* He concentrated on the sensations coming from outside his body. There was noise, a series of *wha-wha-wha* sounds that reminded him of what passed for talking by adults in a Charlie Brown cartoon.

Maybe he was in the cartoon right now. He felt like he could be. Flat. Two-dimensional. Or maybe he'd died and this was his purgatory. He hoped Mary-Kate and Joe did a good job on his funeral. Uncle Mike could run the bar again, and he'd serve the good whiskey. The thought of whiskey reminded Mick of something . . . someone.

The finger squeezer was at it again, and this time Mick managed to pry his eyelids open long enough to catch a glimpse of gray. Gray walls. Gray curtain. Gray chair. A woman sat in the chair. Kat. She was the finger squeezer.

He tried to speak to her, to call her name and let her know he was awake, but his lips wouldn't move. It was like his mouth had laggy Wi-Fi. At least his ears seemed to be online now, and the muffled sounds from before grew more distinctive.

Kat was talking. To herself, or him, or someone else entirely, Mick couldn't tell. She was rambling, a string of barely coherent words tumbling from her mouth one after another. Mick concentrated, waiting for the sounds to turn into words. It was like turning the dial on a radio, trying to nail the frequency.

"Hey," he croaked. *What the hell?* Why did his voice sound like that? Like he had a two-pack a day habit and had spent all day screaming his lungs out a Bears game. He sucked in a breath and tried again. "Kat?"

"You're awake! Oh thank god." She released her death grip on his fingers.

Suddenly Mick could feel his face because Kat was touching it. Her hands patting his cheeks with nervous energy.

"What happened?" His voice was starting to sound better. Maybe if he kept talking he'd clear out all the cobwebs that seemed to be caught in his throat.

"You fell." She brushed his hair off his forehead.

Mick hoped she would do that again. It felt nice. "I fell?"

"Well, actually, I fell first. Into the sink. And then you helped me out of the sink but there was water all over the floor and I slipped and grabbed on to you for balance and you slipped and to make a long story short—too late, I know—you cracked your skull on my bathtub."

"I did?" He blinked. *Okay, ow.* Blinking hurt. How could blinking hurt?

"You didn't literally crack your skull. I mean, not like Humpty Dumpty or anything. But you did hit your head pretty hard. There was a lot of blood. Luckily this all happened in my bathroom so it should be really easy to clean. What the hell am I saying, I don't care how easy it is to clean. I'm just glad you're awake and alive and not suffering from amnesia or something." She paused her diatribe to peer down at him suspiciously. "You don't have amnesia, do you?"

"I called you Kat, didn't I?"

"True." Her eyes narrowed. "But maybe you retained your short-term memory and lost your long-term."

"That's not how brain injuries usually work," he said. "Last in, first out."

"Is that so." Her lips pursed, and then her eyes brightened, as if an idea had just occurred to her. "What's the last thing you remember?"

Kissing you.

He remembered their kiss clearly. In crisp, achingly sharp detail. Maybe it was the result of possibly suffering from a traumatic brain injury, but Mick was on the verge of telling her everything. Of letting it all spill out of him. Not only that he was attracted to Kat, but how very much he liked her.

"What's wrong?" She asked. "What are you thinking about?"

Mick blinked. Yep. Still hurt. He took a slow, painful glance around the room. "Where are we, anyway?"

"I took you to the closest trauma center. There was so much snow, I was worried an ambulance would take forever. So I drove you myself."

"How did you get me out of your apartment?"

"You *were* pretty out of it. You sort of walked, sort of leaned on me." Kat tugged at her shirt, showing him a streak of blood where his head must have rested on her shoulder. "Don't tell Allen, but I used the elevator. And then I . . ." She paused, mouth twitching.

"Then you what?" Mick tried to imagine what about this situation she found amusing. It did not bode well for him.

"I borrowed a sled from some kids playing in the alley, stuffed you in it, and towed you to the delivery van. After that, I kind of jimmied the sled up into the van."

"Let me get this straight," Mick said, words coming slowly as his thoughts processed. "You dragged my bloody, unconscious body around in a sled?"

Kat nodded. "Semi-unconscious." She pursed her lips and

maintained a serious tone. "And it was one of those, long hot-dog sleds, not the saucers."

Now Mick's lips were twitching. Picturing it, he had to admit, it was pretty funny. "That was very resourceful of you," he said. "Thank you."

"It was the least I could do. I mean, what other option was there, let you bleed out in my tub? Then get a fake passport and move to Iceland?"

"Why Iceland?"

"I dunno." Kat shrugged. "It was the first place that popped in my head." She glanced around the room, lowering her voice. "When I brought you in to the ER, I was sure I was going to have to make up some story so I could come to triage with you. Like I was your sister or fiancé or something."

"So, which are you? My sister or fiancé?"

"Neither. They didn't care." Kat sat back, crossing her arms. "I guess that sort of thing only happens in the movies."

"Huh. Guess so." Mick rubbed the bridge of his nose.

"Do you have a headache?" she asked. Then she snorted. "What a dumb question. Of course you have a headache. Do you want me to have the nurse shoot you up with more pain meds?"

"As pleasant as that sounds, no. Thank you." Mick hesitated a moment. "But maybe you could rub my forehead again?"

"Oh," Kat stammered. She dropped her gaze, apparently suddenly fascinated with the hospital's floor. "I didn't realize you knew I was doing that."

"It really helped with the pain," Mick admitted. "Please?" he begged, hating himself a tiny bit for taking advantage of the situation. But he wasn't lying. Her touch made him feel better.

"Um. Okay." She shifted on the chair, scooting closer. A moment later, she brushed her hand across his brow, fingertips feather light.

He sighed and closed his eyes.

"I should probably tell you, I dug around in your wallet for your insurance card, so that's taken care of," Kat said as she continued to stroke his forehead. "And I called your family too. Let them know what happened, and where to find you."

Mick's mood soured. He could only imagine what Joe must have thought when he hadn't come back to help wrap up the event last night. And when Mick didn't show in the office this morning for their meeting to go over numbers . . .

At the moment, Mick was glad he might have a concussion. At least it gave him a good excuse. Much better than, *Sorry I missed our meeting, big bro. I was too busy shoving my tongue down our new business partner's throat.*

Which brought Mick back to the reason he was here. In an ER bed.

Their kiss.

Were they going to talk about what happened? Mick wanted to. He ached to tell Kat how it felt to kiss her. How he knew she felt it too. But confessing his feelings while suffering from head trauma and doped up on painkillers was probably not the wisest move. She'd made him promise that their kiss wouldn't ruin their friendship. And Mick intended to keep that promise. Even if it meant keeping the memory of their kiss locked away.

Besides, what if he spilled his guts right now—laid everything on the line—and she still rejected him? Mick wanted to think he was man enough to take it, but he wasn't sure. Especially if she ended up choosing Joe instead.

But if he kept his feelings to himself. If he pretended the kiss never happened. Then he and Kat could go on as they had been. As friends. Being her friend was important to him. Important enough that he was willing to set aside anything else he may have hoped for.

A knock at the glass partition dividing the triage rooms interrupted his thoughts.

Kat pulled her hand away and sat back in her chair.

Mick eyed the sliding door with trepidation. His concern was warranted, because a moment later, the O'Sullivan clan burst in, surrounding his bed, all of them talking in a rush, Mary-Kate and Joe and even Gran. The only one missing was Seamus, and Mick half expected to see Gran pull the bird out of the enormous handbag she was carrying.

The collective volume of their chatter was overwhelming. Mick winced. He appreciated that his family cared about his well-being and had rushed here to check on him. And in the snow, no less. But right now, he wished they'd all—to quote his Granda—bugger off.

Kat stood and greeted his family, offering Gran the one chair in the tiny room, and Mick's insides went as gooey as sticky pudding.

"What in the saints happened to you?" Gran asked as she settled into the seat Kat had vacated.

"Yeah, Mickey," Joe chimed in. "When you didn't come home last night, we were worried."

Mick snorted, immediately regretting it when a burst of pain bloomed between his eyes. It was hard to be snarky when your head felt like a bruised melon.

"It's my fault," Kat said. "I, um . . . wasn't feeling well last night and Mick offered to give me a ride home, and then it started snowing and he decided to stay the night—in my papasan chair—" she added, glancing at Gran.

"Is that how you got the head wound?" Mary-Kate guessed. "You fell out of the papasan? Those things are death traps."

"Tell me about it," Mick said, lips quirking. His sister understood. And she'd conveniently provided a solution to the problem of how he was going to explain what happened. And he didn't even have to lie. Assuming Kat played along, that is. He glanced in her direction.

She licked her lips. A habit Mick was beginning to realize was a tell that meant she was hiding something. "Yep. A freak accident," she said with an awkward, forced smile. "The doctor has been by twice. They gave Mick some pain meds and stitched the wound—he has a small gash on his head—and a mild concussion. Beyond that, they don't think it's anything too serious, but want to run a few more tests to make sure before they release him."

All of this was news to Mick. He ran a hand along his scalp. Sure enough, there was a bandage on the back of his head below his left ear. "Did they shave my hair?" he asked.

"Only a little," she assured him, her smile more relaxed this time. "Don't worry. Undercuts are very in right now."

"I can't believe I was zonked out during all of that."

"You must have clocked yourself pretty good," Mary-Kate teased. "You better spend the night at Gran's so we can watch over you. Even if it's only a mild concussion, you're going to need to take it easy the next few days."

"But the plans for the bar—" Mick began.

"Don't worry about that right now," Joe said, cutting in. "We'll talk more when you're feeling better."

Mick scowled. His brother was probably all too happy to put the proposal on hold.

"I took some notes last night that I think will improve the bottom line," Kat chimed in. "I'd be happy to set up a meeting and share my thoughts."

"We can grab a coffee now and talk if you like," Joe suggested. "Gran and Mary-Kate can keep Mick company."

Mick's scowl turned even darker. How fucking convenient. He wasn't thrilled by this turn of events, but what was he supposed to do? It's not like he could get up and go with them, bare ass flapping out the back of the hospital gown he was wearing. He glanced down, wondering how he'd gotten this stupid thing on in the first place. Had Kat been the one to undress him? It was an intriguing possibility.

Get over yourself, you idiot. Mick shook his head. If Kat had helped him, it was because he'd been unconscious and bleeding.

It's not like she would be checking out the goods. Mick sighed and dropped his head back on the pillows. Distracted by his thoughts, it took him a moment to realize Kat was gathering up her things and saying goodbye.

"You're not going with Joe for coffee?"

"Not today." She shook her head. "Monday is my day to see my grandmother. We usually go out for lunch, and I'm already late. Now that your family is here to take care of you, I don't feel bad about ditching." Her blue eyes shadowed with guilt as she stared down at him. "Not too bad, anyway."

"Do you hear that?" Gran asked. "She visits her grandmother every Monday."

"Aw Gran, I see you every day," Mary-Kate protested.

"Yes. But when's the last time you took me to lunch?"

Gaze still fixed on him, Kat mouthed the word "sorry."

Mick's lips quirked. He wasn't sure if Kat was aware of this, but she'd scored major brownie points with his grandmother.

She crossed to the bed, brushing her hand over his forehead one last time. "I'll call to check on you later, okay?"

The smile she gave him was sweet, but with a bit more pity than Mick was comfortable with. He nodded gingerly. "Thanks."

"Let me walk you out," Joe said, accompanying Kat to the door.

Smooth motherfucker. Mick gritted his teeth. Gentleman Joe strikes again.

Gran nodded approvingly after Kat. "I like that one." She gave his knee a squeeze through the thin hospital blanket. "She's good for you."

"We're friends, Gran. That's all."

"Your grandfather and I started out as friends too, you know."

"Yes, Gran, we know," Mary-Kate replied for both of them, rolling her eyes at Mick in sibling solidarity.

It was true. They'd heard the story of how Gran and Granda met countless times.

"Besides," Mary-Kate added, "Kat's interested in Joe."

Mick glared at his sister. So much for sibling solidarity.

"Our Joseph?" Gran asked.

"Who else?" he grumbled.

Gran's eyes pinned him with a shrewd look. "What do you think of that?"

"It doesn't matter what I think." Mick squirmed on the narrow bed. He didn't know why he didn't realize how uncomfortable it was until now. "Mary-Kate is right. Kat is interested in Joe. She said so herself."

"Hmm." Gran made a noncommittal noise in the back of her throat. One of those truly Gaelic sounds that implied everything while saying nothing.

And Mick knew he hadn't heard the last of this conversation.

CHAPTER 20

Kat

Kat made her way up to Babcia's apartment, juggling take-out bags from her grandmother's favorite Chinese restaurant. She'd texted Babcia from the hospital, simply saying she'd been delayed and rather than going out to lunch, Kat would bring dinner over. Then she'd followed up with Ronnie and asked if they were cool to keep JoJo a little longer. Ronnie had sent back an enthusiastic reply, offering to do another sleepover, complete with pleading praying-hands emojis.

Who was Kat to steal Ronnie's joy? She was glad they were having fun and hoped JoJo didn't mind all the excitement. As if reading her mind, Ronnie sent a photo of the hedgehog blissfully cuddling a banana. Kat melted at the cuteness and then immediately texted back like the pet mom she'd become, warning Ronnie not to go overboard on the treats.

"Kasia! You made it." Babcia kissed Kat's cheeks. "I've been worried."

"Sorry I'm late." Kat set the take-out bags down on the dining room table.

Babcia shook out Kat's coat before hanging it in the hall closet. "Was it the snow?"

Kat considered blaming the weather for her delay. In a very roundabout way, it was sort of the truth. She hadn't said anything earlier about Mick or the hospital because she didn't have the energy to try explaining over the phone.

But messy and complicated as her current situation might be, Kat had never kept anything from her grandmother, and she wasn't about to start now. "Um, no." She rinsed her hands in the kitchen sink and grabbed some plates and silverware.

Babcia gasped.

"What?" Kat glanced up in surprise.

"You're bleeding!" Her grandmother pointed at Kat's shoulder.

"Oh no. That's not my blood." And this was why it was a good thing she didn't lie to her grandmother. "It's from my friend."

"Is she all right?' Babcia sank into one of the dining room chairs. "What happened?"

"*He* is fine. Mostly. He fell and hit his head in my bathtub." Kat started pulling containers from the take-out bags.

"Kotku," Babcia's tone was careful, "who is this *he* and why was he in your bathtub?"

"Should we have some wine?" Kat asked. "Let's have some wine." She probably should go easy on the booze after last night, but one glass of Babcia's pinot grigio wouldn't hurt. Handing her grandmother a glass, Kat filled one for herself and took a spot across the table.

"Do you want an egg roll or some dumplings?" Kat asked, sorting through the containers. "I think I'm going to have both."

"I want you to tell me what's going on," Babcia retorted saucily. "And I want some dumplings."

"Nothing is going on," Kat insisted, scooping food onto Babcia's plate. "And he wasn't *in* my bathtub, he was in the bathroom and slipped and knocked his head on the tub. He gashed his head open. It wasn't too bad, but it bled a lot." She pointed to her shirt. "I took him to the hospital, and they stitched him up."

"And he is still there now? At the hospital?"

"I'm not sure." Kat bit into a dumpling. "Maybe."

"Kasia." Her grandmother clicked her tongue. "How is that any way to treat your friend? Leaving him at the hospital all alone and bleeding."

"Okay, Babcia, first of all, he isn't bleeding anymore. I told you, they stitched him up. And second, he's not alone. His family is there. I called them and waited for them to come." Kat pursed her lips. "Give me a little more credit, huh?"

"It might be nice if I knew this poor young man's name," Babcia muttered, picking through her cashew chicken. It was a whole thing with her grandma. She ordered the cashew chicken because she said she liked the flavor the cashews gave the dish. But then she picked all the cashews out and never ate them.

"Mick."

Babcia frowned. "Mick. What kind of name is that?"

"Mick O'Sullivan."

"Ah. Irish." Babcia nodded as if that explained a variety of things.

Kat chose to ignore that and turned her attention to the mountain of fried rice she'd scooped onto her plate.

"Is there anything else you'd like to tell me about this Mick fellow?" Babcia asked.

I kissed him.

Kat didn't say that, though. She wasn't going to lie to her grandmother, she simply wasn't going to provide any details. Details like: *I kissed him, and it was so incredibly hot that even though I said I'm not looking for a relationship based on physical attraction and in fact have a plan to pursue a serious relationship with his older brother it's really hard to stop thinking about him and his mouth and that kiss.* Nope, not sharing any of that.

"His family owns a funeral home. I'm helping him put together a business proposal for a new concept he wants to implement."

"It's nice to see you use that fancy degree of yours," Babcia noted.

Kat's smile was tight. Her grandmother meant well. Her comments came from a place of love, but sometimes Babcia's lack of a filter could be a lot to handle. Still, Kat would take her grandmother's occasionally judgy observations over her parents' indifference any day. At least she knew Babcia cared.

After dinner, Kat wrapped up the leftovers and loaded them into her grandmother's fridge. Then she hurried through her other usual chores. She was finishing up putting fresh sheets on Babcia's bed when her phone buzzed. It was Mary-Kate, letting Kat know that Mick was home and resting on their grandmother's couch.

Kat returned to the dining room to find her grandmother had brewed them some tea.

"You forgot to read your fortune," Babcia said, handing Kat a fortune cookie.

"Thanks." Kat broke the cookie open and read the slip of paper hidden inside.

"Well?" Babcia prompted, the picture of innocence. "What's it say?"

Though she had no way of proving it, Kat swore her grandmother had somehow messed with the fortunes. She reread the one that had been curled inside her cookie. "'Love comes to those who seek it.'"

"Is that so?" Babcia said, blue eyes wide. "How interesting."

Yep. Kat sipped her tea. Her grandmother was totally trolling her. Wouldn't things be so much easier if that fortune were true, though? All her life Kat felt like she'd been seeking love. Searching for it in books and movies, from romance novels to romantic comedies. Not to mention all her failed relationships. The guys she'd dated, telling herself over and over again that this time it would work. This time, she'd found the one. In the end, Kat was left wondering if "the one" even existed. Maybe it did for some people, but not for her.

"What about you?" Kat asked, crunching on a piece of cookie. "What's your fortune say?"

Babcia waved her tiny paper in the air. "'What's for you will not pass you by.'"

Kat snorted.

"My fortune amuses you, Kotku?"

"It's kind of the opposite of mine, don't you think?"

"How so?"

Kat pointed a finger at her paper. "In mine, the message is that in order for love to find you, you need to go out and look for it." She slid her finger across the table to Babcia's fortune. "In yours, the message is wait long enough, and whatever you're meant to have will eventually show up." She drummed her fingers on the table. "So, which is it?"

"Maybe it's both," Babcia suggested. "But love isn't going to find you here, in your grandmother's apartment, no matter how long you wait."

"Are you kicking me out?"

"I'm suggesting you go check on that sad boy with the head wound."

Kat bit her lip. Babcia's description of Mick made him sound like an extra in a dystopian movie. "I did get a message that he was released from the hospital . . ."

"See?" Babcia rose from the table and ambled into the kitchen. "Go to him. Make sure he's comfortable." She returned with a plastic container. "And bring him some cookies."

Her grandmother set the container down. Kat stared at it. Babcia used this particular kind of container for only one particular kind of cookie. "Are these . . . ?" She opened the lid. Yep. "You started baking kolackies already?"

"A few batches," Babcia said, swatting Kat's hand when she reached inside the container for a cookie. "Save those for your young man."

"He's not my young man," Kat grumbled. If Babcia thought Kat had the willpower not to cram a few of those cookies in her mouth before she got to Mick's, then she didn't know her own granddaughter. Kolackies were one of Kat's most favorite things in the entire world. And her grandmother only made them around the winter holidays. Kat waited all year for them. "You're going to show me how to make these soon, right?"

"Next week. Before Thanksgiving. I promise, Kasia." Babcia patted Kat's hand. "Now go take care of your boyfriend."

"He's not my boyfriend, Babcia."

"We'll see." Babcia shrugged.

The woman was incorrigible. Kat rolled her eyes and kissed her cheeky grandmother's cheek.

......

On the drive over to O'Sullivan's, Kat exercised amazing restraint and only ate two—okay, three—cookies. Mick had mentioned that his grandmother lived above the funeral parlor, but Kat wasn't sure of the logistics, so she texted his sister from the parking lot.

"How's he doing?" Kat asked Mary-Kate when she met her at the entrance.

"Fine. All the tests came back clear but he needs to take it easy for a few days." Mary-Kate led the way upstairs. "Of course, he's milking the situation for all it's worth. He's already got us waiting on him hand and foot. Gran is sitting with him now, and Joe went out to pick up a prescription."

They reached the second floor, and Kat was surprised to discover that it looked like any floor in dozens of similar turn-of-the-century apartment buildings in the city. She wasn't sure what she'd been expecting. Something with an *Addams Family* vibe, maybe. Which she realized was ridiculous. "You all grew up here?" she asked.

Mary-Kate nodded. "My family owns the building."

"Mick mentioned that."

"He lives across the street now." Mary-Kate waved in the general direction, as if Kat could see through the wall.

"Yeah, he mentioned that too."

"Both my brothers moved out, so it's only me and Gran."

"And your parents?"

"They kind of live all over."

"Oh." Kat frowned. Maybe that meant they were like her

parents, then. Forever off doing their own thing. Totally self-absorbed and completely disconnected from the lives of their children.

"They'll be home soon, though." Mary-Kate opened the door to the apartment and gestured for Kat to go ahead of her. "They always come back for Thanksgiving and stay through New Year's."

"That's nice," Kat said. And nothing like her parents after all. Kat couldn't remember the last time she'd spent a holiday with them. In high school, maybe.

"I'm going to make some tea. Would you like some?"

"I'd love a cup, thanks." Kat offered Mary-Kate the container. "Here. Some kolackies. From my grandmother."

"I don't think I've ever had one before."

"They go perfect with tea." Was that a hint Mary-Kate should serve them? Yes. Yes, it was. Kat was shameless when it came to kolackies.

"Sounds good to me. I'll be out in a sec." Mary-Kate pointed. "The patient is down the hall."

Kat followed the sound of familiar squawking. Sure enough, Seamus was perched on the top of the sofa, watching over a sleeping Mick like a guard dog. Kat waved at the bird, not wanting to wake Mick.

"Hello, gorgeous!" Seamus cawed.

"Shhh!" Kat placed a finger to her lips and whispered, "Hello, Seamus."

"I thought I was your only girl, you feathered Casanova."

Startled, Kat turned to see Mick's grandmother ensconced in an easy chair across from the couch. "Hi, Mrs. O'Sullivan. Nice to see you again."

"Call me Ava, or better yet, Gran."

"Um, okay . . . Gran." Kat smiled tentatively, surprised how comfortable that felt.

Gran gestured at the other easy chair. "Have a seat."

"Thanks." Kat settled in. She glanced over at Mick, buried under a mountain of colorful crocheted blankets that would give Laura yarn envy. "Mary-Kate said all the tests came back clear?"

"All clear," Gran confirmed. "Doctor's orders were to get some rest." She nodded wryly toward the sleeping form on the couch. "As you can see, that's not going to be a problem."

Kat grinned as the last thread of worry that had still been wrapped around her heart unraveled. "The important thing is he's okay."

"Believe me, he's fine." Mary-Kate appeared in the doorway carrying a tray stacked with a teapot, cups, and a plate of cookies. "It's going to take more than a knock on the noggin to damage that thick skull." She set the tray on a table.

"My goodness, how lovely," Gran said, surveying the tray. "Are those kolackies?"

"Mm-hmm." Mary-Kate nodded. "Kat brought them."

"Oh, I haven't had a kolacky in ages." Gran took one, a look of ecstasy crossing her face as she bit into the cookie.

Kat knew the feeling well. "My grandma made them."

"I've always wanted to learn how to make these," Gran confessed, taking another from the tray.

"Me too." Clearly, this was a woman after her own heart. "Babcia—that's my grandma—is going to be teaching me next week. You should come."

"Oh no. I couldn't intrude on family time."

"You wouldn't be intruding," Kat said. "And I think my grandma would really like you."

"You should go, Gran." Mary-Kate snagged a cookie from the plate. "Then you can come home and make these for me."

Kat laughed.

"What's so funny?" Mick mumbled from the couch.

"Oh god. Mick. Sorry." Kat covered her mouth, embarrassed. "I didn't mean to wake you."

"I'm not awake," he said groggily, eyes still closed.

"Um . . . okay." Kat turned to Gran, eyebrows raised in concern.

"He's fine," Gran assured her. "Go back to sleep, Michael."

"Go to sleep, Michael," Seamus echoed.

Kat giggled. "He's a bossy thing, isn't he?"

"Always has been." Gran nodded. "Same as my husband."

"You all must miss him very much." Kat accepted the cup Mary-Kate handed her.

"Every day." Gran sighed. "He was my rock."

"How did the two of you meet?"

Mary-Kate settled back with her own cup of tea. "Granda handled the funeral arrangements for Gran's parents."

"They both passed at the same time," Gran explained.

"Oh my goodness." Kat hadn't expected this to take such a dark turn. "May I ask what happened?"

The old woman said simply, "Train accident."

"I'm so sorry," Kat said, heart lurching at the tragedy those two words conjured.

"Thank you, but it was a very long time ago." Gran sipped her tea. "I was so young and suddenly alone in the world."

"I can't imagine . . ." Kat broke off, at a loss for words.

Gran shook her head, mouth curving gently. "I realize such tragic circumstances might not seem like the origins for a romance, but love blooms in the strangest of places."

"That's a beautiful sentiment." Kat matched the older woman's smile. "And I'm not saying that because I'm a florist."

"Kat's also been helping Mick and me with our business proposal," Mary-Kate chimed in. "And she even convinced Joe to sign a partnership deal for flowers."

"Is that so?" Gran gazed at Kat, shrewd green eyes twinkling. "I have a feeling we'll be seeing a lot more of you around here, then."

"I hope so," Kat agreed, gaze drifting to Mick's sleeping form, as his chest rose and fell beneath the blanket in a slow, easy rhythm.

﹒﹒﹒﹒﹒﹒

It was late by the time Kat made it back home. She slowly climbed the stairs to her apartment. It had been a very long, strange day. She yawned, grateful Ronnie had agreed to the extended slumber party. At least she'd be able to indulge in one more night of sleep undisturbed by a certain spiked critter and her beloved squeaky wheel.

Still, she missed her little companion. Three days. She hoped JoJo hadn't forgotten all about her. Kat was looking forward to seeing her tomorrow. Even if it meant losing sleep. Parenting. It was all about sacrifice, right? Kat glanced fondly at the pink palace in the corner. And it was then she noticed the piece of notebook paper taped to the side. "What the . . ."

Ronnie had a key, maybe they'd stopped by to stock up on hedgehog provisions. Kat tugged the note free. Her name had been scrawled across the front, but the handwriting wasn't Ronnie's. Curious, she flipped the note open and read.

Princess.
I took care of the pea.
Hope you sleep better tonight.
               —M

Kat frowned. The note had obviously been left by Mick. But when did he write this, and what was he talking about? What pea? She thought back to their conversation last night. On a hunch, she reached into the cage and gave the wheel a spin. To her surprise, it was completely silent.

Kat spun it again, listening carefully. Nothing but the slightest rush of air. He'd fixed it. That sneaky devil. A warm glow spread through her. She shook her head, smiling to herself. At some point in the night, while she—according to certain sources—was sawing logs on the couch, Mick had taken the time to do this. For her.

Kat clutched the note to her chest. His thoughtfulness didn't surprise her, but it did take her unaware. Her feelings were already a jumbled mess, and this sweet, endearing bit of kindness wasn't helping make deciphering her feelings any easier. She decided to tackle something she could control and spent the next hour or so cleaning up the crime scene in her bathroom. Once the tub was freshly scrubbed and blood-free, Kat took a long shower and crawled into bed, still smiling. And that night, the princess did indeed sleep better, her dreams filled with a certain dark-haired, scruffy prince in mismatched socks and wrinkled armor.

CHAPTER 21

Kat

The following Monday Kat woke with the kind of excitement usually reserved for a birthday. *Today is kolacky day!* She hit the grocery store, a list of ingredients from Babcia saved on her phone. As she filled her basket with butter, cream cheese, and flour, she debated whether Mick's grandmother was going to take her invitation seriously and join them. Kat had followed up this morning, sharing the address for Babcia's apartment and asking her to say hello to Mick and Seamus.

Her gut twisted at the thought of Mick. Ever since "the incident" (as she'd started mentally referring to their kiss and his consequent concussion), Kat had been finding ways to avoid spending too much time with him. She hadn't ghosted him. She checked in every day to see how his head was doing. But Kat couldn't deny she was almost grateful for the space his injury allowed her to keep while he recovered.

She was a terrible person. Maybe not terrible, but cowardly, for sure. On the upside, Kat's guilt had driven her to double down on work, and she'd teamed up with Mary-Kate, launching a campaign to bombard Joe with texts and emails until he'd finally caved and agreed to sign off on the proposal. Which meant, once Mick was feeling up to it, he could move forward with his plans for the new reception hall.

Overall, Kat was pleased with the progress she'd made. Now, if she could decide what she wanted to do about Allen's offer and get the same forward momentum going with the shop, then she'd be able to end the year in a very good place. Professionally speaking, anyway. Her personal life had never been more of a mess.

But today was not a day to worry about any of that. Today was a day for cookies. And the only mess Kat intended to think about was the one she was now making in her grandmother's kitchen. Kat wiped her hands on her apron, taking a minute to stretch her arms over her head. She knew kolacky baking was an all-day affair, but she hadn't realized what a workout she was going to be getting.

As she started to roll out another ball of chilled dough, the buzzer for Babcia's apartment rang. "I'll get it." Kat scooted around the table to the intercom.

"We're here," Grandma O'Sullivan announced.

We? Kat buzzed them in, wondering if Mary-Kate had tagged along. She hoped so. Kat liked Mick's sister and knew she often drove their grandmother places. But when she opened the door, Kat was surprised to see the O'Sullivan matriarch accompanied by—"Mick!" She froze. "Um, hi!"

"You're not planning to give me another concussion, are you?" he asked.

"What?"

He pointed at the rolling pin still gripped in her hand.

"Oh no." Kat grinned sheepishly and lowered her arm. "Sorry." She stepped back, opening the door wider and inviting them in. *Shit. Shit. Shit. Shit.* What was Mick doing here? *Cool. Be cool.*

"Kasia?" Her grandmother appeared from the kitchen. "Are you going to introduce me to our guests?"

"Yes." Kat plastered a smile on her face. "Um, Babcia, this is my friend Mick, and his grandmother, Ava O'Sullivan."

"Welcome, welcome," Babcia said. She exchanged kisses on the cheek with Mick's grandmother.

"It's wonderful to finally meet you," Mick said. He wrapped

his arms around her, squeezing her in one of his signature hugs. "Kat talks about you all the time."

"Aren't you lovely," Babcia said, patting Mick's shoulder. Then she stepped back and gave Mick the once-over. "But your haircut is terrible."

"Babcia!" Kat gasped.

Mick's laugh was easy and unoffended. "She's right, it is." He leaned toward Babcia and said, "Who knew ER doctors made such terrible barbers."

"You're the one who conked his head?"

"That's me," Mick said, grinning again.

As her grandmother turned to lead her guests into the kitchen, she paused next to Kat, one finely penciled brow arching. "This is who was in your bathtub?"

Kat made a noncommittal sound and busied herself with locating aprons for the newcomers. Soon, everyone was settled into an assembly line of sorts. Mick took over rolling the dough, Kat cut the dough and placed the individual squares on cookie sheets. Gran was on filling duty, adding a dab of preserves to each square, and Babcia saw to the delicate task of pinching the dough closed. With four people, the process went much faster. Before long, Babcia's kitchen was overflowing with trays of cooling kolackies.

"It smells amazing in here," Mick said, unwrapping a fresh ball of chilled dough.

"My favorite smell ever," Kat agreed, trying not to stare at the curve of muscle flexing in Mick's forearms as he rolled the dough flat. He looked good. A smile tugged at her lips. Even in one of Babcia's frilly aprons. Apart from the impromptu trim he'd gotten courtesy of the ER, he didn't seem the worse for wear. If anything, he seemed better than before. More relaxed. She supposed a week of required rest could do that for a person. "What about you? Do you have a favorite smell?"

"I don't think I've ever thought about it." Mick shrugged. "Pizza, maybe?"

Kat laughed. "Spoken like a true Chicagoan." She'd been nervous when he'd first arrived, worried that things would be awkward. Between the kiss, the injury, and the fact she'd not really talked to Mick about anything but sports, weather, and the bump on his head for the last several days, Kat had plenty of reasons to feel nervous, but none of that seemed to get in the way. Mick had settled right in, and Kat appreciated his company.

The only thing she worried about now was one of them saying or doing something foolish. Something that would set off Babcia's radar and confirm her suspicions that Mick might be more than a friend. She'd told her he wasn't. But that wouldn't stop her grandmother from jumping to conclusions.

She glanced over at the kitchen table where Babcia and Mick's gran were working in tandem, chattering away as they filled and folded. "What do you think they're talking about?"

Mick followed the direction of her gaze. "Us, obviously." He leaned closer, speaking low in Kat's ear, "They're probably picking out names for our kids."

"Ugh, I bet you're right." Kat shook her head. "I think I've made a grave error in judgment by inviting your gran here."

Mick snickered.

"I'm serious! The two of them are bound to be diabolical together. Watch them start their own matchmaking service."

"Or solve global warming,"

She smirked. "I'll alert Allen."

Mick set the rolling pin down and leaned back against the counter. "How's that going, by the way?"

"How's what going?" she asked, trying to focus on the squares she was cutting and not on how the weight of his gaze warmed her from the inside out.

"The acquisition. Allen's offer to sell you the shop."

She glanced up, surprised. "You remember that?"

"It's a pretty big deal for you, Kat. Why wouldn't I remember?" His dark brows drew together. "I had a concussion, not amnesia."

"I know that." Kat bit her lip, wondering how to tell Mick that she didn't expect him to remember something simply because it was important to her. Over and over again, she assumed he'd behave a certain way, and over and over again, he proved her wrong.

"Katarzyna," Babcia called, interrupting her thoughts.

Kat blinked, turning to see both her grandmother and Mick's waiting for the next tray.

"Sorry," she said handing it over.

"Katarzyna," Mick repeated slowly, as if tasting it on his tongue like the first bite of a cookie. "So that's your full name. I wondered what Kat was short for."

"Well, now you know. *Michael.*"

"Nobody calls me that."

"Your grandma does."

"You're not my grandma and I stopped going by Michael the first day of first grade."

Kat blinked. "What happened the first day of first grade?"

"Attendance," he said simply.

She cocked her head, waiting for him to elaborate.

"Do you know how many Michaels there are in a Catholic school? Especially a Catholic school in a predominantly Irish neighborhood?"

"I'm guessing about as many Jacobs as there are in a Catholic school in a predominantly Polish neighborhood."

"You went to Catholic school too, huh?"

"All twelve years." Kat pointed a finger at herself. "Eight at St. Mary of the Angels and another four at Holy Trinity."

"You get it, then." Mick chuckled. "There were at least half a dozen Michaels in the O's alone. Michael O'Donnell, Michael O'Rourke, Michael O'Shaughnessy . . . you get the picture." He lifted one shoulder. "I decided I was going to be Mick."

"Why not Mike?"

"Just as bad." He made a face. "Maybe even worse. Everyone goes by Mike. You've met my great-uncle Mike already. There's also an uncle Mike. And at least three of my cousins are called Mikey." He crossed his arms. "That very first day of first grade, I decided to claim Mick for my own."

"You 'claimed' it?" she asked. "What did you do, beat all the other little Michaels up?"

Mick chortled.

Kat grinned. She liked making him laugh. "I'm glad you came today."

"So am I." He nicked a kolacky from one of the cooling trays. "Because these are amazing."

Kat was sneaking a cookie for herself when her phone chimed. She glanced at the screen. Ronnie. Popping the cookie into her mouth, she excused herself and headed into the living room to take the call.

"Hey, Ronnie, what's up?"

"I hate to have to tell you over the phone like this, but I knew you'd want to know right away."

The tone in Ronnie's voice turned the cookie Kat had swallowed into lead in her stomach. "Is everything okay at the store? Did something happen to Allen? I know he's planning to spend Thanksgiving in Alaska, but I thought he wasn't leaving until—"

"It's not Allen. It's Mr. S." Ronnie took a breath. "Kat, he's gone."

CHAPTER 22

Mick

"Take off your shoes," Mick instructed quietly, removing his as well. Kat did as he said, slipping off her low-heeled black pumps. Mick took their shoes and added them to the row of others lined up under a bench on the porch of the Schwartz's house.

"You're matching," Kat noted, voice soft.

"Huh?"

She gestured at his feet. "Your socks. They match. I thought you said your socks never match."

"Oh. Sometimes, I'll make an exception." Mick glanced down at the identical black socks. "I probably stole these from Joey."

Her lips twitched with the ghost of a smile. "I think Mr. S would have appreciated the effort." She tightened her grip on the box of cookies and sucked in a shaky breath.

"When you're ready, go on in."

"What?" Kat asked, blue eyes wide in surprise as she turned to look at him over her shoulder. "I can't just walk into someone's house. I've never been here before."

"It's tradition," he explained. "When sitting shiva, visitors don't knock or ring the bell." He reached past her to open the door. "This way we don't interrupt the mourners in their grieving."

Kat tensed next to him.

"There won't be a body here," he hurried to assure her.

"I know," she said, voice strained. "They buried him yesterday."

Mick reached for her hand, cognizant of the fact she was working through her trauma. Since starting the partnership at

O'Sullivan's, she'd been doing a better job controlling her anxiety, but that didn't mean this was easy. The best he could do was be there for her. Lacing his fingers with hers, he guided her through the door.

"Anything else I should know?" she whispered, still tense.

"There will probably be coverings over any mirrors, don't disturb them. Not even in the bathroom. And the family will likely be sitting on the floor. You can sit on the floor too, but it's not required."

"Thanks." She squeezed Mick's hand. "And thanks again for coming with me."

"Of course." Mick had been there a few days ago when Kat first heard the news that one of her favorite customers had died. He'd seen her face crumple in grief. She'd been frantic, wanting to do something, anything. Her first thought had been to rush to the flower shop and put together a large bouquet, but when Mick learned the family was Jewish, he'd gently explained that flowers were not part of their burial customs.

Aghast at her near faux pas, Kat had begged Mick to accompany her today. Which wasn't necessary as he'd been ready to offer.

Mick paused in the hallway and untangled their fingers. "I'll find out where they want the food while you go find Mrs. Schwartz."

Kat nodded. She handed the box over to Mick, then wiped her palms on the sides of her black velvet skirt and went in search of Mr. S's beloved wife.

※※※※※※

"Thanks again for your help today." Kat kicked off her shoes with a heavy sigh. "I would have screwed up in so many embarrassing ways without you."

"It was nothing, really." Mick reached out and squeezed her hand. "It's what friends are for."

"Well, you're a good friend." She squeezed back, gripping

his fingers tight before letting him go. "And you're really good at that."

"At what?"

"Offering comfort." She shrugged, teeth working her lower lip as she stared up at him. "And making me feel comfortable too."

"I'm glad I could be there for you." Mick watched as Kat headed into her living room, her shoulders slumped. "You okay?"

"I think so," she said. "Just tired."

He stood awkwardly for a moment, glancing around the apartment. "Do you want me to get you a drink?"

"No thanks."

"Some hot, wholesome, booze-free tea?"

She smiled wanly and shook her head. "I'm good."

"Are you?"

"Maybe?" Her voice caught on a sudden sob. "Maybe not."

Mick crossed the room and wrapped his arms around her, holding her tight. Only when her body had stopped shivering did he release her.

Letting out a shaky breath, she collapsed into the giant papasan chair. "I'm sorry," she said, blue eyes red-rimmed and wet with tears. "I was fine. I don't know why I'm crying now."

He knelt on the floor beside her and reached for her hand. "It's a perfectly normal reaction," he assured her.

"I keep picturing Mrs. S sitting there, all alone . . ." Kat swiped the back of her hand across her face, wiping away fresh tears.

"Hold on," Mick said, rummaging in his pocket for the pack of tissues he'd packed for just such an emergency. "Mrs. Schwartz isn't alone. She's surrounded by family and friends."

"But when they go home, when the last person leaves, she *will be* alone. All alone in the home she's shared with her husband for over sixty years. And she will have to get into bed alone, knowing she'll never see him again, never hold his hand again . . ." She trailed off, voice thick with tears.

Mick started to pass Kat another tissue, then decided to press the whole pack into her hand.

For some reason, this made her laugh.

"What's so funny?"

"I'm not sure," she admitted, more helpless laughter mixing with her tears. "How did you know I was going to end up a blubbering mess?"

Mick leaned closer, lowering his voice as if divulging a secret. "It may surprise you, but I do have some experience with this kind of thing."

"Of course." She laughed again, and this time there was more humor and less tears. "You probably think I'm silly."

"Absolutely not." He squeezed her hand. "I think you care."

"I do. Mr. S was such a grump, but he loved his wife so much." Her lip trembled, and for a moment Mick thought she was going to start crying again, but she pulled herself together and smiled at him. "He came into the shop a while ago—he's the one who brought the latkes we ate—and told me he was dying. At first, I thought he was pulling my leg, but he insisted on making arrangements to keep having flowers delivered to his wife for as long as she lived."

"That's incredible," Mick said. Attempting to lighten the mood he added, "Watch. Now she's going to live to at least one hundred and ten."

"Fine with me." Kat dabbed at her cheeks. "I already gave away Mr. S's money."

"What?" He blinked.

"Gave it to a research foundation," Kat explained. "I'll be buying the bouquets for Mrs. S myself." Her voice turned steely with determination. "As long as she's alive, I intend to make sure she gets those flowers every Saturday."

"You know something?" Mick asked, throat tight as his heart clenched inside his chest. "*You're* incredible."

She stared at him, blue eyes bright with more unshed tears. "Nobody has ever told me that before."

"Impossible." He snorted, honestly stunned.

"Oh, people have said I *look* incredible," she said, the words thick with bitterness, "but never that I'm incredible."

"Well, you are." Mick took the tissues from her, gently wiping away the remaining tears. "You're smart, especially when it comes to business proposals."

A bark of laughter escaped her. "Okay," she said, settling deeper into the papasan. "Anything else?"

"You're also thoughtful and generous and kind. You are incredible in so many ways that have nothing to do with your appearance . . ." He paused, a sheepish grin tugging at his mouth. "Though I gotta be honest. You're incredibly gorgeous too."

She rolled her eyes but didn't bother trying to deny it.

He liked that about her. Kat didn't play coy or engage in mind games, refusing compliments while fishing for more. She simply accepted her good looks as part of who she was. Mick wished she could so easily accept all the other good things about herself as well. "You did great today."

"I didn't *do* anything," she mumbled, thrusting a leg out and nudging him in the shoulder with her toes.

"Sure, you did." He grabbed her foot, holding on to it. "I saw how you talked about Mr. Schwartz, told them about his weekly visits to the shop. By sharing your memories of him, you gave his family a piece of the person they loved that they didn't have before." He pressed his thumb against her instep, rubbing gently. "That's a priceless gift."

Kat sighed. Her mouth puckered in contemplation. "I never thought about it that way, but I guess you're right."

"Of course I am." He reached for her other foot and began to massage that one too.

"Oooh." She closed her eyes, moaning softly.

"Good?" he asked, thumbs moving in slow, tender circles on her soles.

"Very good," she confirmed, eyes still closed.

Mick smiled. He could see as well as feel her start to relax, the tension leaving her body, arms and legs splayed loosely at her sides. He let his fingers trail up and down her calves, stroking over the smooth line of her tights. Realizing he was starting to enjoy this a little too much, he wrapped his hands around her ankles and gave her one last quick squeeze before letting go.

"Don't stop," she croaked.

"Hmm?"

"Please." Kat opened her eyes. "It feels so good to be touched right now . . ." She paused, mouth working for a moment, as if struggling to find the right words. "So nice to have your hands on me . . ."

"Shhh," he whispered. "It's all right." Mick understood. She needed comfort. And while words offered some solace, nothing soothed the soul quite like human touch. It was a scientific fact. He knew that. Knew he could give her that. "Should I . . . ?" he began, plucking at her tights.

She wriggled, reaching under her skirt to help him peel her stockings off. He tossed them aside and scooted closer. The moment his palms brushed her bare skin, they both gasped.

His pulse picked up and Mick tried to douse the fire flaring to life in his veins. He needed to be chill. This was for Kat, he reminded himself, as he continued to run his hand up and down her legs. He was doing this for her.

"You have nice hands," she murmured, eyes heavy lidded as she watched him touch her, gaze following the path of his fingers. "I like your hands."

He forced himself to relax, not an easy task, as he continued touching her, long slow strokes from knee to ankle. Over and over and over again.

"That feels so good," she sighed softly. With each caress, she seemed to melt a little more, body growing heavy and loose limbed.

Beneath the hem of her skirt, his thumbs stroked the warm flesh of her inner thighs.

"Mick." She shivered and began to squirm beneath his touch.

His hands roamed higher, stroking over the heat at her center.

"*Mick*." His name was a moan deep in her throat. She lifted her hips, asking for more.

He could give her what she was asking for. He wanted to. But only if she wanted it. He nudged her knees even farther apart, settling himself in front of her. Mick lifted his head, meeting her gaze. "Do you want me to . . ." He brushed his hands over her, letting his touch ask the question for him.

Her teeth worked her lower lip. "You don't have to—"

"Do you *want* me to?"

She stared down at him, blue eyes intent on his.

Mick didn't move. On his knees before her, still and patient, he waited. Letting her decide what she wanted. Her needs. Her choice.

The sound of her breaths filled the space between them. Inhale. Exhale. One breath. Then two. On the third breath, she nodded answering him by spreading her legs and urging him to come even closer.

He complied immediately, fingers caressing, exploring. She was so soft. So warm and so fucking soft. Her skin like living silk. He bent his head, wanting to feel that silky softness against his lips, wanting to taste it, to taste her. Hands braced on her thighs, Mick pressed his mouth to her center.

"*Oh*," she whispered.

He flattened his tongue, lapping her up in slow lazy licks. Nipping her with his teeth, he switched up the tempo, flicking the tip of his tongue over her clit in rapid-fire strokes.

Kat made a choking sound, half gasp, half moan. Beneath his

palms her legs twitched as her hips lifted from the cushion, rising to meet his mouth in quick little thrusts, matching the rhythm of his kisses.

Mick sensed the change in her, the tightening of her muscles, and doubled his efforts, pushing her over the edge. She let out a tiny cry of surrender, entire body quivering. He welcomed her release, savoring each tremor of her climax, hot and wet and sticky sweet as it danced across his lips and fingertips. When she finally went limp, he pressed one more kiss to her still trembling flesh.

He hadn't planned to do that. Hadn't intended to take things so far. But when he glanced up and caught Kat watching him, the taste of her fresh on his lips, he knew he wanted to go even further. He *needed* to. Mick shifted, joining her on the chair. Hands braced on either side of her beautiful face, he hovered over her.

Again, she answered him with her body, rising up on her elbows and lifting her head to kiss him. She brushed her mouth over his and he knew she was tasting herself on his lips. Mick groaned, he'd wanted to kiss her again for so long. But he'd never imagined it would be like this.

He shifted his weight, moving closer so he could deepen the kiss. The frame of the chair creaked beneath them, and a moment too late, Mick realized his mistake. The giant papasan saucer tilted, flipping over, and taking them with it.

They both yelped as their bodies tumbled to the floor. He landed first, grunting when his back slammed into the hardwood floor of Kat's apartment. Of course, it had to be hardwood; what did people have against carpet? The random thought was knocked out of him along with all the air in his lungs as Kat landed on top of him. Followed quickly by the entire chair crashing down on top of both of them. Fortunately, the damn thing was so big it landed over their heads rather than cracking their skulls, and the thick cushion softened the blow where the wooden frame smacked into his shins.

"Fucking death trap," Mick muttered. He peered into the muffled darkness under the dome of the chair. "You okay?"

Her body jerked against his, shaking.

"Kat?" He patted his hands down her sides. The shaking increased, her rib cage heaving beneath his fingers. *Shit.* Mick tensed. She was crying again. "Are you hurt?"

A peal of laughter escaped her, her entire body convulsing with giggles.

"Oh." He went limp with relief. "You're laughing." A chuckle rumbled in his chest as the bizarreness of their predicament washed over him. Soon, they were both cracking up.

When the wave of hysterical humor subsided, the psychology major in Mick recognized this for the emotional catharsis it was. A release of all the stress and emotions of the day. In the midst of great sorrow, sometimes the best thing to do was let loose and laugh your fucking ass off.

He threaded his fingers through her hair, gently massaging her scalp. "Better?"

Face pressed to his chest, she bobbed her head, a hiccup escaping her.

His heart squeezed reflexively, almost as if it had hiccupped too. Mick ginned into the shadows of the shallow space under the dome of the upside-down papasan saucer. "It's not so bad under here. I feel like we're in a blanket fort."

"I love my papasan." Kat's voice was a quiet hum in his ear. "It was my first official purchase as a full-fledged adult. One of those things I'd always wanted as a kid but never got." She snuggled against him. "It's my cocoon. My place to curl up and just be."

"Be what?" Mick asked.

"Be whatever I am in the moment." Her whole body seemed to shrug. "Whatever mood. Whatever thoughts or feelings. I can sit with them in this chair."

"Or under it," he suggested, chuckling.

"Except, with this thing propped on top of me, I sorta feel like a turtle," she mumbled.

Another chuckle rumbled through him at the mental picture. "Should we move?"

"No," she said, and he felt more than saw the shake of her head. "I like it here."

"I do too," he admitted.

They stayed like that for some time, curled together in the quiet darkness under their turtle shell. Mick had begun to think Kat had fallen asleep on top of him when she shifted, tilting her head to whisper in his ear.

"Thank you."

"For what?"

"For everything. For going with me today. For listening to me after."

"Happy to do it," he said, meaning every word.

"And . . . ," she continued, her hand finding his. "Thank you for that other . . . thing."

"Very happy to do *that*," Mick assured her. And hell, did he mean it.

"I am curious, though," she said, a teasing note in her voice now. "If this is the kind of grief counseling services O'Sullivan's is going to offer, I have questions."

Reluctant laughter rumbled through his chest. His body was strung tight with lust, but Mick recognized the moment had passed. He still wanted her. Badly. But it felt pretty damn good to know he'd been able to ease her grief. Take some of the pain away and make her feel better. The sensation floating through him was almost as good as sex . . . almost.

Mick stroked her back gently, not in an I-want-to-fuck-your-brains-out way, but simply because he liked the contact. The connection. He liked touching her and he liked talking with her. He liked making her laugh. Whether it was baking cookies with her and her grandmother, accompanying her to a memorial service, or . . . other stuff. He liked being with Kat. Period.

His gut twisted. Things had been so strange lately. They hadn't discussed the kiss since it happened. And now . . . well, now things were more complicated than ever. Mick couldn't deny he felt more than friendship for Kat. That he wanted more. But did Kat? That was the real question.

She'd wanted him in the moment today, but he couldn't count that. Emotions had been running high and he'd been there. Part of him felt guilty, like he'd somehow taken advantage of the situation. Maybe he hadn't then, but to push her for more now, that would be wrong.

Mick pressed a kiss to the top of Kat's head. He'd promised to be her friend and he'd been trying his damn best to keep that promise. He wasn't sure he could go back to the way things were—keep on as they've been keeping on—situation normal. Nothing was normal about this, and it was slowly killing him to pretend that it was.

But for now, he'd try to continue. Allow Kat the space she needed to sit with her feelings. Give her time to figure things out. He'd wait and let her decide what she really wanted.

He only hoped that sooner rather than later, she'd realize what he already knew.

CHAPTER 23

Kat

Late on Thanksgiving afternoon, Kat pulled into O'Sullivan's and was greeted by the view of a giant RV stretched across the funeral parlor's parking lot. She blinked, befuddled for a moment by the incongruous sight. Finally, it clicked, and she realized who the massive retirement home on wheels must belong to. Mary-Kate had mentioned her parents would be taking a break from their cross-country adventures to spend the holidays at home.

Yep. She was about to meet Mom and Dad O'Sullivan.

Well, this adds an exciting extra layer of stress to the situation. Arms loaded with a bottle of Beaujolais, a beribboned flowerpot, and a box of kolackies, Kat got out of the van and made her way across the parking lot. She contemplated chugging the wine. If it had been a screw top, she might have. But since the bottle was corked, she resolved to pull her shit together.

Damn Mick for getting her vagina involved and doing such a phenomenal job of it. And damn her for letting him. Should she have let the man she was determined to keep in the friend zone fingerbang her on the papasan? Probably not. But after the shiva, she'd been so overwhelmed with emotion—a powder keg of pent-up feelings—and Mick had provided the match.

Even now, the memory of what he'd done to her that afternoon caused sparks of residual heat to flicker between her legs. No. Nope. No sparks. She was not going to revert to the old Kat, the one who let her body call the shots. A mind-blowing orgasm, no matter how incredible, wasn't enough to build a future on.

There was more to it than that, and she knew it. Kat was honest enough with herself to admit she'd started to consider the possibility of pursuing more with Mick. But she wasn't sure where he stood. Obviously, there was something happening between them, but that could be hormones or pheromones or whatever-mones.

Her number-one mistake in every failed relationship had been conflating lust with love. Assuming physical intimacy meant emotional connection. She'd been wrong every time.

But things with Mick were different. He was a friend. A real friend. And that made Kat even more wary. If Mick showed a genuine interest in being more than friends—and she didn't mean friends with benefits—then maybe . . .

A familiar voice shouted her name. Kat turned to find the youngest O'Sullivan waving at her as she exited a small building on the other side of the parking lot. "Here, let me carry something for you," Mary-Kate said, hurrying to Kat's side and taking the flowerpot. She eyed the naked bulb sticking up out of the dirt. "What is this?"

"An amaryllis," Kat explained. "I know it doesn't look like much now, but put it by some sun, give it a bit of water, and by Christmas you'll have a glorious surprise."

"Speaking of surprises, are you ready for this?"

"This?" Kat repeated.

"Dinner with the entire clan." Mary-Kate held the door open and followed Kat inside. "Well, not the *entire* clan. Back when Granda was alive, we used to host these huge gatherings. Every aunt, uncle, cousin, second cousin, and people I'm not even sure were family would come here for holiday meals."

"I'm guessing you had to use that big space downstairs," Kat said, wondering if that was where the seed for Mick's idea to host events was first planted.

Mary-Kate led the way to the private living quarters. "You would think so, but no. We all crammed in up here. There'd be folding tables set up in every room and people everywhere." Mary-Kate wrinkled her nose, freckles scrunching. "I remember one year my cousin Kathleen and I ended up eating dinner in my closet."

"It sounds like fun," Kat said, trying to imagine being surrounded by that much family—or even having that much family.

"It was absolute chaos." Mary-Kate laughed. "Everything changed after Granda passed, though," she added, face sobering. "He was like this big magnet, drawing us together. The sun that we all orbited around." She gave a melancholy little shrug. "Without him, everyone started drifting off, doing their own thing."

"I'm sorry," Kat said, thinking of her grandfather, of Mr. Schwartz, of the void created when a loved one is gone. The changes that ripple through your world in their absence.

"Thanks. I was pretty little when he died, but I do miss those wild holiday gatherings. I miss him." They'd reached the landing and sounds of laughter and music could be heard drifting from down the hall. "It might be a smaller party now," Mary-Kate said, lips curving in a smile that swept the sadness from her eyes. "But it's still a party."

A party indeed. Kat had never thought of Thanksgiving as a party kind of holiday. She tried to picture what Thanksgiving was like when she was a kid, but to be honest, she wasn't even sure her family celebrated it most years. She remembered getting time off from school and watching the parade on TV, but there had never been any family gatherings, not even with her immediate family.

There was no magnet, no sun to bring them all together. Her parents were too self-involved to orbit around anything but their work and each other. The closest thing Kat had to what Mary-Kate described was Babcia. Her grandmother had been the one constant in her life, always there.

"Kat?" Mary-Kate asked. "You okay?"

"Huh?" Kat glanced up and realized they were at the door to the apartment. "Sorry, I must have gotten lost in my thoughts."

"Nervous about meeting the fam?"

"A little." Which was true, even if not the reason for her current distraction.

"Don't worry." Mary-Kate reached for the doorknob. "Mom and Dad are going to adore you." She opened the door and shouted into the entryway, "I'm here and I brought company!"

The moment Kat entered, she was bombarded by a flurry of enthusiastic greetings. Even Seamus was there, adding his usual affectionate but foulmouthed salutations to the chaos.

Gran enveloped Kat in a warm hug. "More kolackies?" she asked, eyeing the box in her hands.

Kat nodded. "With Babcia's compliments."

"It's a shame she couldn't join us for dinner," Gran sighed.

"She appreciated the invitation but told me she can't miss Polish Thanksgiving at her church."

Mary-Kate set the flowerpot on a shelf near a window. "What does Polish Thanksgiving have?"

"Plenty of pierogis and polka music." Kat grinned.

"Well, let me welcome you to Irish Thanksgiving, where we have plenty of whiskey," Joe said and lifted his glass with a grin that bordered on goofy.

Kat returned the smile. Was Joe tipsy? She'd never seen the man so . . . relaxed before. Oh boy, tonight was going to be interesting.

"Would you like some?" Mick appeared behind her.

Kat's body went on high alert and her thoughts scattered like a puff of dandelion seeds blowing in the breeze. "Some what?"

"Whiskey." A hint of a smirk flickered across his face as he gestured at the decanter on the table.

"Um, no thank you." Kat blinked and held up the bottle in her hands. "I think I'll stick with wine tonight."

"Suit yourself."

Kat doubted anyone else caught the teasing note in his voice or the challenge in his lifted brow as he slipped the bottle from her grip, but she did. She took off her coat and glanced around the room nervously. "Um, Mary-Kate said your parents are in town?"

"Yep." Mick nodded, hanging her coat on a rack by the door. "Come on, I'll introduce you."

Heart pounding with a fresh burst of nervous energy, Kat followed him toward the kitchen. She wasn't sure what to expect, but the sight that greeted her wasn't it. The music she'd heard in the hall was louder here, coming from a small speaker set on the island. And dancing around the island, doing what looked like the tango, were Mr. and Mrs. O'Sullivan.

If Kat had to describe Mick's parents, she'd say they reminded her of Gomez and Morticia Addams. How's that for irony? When Mick had first told her his sister was a mortician, Kat had pictured someone like Wednesday Addams, or that girl from *Beetlejuice*, but Mary-Kate wasn't anything like either. Their mother, however, was all those characters rolled into one elegantly melodramatic package.

The song ended and Mr. O'Sullivan swept his wife into a dramatic pose, bending her backward over his arm and kissing her neck. And . . . was he growling?

Mick set the wine on the island and clicked off the speaker. "Mom, Dad, we've got company."

The growling and kissing continued.

Kat averted her eyes, focusing on the wine bottle. This would have been awkward even if the man standing next to her hadn't recently had his tongue on her clit. Maybe she should have said yes to that whiskey.

As if reading her mind, Mick took a corkscrew out of a drawer and opened the wine. The sound of the cork popping seemed to finally catch his parents' attention. Still locked in their embrace, the pair halted their amorous activities and glanced up.

Not knowing what else to do, Kat gave an awkward little wave.

"Michael!" Mrs. O'Sullivan exclaimed, straightening the collar of her blouse. "You didn't tell me we had company."

"Um, yeah. Mom, Dad, I'd like you to meet Kat. My . . . friend." Mick turned and looked at her, and the pained expression that crossed his face was gone so fast she might have imagined it, like she might have imagined the pause she heard before he said the word friend.

Kat nodded and smiled. Right. Friends. Very good friends. Friends who'd almost fucked on the floor of her apartment—Kat abruptly cut off that thought like she was pinching a dead bud from a stem. "Mick's friend, that's me," she said brightly and stuck out her hand. "Hello!"

"My goodness, aren't you lovely," Mrs. O'Sullivan said, her melodic voice almost a caress as she took Kat's hand. But rather than shake it as Kat had expected, Mick's mom pulled her into an exuberant hug.

"Moira, dear, don't suffocate the poor thing." Mick's dad wedged between them, untangling Kat and wrapping an arm around her shoulders. "Nice to meet you. I'm John O'Sullivan, but you can call me Jack."

"How about we all give her some room to breathe, okay?" Mick said. He glanced at Kat, and the look he gave her as he held out a glass of wine seemed to say, *Brace yourself.*

Kat accepted the wine gratefully. She already knew she was going to like Mick's parents, but they were a lot to take in all at once.

"Tell me, where did you two meet?" Mrs. O'Sullivan asked.

Before Kat could finish swallowing her first sip, Mick replied, "Here." He gestured at the floor. "Well, not *here*. But downstairs. Over a corpse."

Kat choked, sputtering wine.

"Oh, my poor sweet child," Moira said. "Was it someone very close to you?"

Still coughing, Kat shook her head, but Mick's mother must have interpreted her reaction as grief because she clucked her tongue and started rubbing Kat's back.

"That's how Gran met your granda, you know," Mr. O'Sullivan said to Mick. "Her parents' funeral."

"Yes, Dad, I know."

"Terrible tragedy," Mr. O'Sullivan continued.

"We've all heard the story," Mick said, voice taking on an edge of exasperation. "Many times."

"Even I've heard it," Kat admitted. "Love blooms in the strangest of places," she added with an awkward smile, not sure what possessed her to quote Mick's grandmother.

"It does indeed," Mr. O'Sullivan—Jack—said. "That's how I met Mick's mom too, you know."

"Really?" Kat asked.

Jack nodded, the trademark dark brown eyes he'd passed on to all three of his children sparkling as he gazed at his wife. "Our first week at mortuary school, we shared a cadaver."

Kat swallowed. "How . . . romantic."

"And now fate has intervened in the O'Sullivan clan once again," Moira added dramatically, reaching out to clutch her son's arm in one hand and Kat's in the other.

"It wasn't fate, Mom," Mick grumbled. "It was the Murphy widows."

Moira blinked. Unlike the rich dark brown of her children's and husband's eyes, Mick's mother's eyes were bright blue. Actually, they reminded Kat a bit of her own eyes. Eyes Mick had said were beautiful. Was that weird? She shook her head. This whole situation was weird. And plenty of people had blue eyes. It didn't make Mick's attraction to her an Oedipus complex . . .

Kat realized she was looking for excuses. Reasons for why Mick might be into her. Because of course, he couldn't be into her for herself . . . guys had always been into her for some reason, usually sex. She'd thought Mick was different, but after what had happened between them at her apartment, she wasn't sure. And the fact he was acting like nothing had happened at all made her even more confused.

"How are you related to the Murphy family?" Moira asked.

Maybe it was because she'd been distracted, but Kat had no idea what Mick's mother was talking about. She did a quick replay of their conversation and shook her head as the question clicked into place. "Oh no. I was hired at the last minute by the first widow Murphy."

"Well, that's not like Gran's story at all," Jack said, petulant, as if something had been taken from him.

"Nobody said it was, Dad." Mick rolled his eyes.

"I'm confused," Moira said.

"That's makes two of us, sweetheart," Jack added.

Three of us. Kat cleared her throat and decided to give this game of Who's on First? one more shot. "I'm a florist. I was dropping off a last-minute order when I ran into Mick."

"Literally," Mick added, chuckling. "But it all worked out in the end, and now here we are."

"Here we are," Kat agreed. Though she wasn't sure where "here" was. Friends? Business partners? More? She glanced Mick's way and realized his sweater was on inside out, the seams on the sleeves visible, the little tag sticking up at the collar. Her heart contracted with affection.

Maybe they could be more.

No. This sweet, warm, squishy feeling is what Kat would have for a cute puppy or a hedgehog in a tutu. She was making more out of it because of what happened. But if Mick thought there could be more between them—if he wanted more—why hadn't he said anything?

Joe appeared in the doorway to the kitchen. "How's it going in here?"

"Great," Mick said.

"Great," Kat echoed.

"Well, that's really great!" Joe beamed at both of them. In contrast to his habitually disheveled brother, even loosened up by a bit of whiskey, Joe's tie was still knotted tight at the throat and his buttons were all straight. His shirt neatly pressed and tucked into equally neat dress pants.

"We were talking about fate," Moira said, sashaying forward. There was something about the way Mick's mom moved that was mesmerizing. She didn't walk, she flowed.

"Fate?" Joe repeated, shooting a quick *Should I be worried?* glance in Mick and Kat's direction.

"Yes, fate." Moira floated to a stop next to Kat. "This lovely creature has come into your brother's life, and I believe it's destiny."

"Mom," Joe said, eyebrows drawing together. "Stop being weird in front of our guest." He shifted his attention to Kat and mouthed an apology.

Kat waved a hand, dismissing his concern. The situation was awkward and yes, embarrassing, but also kind of flattering. It was sweet Mick's mom believed Kat was destined for Mick. She shifted her gaze to Mick, wondering what he thought of his mother's speculations. But before she could get a read on him, the oven timer started beeping.

"Turkey's done!" Gran declared, barreling into the kitchen.

From the other room came the sound of Seamus shouting, "Tukey's done! Turkey's done!" Kat could have sworn she heard the bird making gobble-gobble noises, which was hilarious and also disturbing.

Mass chaos ensued as everyone began hustling around the kitchen. Kat hovered near the island, surrounded by bustling activity. From taking out the turkey, to stirring pots on the stove, to pulling items from the fridge, each person seemed to have a job to do. The O'Sullivans were a team, working together. Kat wanted to help. Wanted to be a part of the team. Part of the family.

"Here," Mick said, joining her at the island. He set a steaming pot on a trivet and handed her a masher. "You can help me with the potatoes."

"This Polish girl can handle that." Kat grinned, happy to be included. She set to work mashing the boiled potatoes while Mick added gobs of butter and a dash of milk. It was nice, working alongside him. Comfortable.

Before long, the meal was ready, and Gran ordered everyone to find a seat in the dining room. Kat glanced around at the faces gathered at the laden table and tried to imagine what it must have been like in years past, the way Mary-Kate described it, the apartment packed wall to wall with people. Rooms full of family, laughing and eating and talking and celebrating together. It must have been wonderful.

But Kat found even this smaller gathering to be enchanting. Despite the squabbling and disagreements between Mick and his siblings, the love they had for each other was obvious. A familiar ache burned in her chest, hot and hollow, a longing for something she'd never had, something she'd always wanted.

"Now then," Gran began from her place at the head of the table. "I know we're very grateful for all this wonderful food we're about to stuff in our faces, but before we dig in, you know the rules."

Kat tilted her head toward Mary-Kate, seated on her left. "What are the rules?"

"We have to share something we're grateful for that happened this year," Mary-Kate replied. She grinned at Kat. "You should go first."

"Me?" Kat froze.

"That's an excellent idea," Gran said. "Yes, the guest of honor should go first."

Kat's mouth went dry as all eyes shifted in her direction. She would hardly have considered herself the guest of honor. She reached for her wineglass. "Well," she began, "there's been some changes in my life this year, and I know more changes are probably coming soon. To be honest, it's been pretty scary, but it's also exciting." She paused to take a sip and consider her words. "I think what I'm most grateful for are new opportunities."

"Here, here," Moira called from the other end of the table, clanking a spoon against her water glass like she was at a wedding, not her family's Thanksgiving. She clasped her husband's hand in hers and said, "I think I speak for both of us when I say we are grateful to share this grand adventure that we call life."

"Is it me, or does my mom sound like the back of a granola bar wrapper?" Mary-Kate said under her breath to Kat. Her playful tone took any insult out of the comment.

Kat bit back a grin. "What about you?" she asked. "What are you grateful for this year?"

"Honestly?" Mary-Kate cocked her head and looked at Kat. "You."

"Me?" Kat sputtered. "Why me?"

"You're the best thing to happen to O'Sullivans in ages."

"Here, here," Mick added, mimicking his mother with a well-timed cheer. "I agree, MK." He turned to look across the table, directly at Kat. "This year, I'm most grateful for you." Heat flickered in his gaze, lit with candle glow and something more. Something that made her belly tickle.

"You too?" She shook her head. "You shouldn't waste what you're most grateful for on me."

"It's not a wish," Mick said. "Besides, it's true."

As he continued to stare at her across the table, the tickle in her belly became a flutter in her heart. Again, the idea of *maybe* drifted through her mind. Maybe they could try for something more.

Kat had been so worried about repeating her past mistakes, falling into her old patterns, but she'd never had a relationship with a guy like the one she and Mick shared. Could he be her friend *and* her lover? Wouldn't that be perfect? The problem was, if Kat tried to have both with Mick, she could wind up with neither. And one thing she knew for sure—she could not lose him as a friend.

If he would give her some signal . . . some little sign that she wasn't making this all up in her head. Help her be sure she wasn't doing what she always did and assuming sex meant more. What had Julia called it? Groundhogging. Over and over again, the same situation played out in her relationships. Kat was done with that.

But if Mick's feelings for her didn't extend beyond friendship (and the occasional bout of horniness), then she needed to consider sticking to her original plan. Kat shifted her attention to Joe. The brothers were seated next to each other, both men directly across from Kat, regarding her with their nearly identical pairs of rich dark eyes.

They were similar in height and build as well, though Joe was taller while Mick was broader through the chest and shoulders. Between the candles on the table and the chandelier above, Joe appeared almost angelic, the soft chestnut of his hair shining like a halo. In contrast, Mick's jet-black locks seemed to absorb the light.

Kat cleared her throat. "What about you, Joe?" She leaned forward, genuinely curious. "What are you grateful for this year?"

"I think I'm going to have to agree with my siblings," Joe said, smiling at her. "I'm grateful to have met you, Kat." Maybe it was the whiskey, but there was a warmth in his gaze Kat hadn't seen before. "You're a real asset to the business," he added.

Okay, so not the most romantic of declarations, but it was a start.

"To Kat," Joe said, lifting his glass.

"To Kat," the rest of the O'Sullivans repeated, toasting her as well.

Kat murmured an awkward thank-you and downed the rest of her wine. Pleasure glowed warm and bright in her. She'd never been surrounded by so much respect and admiration. So much love and attention.

"Sláinte." From the head of the table, Gran rounded out the toast. "And I'm grateful to have all my family together, under one roof," she said. "Now let's eat."

CHAPTER 24

Mick

Dinner was surprisingly less awkward than Mick had anticipated. Mom and Dad kept everyone entertained with tales of their travels, and the generous amounts of food and alcohol everyone had consumed seemed to cocoon his family in a pleasant buzz. They'd all moved from the dining room to the parlor for coffee and dessert. Now Dad was snoozing on the settee while Mom serenaded them with a slightly drunken rendition of "Danny Boy," accompanied by Seamus, of course.

Mick should be relaxed too. But right now, he was tense as hell. He glanced across the room to where Kat was seated next his sister and grandmother. His heart turned to Jell-O at the sight. All wobbly. She'd settled in so easily with his family. So naturally.

As if she felt his gaze on her, Kat turned and met his eyes. Her lips curved gently, and the warmth of that smile melted Mick's insides. Good thing his heart wasn't made of Jell-O, or it would be a sticky puddle of goo right now.

"Cookie?" Joe asked, holding out the tin Kat had brought.

"No thanks." Mick shook his head. "I'm stuffed." That, and thinking about Kat had his stomach in knots.

Joe dropped onto the couch next to Mick. "Me too," he admitted. "But I can't stop eating these. They are so good." Joe bit into another cookie. "What are they called again?"

"Kolackies," Mick said, grinning despite himself. Joe rarely overindulged. It was nice to see his brother relax his strict standards, even if it was only an extra cookie or two. Or three. His grin widened as he watched Joe take another cookie from the tin. "I helped make those, you know."

"Gran mentioned that." Joe brushed crumbs from his spotless slacks. A twinkle of mischief appeared in his eyes as he added, "I also heard something about you in an apron."

"Hey, I rocked that apron."

"I'm sure you did." Joe plucked at something on the back of Mick's collar. "Did you know your sweater is on inside out?"

"It's not inside—" Mick glanced down and realized his brother was right. "Oh." He shrugged. "Well, at least if I spill something on it, I can turn it inside out. Or right-side in. Whatever." Mick was expecting Joe to make some snarky comeback to his suggestion. When it didn't come, he realized it was because his brother's attention was elsewhere. He followed the direction of Joe's gaze. It was fixated on Kat.

Mick's heart froze. A Jell-O ice cube now.

"You and Kat have been spending a lot of time together, huh?" Joe asked.

"I suppose." Mick did not like the direction this conversation had taken. "We're friends," he said carefully.

"*Just* friends?" Joe asked, shifting his focus back to Mick.

Mick fought the urge to squirm under his brother's scrutiny. Yes, Kat was a friend. A friend whose gasps and sighs as he made her come still echoed in his ears. A friend whose smile turned his insides to mush. A friend who saw Mick in a way no one else ever had.

His mother and Seamus had switched from ballads to ditties and were deep in a raucous rendition of a famous Irish limerick. The suggestive lyrics were not helping the situation. Mick cleared his throat. "Yep." He nodded. "Just a friend."

He wanted her to be more than a friend, so much more, but by the way she was acting tonight, it was obvious she didn't feel the same. After what happened in her apartment, Mick had thought there was a chance for more between them. The door had been opened, and he was hoping Kat would walk through it.

Tonight, however, when she'd literally walked through the door, Kat had treated him the same as always. Mick had been ready to pursue something more, to take the first step, if only she'd given him a sign she wanted him to. She hadn't. So he'd taken his cues from her and acted like nothing had changed.

He watched Kat for a moment now, talking to his sister, and realized she'd spent more time with Mary-Kate tonight than she had with him. Kat had become more than his friend. She was a friend of his family. In some ways, she'd started to feel like family.

With that in mind, Mick had to let what happened between them go. She'd needed comfort, a release from the stress of the day, and he'd provided it. That's all. He shouldn't have read into it. Maybe, like he'd done so many times before, from their first meeting to karaoke to the kiss that had landed him in the hospital, he'd seen what he wanted to see.

Mick shifted his attention back to Joe. "Why do you ask?"

His brother fiddled with the piece of cookie remaining in his hand.

"Joey," Mick asked, keeping his tone light as his gut grew heavy with dread, "are you thinking about mixing business with pleasure?"

The cookie crumbled between Joe's fingers. "Shoot."

"Don't worry," Mick said, scooping up the crumbs and setting them on the edge of the coffee table. "Seamus will take care of it."

"Thanks." Joe wiped his hands on his pants, a sure sign he was more than a little nervous. "I asked about you and Kat because I know there's been some confusion in the past . . ."

"By confusion do you mean you stole the only serious girlfriend I've ever had?" Mick asked.

Joe winced.

Despite his lingering hurt, Mick knew he wasn't being fair. Joe hadn't stolen anyone. Elsi had made her choice. Mick shouldn't be surprised to see history repeating itself. Especially since Kat had made her intention to try and date his brother clear.

He couldn't blame her. Why would Kat want him, a guy who never matched his socks and wore his sweater inside out, when she could have Joe, a man who organized his sock drawer and had a suit for every day of the week. As a friend, a true friend, the best thing Mick could do was get out of her way—out of *their* way. If Kat truly wanted Joe, Mick vowed to do whatever he could to help ensure that his brother reciprocated those feelings . . . even if that meant putting his own feelings aside.

Mick turned to his brother. "The partnership with O'Sullivan's is important to Kat, so that has to come first." He sucked in a breath. "Do you think you can handle a personal relationship with someone you work with?"

"Relationship?" Joe raised his eyebrows. "Whoa. I was only thinking about asking her out for coffee."

"I'm serious, Joe," Mick said, jaw clenching. "And you should be too."

"You care a lot about her, don't you?" Joe asked. He hesitated, as if debating the next question. "Are you sure there isn't more between the two of you?"

Mick nodded, jaw still tight. "I'm sure."

"Okay, then." Joe patted Mick's shoulder, and if he noticed the lingering tension in the stiff line of his brother's back, he didn't mention it.

"Does that mean you're going to ask her out?" Mick couldn't help himself. He needed to know.

"I think so." Joe's gaze shifted back across the room to Kat. "To be honest, I've been considering it for some time now. Since Halloween, actually."

"Really?" Mick asked, impressed with his ability to sound so calm.

Joe nodded. "At first, the idea seemed painfully inappropriate. As you mentioned, we're business partners." He adjusted his glasses. "But watching Mom and Dad tonight reminded me that O'Sullivan's is a family business. This place has been run by husband-and-wife teams for generations. I mean, think of Gran and Granda."

"Husband and wife?" Mick was going to puke. "What happened to asking her out for coffee?"

Heat crept up Joe's neck, rising above his tightly collared shirt. "That came out wrong. I simply meant that I didn't think it would be out of place if we . . . that is, if I pursued, as you said, a more personal relationship with her."

Joe fiddled with his tie, and for a moment Mick thought his brother might actually loosen it. But instead, Joe smoothed his hand over the silk, straightening what was already perfectly straight. "I'm getting older, and as the head of the family I should probably start considering settling down."

Leave it to Joe to turn the prospect of marriage into a sensible solution. "You're such a romantic, Joey."

"You know I'm not," Joe said, missing the sarcasm completely as he brushed invisible crumbs from his lap. "Marriage is good for our reputation; it sends a message of stability to the community. Besides, if we want to keep the business in the family, someone needs to get started on the next generation of O'Sullivan's."

"Oh, Gran's going to love that." Yep, he was definitely going to puke.

"Does this mean I have your permission?"

"You don't need my permission." Mick laughed. It was either that or cry. "I'm her friend, not her keeper." He glanced at Kat, who must have realized they were talking about her, because she was looking at them, a question in her blue eyes. "Knock yourself out."

"Yes, well, hopefully I don't end up in the hospital with a head wound," Joe teased.

When Mick didn't laugh, he sobered. "I'm kidding, Mickey."

"I know, Joey." Mick ran his fingers over the spot behind his ear. The stiches had dissolved, but he could still feel a slight bump from the scar tissue.

What might have happened if he hadn't fallen? If he hadn't bumped his head. That kiss . . . Mick closed his eyes. That kiss had been incredible. And something else he and Kat hadn't talked about. Not that it mattered now. A dull ache throbbed in his chest. He pressed his hand over his heart, sensing new scar tissue forming there too.

Seamus fluttered across the room, landing in front of him on the coffee table and pecking at the cookie crumbs. Mick stroked a thumb over the bird's crest. "Happy Thanksgiving, Seamus."

"Gobble-gobble," Seamus chirped.

"You don't want to be a turkey today, buddy," Mick warned, laughing despite himself.

From across the room, Kat laughed too.

The sound pierced his chest, sharpening the ache that had begun to fade. This was going to suck. But it was his own stupid fault.

She crossed the room, scooting between Mick and Joe on the couch.

"Hello, beautiful," Seamus cooed.

"Hello, you handsome turkey." Kat tickled the feathers on his chest. "I thought I heard you making gobbling noises."

"Does anyone else think it's strange he isn't making actual turkey sounds?" Joe asked. "They are both birds, after all."

"When would Seamus have ever heard a real turkey?" Mick shook his head. "Granda taught him how to gobble."

Either to prove a point or to impress Kat or simply because he was buzzed on whiskey and sugar, Joe leaned forward and proceeded to gobble. Or . . . Mick assumed that's what his brother was trying to do.

Seamus cocked his head at Joe, turning it to the side in that odd bird way of his until it was almost perpendicular to his body.

"See?" Joe said. "He just needs someone to show him how. Listen to this, Seamus." Joe made the questionable turkey noise again.

The cockatoo straightened, blinked its beady eyes, and said, "Shut up, fucker."

Mick pressed his lips together, trying to contain the fizz of laughter.

Beside him, Kat had no such luck. She burst into a fit of giggles that ended on a snort.

Seamus proceeded to mimic the sound exactly.

"Hey," Kat said, giving the bird a soft poke.

"Wait until he hears you snore," Mick teased.

"Please," Joe huffed. "I highly doubt a lady like Kat snores."

Mick met Kat's eyes and held her gaze for a moment. What he wanted to say was, hell yes, the lady snored. She snored like a lumberjack, and it was adorable, and he'd be perfectly content to fall asleep to the sound of her snores every night. But instead, Mick shifted his attention to his brother and said, "You're probably right."

Kat smoothed her skirt and didn't contradict him.

After an awkward pause, Mick cleared his throat and stood up. "I'm going to get a start on those dishes."

"Do you need some help?" Kat asked, beginning to stand.

"No, no. You stay here." Mick forced the words around the lump forming in his throat. "I think Joe has something he wants to talk to you about." He held out his arm to Seamus. "Come on, buddy. I'll let you play in the bubbles."

The bird perched on his wrist and Mick turned, heading for the kitchen before he could change his mind. He'd barely started to fill one side of the sink with water before Mary-Kate joined him.

"What's up?"

"The sky," Seamus squawked.

Mary-Kate chortled. "That was one of Granda's favorite jokes."

"Got me with it every time." Mick grinned, shoulders easing a bit.

"What are you doing in here all alone?"

"I'm not alone." Mick reached for the soap and squeezed a generous amount into the water. "Seamus is here too. He's going to help me wash the dishes." Big foamy bubbles began to form, and the cockatoo hopped over, popping them with his beak.

"Mm-hmm." His sister's response made it clear she didn't believe him.

To prove his point, Mick reached for the stack of dinner plates and began setting them gently in the warm, soapy water to soak. The fine bone china was a family heirloom, too delicate for the dishwasher.

"Gran will kill you if you break one of those," his sister warned.

"Then why don't you get a towel and help me," Mick shot back, handing her a freshly scrubbed and dripping wet plate.

They worked in tandem for a few minutes, washing, rinsing, and drying, the silence only broken by the sounds of splashing water and Seamus's happy chittering as he played. From the other room, the soft murmur of conversation was a blur, the voices of his mom and Gran and Joe and Kat blending together. Mick wondered if his brother had made his move yet. He shoved the last plate at his sister.

"Hey, easy," Mary-Kate said.

"Sorry." He pulled the plug and watched the sudsy water swirl down the drain.

"What's with you?" Mary-Kate asked, drying her hands on a towel. "You're being very mopey."

"I have a lot on my mind."

"Like what?"

Like the fact my brother is currently asking out the girl of my dreams. Mick leaned against the counter and crossed his arms. "The business."

Mary-Kate studied him, one auburn brow arching.

"I'm serious. I have an idea."

Her second eyebrow joined the first. "Another one?"

He nodded.

"Mick, we finally got Joe on board with our plans. I'm not sure it's a good idea to tempt fate and push it with something else."

"Funny you use the word 'fate,'" Mick said. "That's exactly what Mom said earlier. That fate had brought Kat into our lives."

"Mom has a tendency to be melodramatic." Mary-Kate wrinkled her nose, freckles scrunching. "Also, I think she and Dad have been smoking weed."

Now it was Mick's turn to raise an eyebrow.

"I'm serious! Who knows what the two of them have gotten into while on the road." She shook her head. "As long as they don't join some death cult, I don't care."

"Other cults are fine, but no death cults," Mick said, never able to resist razzing his sister.

"Shut up and tell me about this business idea," Mary-Kate demanded and pulled a can of whipped cream out of the fridge.

"What are you doing?" Mick asked.

"Stress eating." She cut a slice from the pie still sitting on the island and began spraying whipped cream on top.

Mick waited until she stopped. "My plan is to—" He was cut off by another blast of whipped cream. "Are you done?"

"Yes," Mary-Kate said, but before Mick could open his mouth to speak, she pressed the nozzle again, topping off her mountain of whipped cream with one last dollop. "*Now* I'm done."

"I want to offer grief counseling services," Mick said, spitting it all out in a rush in case she changed her mind.

Mary-Kate stared at him, whipped cream–laden fork hovering midair.

"Here. At O'Sullivan's," he added.

She set the fork down. "Mick that's . . ."

"Bananas, I know. But—"

"I was going to say genius."

"Well, yes, that too," he agreed, relief coursing through his veins.

"I can't believe you've never suggested this before." She shook her head. "What prompted this?"

"Kat," Mick admitted. "She put the idea in my head."

Understanding flashed across his sister's face. "That's why you mentioned fate." She nodded. "For a moment I thought maybe . . ."

"Maybe what?"

"Nothing." She picked up her fork again.

"MK," Mick said, adding the wheedling tone to his voice he knew his sister couldn't refuse.

She shoved a giant forkful of whipped cream–slathered pie into her mouth.

Mick crossed his arms, waiting while she chewed. Seamus joined them at the island, whistling the naughty ditty from earlier.

Finally, she swallowed, and Mick made his move, snatching the fork away before she could cram another bite into her mouth. "Talk," he ordered.

"Pretty bird. Seamus is a pretty bird."

Mary-Kate snickered. Mick rolled his eyes. "Not you, bird-brain." He pointed the fork at his sister and speared her with a look. "You."

"I thought maybe something was going on between you and Kat."

"Why would you think that?"

"I dunno." She shrugged. "I guess because of all the time you two spend together."

"We're friends."

His sister snorted.

Seamus immediately mimicked the sound. Mary-Kate turned her attention to the bird. "I know, right?" she said. "I've never seen two 'friends' look at each other that way either."

"She doesn't know what she's talking about, Seamus," Mick

said, taking a page out his sister's playbook. "Because Joe is the one Kat is looking at. In fact, he's asking her out on a date right now."

"What?" Mary-Kate yelped, giving up the pretense of conversing with the bird and jerking her gaze back to Mick's. "He is?"

"Yep." Mick nodded.

"Are you sure?"

"Yep," he said again.

"And you're okay with this?" his sister asked.

Nope. But he couldn't say that. He had to be okay with this.

"Mick?" his sister pressed, voice gentle now. "No regerts?"

A soft laugh snuffled out of him. "No regerts" was a long-standing inside joke. A bit of irony they could appreciate a little more than most. "No regerts" meant all in. "No regerts" meant regardless of how impetuous or ill-advised an idea was, if you believed in it wholeheartedly, it was worth going for. Life was too short to sweat the details. Better to do something and mess it up than not do it at all.

Mick had thought that's what he wanted with Kat. To take a chance. See if there was more between them. It's why he'd finally kissed her. But this wasn't just about him. This wasn't just his life. He might be willing to risk their friendship, but she'd made it clear she wasn't. And he had to respect that. To be the friend he'd promised her he could be.

"Yeah," he finally said. "No regerts."

CHAPTER 25

Kat

On the Monday following Thanksgiving, Kat headed to Babcia's for their usual afternoon of lunch and shopping. After Kat finished up the last of the chores, Babcia invited her to sit down for a cup of tea before heading home.

"It's so cold outside today Kasia, a cup of tea will keep you warm."

Kat followed her grandmother into the kitchen with a suspicious eye. Tea was never simply tea with Babcia. Her grandmother should work for the CIA or something. One cup of tea with Babcia and she knew all your secrets.

Which was how, even though Kat had managed to keep a few specific details about Thanksgiving dinner with the O'Sullivans to herself all afternoon, three sips of tea and she was telling Babcia how Joe had asked her out on a date.

"Oh, that nice young man who came to make cookies?" Babcia asked. "I really like him."

"Um, no," Kat admitted. "His brother."

Babcia made a face. It was a face Kat swore Polish grandmothers were taught in some secret society, where they learned how to show great disappointment, disdain, and disinterest all at the same time so you were left feeling guilty, defensive, and ignored in one swoop.

Today, Kat got that look twice. Once when she told Babcia about Joe, and again when she mentioned her possible deal with Allen.

"Are you sure this is what you want, Kasia?"

Kat tilted her teacup, stirring the dregs remaining in the bottom. "Is it exactly how I dreamed things would happen? No. But I'm learning that sometimes getting what you want isn't about getting exactly what you imagined."

Babcia sighed and set her teacup down. "That's a tough lesson, Kotku."

"Tell me about it," Kat muttered. "I always thought that settling for anything less than what I imagined in my dreams was giving up."

"That's not giving up, that's compromising," Babcia said.

"Isn't compromising the same thing as settling, though?"

"No, Kotku." Babcia clicked her tongue. "Compromise isn't settling, it's figuring out the most important parts of your dreams and making sure you get them."

Kat sat straighter in her chair, absorbing her grandmother's words. The truth of them settled into her soul. "You're right, Babcia."

"Of course, I am." Her grandmother pursed her lips and sipped her tea. She set the cup in the saucer and asked in a casual tone that was anything but, "What's most important to you?"

Should've seen that coming. "I've always dreamed of building my business from the ground up, having a hand in every step of the process, from choosing the location to construction to building a loyal customer base. I wanted every piece to be mine."

"But now?"

"Now I know I don't need all that. By taking over Allen's business, I don't get to start from the ground up, but as long as I can still start fresh, I'm okay with that. When it comes down to it, what's most important to me is making the business my own."

"Do you think that man will let you do that?"

As always, the way Babcia called Allen "that man" was like a curse. Allen wasn't a bad boss, he was just . . . Allen. Kat shrugged. "Honestly, I don't know. I'd like to think he would, but I'm not sure." That uncertainty is why she'd been dragging her feet on the deal.

"Is there any way you can find out?" Babcia spooned more sugar into her tea.

"You mean like a test?"

Babcia gave one of her little shrugs. "If that's what you want to call it."

Kat chuckled. Her grandmother was not someone you wanted to fuck around and find out with. Babcia's suggestion was a tad vicious, but effective.

As she considered the possibilities, Kat's attention drifted to the vase of flowers on the table. The bouquet she'd brought her grandmother today was full of French hydrangeas in her favorite shade of pink. She'd always wanted to paint the walls of the shop, but wasn't sure Allen would allow it.

An idea bloomed in her mind and Kat jerked her chin up, grinning at her grandmother. "You know what, Babcia? I think that's an excellent suggestion."

······

Kat didn't waste any time putting her idea into action. The next day she showed up at the shop with paint and a plan. Today was the day she'd figure out if her dreams could come true. With every stroke of color, her hopes rose a little higher. She rested the roller in the drip tray and stepped back to admire her handiwork.

"Are you done yet?" Ronnie called from the back room.

"Almost," Kat said. "Come tell me what you think."

Ronnie emerged from the back room, JoJo clutched in their arms, dressed in a Sugarplum Fairy costume, complete with crown and sparkly tutu. "Wow," they said, staring at the walls. "It's very . . . pink."

"French hydrangea," Kat explained.

"I think it looks nice." Laura added her two cents from her spot behind the counter, where she was busy crocheting away.

They'd launched her new products for the holiday season online last week, and orders were pouring in. Kat had a feeling a lot of people would be sipping their hot cocoa from candy cane–striped cozy cocks this winter.

"I didn't say it doesn't look nice." Ronnie set JoJo on the floor and stood, hands fisted at their sides, gaze scanning the shop walls once more. "Just that it was very pink."

"I like pink," Kat said.

"I know." Ronnie smirked. "Ninety percent of your wardrobe is pink."

Kat would argue it was probably closer to eighty, but their point was valid. "And this is environmentally friendly paint," she added, "so fingers crossed Allen approves." If he didn't, then Kat would have her answer.

Ronnie glanced over their shoulder and stared at Kat. "You didn't ask him beforehand?"

"Nope."

"Seeking forgiveness rather than permission." Laura chuckled. "Ballsy."

"Something like that."

The chimes over the front door jangled.

Laura jerked her gaze toward the entrance. "Allen!" She waved, giant Christmas cozy cock in hand.

"We were just talking about you," Ronnie said, crouching to retrieve JoJo from the floor.

Allen stood in the doorway to the shop, mouth agape as his gaze shifted from the fairy-princess hedgehog to the crocheted penis to the bright pink walls.

Whether it was a look of shock, wonder, or horror on her boss's face, Kat wasn't sure. "What do you think of the new paint?" she ventured.

Allen's mouth opened and closed, but no sound came out.

"It's called French hydrangea," Laura said helpfully.

Ironically, Allen's complexion was turning a similar shade.

"And the brand is environmentally friendly," Ronnie added.

Kat cleared her throat, glancing nervously at Ronnie and Laura as Allen began to pace around the shop.

"Why wasn't I consulted about this?" he demanded, waving a hand at the walls. "I didn't give my permission to do this."

"Um," Kat began, hating the stammer in her voice, "I didn't think I needed your permission."

He whirled around to gape at her. "Of course, you need my permission. It's *my* shop."

"But it's going to be *my* shop," Kat countered. Her heart was pounding, and she felt like she was going to throw up, but she held her ground. "Remember the arrangement we discussed?"

"Discussed but not decided."

"Fair," she conceded. "But if I accept your deal, then the shop is going to be mine. And there will be some changes."

"It won't be yours until the down payment is paid in full." Again, he waved a hand, gesturing angrily at the fresh paint. "Which means you still need my approval to make changes to the building."

Kat stiffened. "My understanding was that once I'd accepted your offer, you'd hand over control of the business to me."

"You must have misunderstood." Allen frowned, forehead furrowing so deeply his eyebrows disappeared behind his glasses. "The store is in my name. I'm still the owner, and until you buy me out in full, it's technically mine."

"'Technically'?" she repeated, heart sinking. "Are we going to get technical, Allen?" Forcing her voice to remain calm, Kat said, "I promised you I would do my best to continue to run the business in a way that upholds your commitment to conservation, and I will, because I believe in that too. But I also have my own ideas, my own plans. As owner, it will be *my* vision I carry out, not yours."

Kat bit her lip and looked around the shop. She'd been so hesitant to take Allen's deal because she feared it would never feel like it was truly hers. Never be the dream she'd always imagined.

And now, she'd finally come around to the possibility that she could make the business hers, had started to believe her dreams would be a reality, only to have her worst fears confirmed instead. Her shoulders sagged, hopes wilting like a flower past its bloom.

Kat sucked in a slow, deep breath. She'd known this might be a problem. It's why she'd resorted to this little experiment in the first place. Allen was great about a lot of things. He was a brilliant mentor. Generous and fair. But he was also incredibly possessive. She sighed. "I don't mean to seem ungrateful, but I think it's obvious this isn't going to work out."

He harrumphed and crossed his arms. "What are you saying?"

"I'm saying, as long as you own the store, as long as you retain control, it will never really belong to me."

"But what if we helped?" Ronnie suggested.

"Yeah," Laura chimed in. "Ronnie and I have been talking. We figured we can chip in and help you buy Allen out."

"I can't ask you to do that," Kat said, shaking her head even as her heart wrenched with gratitude.

"You're not asking," Laura pointed out. "We're offering."

"And I appreciate the offer." Kat sighed. "But it's too much."

"Not if Allen is willing to honor his original offer of splitting the down payment into installments," Ronnie insisted.

"Of course I am." Allen crossed his arms. "I made that offer in good faith."

"We're sure you did," Laura said gently. "But you've gotta give Kat control. Full control," she added sternly. "You're moving to Alaska, anyway. Sooner of later, you're going to have to accept the fact you need to let this place go."

"I built Allen's Arrangements myself," Allen said, expression thoughtful as his gaze shifted to the bright pink walls. "But I suppose you're right. If I'm gone, is it really Allen's Arrangements anymore?"

"That has to be hard to imagine," Kat said, voice thick with empathy. "This place means a lot to you."

"I know it means a lot to you, too." Allen dropped his arms. "The shop should belong to you."

"No," Kat declared impulsively. "It should belong to us. To me and Ronnie and Laura."

"So we'd be like business partners?" Laura asked. "The three of us?"

Kat nodded. It felt right. "The place means a lot to all three of us. Ever since Allen first made his offer, whenever I envisioned the future of this shop, you both were always part of it. Why not make it official? What do you say, Allen?"

Eyes bright with respect, Allen's usually stern mouth quirked slightly as he held out his hand. "I say it sounds like a deal."

"Then on behalf of my colleagues"—she beamed at Ronnie and Laura—"and business partners," she added before shaking his hand, "I accept in good faith."

......

Later that night, still riding the high of the day's success, Kat bounced around her apartment and wished she had an exercise wheel like JoJo. Some way to help burn off all the excess energy she was feeling. Kat settled for watching her hedgehog zoom around in circles while giving her thumbs a workout texting her best friends about what had happened.

It still felt strange, not seeing Andie and Julia all the time. So much had happened these past few weeks and Kat felt like she'd barely covered the highlight reel with them. Checking in via text wasn't the same as chatting over lunch and not even close to catching up on a CCC night.

A gloomy cloud of sadness swept over Kat, casting a shadow on her good mood. She missed her besties. But more than that, as Kat scrolled through her favorite contacts, she realized the person she most wanted to share today's success with was Mick.

Her heart clenched and she hesitated, thumbs hovering over her screen's keypad. Across the room, JoJo was still running her spiky little heart out on the now silent wheel. She still hadn't thanked Mick for fixing it. She'd meant to say something to him about it but had never seemed to find the right time.

Kat pulled out the note he'd left her that night, smiling to herself as she unfolded and reread his message. Guilt pricked like a thorn in her side. Her smile faded and she refolded the note and tucked it away again. Was it wrong of her to keep it? She didn't think so. Mick was a friend. Kat had plenty of notes she'd kept from Andie and Julia. So why not one from him?

Still, the guilt lingered. She'd been pleased when Joe had asked her out on Thanksgiving. Relieved, actually. Following her plan to date Joe was simple. Easy. Nothing like the complicated web her thoughts and feelings for his brother had become

Rather than try and untangle that emotional snarl, Kat decided it was easier to set the whole situation aside. If she was lucky, given enough time, things would work themselves out. Look what had happened with the flower shop today with Ronnie and Laura. An unexpected solution had presented itself when she needed it most. She could only hope for something similar to happen with Mick.

With eerie timing, her phone began to vibrate. Kat glanced at the screen, recognizing the number at once. O'Sullivan's. Her heart hiccupped, coming to a stop and then speeding up again, like JoJo stumbling inside her wheel. "Hello?"

"Kat?"

It took her a moment to register the voice on the line belonged to Joe, not Mick.

"That's me." Kat swallowed. Of course, it was Joe. Why would Mick be calling her? Just because she felt there were a whole lot of things they'd left unsaid didn't mean he felt the same. From what she could tell at Thanksgiving, he didn't feel the need to say anything. She'd even tried to find a moment alone with him, offering to help with the dishes, and he'd told her no. He'd told her to stay with Joe.

I think Joe has something he wants to talk to you about.

The dots connected and Kat realized Mick must have known Joe was going to ask her out. He'd known, and he'd not gotten in the way. Had, in fact, helped facilitate it. A moment ago, Kat had hoped for a solution to present itself. Well, here it was. Mick obviously wanted her to be with Joe. They were friends and nothing more.

"How are you?" Joe asked.

"Fine. Good." Mind still whirring, Kat scrambled for something to say. "How are you?"

"Good. Fine."

Thrilling conversation so far. She licked her lips, trying to summon more excitement. This is what she wanted, after all. "How are—" Kat stopped, she'd almost asked Joe the same question again. "How was your day?"

If he said "good" or "fine," she might scream.

"Great, thanks."

"Great" was better. Not much, but she'd take it.

"Look," Joe continued, finally taking the reins, "I was calling because I'd like to follow up on what we'd talked about the other night. You know . . . our date?"

"Sure," she said. "What did you have in mind?"

"This might sound odd, but how would you feel about having dinner with my family again?"

"Um, okay." Not what she was expecting for a first date but . . .

"I know it's probably not what you were expecting for a first date."

Kat laughed, relaxing into the conversation. "Not exactly," she admitted.

"My folks are in town for only a few weeks. I want to spend

as much time with them while I can, but I also would like to see you . . ."

"It's fine," she said. "And sweet. I like your family."

"Well, they like you too," he said.

There was that warm glow again. Kat felt a silly grin creep across her face. She couldn't recall ever meeting the family of a guy she'd dated, let alone being liked by them.

"We're having game night on Friday, and I'd love for you to come."

"Sounds fun." A family that had game nights. That's what she wanted. "What time?"

•••••

At seven that Friday, Kat arrived at O'Sullivan's. A twinge of nervous energy dogged her steps as she made her way up to the family apartment on her own. She wasn't sure what to expect tonight. Joe had said the family would be there. Did that mean the *whole* family?

She shouldn't be nervous. The prospect of seeing Mick should be the same as seeing Mary-Kate. Her friends and the siblings of the man she was dating. If this was going to work, Kat needed to get used to that.

Mary-Kate greeted her at the door with a hug and a smile, instantly making Kat feel more at ease. The glass of wine that was soon pressed into her hand didn't hurt either.

"So wonderful to see you again, lovely," Moira said, floating into the room and kissing Kat on each cheek. In keeping with her Morticia motif, she was draped all in black, wearing a long black sweater shot through with threads of silver and an ankle-length black velvet skirt.

Kat wondered if all the black was a personal choice or a hold-over from her profession. She glanced at Mary-Kate, who was dressed in a bright combo of spring green and sunny yellow. Must be personal then.

Mr. O'Sullivan joined his wife in greeting Kat, wishing her a good evening and pressing a gallant kiss to her wrist.

"You need to teach your sons some of your tricks," Kat said, giving Jack a wink.

"Don't worry," Joe promised her, stepping in front of his dad to take her hand. "I have a few tricks of my own."

The words were sweet, and spoken in a low, flirtatious timbre that should have set off a flurry of butterflies. Even though she said she wanted a relationship that wasn't based on attraction, she had to admit she was disappointed at its absence. And speaking of absences . . . She glanced around the living room.

"Mick's not here tonight," Mary-Kate said, a knowing look in her eyes.

Kat's attention snapped to her friend. It took all her willpower not to ask where Mick was. Instead, she let her gaze drift around the room again, landing on the flowerpot by the window. "Ah!" she said, as if that was what she'd been looking for the entire time. "I see the amaryllis has begun to sprout."

"Yes," Gran said, shuffling over to the plant and rotating the pot. "I've been keeping an eye on it."

"That's putting it mildly," Joe added. "She's been showering that bulb with so much love and attention you'd think it was her first great-grandchild."

"What else am I supposed to do until you give me one of those, Joey?" Gran asked cheekily.

Joe's face flushed, and he shot Kat and embarrassed glance. "Should have seen that one coming."

Kat grinned. "Indeed."

The evening passed in a blur of laughter and conversation, and Kat stayed long past when she should have, considering she had to open the shop early the next morning. Joe walked her to her van, and for a moment she thought he was going to kiss her. He did, but only a soft touch of his lips to her cheek.

A memory rippled through her, and Kat realized that was exactly how she'd kissed Mick that day he'd taken her to Fidel's for breakfast. The day he'd agreed to be her wingman. The kiss of a friend.

Which was a good thing, Kat worked very hard to remind herself. Joe was a gentleman, exactly like she'd wanted.

CHAPTER 26

Kat

The O'Sullivan Christmas Eve party was a small, intimate affair. Kat had thought it might be more like the Thanksgivings of old that Mary-Kate had described, but it appeared to be a casual gathering of friends and family. Ever the gentleman, Joe had insisted on picking Kat up at her place. After they arrived back at his family's apartment, he took Kat around on a little tour of all the guests, making introductions as needed.

Gran was seated in the parlor with some friends from bingo. Mary-Kate was in the kitchen with another redhead Kat recognized as Kathleen, the cousin she'd met at the funeral reception. Kat waved, watching with a mix of horror and respect as they filled a punch bowl with obscene amounts of whiskey. Against her better judgment, she accepted the glass Mary-Kate offered her. 'Tis the season, after all.

The dining room had been turned into a makeshift karaoke stage, the long, oval table pushed to one side and the chairs arranged to form an audience. In full Morticia and Gomez mode, Moira and Jack were performing a jazzy Christmas number together for a small crowd of enthusiastic onlookers. Seamus, of course, was providing backup vocals.

Kat squinted. "Is your dad wearing an emerald velvet suit?"

"Unfortunately, yes." Joe nodded. "He's had that thing since the eighties."

Kat tugged awkwardly on the hem of her sweater. She'd been sure other people at the party would be wearing ugly holiday knits as well, but nope. She was the only one. It was like a scene from one of her favorite rom-coms, save for a very important detail: her Mark Darcy was dressed, as always, in neatly pressed slacks, button-down shirt, and tightly knotted tie. Joe had added a sweater vest to the ensemble, but there was nothing remotely kitschy or cute about it.

This shouldn't surprise Kat; "kitschy" and "cute" were not words that came to mind when she thought of Joe. And that was fine. He made her laugh, in his own way, though Kat had a feeling it was often unintentional. He was a hard worker. Loyal. And above all, he was kind.

She'd seen that kindness in action many times. In the past month, as she and Joe worked on establishing the partnership with O'Sullivan's, Kat had many opportunities to observe how Joe handled grieving clients with a kindness that went beyond professionalism. He had a tendency to be stiff, sure, but there was a softness beneath the polished exterior.

Maybe it came with the territory, but Kat found all the O'Sullivans, each in their own way, to be unerringly kind. She'd felt more welcomed and loved and at home here than she'd felt anywhere else, save with her best friends and Babcia. Kat could easily picture a future filled with O'Sullivan family gatherings, nestled in the warmth of their love, basking in the glow of their respect and admiration.

But was that enough? The question seemed to creep out of the hollow space in her chest, whispering in her ear. Kat ignored it and sipped her punch. Considering all the whiskey she knew had been added, the drink was sweeter than she expected, with notes of citrus and honey and something else . . . anise, maybe. Whatever was in it, it was delicious, and she downed the festive beverage much faster than she'd planned.

"Should I get you another?" Joe asked.

Kat nodded and handed him her glass. "Why not." The seal

had been broken, the night was still young, and she was really enjoying the tingly feeling seeping through her veins, filling that troublesome void with a pleasant warmth.

"Are you sure that's a good idea?" a familiar voice asked.

Familiar, even if she hadn't heard it recently. *Mick.*

Kat turned. The sudden move made her slightly dizzy, just enough for it to take her a moment to get her bearings, focus on Mick, and realize what he was wearing.

Ha, ha, universe, very funny.

This was too much. Kat pressed her lips together, trapping the laugh before it could escape.

Mick stood facing her, tall, dark, and disheveled, and dressed in an ugly sweater identical to hers.

A full body flush crept over Kat's skin, a rush of heat she couldn't contribute to the whiskey. This . . . *coincidence* didn't mean anything. Not a thing.

Except it did . . .

Once upon a time, she and her friends had dreamed what their dating life might look like if it could be more like a romantic comedy. And bumping into the man of your dreams—your Mr. Right, to quote Bridget Jones herself—in an ugly sweater at a holiday party, was exactly the kind of moment Kat had fantasized about.

But this wasn't a fantasy. And the man before her wasn't her Mr. Right.

"You might want to reconsider that second glass of punch, princess. I've seen how you handle your whiskey," Mick reminded her.

"Hello to you too," she said, serving him her frostiest glare.

"You're right, I'm sorry." Mick acknowledged with a nod. "That was rude of me. Hi, Kat."

No. No, goose bumps did not prickle her skin at the sound of Mick saying her name. She'd heard him say her name countless times before, why should now be any different? "Hi," she said, voice as cool as her eyes.

The tension built between them, the same invisible friction she'd felt every night she'd come to visit the past few weeks as Joe's date and Mick had been there. Those nights he'd all but ignored her. Rarely looking at her and barely speaking to her. Kat hated this. She hated the distance between them. She was about to reach out and say something when Joe reappeared from the kitchen, punch glasses in hand.

Like a baby fawn obliviously stumbling into the line of fire, Joe walked right in between Mick and Kat. "Hey," he said, glancing back and forth. "You two are wearing the same sweater."

"We are," Mick agreed, scruffy jaw stiff.

Joe glanced between them again. "Did I interrupt something?"

"No," Mick said.

At the exact same time Kat said, "Yes."

"I see." Joe eyed the two punch glasses in his hands. "Well, I'm going to have a seat while you two figure out which it is."

The glum tone in his voice caught Kat by surprise, and she realized she was being a terrible date. She hurried after Joe, shooting Mick icy daggers over her shoulder. But it wasn't his fault. He'd tried to leave things alone. She was the one who couldn't drop it. "Joe," Kat said, joining him on the couch. "I'm sorry about that."

Joe had already slammed one glass of punch and had started on the other. Probably best Kat didn't have any more, anyway. She needed her wits about her if she was going to pull herself out of the mess she currently found herself in.

Because this was a mess. She was a mess. A hot mess.

The stupid sweater had been the tipping point, a manifestation of all her romantic hopes and dreams. A physical, in-her-face reminder of all the ways Mick was the one she really wanted to be with. Not because of a list or a set of rules, but because being with him felt right in a way it never had with anybody else.

Her gaze snagged on the amaryllis blooming by the window. A month ago, when she'd brought the bulb as a gift, it hadn't been much more than a blob half buried in a pot of dirt. Under-whelming. Only the barest hint of green as the first leaf began to sprout.

It was one of the things she loved most about these flowers, each one like a little Christmas miracle. Kat had cultivated holiday amaryllis bulbs for years, but the magic of watching one bloom never got old. It seemed to happen so slowly, the shoots rising into the air, day by day, inch by gradual inch. For weeks, there'd be no sign of anything more interesting than a plain green stalk. And then all of a sudden, seemingly overnight, the blooms appeared, bright and bold and breathtakingly glorious.

Kat always believed falling in love had to be this overwhelm-ing feeling. Waves crashing, fireworks bursting, the earth mov-ing. She'd had those big explosions of emotion before, but they'd always fizzled out as fast they'd occurred. On the surface, Kat's discovery of her feelings for Mick seemed sudden, but the seed of emotion had been planted months ago. And like the bulb of an amaryllis, those feelings had quietly grown, easy to dismiss or ignore until they burst into bloom.

"Darlings," Moira crowed, gliding across the room in a swirl of ebony satin, her gown trimmed in emerald velvet. "Merry Christ-mas, my two turtle doves," she said to Kat and Joe, tapping them each on the cheek. "Are you enjoying the party?"

"It's lovely," Kat said, nodding. "Thank you for inviting me."

"Of course, of course." Moira settled herself on a chair across from them. "You should come for brunch tomorrow."

"Oh no . . . ," Kat stammered, "I wouldn't want to intrude on your Christmas morning."

"Nonsense!" Moira declared. "It's my favorite holiday celebra-tion and you practically feel like family already. Unless you have plans with your own family?"

Kat's heart dipped a fraction. "My grandmother and I do Christmas dinner together, but I I don't have plans in the morn-ing, no."

"Alone on Christmas morning?" Moira gasped. "I won't hear of it. You must come."

"Well . . ." Kat glanced around for Joe, who'd drifted off toward the kitchen. "If you insist."

"I do. Absolutely, I do. It's our last day home tomorrow. After that, Jack and I will be headed west for the rest of the winter. There are some intriguing ghost towns in Wyoming I'm dying to explore."

"That sounds . . . nice," Kat managed.

"Nice." Moira beamed at her. "It's been nice getting to know you, dear girl." She stood, satin skirts swishing around her like the flutter of raven's wings. "Hopefully I'll be seeing you again next year." She winked. "Merry Christmas."

"Merry Christmas," Kat said, watching as Moira sashayed across the room, where Gran and her bingo ladies seemed to be holding Mick hostage. *Sorry, ladies, he's mine.*

She hoped. But first, she had to untangle the mess she'd made. Kat turned back to Joe.

"Sorry," he said, settling onto the sofa with a freshly refilled glass of punch. "My mom can be a tad melodramatic."

"I like your mom. I like all of your family, including you, Joe." Her earnest smiled turned somber. "I have a confession," she began.

Joe nodded, sipping his punch in silence as he waited for her to continue.

"My dating track record isn't the greatest. I've not always been the best judge of character."

"Ow," Joe said.

"No, not you!" Kat hurried to add. "You're different. Totally different from any of the guys in my past. That's the whole reason I wanted to go out with you." Kat cleared her throat. "Recently, I decided I needed a change. I knew that if I ever had any hope of finding the right man for me, I needed to reevaluate my . . . qualifications."

Joe took another pull on his drink. "You make it sound like you were putting together a business proposal."

"In a way, I suppose I was," Kat admitted. "I made a list."

"A list?" Joe finished his drink.

She nodded. Kat hadn't planned to tell Joe about the list, but now that she'd started explaining, she couldn't seem to stop. "A list of all the things I believed would make up my perfect Mr. Right." She gazed at him. "And you checked off every box."

"Does this mean I'm your Mr. Right?" he asked, leaning back on the sofa.

"I thought so . . ." She hesitated and picked up a candy cane, twisting it in her hands. "You're perfect on paper. Everything I believed I wanted."

"But . . . ," Joe prompted. "I'm sensing a 'but.'" He snorted. "Butt sensing."

Kat cocked her head. Joe never snorted. Certainly not at butt innuendos. She eyed the empty glasses on the table. He'd had three glasses of punch that she knew of. Could he be tipsy? Maybe the conversation was making him uncomfortable, and he was handling it with bad jokes? She'd been guilty of that tactic a time or two.

But Kat was trying to be serious right now, so she soldiered on. "But I realized tonight, despite how perfectly you match my list, there is something to be said for qualities that can't be measured." She reached out and squeezed his hand. "Joe, you are right in so many ways. And you are someone's Mr. Right . . . you're just not right for me."

Joe was quiet for a moment as he stared down at her hand covering his. Finally, shifting his gaze to meet hers, he said, "I have a confession to make too."

"Okay . . . ," Kat said slowly.

"I don't have a list or anything, not on paper anyway, but I'm guilty of the same thing." The ice cubes rattled in his empty glass. "I decided it was time to take the next step on the ladder of adulthood, you know, marriage, kids, the works, and you seemed like the perfect fit. You're smart, have a good head for business, and aren't bad on the eyes either."

"Um, well . . . thank you?" Kat said, not sure where he was going with this.

"I love you, Kat," Joe admitted.

Kat's face fell and her stomach plummeted. "Joe, I . . ."

"Don't worry." He held up a hand and flapped it at her. "I'm not *in* love with you. I've loved spending time with you, and I realize I love you like a sister."

"I feel the same," she admitted. "You're like a brother to me." Which explains why she'd never once felt a spark of attraction to Joe, much as she genuinely liked him.

"My brother on the other hand," he continued, leaning closer to whisper in Kat's ear. "I don't think he could say the same."

"You don't think he loves me?" Kat asked.

Joe gave her a look that seemed to imply she was being an idiot. "Do you love him?" Joe asked.

Was it possible to feel like you were falling when you were sitting down? Kat gripped the couch cushion, holding on with both hands. Joe's question pulled the rug out from under her. "I . . . I don't know."

Then he did something Kat was completely unprepared for. He stuck out his tongue and said, "*Pbbbbbbbt.*"

Kat blinked. Did that just happen? Joseph O'Sullivan had blown raspberries at her. "Joe," she said slowly. "Are you feeling all right?"

"I'm fine," Joe said, beaming angelically. "Ffffffine," he repeated, drawing the *eff* sound out in an extended whistle of air.

Kat stared at the notoriously calm, cool, collected oldest O'Sullivan brother. Joe's usually pleasant, albeit restrained smile was wide and goofy, and his dark brown eyes shone. "You're definitely not fine," Kat said. She glanced at the punch glasses again, relieved she'd stopped at one.

"Hey," Mick said, appearing without preamble next to Kat. "Is Joe okay?"

"I think he's drunk." She pointed at the empty glasses. "What did your sister put in that punch?"

"Enough whiskey to fell a horse," Mick grumbled. "Or an O'Sullivan." He gave Kat a once-over. "How are you feeling?"

Aside from realizing I think I'm in love with you? "Fine. I only had one glass."

"That's one glass too many, with your tolerance," Mick said. "I'm taking you home tonight."

CHAPTER 27

Mick

"Thanks for driving me," Kat said as Mick opened his car door for her.

"Well, my brother was certainly in no condition to do it." Secretly, he was grateful for the excuse to be alone with Kat. After nearly a month of avoiding her, it was time they talked. Cleared the air. At least got back to being friends.

Mick glanced at her. How was it was possible she'd gotten even more beautiful? Her blond hair fell in soft waves over her shoulders, cheeks pink from the December air.

These last few weeks had been agony, watching Kat spend time with his brother. In reality, she was spending time with his entire family. But Mick couldn't help scrutinizing every interaction between Joe and Kat. Trying to decipher every look and every touch they shared.

From what he could see, there didn't seem to be anything there—not a single spark of attraction—definitely not what had been there when he'd kissed her, when he'd touched her.

Mick had tried to think of Kat as a sister but quickly realized that was never going to happen. Instead, he'd done his best to avoid her. Which was shitty of him, considering he had promised to be her friend.

But it's not like she'd reached out to him either. From the moment on Thanksgiving when he'd pushed her toward Joe, Kat had given Mick the cold shoulder. There'd been a second tonight, when they'd first run into each other and made the awkward discovery they were wearing the same sweater, that he thought she was going to open up to him, to say something more than the cursory greetings they'd been exchanging. And then Joe had reappeared, and Mick was reminded of the fact she wasn't there to see him.

"Did you have fun tonight?" he asked, more to break the awkward silence than anything.

"I did," she chuckled. "Even without the massive amounts of whiskey, your parents know how to throw a party."

"They have definitely embraced the motto to live life to the fullest," Mick agreed, and found himself chuckling too. "What about your parents?" he ventured. "How are they doing?"

The mood in the car immediately shifted, and Mick swore the temperature dropped a good ten degrees.

"My parents are fine," Kat said. "Very busy." She looked out the car window and muttered, "Very, very busy."

Kat still did not like discussing her parents. Noted.

Luckily, they'd arrived at Kat's place. Mick pulled around to the back. "Can I walk you up?" he asked, finagling for at least a little more time with her.

She nodded.

As their footsteps echoed on the cold pavement, Mick sent up a prayer for snow. Any excuse for him to stay the night again.

Kat paused and glanced up at the sliver of clear night sky visible between the buildings. "It's almost midnight," she said. "Nearly Christmas."

"Looking for Santa?" Mick asked, following her gaze.

"Actually, I was looking for snow," she admitted.

Mick's heart skipped a beat. Was she hoping for the same thing? Then he recalled what she'd said before. How she always wanted it to snow on Christmas. "I hope you get your Christmas snow," he said, throat tight. "I hope you get everything you want."

She chuckled softly. "Sometimes, it takes me a while to figure that out."

"Figure what out?"

"What I want." Kat turned to look up at him. In the shadowed light of the entryway, her eyes seemed so blue he felt like he was standing at the edge of a pool, the depth unknown. He wanted to dive in and explore those depths. "And right now," she said, her voice low and husky, "I want you to come upstairs."

A shiver of need raced up his spine. "What about Joe?" he blurted out. "Sorry," he added immediately after. "That was presumptuous. You could be inviting me up for coffee. Or need me to fix you hedgehog's wheel again."

"JoJo's wheel is working perfectly. Thank you for that, by the way."

"You're welcome."

She licked her lips. "As for me and Joe, well, there is no me and Joe."

"Oh."

She turned and entered her building.

Oh. Mick followed her inside and up the stairs, mind buzzing with questions. What had happened at the party tonight?

"You're thinking so loud I swear I can almost hear you," Kat said, unlocking the door to her apartment. "What's wrong?"

"I thought Joe was everything you wanted. You had your Mr. Right in the bag. Wasn't that the plan?"

"That was the plan," she agreed, closing and locking her door. "If I sealed up my list for Mr. Right and mailed it to Santa, Joe would be who I'd find under the tree." She turned to face him. "Until I realized he was all wrong for me."

For a moment, his heart stopped beating. "What made you change your mind?"

"You."

That one word jump-started his heart, sending it into overdrive. "Me?"

She nodded. "The reason it was so clear to me that Joe was wrong was because I finally realized what I should have known all along. What I refused to see even when it was staring me right in the face. What you even tried to make me see."

Mick thought he knew the answer, but he still had to ask. Had to hear her say the words. "And what's that?"

"The right one for me is you."

The blood was rushing in his ears, heart pounding so fast he thought he might pass out. "Are you sure?"

"You're the one I want, Mick," Kat said bluntly. "Is there a chance you still want me?"

Kat didn't need to ask Mick twice. She barely needed to ask him once. The words had hardly left her lips before his mouth was on hers. Mick groaned. "God, yes." His hands braced against the sides of her face, as if to make sure she was real. He'd been fantasizing about kissing her again for so long, this could be a dream.

But it wasn't. Kat was real and warm and solid. She smelled like flowers and winter moonlight and tasted like licorice and honey and lemon and whiskey, and Mick couldn't get enough. He walked her backward, moving her toward the couch because there was no way he was braving that papasan again.

Kat collapsed onto the cushions. He was about to join her, but she stopped him with a hand on his belt. He stood, watching with rapt attention as her deft fingers unfastened his buckle and tugged the button of his fly open.

Holy shit, they were moving fast. Mick swallowed a groan as she slid his zipper down over his growing erection. Or maybe this wasn't fast, considering all that had passed between them already.

"Mick?" Kat asked.

"Yeah?"

Her fingers slid beneath the waistband of his boxers. "Can I touch you here?"

"You're asking permission?"

"Mm-hmm." Her hand inched closer to the tip of his achingly hard shaft. "Well?"

"Yes." He nodded vigorously. "Please and thank you."

She laughed, the sound still vibrating in her throat as she took him in her mouth.

Oh fuck. Mick dropped his head back and closed his eyes. Her tongue swirled around the hood, and his balls clenched in response. *Oh sweet Jesus.*

Kat shifted on the couch, moving closer, taking him deeper. Her hair tickled his belly and her full breasts pressed firmly against his thighs. Her breasts. Oh god, her sweet perfect breasts. Mick's eyes snapped open. He wanted to see her, touch her.

But as his gaze adjusted to the dimly lit room, his attention was caught by the fixed stare of Kat's pet hedgehog. *Well, this is awkward.* Mick tapped Kat on the shoulder. "Uh, Kat?"

She released his cock, rocking back to look up at him. "Is something wrong?"

The sight of Kat's wet full lips, swollen from sucking him off, almost pushed Mick over the edge right there, but their unexpected voyeur held him in check. "I hate to interrupt, believe me I do, but, um, we have an audience." He gestured in the direction of the cage.

Kat turned, giggling when she realized what he meant. "JoJo, you prickly perv." She scooted off the couch and headed for her bedroom, clothes dropping as she went. "Are you coming?"

"Dear god, I hope so," Mick muttered, following after her. By the time he caught up to her, she was already nearly naked, kneeling on her bed in nothing but scarlet panties and matching bra tied with a bow across the chest that made her tits look like a present.

"Holy shit," Mick wheezed. "Merry Christmas to me."

"Do you like it?" Kat glanced down at herself. "I thought it was so cute."

"Cute?" Mick croaked. "Your pervy hedgehog is cute. This." He traced a finger over the neatly tied ribbon covering her nipples. "Is fucking sexy as fuck."

"Fucking sexy as fuck?" Kat echoed, snickering.

"Sorry." Mick tugged on the ribbon. "Your incredible tits are making my brain short circuit."

"Ah yes. Boob Brain," she said, clucking her tongue. "I've seen this condition before."

"Any suggestions for a cure?" he asked.

The corner of her mouth quirked in a teasing grin. "Take two and call me in the morning."

Mick guffawed. "That was terrible," he said.

"Yeah, but you're laughing, aren't you?" she shot back.

"True," he admitted. He liked this. This playful teasing between them. The easy banter. The friendship Mick thought he'd lost was still there between them. He finished untying the ribbon, baring her breasts to his hungry gaze. *Feast*. That's the only message his brain was sending.

Maybe there was such a thing as Boob Brain. Because all Mick could think about was burying his face in her breasts, licking, nipping, sucking, biting. "I want to taste you," he said and dipped his head, circling his tongue around one taut rosy nipple.

Kat let out a sharp exhale, arching her back, filling his mouth with more of her soft, sweet, flesh.

She moaned. "That feels so good."

"You taste so good," he said, guiding her down to the pillows. He paused to strip off his sweater.

She propped herself up on her elbows, watching him. "We wore the same sweater tonight," she said.

"I know." He shucked off his jeans. "Weird, huh?"

"Maybe it was fate," she suggested.

He kicked off his boxer briefs and joined her on the bed. "You sound like my mother."

"Ack! Don't tell me I sound like your mother while you're crawling into bed *naked* with me." Kat swatted at him. "Quick, save the mood with some dirty talk."

"Um, okay." Mick drew a blank. Finally, something popped into his head, and he lowered his voice into what he hoped was a tone that sounded erotic and sensual and said, "I'm going to fill your moist cave."

"NO!" Kat shrieked, giggling. "No using that word—ever."

"What word?" Mick asked, though he knew exactly which

one she meant. "How about I say something about my turgid rod instead?" He crawled toward her on the bed and growled, "I'm going to put my sword in your sheath."

She giggled again. "You sound like one of Babcia's romance novels."

"Probably because I got the idea from my gran's romance novels." Mick slid her hair back so he could press his lips to the delicate curve of her neck.

"Wait." Kat backed out of kissing range. "You read romance novels?"

"I used to," he said, inching forward, intent on getting another taste of her. "You're so soft. Do you know how soft you are? Your skin. Your hair. Silk and satin."

"Yes, I know. I'm very particular about my bath products." Kat dodged his advances, nudging his chin to look at her. "Do you still read romances?"

"Sometimes," he admitted. "Don't laugh."

"Why would I laugh? I read them too." The corner of Kat's lip curled with mischief. "I would sneak them from Babcia's shelves until eventually she caught me."

"What did your grandma do?"

"Took me to the secondhand shop and let me pick out five of my own."

Mick grinned. "I knew I liked Babcia."

"Well, she likes you too." Kat tugged on his shoulder, urging him to snuggle closer again.

"Really?"

She nodded.

His grin stretched so wide his cheeks hurt. "Now, that's some dirty talk."

"Did your gran know you were reading her romance novels?"

"I think so." Mick stroked a hand over Kat's shoulder, letting his fingers drift lazily down the silken skin of her bare back. "I'm not sure, but I always had a feeling Gran would leave them lying around on purpose for me to find. Like she thought she was providing some kind of sex-ed course."

"Oh dear." Kat smirked. "So how long before you discovered that simultaneous orgasms aren't real?"

"What?" Mick asked in faux shock. He lifted his head and stared down at her. "They're not?"

"Not all the time, anyway." Kat shoved his head back into the pillow. "They're like a sexual unicorn."

"I read a unicorn romance once," Mick said, struggling to maintain a straight face. "If I recall, the horn came in very handy."

"Argh!" Kat groaned. "Now you're ruining unicorns for me."

"Maybe it wasn't a unicorn book," he conceded. "But there was definitely a horse on the cover."

"There's always horses on the cover," Kat insisted haughtily. "Stallions," she added, eying him saucily. "It's a metaphor."

"I see," Mick said.

"For the hero's studliness," she explained. "Get it? *Stud*-liness."

"Oof." Mick cringed. "That might be worse than your boob brain joke." He dug his fingers into her ribs, tickling her.

Kat burst into giggles again, wriggling and writhing beneath him.

All that squirming around was having an effect. "Hold still," he ordered, fighting for control as his cock sprung up between them, heavy and thick, and entirely too eager.

"Oh my," Kat whispered. The lightness of the mood shifted. Still playful but edged with hunger. Her fingers wrapped around his shaft. "Well, this feels very . . . *turgid*."

A husky laugh escaped him as his hips twitched.

"Slow down, cowboy," she said, pulling away to dig in her nightstand drawer. "We need a sheath for that sword."

"You're mixing your metaphors," Mick teased, impressed his brain was working at all as she rolled a condom down his hard length.

"Am I?" Kat guided him between her legs, nipping his earlobe as she whispered, "Then let's try and catch ourselves a unicorn."

CHAPTER 28

Kat

Early morning sunshine drifted across Kat's face, the warm light flickering against her eyelids. She stirred and stretched luxuriously, enjoying the pull on her muscles, the tenderness between her thighs. Kat rolled to her side, but when she opened her eyes, Mick wasn't there.

Did he leave? Her heart gurgled, sputtering like it was Mr. Pokey the coffee maker. She clutched her chest, feeling the beats chug along erratically. They'd slept together, and he bailed. It had happened before. With guys she'd believed had cared about her. So why wouldn't it happen again?

The fear she'd tried to smother roared to life, devouring all the oxygen in her lungs. Kat struggled for air, her breaths coming shorter and faster. She was on the verge of a full-blown panic attack when she heard Mick's voice drifting in from the living room. She grabbed the sheet off the bed and wrapped it around herself. As she came around the corner, Kat nearly melted at the oddly domestic scene taking place before her.

Mick was crawling around on his hands and knees, building an obstacle course for JoJo.

Brain still recovering from her moment of panic, Kat blurted out the first thing that came into her head. "You're wearing my sweatpants," she said, noting her college mascot stamped across his ass.

"Morning!" Mick's gaze was warm, his smile tender as he greeted her. "Merry Christmas."

"Merry Christmas," Kat said, heart percolating smoothly now.

It dawned on her that she'd never spent Christmas morning with a guy before. Ever. She placed a hand on her chest. The ache was still there, but different—sweet instead of bitter. The hollow space felt like it had been filled with dandelion fluff. Hundreds of tiny seeds waiting for her to exhale and make a wish. Nearly weightless, but full of possibility.

Kat took in the elaborate setup spread out over her living room. "How long have you been working on this?"

Mick shifted to his knees and rocked back, resting on his heels. "Since four. I woke up and couldn't go back to sleep so I decided to keep JoJo company." He adjusted the track the hedgehog was scooting along on, making sure it connected to the next. "Your pet really loves to run."

"JoJo can go all night long." Kat grinned and circled behind Mick, bending down to whisper in his ear. "Lots of stamina." Then she leaned forward, pressing her breasts against his back. "Maybe we should test your stamina."

A gurgle of sound escaped Mick. From her vantage over his shoulder, Kat had a birds-eye view of the effect her suggestion had on him. Her sweatpants didn't leave much to the imagination. Turgid indeed.

She moved against him, letting the sheet drop so the tips of her nipples scraped across the bare skin of his shoulder blades. "What do you think?"

"I think, if you keep that up, we're going to be going for speed, not distance," Mick warned her. He quickly deposited JoJo into her cage and tugged Kat toward the bedroom.

His eagerness pleased her. Made her feel wanted. Desired. But it was more than that. Mick seemed to cherish her. Kat felt it in every kiss he pressed to her skin. Sensed it in the way his eyes held hers as his arms wrapped around her.

He was looking at her now, dark gaze brimming with admiration. "You're so beautiful," he whispered, stroking her cheek. "So very, very beautiful."

While Kat appreciated the compliment, a twinge of discomfort stirred. An echo of old wounds. Past fears.

As if sensing the shift in her mood, Mick pulled back. Sitting up, he said, "I know it can be difficult for couples when one person is much hotter than the other," he said, and then paused before adding, "I hope you're okay dealing with the fact that I'm the hot one."

It took Kat a moment to register what he'd said. Then she snorted with laughter.

"What's so funny?" Mick demanded, thrusting his hips against her. "I thought I proved to you last night that I was a sexy stud."

"Very sexy," she agreed, meeting his next thrust.

A blast of music filled the room.

"Fuck!" Mick rolled off her so fast he tumbled from the bed. "Fuck," he cursed again.

The music continued playing. "What is that?" Kat asked, peeking over the edge of her bed, bemused.

"It's whatever crap my sister listens to," Mick grumbled, searching the chaos on the floor for his phone. The music stopped. "Shit, I missed her call," he said, finally locating his phone in the pocket of his jeans. A chime came a second later and Mick checked the text.

"Everything okay?"

Mick nodded. "Mary-Kate is reminding me to get my 'sorry ass home in time for brunch,'" he said, making air quotes with the fingers of one hand while he read.

"How much time do you have?" Kat asked, letting the sheets slip from a few strategic areas.

He shifted his gaze back to the bed, eyes traveling slowly over Kat's body. Mick licked his lips. "Not enough time for that," he said hoarsely. "Why don't you come with me?" He suggested as he began pulling on his clothes.

"To Christmas brunch?"

Mick nodded and tugged the sweater over his head. He stared down at it in confusion, it was much too snug.

"You look like Winnie-the-Pooh." Kat's lips twitched. "I believe that one's mine."

"Oh." He chuckled, pulling off Kat's sweater and retrieving his own. "Right."

"Your mom did invite me," Kat admitted.

"When?" Mick asked, smoothing the properly fitting sweater over his torso.

"Last night. When I was at the party. Before . . ." She paused.

"Before you realized Joe wasn't the right brother for you and you banged me instead?"

"I don't know if I'd phrase it quite so poetically," Kat grumbled.

Mick sat on the edge of her bed and began pulling on his socks. Mismatched, as usual.

The sight brought a soft smile to Kat's lips, but her heart was heavy with sudden doubts. Was she falling back into old habits? Mick's summary may have been a little crude, but it was accurate. Last night, she'd told Joe she wasn't interested in dating him and then immediately found herself in bed with Mick.

Kat retraced the evening's sequence of events. At every turn, she'd been the one to push for more with Mick. At first, when Joe had sensed something was going on and asked if they'd needed a minute, she'd said yes, but Mick had said no. And if Joe hadn't gotten wasted on his sister's punch, Mick probably wouldn't have driven her home last night, and none of the things that followed after would have happened. Even when they'd arrived at her place, Kat had been the one to invite Mick upstairs. She'd basically thrown herself at him.

Sure, Mick had reciprocated immediately and seemed more than happy to run the bases with Kat once she'd thrown the first pitch, but what if she hadn't? What if she'd left it up to him? Would he have said anything? Would he have come upstairs? Would he be with her now?

At Thanksgiving, she'd waited for Mick to give her a sign.

Show her in some way that he wanted to be more than just her friend. But instead, he'd basically handed her off to his brother.

The fact that at the time, Mick thought that's what she wanted was irrelevant. If he wanted her, why didn't he fight for her? And what about now? Their time together had been amazing, but had Mick ever said he had feelings for her? Did she admit she had feelings for him? She'd said she wanted to be with him, but she'd never said she loved him. And he hadn't said the words either.

No . . . they'd jumped right to the fucking. Typical Kat.

Kat smoothed a hand over the mattress. "Maybe it's better if I don't come with you."

"Why?" His hand traced the curve of her hip. "Are you worried they'll know you spent Christmas Eve riding my sleigh?" He leaned forward to give her a kiss, but Kat recoiled.

"Sorry," he said, immediately contrite. "Was that euphemism too much?" Mick brushed a strand of hair from her eyes, concern stamped on his features as he studied her face. "If you really don't want to come, I won't push you," he finally said. "But I hope you will. It would mean a lot to me. And I know it would mean a lot to my family."

His family. Mick's family had started to feel like Kat's family too. She'd never had a big Christmas morning, and the thought of spending time with them, of being wrapped in their glow, was something she wanted very much. "Okay," she finally said. "I'll come with you."

Twenty minutes later, Kat was ready. She'd washed up, barely doing more than scrubbing the important bits, before brushing her teeth, yanking on some fresh clothes, and dabbing on some makeup.

Kat found Mick waiting for her in the living room. He'd added another feature to the obstacle course and was currently walking JoJo through how to navigate it. As muddled as her feelings were about herself and Mick and the entire situation, she was still charmed by the interaction between this scruffy man and her spiky pet.

"I'm ready," she finally said, announcing her presence.

Mick turned in her direction, his deep brown eyes flickering with heat as he took in her outfit with obvious appreciation. "You look great," he said.

"Thanks."

"I'm glad you decided to come with me."

"I had planned to spend Christmas morning with my hedgehog." She glanced at JoJo, still running the new course Mick had set up. "But thanks to you, I'm sure she'll have fun without me."

"Let's bring her with," he suggested.

"Won't your family mind?"

"Please," Mick teased. "You've met my parents, right? A hedgehog at Christmas brunch will be the least weird thing to happen today."

"Okay," Kat said with a grin. "Sure. It will be fun to show JoJo off to your family."

"I'm excited to show *you* off," Mick said, pressing a kiss to her cheek. He wrapped an arm around her shoulders. "This time, I got the girl."

Kat stopped cold. "What's that supposed to mean?"

"Uh, nothing," Mick stammered.

But the look on his face told Kat there was more to it. She stared at him, waiting for an explanation, hoping she was wrong.

"I had a girlfriend who dumped me for Joe," Mick finally admitted. "But it happened a long time ago. It doesn't matter."

"It matters to me." *Let's just say there's a complicated history between my brothers when it comes to dating.* Mary-Kate's words floated through her memory. "Has this always been some kind of competition for you?" Kat asked, thorns twisting in her gut. "A game?"

"No," he said, throat working. "It's not like that."

"I am not a prize. A trophy to be paraded in front of your

brother." She shook her head. "I should have seen this coming. My radar has always been terrible." The bark of laughter that burst from her was caustic and cold. "No wonder I was attracted to you from the beginning." She'd been so worried she was focused on being with someone for the wrong reasons; that *her* issues would be what led to things not working out. But this wasn't her fault. This was Mick's insecurities getting in the way. His issues messing things up. "At least, now it all makes sense."

"Wait," Mick said, reaching for her. "You were attracted to me since the beginning?"

Kate gaped at him, dodging his hand. "That's all you heard?"

His face fell as he realized his mistake. "I'm sorry, Kat." Mick tried to stumble through an apology. "That's not what I meant. What I said was stupid. I wasn't thinking."

"You got one thing right," Kat said bitterly. The thorns spread through her chest, piercing her heart, sharp and stinging. "Maybe you weren't thinking, but that's how you really feel, isn't it?"

"No, not like that," Mick insisted again, then stopped. "Okay, yes, I'm not going to lie. It felt really damn good when you said it was me you wanted, not Joe. But this is not a game to me. You are not a prize."

Mick licked his lips, speaking faster, like he thought if he could get the words out quick enough, she'd believe him. "I wanted you to be happy, Kat. Whatever you wanted. Whoever you chose. And when I thought that was Joe, I was ready to walk away. But if it's me . . ." Mick's voice broke. He punched a fist to his chest. "If the person you want is me, Kat, please don't walk away from that—from us."

The ice in Kat's veins started to melt. Mick's words were so raw, and they rang true. She could feel her resolve crumble, her heart softening. But as Kat replayed Mick's words in her head, her thoughts snagged on one detail. "If you felt this way at Thanksgiving, why didn't you fight for me then?"

"I told you, I thought Joe was who you wanted."

"But you didn't even try!" Her voice was rising, but Kat didn't care.

"Why should I?" Mick said, voice rising too. "You didn't give me any reason to—"

"You needed me to *give* you a reason before you could act?" Kat scoffed. "I thought you said you had feelings for me. Isn't that reason enough to at least try?"

"You're twisting my words," Mick said, voice harsh with frustration.

"So you *don't* have feelings for me?"

"I do, but . . ." Mick hesitated.

"*But* what?" Kat echoed. "I'm not worth fighting for? Is that it?" The sting of those words was familiar, an old wound reopened. Kat didn't want someone who walked away when things got messy, who gave up when things got too hard. She wanted messy and real in for the long haul. And above all, Kat wanted someone who was willing to stay and fight. Fight with her and fight for her. This, Kat realized, was what she wanted most. The thing she couldn't compromise on.

"I picked *you*, Mick. Period," Kat said, voice breaking, mirroring the crack in her heart. "I wish you could see that . . . could understand." She shook her head. "But now I realize I made a mistake. I was wrong about you."

"Kat, please . . ."

"Forget it." Gathering herself together, she met his gaze. "I think you should leave."

He stared at her, face drawn with frustration.

Kat held her breath, wondering what he would do.

Mick grabbed his coat and, confirming her fears, walked out the door.

And Kat's heart broke just a little bit more. She reached for JoJo, curling the spiky warm ball against her chest. "Maybe he'll come back," she whispered. "He'll come back for us." Kat still wanted to believe Mick would fight for her.

She waited, even leaving the door to her apartment cracked open, ears straining, listening for his footsteps in the stairwell. Any second now, Mick would come running back down the hall, breathless, telling her he can't let her go.

But he didn't come. The next thing Kat heard was the slamming of a car door. She hurried to look out her window, just in time to catch Mick backing out of the parking space.

"It's for the best," she told JoJo, rubbing her pet's soft underbelly as she watched Mick's car speed out of the alley. "I did the right thing."

It was better this way. Kat told herself. Better to know now. Better to let go before she had anything to hold on to. But as Kat stared at the empty parking spot, she couldn't help wondering; if telling Mick to go had been the right thing to do, why did it feel so wrong?

CHAPTER 29

Kat

Kat contemplated hiding in the shower forever . . . or maybe at least until next year. She let the water pour over her, willing it to rinse away the memory of this morning, take all the pain and frustration and hurt and confusion and wash it down the drain. In the end, she finally had to turn off the faucet. The water stopped, but the memories remained, heart feeling as cold and shriveled as her pruney skin.

But it was Christmas, and Kat was determined not to be sad on Christmas. Though she'd missed out on brunch with the O'Sullivans, she still had dinner with Babcia to look forward to. Between church and her friends at the retirement home, her grandmother's holiday schedule was very busy, but she always reserved Christmas dinner for Kat.

Considering how well Babcia could read her moods, Kat decided it was impressive that she made it all the way to dessert before her grandmother set down her napkin and declared, "Okay, Kotku, tell me what's wrong."

Kat was also impressed with herself when she managed not to cry as she told her grandmother what had happened with Mick.

"Mick?" Babcia narrowed her eyes, the icy blue of her gaze piercing Kat. "I thought you said you weren't seeing him. That it was the other one you were interested in . . . his brother."

"I thought I wanted Joe . . . he's everything I believed I was looking for." Kat shook her head. "But it didn't feel right, no matter how much I wanted it to be."

"And Mick feels right?" Babcia asked carefully. "Are you sure, Kasia? You've thought you found the right one before."

"And been wrong, I know." The tears pricked her eyelids. So much for not crying. "For as long as I can remember, I've wanted to fall in love, wanted to believe I found the right person for me. I wanted it so badly, that over and over again, I pushed myself to imagine feelings were there that weren't . . . but with Mick, I *didn't* want to have those feelings but they are just *there*, and I don't think I can change them or make them go away."

"Why should these feelings have to go away?" Babcia asked.

"Because I messed things up! Everything is all messed up." Kat sniffled. "Or maybe it's me that's messed up."

"Nonsense." Babcia clicked her tongue. "But if there is a mess, we'll fix it." She pushed the plate of kolackies toward Kat and rose slowly to her feet. "First, I'm going to make us some tea. Then, you're going to start from the beginning and let's see what we can do about the ending, eh?"

Kat crammed a kolacky in her mouth and nodded. Between bites of cookie and sips of tea she told Babcia everything. Her grandmother already knew bits and pieces, and Kat filled in the missing details. By the time her teacup had been emptied twice, she'd caught Babcia up to the point when she'd kicked Mick out of her apartment.

"And now?" Babcia asked, looking at Kat thoughtfully. "What are you feeling now?"

"Sad," Kat admitted. "And confused. Usually, a breakup brings me a sense of clarity. Make me face issues that had always been there. See what was wrong in the relationship. Things I'd missed or ignored because I'd wanted it to work so much." Kat fiddled with the last cookie on the plate. "But this time, it's different."

"Maybe because Mick is different?" Babcia suggested.

Kat ate the last cookie, mulling over her grandmother's words as she chewed. Mick *was* different. Unlike anyone she'd been with. Someone she could count on and confide in. From the beginning, first and foremost, he'd been her friend.

Over and over again, she'd told him that's all she wanted. A friend. And Mick had honored that. Even this morning, when she'd told him to leave, he'd respected her wishes then too. That's what she wanted, right? Someone who listened to her, who put her wishes above their own. Made her happiness a priority.

Understanding flashed through Kat, and she swallowed hard, bits of crumbs stuck in her throat. She'd been upset because she felt like he wasn't fighting for her, when the truth was, he was fighting himself in order to give her what she wanted. Mick fought his own desires, put his own feelings aside, all for her.

And Kat had told him to get out.

She'd been wrong. And now she needed to try and make it right.

......

Boxing Day was not an official holiday in the United States. In fact, Kat wasn't exactly sure what Boxing Day was. All she knew was that the day after Christmas was always a busy day at the shop.

Kat was grateful for the excuse to stay busy. She threw herself into the chaos, rotating with Ronnie, assisting customers, and arranging orders. Work was so successful at helping Kat keep her thoughts at bay that when she turned around to see Mary-Kate walk through the door, she waved brightly, momentarily forgetting that everything was a clusterfuck.

Mary-Kate returned the wave and took in her surroundings, studying the shop with interest. "Wow, this place has some fabulous eco-friendly elements," Mary-Kate tapped her foot, "I'll bet this is bamboo," she said, then shifted her gaze from the floor to the ceiling. "Are those mineral-fiber ceiling tiles?"

"They are," Kat said with a nod. "Made mostly of recycled newspapers."

"There's a company out of Denmark making coffins from similar materials," Mary-Kate said. "This is fantastic!"

"The owner is really into conservation efforts. We plan to continue his green initiatives when we take over in the new year." A thrill shot through Kat. "I'd be happy to discuss more environmentally friendly options for funeral displays with you too."

"That'd be great." Mary-Kate's dark eyes lit up, and for a moment she reminded Kat of Mick so much it made her heart squeeze painfully. "I was worried you wouldn't want to talk to me."

"Why?" Kat blinked. "Oh, right." Memories from yesterday fell into place and her mood wilted faster than cheap roses. "Mick told you what happened?" Kat's heart squeezed even tighter. Did he send her?

"Mick doesn't know I'm here," Mary-Kate said, as if reading Kat's thoughts. "He'd probably kill me if he found out."

Mary-Kate's admission did nothing to help ease the pressure in Kat's chest.

"Actually, my brothers haven't said much of anything about anything." The youngest O'Sullivan sucked on her bottom lip, looking sheepish as she added, "I don't mean to pry, but . . . you left the Christmas Eve party with Mick instead of Joe and then you didn't come to brunch yesterday. My mom was really bummed not to see you again."

"I'm sorry." Kat's heart sank. "I would have liked to see your mom again too." She glanced around the shop. It was getting near closing. Laura was out on a final delivery run and Ronnie was refilling the display of premade bouquets. "Here," Kat said, moving to gather together some flowers. "Please give these to your mother." She handed the arrangement to Mary-Kate. "An I'm-sorry-I-missed-brunch bouquet."

"That's so sweet, but you don't have to do that," Mary-Kate began.

"No, I want to," Kat insisted. She surveyed the variety of

flowers, considering the meaning of each stem. She wanted to make a bouquet for Mick too, but what would it say? *I'm sorry, I was wrong. I miss you.* Making up her mind that she could at least do this one thing—extend an olive branch, as it were—Kat quickly put together a second bouquet. "And give this one to your brother," she said. "Mick," she added quickly, realizing that might not be clear.

"Oh, I know who they're for," Mary-Kate said slyly.

Kat narrowed her gaze. Had Mick talked to his sister? Mary-Kate had said her brothers hadn't told her much of anything, but she obviously knew something . . . it didn't matter. Mary-Kate was her friend and Kat wasn't going to ask her to get in the middle of anything. Besides playing messenger with flowers.

"Regardless of what happens with my brothers, I hope we can still be friends?" Mary-Kate asked.

"I was just thinking the same thing," Kat admitted. "I'd like that," she said, and meant it.

"Great," Mary-Kate said, relief evident in her voice.

Kat was relieved too. The last thing she wanted was to lose another friend. Mary-Kate had begun to feel like family. A sister, the way Julia and Andie were like sisters. "Hey," Kat said, inspiration striking, "are you busy this Friday?"

"As long as there isn't a work emergency, I'm free."

Kat chose not to think about what a work emergency for Mary-Kate would entail. She was getting better about the whole dead bodies—corpses—thing, but it was a journey. "How would you like to join me for CCC night?"

"CCC night?" Mary-Kate raised an eyebrow. "That isn't one of those direct-sales kind of parties, is it? I'm not going to end up going home with a bunch of leggings or nail stickers or essential oils, am I?"

"What?" Kat snorted. "No."

"Good, because I'm a sucker for that stuff."

"CCC stands for 'cocktails, carbs, and comedies.' It's a movie night where we watch rom-coms and binge on snacks."

"Where has this been all my life?" Mary-Kate said.

Kat grinned. She knew she liked her. "It's something I've been doing since college with my best friends—Andie and Julia—you might remember them from Halloween?"

"Of course, I remember them."

"Well, this Friday is our last CCC night before the new year." *And hopefully, not the last official CCC night ever,* Kat thought dismally.

She and her friends planned to stick to their monthly schedule, but with Julia living with Luke and Andie engaged and moving to Milwaukee, who knew how long before one month became two, then three, then six, then never. The thought didn't cause the panic it once had, but still left Kat feeling . . . bereft. The new bonds her friends were forming didn't cut the bonds they held with her, but they did pull everyone in different directions. She just had to trust the connection they shared would remain strong enough to stretch and not break.

And maybe, Kat thought, smiling at Mary-Kate, she could form some new bonds of her own. "So you'll come?"

"Wouldn't miss it," Mary-Kate promised.

CHAPTER 30

Kat

Three days later, Kat had reached her breaking point. Mick still hadn't called. Not even a text to thank her for the flowers. Kat wasn't expecting a big thank-you, but she had hoped for some kind of acknowledgment from him. The fact his silence cut so deeply told her she'd been holding out hope more than she realized . . . or at least more than she'd let herself admit.

She'd told him to leave. And as much as it frustrated her, Kat could, on a logical if not emotional level, understand why Mick wouldn't want to be the one to reach out. But she'd made the first gesture. Taken the first step. Held out her hand, filled with flowers, no less.

It had taken every ounce of self-control Kat had not to call Mick and ask him if he'd gotten the bouquet. She'd even managed to refrain from calling his sister. Mary-Kate had promised to give Mick the flowers, and Kat didn't want to put her friend in the middle of things more than she already had. It wouldn't be fair. So Kat waited. And waited some more.

She tried to bury her frustration with work. But even that backfired, because by Thursday afternoon, Ronnie had finally had enough of Kat's moping and ordered her to take the following day off. "Your crappy mood is messing with the store's energy," Ronnie declared. "Go home. Have a good cry. Wrap yourself in a cocoon of wine and chocolate and emerge like the bold, beautiful, badass butterfly I know you are."

Arguing with Ronnie was pointless. Kat had tried to tell them she didn't need a day off, but even Laura had agreed. Outnumbered, Kat had finally acquiesced. She knew the two of them could handle the store without her for a day, and maybe Ronnie was right. Maybe some time wallowing was exactly what she needed to shake free of her bad mood. Get as sad and low as she needed so she could crawl out on the other side.

That night, Kat decided to take Ronnie's advice. If she was going to wallow, she might as well do it properly. First, she opened a bottle of wine and put in an order for an obscene amount of sushi. Then she dug in her drawer for some appropriately grungy lounge clothes.

She sniffled at the memory of Mick wearing her sweatpants, the elastic cuffs only reaching mid-shin, her school's mascot stretched across his backside while he crouched on all fours, building JoJo an obstacle course as a Christmas gift. Kat tried to reel her emotions in, but her chin wobbled, lips trembling. He was such a sweetheart. And a weirdo. Why had he put a pair of her pants on in the first place? For some reason, the thought she might never get a chance to ask Mick about that made Kat cry harder.

By the time her sushi arrived, Kat was a sniveling mess. She thanked the delivery guy with a tearstained tip and proceeded to cry all over her shrimp tempura roll while watching *The Notebook*. No romantic comedies tonight. She needed angst. She needed melodrama. She needed the unabashed manipulation of heartstrings. Proper wallowing called for a Nicholas Sparks marathon.

The hours passed in a haze of chardonnay and conventionally attractive white people having emotional outbursts in the rain. Kat must have fallen asleep at some point, because she snored loud enough to wake herself up. She blinked, bleary-eyed, and glanced around the room. JoJo was running on her nearly silent wheel. Kat almost wished the darn thing would start squeaking again. The fact it didn't was another reminder of Mick. Another example of his thoughtfulness.

He'd called her princess. Kat's heart folded in on itself, as if she could tuck away the note he'd left her inside one of its chambers.

Her mood dipped even lower, and Kat pried herself off the couch and foraged for some chocolate. After successfully locating a bag of peanut butter cups, she decided it was time to break out the big guns. It was time for *Titanic*. She'd watched the epic love story of Jack and Rose for the first time with Babcia. She'd been about six when her grandmother had brought home the VHS tapes. A little young for the content of the movie? Maybe, but this was the same grandmother who let her read Johanna Lindsey when she was in grade school.

For years, even though Kat was abstractly aware that the historic ship sank, she didn't realize the movie ended in tragedy, because Babcia refused to play the second tape. It had been at a slumber party in high school when Kat finally watched the full version and bawled her eyes out.

She was bawling her eyes out now, as Rose clung to Jack's hand while he slowly froze to death. Kat climbed onto the coffee table with JoJo cuddled in her arms. "Don't worry, I won't let you go," she whispered to the hedgehog. And she didn't. She held on tight. Lying on her side, Kat curled her body around JoJo and closed her eyes. She drifted off again, only to startle awake at the sound of an Irish tin whistle.

Still groggy, Kat recognized the music of the closing credits. "The movie's over, JoJo," she murmured, shifting to pet the hedgehog. With a start, Kat realized that JoJo was no longer snuggled up next to her.

Fear shot through Kat like she'd been plunged into the icy waters of the Atlantic. "JoJo?" Kat torpedoed into a sitting position. Her head swished and her stomach heaved like she was on the deck of the sinking ship. She groaned, immediately regretting the sudden movement.

But she had to focus. JoJo was missing. Kat glanced around frantically. "JoJo? Where are you?" Oh god, she'd promised to never let go and she had. She was as bad as Rose, letting Jack turn into a popsicle and sink into the ocean when everyone knew there had to be some way both of them could have survived on that damn piece of wood. "JoJo?" she called, almost hysterical now.

A scratching sound came from below her. Kat slid to the edge of the coffee table and peered underneath, relief washing through her at the sight of the chunky ball of spikes puttering around inside the empty candy bag. She scrambled off the table and picked up her hedgehog, dancing around the room as Celine Dion sang about her heart going on.

Unable to resist, Kat joined in, singing along as if her life depended on it. She held JoJo aloft like she was Jack standing at the bow, encouraging Rose to close her eyes and feel the wind. It felt good to let go, to let loose and fly.

Kat twirled around in time with the music, promising JoJo there was nothing to fear. But as she whirled in a circle again, she almost dropped the hedgehog. Hovering in her apartment doorway, wearing twin expressions of shocked bemusement, stood Andie and Julia.

"Ack!" Kat stumbled, almost dropping JoJo. "Haven't you two ever heard of knocking?"

"We did," Andie said, smirking. "Several times."

"And called too," Julia added. "Several more times."

Kat glanced around the disheveled state of her apartment. She had no idea where her phone was at the moment, though if she had to guess, it was lost in the depths of her couch, sinking out of reach like the Heart of the Ocean. "Well, don't just stand there gawking," she grumbled, embarrassment making her snippy, "come on in."

Her friends did as instructed, closing the door and navigating around the flotsam.

"That key was supposed to be for emergency use only," Kat said, cuddling JoJo in one hand and clicking off her TV.

"This is an emergency," Julia said. "We were worried about you. The whole not-answering-your-phone-all-day tends to cause concern."

"I'm fine," Kat insisted.

"That's debatable," Andie snarked, pulling a candy wrapper out of Kat's hair.

"Ronnie told us you took the day off," Julia added. "You *never* do that."

"Yeah, well, I needed to wallow," Kat said. "I took a wallowing day, okay?"

"Hey, wallow away," Julia said. "We've all been there."

"But what happened to make you go all Bridget Jones in here?" Andie asked.

"I did not go all Bridget Jones . . ." Kat stopped, taking in the wineglasses and takeout boxes and peanut butter cup wrappers littering her living room, not to mention her own disgusting state. "Okay, fine. Like I said, I was wallowing."

Julia picked up an empty wine bottle from the floor and set it on the coffee table. "Did something happen with Joe?"

Kat shook her head. "No." She paused and reconsidered that. "Well, yes and no." She settled JoJo in her pink palace. "It's mostly Mick."

"I knew it," Andie crowed. "I told you so!"

"Not a great time to gloat," Julia chided gently.

"Right," Andie said. "But I did tell her so."

"I remember," Kat snapped. "And you were right, okay?" The fact her friends hadn't known she'd been upset enough to lock herself in her apartment and go all Bridget Jones made her even sadder. It wasn't that long ago they would have been aware of everything right after it happened, often even as it was happening, and would have been there to drink and carb load and cry and sing Celine Dion songs badly with her.

Over the past few months, Kat had keenly sensed the distance as their worlds drifted further apart. She shoved her hand between the couch cushions and fumbled around, searching for her phone. "I'm sorry I missed your calls." Her fingers brushed the edge of her phone and she tugged it free. "And texts," she added, as she pulled up the home screen and saw the string of messages. Then she noticed the date.

Shit. Kat sank onto the couch. "It's Friday?"

"Uh, yeah," Andie said, clearing space on a cushion and joining Kat. "Friday afternoon."

"What's going on, Kitty Kat?" Julia asked, taking the seat on Kat's other side.

Bookended by her best friends, Kat wanted nothing more than to curl up in their laps and unload everything that had happened since their last CCC night. At the same time, she didn't want to spend what could be their last CCC night ever rehashing her problems. "A lot," she finally said.

Julia pulled Kat's head down to rest on her shoulder. "I didn't know. I should have checked in more. I've been so busy trying to keep up at work, and now that Luke and I are sharing a place . . . I'm sorry."

"I'm sorry too," Andie said. "I've been so completely focused on packing for the move and prepping for my new job that I haven't thought about anything else."

"That's right." Kat sat up straighter. "You're going to be coaching a new team next year." Kat had forgotten that as part of her move to Milwaukee, Andie had taken a new coaching position. New city, new home, new job . . . "I owe you both an apology as well," Kat admitted. "I've been obsessed with how you're both moving on with your lives and hung up on how it's affecting my life, I never stopped to think about how hard it must be for you to deal with these changes. I've been a crappy friend."

"I think it's fair to say we all could have been better friends lately," Julia surmised. "So tonight, let's cut the crap and hit the refresh button."

"On that subject," Andie glanced at Kat. "Kitty Kat, I'm going to tell you what I tell my players. And I say this with love. Hit the showers, because you are funky."

"You are rather ripe," Julia agreed, nudging Kat toward the bathroom. "Go wash up. Andie and I will take care of this mess."

"We will?" Andie asked.

"Yes, we will," Julia said firmly.

Kat laughed. Their banter made it feel like old times.

When she emerged a little later, showered, dressed, and candy-wrapper free, Kat discovered her apartment was neat as a pin, all remnants of her night of sad-girl shenanigans erased. And the two little elves responsible for the cleanup were currently occupied cooing over JoJo like she was a newborn baby.

The domestic sight triggered a moment of dissonance in Kat. It was strange to think that one of her friends would be getting married, let alone becoming a mother. Not that Kat put any stock in that old love-marriage-baby-carriage rhyme, but it was a pos-sibility, one that had always existed in the distant future but now suddenly seemed much more plausible.

"What?" Andie said, catching Kat staring at her while she cud-dled JoJo in her arms.

"Nothing," Kat said immediately.

But Kat's bemused face must have given her away because Andie looked at her and said, "Don't you dare think it."

"I'm not thinking anything," Kat declared innocently.

"Yes, you are," Andie insisted, handing JoJo to Julia. "You're making those googly eyes that you only do when you're thinking about weddings and babies, and . . . I don't know, freaking blue-birds and shit."

"Julia, do you have any idea what she's talking about?" Kat asked, feigning innocence.

"Sorry, Kat. You were totally making your googly baby face." Julia shifted her attention back to JoJo, speaking in a high-pitched, sugar-coated, talking-to-toddlers-and-puppies voice, "But how can you resist when in the presence of such cuddly cuteness?"

"Ugh," Andie groaned. "I have some important news I wanted to tell you, but now you two are going to make it weird."

"You're pregnant," Kat guessed immediately.

"No!" Andie barked. "Why do you keep guessing that? Knock that shit off. It's weird, and while I don't care, you could hurt someone's feelings."

"Shit," Kat said. "You're right. I'm sorry. I wasn't thinking." Chagrined, she offered Andie an apologetic smile and said, "Let me start over. What's your news?"

Andie looked back and forth between Kat and Julia. After a dramatic pause, she announced, "Curt and I have picked a date for the wedding."

"Aaaah!" Kat shouted, wrapping her friend in a hug.

"When's the special day?" Julia asked.

"February fifteenth."

"Wow, that's great!" Kat nodded, relieved. "A whole year to plan."

"Um, more like a whole month." Andie's smile turned sheepish. "February fifteenth of *next* year."

Kat raised her eyebrows in surprise. "Are you serious?"

"Why the rush?" Julia asked. "Don't get me wrong, I'm excited for you, but six weeks to plan a wedding?"

"I know, it's a lot . . ." Andie brushed her short dark bangs out of her eyes. "I mean, not a lot of time, but a lot to do in not a lot of time," she continued, excitement making her ramble. "But it's going to be fine because Curt and I don't want anything too elaborate."

Julia snickered.

"I mean it! Curt and I agreed the most important thing is that we have all our friends and family there." Andie sobered. "That's why we decided to have it as soon as possible. Curt's grandma isn't doing well."

"Oh, Andie. I'm so sorry." Kat reached out and gave her friend's hand a squeeze.

"The good news is we're having the wedding here in Chicago instead of Milwaukee."

"That does make things easier," Kat agreed. "Especially if you still want me to do the flowers," she paused. "You do still want me to do the flowers, right?" she asked.

"Of course, I still want you to do the flowers!" Andie exclaimed. "And I really am sorry about the date. One of Curt's buddies works over at the Irish American Heritage Center. They had a spot open up unexpectedly, and it seemed like fate."

Fate. Kat got a little shiver at the word. She thought of Moira, declaring it had been fate that brought Kat into her family's lives. She shook herself. "I don't know about fate, but it does seem like too good an opportunity to pass by."

"It *is* lucky," Julia agreed. "That venue is one of the best kept secrets in the city." She shifted her gaze to Kat. "Do you think you'll be able to swing it? I know Valentine's Day is like the Superbowl of the floral industry."

"Not a bad way to describe it," Kat agreed. "But don't worry, I'll manage."

"You know what this means?" Julia asked, eyes flickering with excitement.

Andie and Kat exchanged glances. They knew better than to try and guess when Julia had her plotting face on. "What?"

"Galentine's Day Bachelorette Party!"

"Jules, you're a genius!" Andie bounced on her toes, almost vibrating with anticipation as she squealed, "I can't believe this is really happening!"

In that moment, all Kat felt was pure joy for her friend. She was thrilled to see Andie so happy. "I have some champagne I was saving for New Year's Eve, but maybe I should pop it now." She hurried into the kitchen to grab it but paused before popping it. "Should we open it at your place?" she asked Andie. "We are still doing CCC night tonight, right?"

"Abso-freaking-lutely," Andie said, grabbing the bottle and holding it up. "To the last CCC night ever!"

"The last?" Kat's glow of happiness dimmed at her friend's words. "Ever?"

"No, not the last," Andie immediately backtracked. "I meant the last in the old apartment."

"Right."

"Come on, Kitty Kat," Andie said. "Turn that frown upside down."

"Milwaukee isn't that far," Julia added. "We'll figure out how to keep CCC nights going."

"I know we'll try," Kat said, "but the fact is, we've been doing CCC nights in that apartment for almost a decade, and with Andie moving up to Milwaukee to live with Curt, I feel like this is the beginning of the end."

"Um, that's a touch too melodramatic," Andie said. "Even for you."

"Sorry." Kat swallowed and tried to dial it back, she knew she was being extra.

"If I may make a suggestion," Andie said. "Since we're all here already, let's have CCC night at Kat's place."

"That's a great idea," Kat exclaimed. "It will feel less like an ending and more like the start of something new."

"I like it," Julia agreed. "But what about the cocktails and carbs?"

Andie glanced at the champagne bottle she was still holding. "I guess I could whip up something with this."

"And I've still got a box of Babcia's kolackies left," Kat said.

"We've got the first two Cs covered. What about the comedy?" Julia tapped her chin. "How about a *Bridget Jones* marathon?"

"All three movies?" Andie asked. "That will take most of the night."

"What do you think, Kat?" Julia asked. "Should we turn this into a sleepover?"

She beamed at them. "A slumber party with my two besties is exactly what I need right now." Her smile faltered. "Wait, I almost forgot. Kat hesitated, suddenly nervous. "I, um, invited someone to CCC night."

"What?" Andie asked, the shock in her voice evident.

"Really?" Julia added, sounding equally surprised.

"I know it's always been just the three of us," Kat said, guilt pricking her like thorns. "I should have run this by you both first, but I invited her on impulse and yeah, add that to the list of things I did as a crappy friend."

"Seeing as your equally crappy friends were too busy with their own shit, I'd say you're forgiven," Julia said.

"It's fine with me," Andie agreed. "But you should probably let her know the party is at your place instead of mine."

Kat shook her head. "She was already planning to meet me here. We were going to drive over together."

"Even better," Andie said. "Do you think she can pick up a few things for the cocktails?" Andie asked. "I'll pay her back."

"Oooh, great idea," Julia said. "And ask her to grab snacks too."

"Excuse me," Kat said, feigning offense, "aren't Babcia's kolackies enough for you?"

"They would be," Julia teased, "except I know you're going to eat most of them."

"She's got you there, Kat," Andie laughed.

"Fine," Kat said, knowing full well they were right. When it came to kolackies, Kat was an unrepentant glutton.

By the looks of things when Mary-Kate arrived less than an hour later, she was an unrepentant glutton too. "Whoa," Kat said, greeting a bag-laden MK at her door.

"I went a bit overboard," Mary-Kate admitted. "It's been so long since I've gone to a slumber party, I got carried away."

Kat grinned, happier than ever that she'd invited Mary-Kate to join them. She led the way into her apartment and reintroduced everyone. "Julia and Andie, you remember Mary-Kate."

"From Halloween." Andie nodded. "You were the cereal killer."

"Guilty." MK raised a teasing hand. "Of bad puns, at least."

"Mick's sister, right?" Julia asked, reporter's gaze narrowed in speculation.

To her credit, Mary-Kate picked up on the implication immediately. "Again, guilty. But that doesn't give me the right to pry into his relationships."

"Very noble of you." Julia's mouth quirked. "But trust me, sometimes the best thing that can happen is a prying sibling."

"I'm so glad you said that," Mary-Kate confessed, spine relaxing as she exhaled. "Because when it comes to my brothers, I can't help meddling."

"Don't feel bad. They need you to meddle," Julia assured her. "If my boyfriend's sister hadn't talked some sense into him, I'm not sure he would have ever figured things out." She shrugged. "Luke's smart, so he might have, eventually, but definitely not as quickly."

"What?" Kat asked, genuinely surprised by this news. "Everything seemed to fall into place perfectly for you two. It was so fast, I thought it all happened like magic . . . like in the movies."

"Hardly," Julia laughed. "I mean, you remember how I never believed in fate and finding The One and all that . . ."

"I remember," Kat said, unable to keep the edge of bitterness from her voice. Meanwhile, she'd always believed, for all the good it did her.

"I'm sure this sounds super corny, especially coming from me," Julia admitted. "But I knew Luke was the one the moment I first met him. I had this . . . feeling, I can't really explain."

"There's a Japanese phrase for that," Mary-Kate said. "Not that I can pronounce it, but basically it means you know someone is your person from the moment you meet."

Kat turned to eye Mary-Kate in surprise.

"I've seen it in tattoo form before," she explained.

"I wonder if there's a phrase that says the opposite," Andie mused, smirking as she lined glass rims with sugar, "because I couldn't stand Curt when I first met him."

Kat and Julia both broke into giggles over the memory of that meeting.

"That's right," Kat said, remembering Andie's initial impression of Curt.

"What changed?" Mary-Kate asked.

Andie poured some cranberry juice into each of the glasses. "Not sure, exactly." She shrugged. "There was something about him that got under my skin. And the more I thought about him the more I liked him. I definitely didn't think he was the one when we first met—but when he asked me to marry him?" She nodded and popped the cork on the champagne. "Yeah, then I just knew."

"I guess it doesn't matter when the moment happens that you realize you're with the one," Mary-Kate said, "as long as it happens." She sighed dramatically. "Like a romance novel."

Andie topped off each glass with champagne. "Can you imagine Curt on the cover of a romance?" she snickered.

Julia joined in, laughing as she added, "He'd be in his Packers jersey."

Kat's lips twitched at the image even as her heart hiccupped, recalling her night with Mick and their unexpectedly fun and sexy conversation about romance novels. Before she could get all sad and start feeling sorry for herself, Kat joined in the conversation. "With a mullet," she suggested. "Maybe Curt could grow one in time for the wedding,"

"In six weeks?" Andie chortled. "I doubt it."

"Wait, didn't I watch you two get engaged on Halloween?" Mary-Kate asked.

"Yep." Andie nodded, handing out the cranberry mimosas she'd finished mixing.

"And you're getting married in *six* weeks?"

"Yep." Andie nodded again. "The day after Valentine's Day."

"Wow." Mary-Kate's auburn eyebrows rose so high they

blended into the red curls brushing her forehead. "I guess you're right," she said, shaking her head in admiration. "When you know, you know."

"Cheers to that!" Andie agreed.

"You know," Kat said, sipping her mimosa thoughtfully. "Mick promised he'd my plus-one." Maybe this surprise rush wedding was exactly what she needed. Another unexpected solution to her problem she could chalk up to providence or fate or dumb luck.

"If there's one thing I know about my brother it's that he keeps his promises," MK assured Kat. "Did he explicitly promise he would go with you?"

"Why are you asking that?" Andie frowned, shoulders bunching like a dog whose hackles raise when anticipating a fight. Andie was a caretaker. Fiercely loyal. If she even got a whiff that one of her own was hurt or betrayed, the perpetrator better say their prayers. "Do you think he'll bail?"

"Not at all," Mary-Kate said easily, either oblivious or unintimidated by the waves of tension emanating off Andie. "My brother takes his word very seriously."

"Yeah, but isn't there some unspoken rule that if you're not together those promises are void?" Julia said. "Like an expired coupon or something."

Kat's stomach churned. "But we made a pact. He said no matter what happens, he'd be there for me."

"I guess if you're not sure how he feels about you, this can be the thing that decides it, huh?" Julia asked.

"True." Andie chimed in. "If Mick shows up to be your plus-one at my wedding, it's meant to be."

"I know I promised to stay out of it," Mary-Kate said quietly. "but do you want me to talk to my brother?"

"No." Kat shook her head. "I appreciate the offer, but I'd rather Mick figure this out on his own. Like Andie said, if it's meant to be, it will happen."

CHAPTER 31

Mick

In that surreal hazy week between Christmas and New Year's, Mick spent a lot of time drinking whiskey-laced eggnog and even more time thinking. As the clock struck midnight on New Year's Eve, he made a decision. He was done trying to contort himself to fit into someone else's mold. It was time he made a space for himself that was uniquely his. A role in the family business tailored to fit him.

On New Year's Day, Mick marched into Joe's office and announced to his brother that he planned to start offering grief counseling at O'Sullivan's.

Joe frowned. "Isn't this a bit sudden?"

"If more than six years of college, two degrees, and hundreds of clinical hours is sudden, then yes. Counseling is what I've always wanted to do."

"Why is this the first I'm hearing of it?"

"I needed to be sure before I talked to you," Mick said. "I'm serious about this."

"You were serious about the bar too. And now that we've invested the money in renovations and are booking receptions, you want to switch to something else?" Joe asked, incredulous.

"You already said you want to handle the scheduling," Mick pointed out. "And I've talked to Uncle Mike, he's willing to have the bar sign on as a permanent partner. He'll take the lead on running the event space. He was excited about it, two O'Sullivan businesses working together."

Joe shook his head as if he hadn't even heard what Mick said.

"This is so typical of you. Start something and quit. Are you even qualified to open a practice?"

"Yes, my qualifications are in order."

"Are you sure? You said it yourself. Two degrees. Not three." Joe ticked off his fingers. "You quit before you finished your doctorate."

Mick forced his jaw to unclench and bit out, "I didn't quit my Ph.D. program, I dropped out after mom and dad decided to retire early and left us in charge of the business."

"Please." Joe scoffed. "Mary-Kate and I would have found a way to manage without you."

His brother's words hit a nerve. "I gave up my dreams to be here. Do you really believe my contributions have been worthless?"

Joe sputtered, "That's not what I said."

"That's how I feel," Mick admitted. "I've tried to be whatever the family needed. But it's never enough. I'm never enough. Just like I wasn't enough for Elsi."

"Elsi?" Joe's brow furrowed. "What does she have to do with any of this?"

Like with a sore tooth, Mick was tempted to skirt around the pain. Avoid the raw tender places. But he'd let the bitterness and shame fester beneath the surface long enough. It was time to rip those feelings out. Wash the old wounds clean. "She chose you, Joey. I thought she wanted me. Maybe even loved me. But none of that mattered when she met you."

"Mickey, that was years ago." His brother's voice was quiet, and maybe Mick was imagining it, but he thought he sensed a hint of remorse. "We didn't even date that long."

"Right." Mick shook his head. "Because noble Joe didn't want to hurt my feelings."

"Not exactly." Joe shifted awkwardly. "I know I've let you think that all these years, but the truth is after a few weeks together, Elsi realized she didn't want me after all." Joe met his gaze, mouth scrunched into an awkward line. "She wanted you."

Mick's belly flipped. "Bullshit."

"I'm serious." Joe insisted. "Elsi never came out and said it, but I always got the feeling that she missed you. You were funnier. More interesting to be around. If you hadn't walled yourself off like a wounded troll the rest of that summer, you two might have gotten back together."

Mick shook his head. It was hard to reconcile this version of events with the memories he'd carried for so long. But his brother's words rang true. A snort of laughter escaped him.

"What's so funny?

"I always thought I needed to be more like you. Act like you. Dress like you. And now you're telling me I should just be myself?"

"You didn't know that already?" Joe raised an eyebrow. "The guy who almost earned his doctorate in psychology?"

"As it so happens, I recently figured it out." A slow, determined grin crept across Mick's face. "Regarding my psychology degree, I'm done playing Mick-of-all-trades, filling in the cracks and smoothing things over. I'm launching a counseling practice at O'Sullivan's. You can either get on board or get out of my way, because it's happening."

Joe stared at Mick, a slow smile spreading across his features, a new respect shining in his eyes.

······

Things happened quickly after that. With the full support of his family, Mick felt like he'd hit that rare magical moment downtown when every traffic light simultaneously turns green, and you could coast straight into the heart of the city. Within a month, his practice at O'Sullivan's was up and running.

Midway through February, Mick was spending a rare free afternoon reviewing session notes. The wall behind his desk featured an array of diplomas and certificates arranged in a semicircle. Joe had been the one to suggest it. At first, Mick thought it might be a tad obnoxious to hang all that stuff up, like some desperate attempt for people to take him seriously.

Despite Mick's initial reluctance, he realized his brother had been right. Maybe it was the old fake-it-till-you-make-it mindset, but the wall of wise, as Mick had christened it, did make him feel more accomplished. Worthy of the important work he did in this office. Joe had joked the wall stood in for the suit Mick never wanted to wear, offering a layer of built-in respectability. Since Mick still refused to wear a suit, he supposed the wall balanced things out.

Mary-Kate passed the door to his office, stopping when she noticed he was inside. "Do you have a minute?"

Before he could reply, his sister handed him half of the stack of paper she was holding. "Programs for the Bailey service tomorrow." She dropped into the chair across the desk. "You can help me fold."

They fell into an easy rhythm for a few minutes, creasing, folding, and smoothing, the rustling of paper a familiar comforting sound. His sister glanced around the room. "Looks good," she said, eyeing the wall display. "Very professional."

"That's the point." A half-hearted smile tugged at his mouth. He leaned back in his chair, kicking his feet onto the desk and hiking up his pants to show her his socks. "I even match now."

"Will wonders never cease," Mary-Kate teased, clasping her hand to her chest in mock surprise. She studied him for a moment. "Starting this practice has been really good for you, Mick. I'm proud of you."

"Thanks," he said, fidgeting with a paperweight. As much as he craved it, praise and admiration, especially from his siblings, still sat uncomfortably.

"When do you think you'll figure out the rest of your shit and stop moping around?"

"Excuse me?" Mick protested, the paperweight slipping from his fingers. "I have not been moping."

"You're not excused," MK said. "And you *have* been moping. It's not good for business. You're supposed to be cheering people up, not depressing them even more."

"I'll have you know that a grief counselor's job is not to cheer people up but to help them learn how to process grief," he explained with a touch of arrogance.

"Look, all I know is you're supposed to offer our clients a shoulder to cry on, not cry all over theirs."

Mick stiffened. "I have never cried on a client's shoulder."

"I meant it figuratively," Mary-Kate said, "though you might as well be crying for real, with the amount of pouting you do."

"I don't pout," Mick insisted, crossing his arms.

His sister stared at him. "You're pouting right now."

Mick grumbled and dropped his arms. This time, he didn't bother denying his sister's accusations, because he knew she was right.

"It's Kat, isn't it?" his sister asked quietly.

Again, he didn't bother to deny it. Mick sighed. "It's frustrating. I've been over it again and again, and I still don't understand what went wrong between us. I thought we really had something together."

Mary-Kat quirked an auburn brow. "As far as I can tell, so far all you two had was a one-night stand."

He shook his head. "You don't get it."

"Then explain it to me."

"There was so much more than sex between us. I mean, don't get me wrong, the sex was incredible—"

Mary-Kate covered her ears. "Skip the details, please."

"Fine." Mick grunted. "Bottom line is we had a real connection. It meant something to me. I thought it meant something to her too. I can't believe she walked away from it so easily." Even as he said it, the echo of his brother's words came back to haunt him.

"Oh really? I find that wildly ironic since that's exactly what *you literally did* to her." Mary-Kate stared at him across the desk. "You were the one to walk away." The scorn in his sister's voice was sharp and thick and eerily identical to Joe's.

But Joe was wrong. Mary-Kate was wrong. Fighting for his

place in the family, in the business, was one thing. Fighting for a place in the heart of someone that didn't want you was another. "This is different." Mick could hear the frustration building in his voice. "Kat told me to go."

She'd said Mick must not care for her because he wasn't willing to fight for her, but all he'd done was try to follow her wishes and do what she asked. No. What really must have happened was she'd realized her mistake. She didn't actually want to be with him. She hadn't chosen him over Joe. He'd been a convenient distraction in the moment. And once Kat had been with Mick, she'd realized he didn't measure up to her expectations. He wasn't good enough.

He'd never be good enough.

Kat had made that clear. Her look of disappointment as she'd told Mick he wasn't who she thought he was had been seared into his brain. A thousand times worse than the pain he'd felt with Elsi, Kat's rejection of him was branded on his soul. She didn't think he was the right one for her. He didn't fit that space in her heart, and he wasn't going to try and force his way in. He was done trying to contort himself to fit in, whether it was with Kat or his family. "What else was I supposed to do?"

"For starters, maybe stuck around long enough to tell her how you feel."

"I did!" Mick was shouting, but he didn't care. He was tired of being told he wasn't fighting hard enough. Wasn't doing enough. "I ripped my chest open and showed Kat my heart."

"Did you?" Mary-Kate asked quietly, the drop in tone more compelling than if she'd shouted back at him. "Did you really?"

The fear he wasn't enough crept up, burning in the back of his throat. Mick swallowed hard. It would be easier to give in to that fear, but he wasn't doing that anymore. Instead, he took a moment to sit with Mary-Kate's words. To really think about what she was asking.

To respond instead of react.

"You're right," he breathed. For the first time in all the weeks he'd spent thinking about this, a savage realization struck him. "I never said the actual words to her." He bit his lip. "But it's not like she said the words to me either."

"You do realize how juvenile you sound," Mary-Kate observed.

Ouch. Always nice to have your baby sister tell you you're acting like a child. "It may be childish, but it's true. And like I said before, she was the one who told me to leave."

"Did you want to leave?"

"Of course not."

"Then why did you?"

"Because she told me to!" The helplessness of that moment settled over him again. He'd left Kat's apartment on Christmas morning in a blur of hurt and confusion. And, if he was being honest, a fair share of anger and frustration. The entire drive home, Mick replayed their conversation over and over again. With every block he put between himself and Kat, the conviction he should have stayed gnawed at him a little more. He should have gone back to her apartment, gone after what he wanted— gone after her.

He turned back to his sister. "I didn't want to leave. At every red light, I thought about turning around, going back. Several times I almost did."

"Why didn't you?" Mary-Kate pressed.

Mick shrugged. "Each time I was about to yank the wheel, I heard Kat's voice in my head, telling me to leave. Telling me it was over." *Over? It hadn't even really begun.* "This conversation is going in circles," Mick said, growing testy. "I left because Kat asked me to. It's what she wanted."

"But what about what you wanted?" Mary-Kate pressed.

"Christ, MK, let it go!" She was like a dog with a bone, gnawing away at the wall Mick had struggled to build. "It doesn't matter," he said. "I'm not some asshole who goes around pounding on a girl's door demanding to talk to her after she told me to leave."

Mary-Kate's lip's twitched and Mick had the distinct impression she was imagining the scenario he'd described. "No one is suggesting you go all caveman on her, but you could have at least tried. I think all Kat wanted was to matter enough to you so that you would try." She set her pile of folded programs aside. "I think she pushed you away out of fear, but she hoped you'd push back. To fight for her."

Mick heard the echo of Kat's words in what his sister was saying now. "If Kat was scared, it's because she was worried about repeating bad habits. Making the wrong choices." *Choices like me.* The shameful weight of the truth pressed down on his chest, threatening to suffocate him.

"What are you talking about?" Mary-Kate blinked. "She even sent you flowers, Mick! And what did you do about that? Nothing."

"Those were a pity offering," Mick said. "Because she felt sorry for me. That's all."

"Oh my god." His sister let out a sound of disgust. "You always do this."

"Do what?"

"Think less of yourself and expect others to do the same. You don't think your needs are valid, so you do what everybody else wants. Even if it's not what you want."

Mick's jaw clenched. "Again, sorry for not being an asshole."

"You're kind of being an asshole right now," Mary-Kate shot back.

"Fine." Mick leaned back in his chair and crossed his arms. "What do you think I should have done when Kat kicked me out?"

Mary-Kate glanced around pointedly at their surroundings. "Well, you're sitting in this office because you finally stood up for yourself. How did that feel?"

"Pretty damn good," Mick admitted, "but it's not the same thing."

"Maybe not *exactly* the same. But you're the psychologist

here." Mary-Kate leaned back and mimicked his posture. "I think you know exactly what I'm driving at, so stop being so obtuse. Kat has a problem accepting when things aren't working out according to her expectations and you have the same issue, except in reverse; you're not willing to accept you are worthy of more. You need to be an advocate for yourself."

Again, the near identical thoughts expressed by both his siblings were too much to ignore. Mick could be stubborn, but he could take a hint. Eventually.

"Maybe you're right," Mick muttered.

Mary-Kate leaned forward, one hand held up to her ear. "What was that?"

"I said you're right."

"Damn straight, I am." His sister got up to leave but then stopped and turned to face him. "I'm not sure I should tell you this, because I don't think you deserve to know, but someone recently told me prying siblings are the best thing a brother can have, so consider this a favor."

Mick sat still, jaw tense as he waited for her to continue.

"Remember how Kat's friend got engaged on Halloween?"

Mick nodded. "Of course I remember. I was going to be Kat's plus-one." He frowned. "If she needed me."

"Well, the wedding is today."

"Today?" Mick stared at his sister.

"Yep." She nodded. "And I know for a fact Kat doesn't have a date."

Mick's mind raced. He'd made a promise to Kat that he would be there for her, but that had been before . . .

"Something else occurred to me about that night," Mary-Kate said. "Do you remember the song you chose to sing for karaoke?"

"Yeah." Mick stared at his sister, wondering what point she was trying to make now. "What about it?"

"Do you need someone to hit you over the head?" She rolled her eyes. "Dude, opportunity comes once in a lifetime."

Mick blinked. And suddenly it clicked. All of it. *One shot.*

"You said the wedding is today?"

"Yep."

Mick stood so fast he sent the programs flying. He cursed under his breath.

"Don't worry about those, I'll clean it up," Mary-Kate assured him.

"Thanks." Mick ran a hand through his hair. It was like a pack of wild horses had been set loose, galloping in chaotic circles inside his body, trampling his head and heart. He needed to rein everything in. Focus. One shot. The wedding. Right. "Do you know where the wedding is?"

"As a matter of fact, I do." She scribbled the address on the back of a program.

His sister handed him the paper with a sly smile and the realization hit him. "MK, you little stinker. You didn't need help with folding these, did you?"

A minute later, Mick bolted outside, gasping in shock as a blast of snowy February air smacked him full in the face. *Of course.* Of course, there would be a blizzard today. He dashed through the snow, thinking of Kat, who must be so pissed about this weather.

Mick finally made it across the street and located his car, only to discover he'd been blocked in by the snowplow. "Seriously?" This felt like some sort of passive aggressive taunt from Mother Nature aimed directly at him. He stared up at the sky for a moment, shaking a fist as the thick white flakes continued to fall. "FUCK!"

Now what? Mick rubbed his hands together, warming them as he weighed his options. He could dig his car out, but with the way his luck was going today, the moment he got it clear the plow would come by again. He could call an Uber or try and take a train, but the Heritage Center was all the way across town . . .

His gaze drifted toward the garage housing the funeral home's fleet of hearses. Mick closed his eyes and accepted his fate. There was nothing else to do, and he knew it.

Hoping the universe was enjoying a good laugh at his expense, he hurried back to the funeral home, sliding his feet through the slushy parking lot like he was skiing and hoping he didn't end up on his ass.

He stomped through the foyer, shaking snow from his shoes as he raced down the hall to the main office.

"Watch it, fucker!" Seamus cawed as Mick plowed through the door.

"You watch it," Mick said, his greeting affectionate, if brusque. He grabbed a key fob from a rack hanging on the wall. As an afterthought, Mick also nabbed Joe's coat that was draped over the desk chair. "Don't tell Joey," he said, blowing the sassy bird a kiss as he zipped out of the room.

Rolling up late to a wedding in a hearse in the middle of a snowstorm might not have been Mick's first choice for a romantic gesture—if that's what he could even call this—but it was his only choice. Firing up the engine, Mick pulled out of the garage and flipped on the radio.

It was time to own his moment.

CHAPTER 32

"Okay," Kat said, returning to the dressing room. "The grooms-men all have their boutonnieres, and the flower girls have their baskets of rose petals and are ready to go." She met Andie's gaze in the reflection of the full-length mirror and grinned. "Curt is a lucky man."

"Because his bride is so beautiful?" Andie asked, returning the grin from beneath the scrap of lace covering half her face. Rather than a full-length veil, she'd opted for something simpler, and her short, dark hair was tucked beneath a vintage pillbox hat. Simple or not, the overall effect was stylish and sleek, and decidedly Andie.

"That," Kat agreed, "and the fact getting married the day after Valentine's Day means roses will always be dirt cheap."

"I know," Andie snickered. "I told Curt he could look forward to a lifetime of being able to buy flowers and chocolates on clear-ance to celebrate our anniversary."

"I'm just glad you two will have an anniversary to celebrate," Julia said. She adjusted her own pillbox hat, which kept slipping loose from her mane of auburn curls. "My heart still hasn't recov-ered from that scare you gave us," she scolded Andie.

Two days ago, Andie had gotten cold feet. Ice cold. Colder-than-Lake-Michigan-in-February cold. Smack in the middle of her own bachelorette party, roughly forty-eight hours before she was supposed to be walking down the aisle, the bride-to-be had run full speed out of the restaurant and into the Chicago night.

"Same," Kat agreed. Between the Valentine's Day rush at the shop and the scramble to help track down Andie and convince her she wasn't making the biggest mistake of her life, Kat's nerves were shot. She lifted the satin trim of Andie's wedding gown.

"What are you doing down there?"

"Checking if you're wearing sneakers," Kat said. "If you're planning another runaway-bride moment, I want to know ahead of time."

Andie smirked, poking the toe of one shoe out. "Even in heels, you couldn't catch me."

"That's why we need the head start," Julia teased. "Seriously, though," she moved to wrap an arm around Andie. "If you change your mind again, even at the last minute, you know we'd support you."

"She's right," Kat chimed in, moving to Andie's other side. "For whatever reason, if you decide you're not ready to get married, we got your back." She slid an arm behind Andie and linked hands with Julia. "Jules and I will handle the fallout."

"Don't make me cry," Andie warned them. "I'll fuck up my makeup and this cut crease was a bitch to get right."

Cracking up, they crowded together in front of the mirror, grinning like fools at their reflection. Andie reached for their free hands, squeezing them in hers. "You two are more than my maids of honor. More than my best friends. You're my sisters. I want you to know nothing will ever change that."

Kat nodded, wanting to believe her friend's words with every fiber of her being. Despite her best efforts, she couldn't ignore the cold knot of fear in her belly. Life happened. Things changed. Her fears were valid, but she couldn't let them take over her ability to enjoy the moment. She needed to sit with her feelings, as Mick liked to say.

Mick. Her supposed plus-one. Kat released her friends' hands and stepped away from the mirror, crossing to the window. She gazed out across the parking lot, hope lying dormant in her chest. Mary-Kate had said that Mick always kept his promises. She seemed to think her brother was going to show up today, but Kat wasn't so sure. Personally, she'd never known a man to keep his promises and demonstrate actual follow-through. Not for her. So why should Mick be any different?

Because he *had* been different. They'd been different together. Mick had come into Kat's life right when she'd finally given up on the fairy tale of true love. Being with him made her want to keep dreaming. To hope. To trust that there really was someone out there meant for her . . . the one. She'd started to believe she'd found her person in Mick.

And maybe she had. Maybe Mick was the one.

But it wasn't enough if only she believed. He needed to believe too.

Kat shook herself.

"You're thinking about Mick right now, aren't you?" Julia asked.

"Nope," she lied. Or maybe it was a half truth since she wasn't only thinking about him right now, she was thinking about him always. Kat couldn't get him out her head. Thoughts of Mick kept springing up regardless of what she did. They were like weeds. No matter how hard she tugged and pulled and fought to remove one, more sprouted up.

Kat eyed the gray skies warily. Her gaze drifted east, toward the lake. "I'm thinking it's going to snow."

"Why? Is your left knee twinging or something, old girl?" Andie teased. "Relax, a little snow will be pretty. It will add to the ambience." Her smile was smug, as if she'd ordered the weather especially for her wedding.

"I hope so," Kat muttered.

"I know so," Andie said, joining them at the window. "And snow or no snow, Mick is going to be here tonight. You heard his sister. He promised."

"And if he isn't, you're still going to be okay," Julia said. "Because it means he wasn't the right one after all."

"Right." Kat forced herself to smile. Easy for Julia to say when she'd already found her one. "What about you?" Kat held up the bouquet Andie would toss after the ceremony. "Do I need to start planning your wedding flowers?"

"No way." Julia laughed. "Moving in with Luke was a big enough step for now. Don't get me wrong, I love him and want to be with him forever, but we're happy to keep things as they are." She shook her head. "We'll probably get married one day, but not for a long time." She chucked her thumb at Andie. "I'm not in any hurry to chase this one down the aisle."

The first notes of an Irish wedding song drifted in from down the hall, and Kat's heart leaped into her throat. "Speaking of, that's our cue," Kat said, fussing with the bridal bouquet one last time, checking to make sure the satin ribbon was wrapped securely around the stems.

Satisfied, Kat handed the flowers to Andie. "Ready to get hitched?"

Time seemed to go wonky after that, expanding and contracting in a soft-focus blur while the wedding party huddled in an alcove, waiting for the guests to finish being seated.

"Any sign of him?" Julia whispered.

Kat shook her head, not bothering to pretend she didn't know who Jules was asking about. So far, she hadn't seen any trace of Mick's scruffy dark locks.

Finally, everyone was in place and the ceremony officially began. One eye still on the door, Kat kept watch over the flower girls as they ambled down the aisle, sprinkling rose petals from their baskets.

Then it was her turn. Kat gripped her bouquet tightly, holding out hope with each step she took. She started making little mental checkpoints for herself. Hypothetical moments when Mick might appear. When she reached the front of the room and turned around, Mick will be there. When the groom is asked to kiss the bride, he'll be there. When Andie and Curt are declared man and wife, he'll be there.

But each moment came and went; all without Mick. Three chances, three strikes, Kat was out. It was over. He wasn't coming. Turns out her life really was *not* like a rom-com.

Despite her bitter thoughts, as the ceremony drew to a close and the newly married couple retreated down the aisle, Kat's heart swelled with joy. Her friend had gotten fucking married today! There was no denying Andie and Curt were perfect for each other. But even as Kat rejoiced in their happiness, she couldn't deny the creeping sense of despair. One of her best friends in the entire world was now married, and she had a feeling her other bestie would soon follow. She'd be left behind, single and alone and without Mick as a lover or a friend, because she'd screwed that up too.

The guests stood and crowded together, anticipation growing as Andie prepared to throw the bouquet. Kat was already feeling cynical, so she was not surprised at all when, shocker, Julia caught it. Despite what her friend had said about not being ready, Kat bet Luke already had a ring picked out. After all, Andie had been adamant she was in no hurry to settle down either, and now look at her.

When you know, you know.

Once the excitement simmered down and the guests began to disperse to the bar and buffet tables, Kat decided to go outside for some fresh air where she could continue her pity party alone. She pushed open the heavy door and was met with a frigid blast of February air. Kat blinked the snowflakes from her eyelashes. She'd been right. She *knew* it was going to snow.

The chilly air felt good on her heated skin, and the snow, falling fast and thick, was—as Andie had predicted—very pretty. Even though Kat dreaded snow anytime past Christmas, she had to admit, there was something magical about it. The air was different. The entire world hushed; its edges softened. Streetlamps became enchanted portals, snowflakes dancing in the beams of light like the wisps of a dandelion.

Swept up in the beauty of the moment, Kat stepped into the light of one such portal, closed her eyes, and made a wish. A heartbeat later, the soft crunch of tires on snow filled her ears. Kat opened her eyes and peered through the swirling eddies. Her pulse fluttered in her throat. She'd had her hopes dashed so many times tonight, and yet, she couldn't stop herself from hoping once more.

Was that a . . . hearse? The door opened, and Mick appeared. He crossed the parking lot toward her, and Kat knew he was real by the shadow of snowy footsteps trailing behind him. And then he was in front of her, sharing her little circle of light below the streetlamp.

"I'm here," he said simply.

But there was nothing simple about this moment. Kat glanced back at the hearse. "I thought you said you wouldn't be caught dead driving one of those unless you had to."

"Well, I guess I had to, then, didn't I?" The corner of his mouth lifted, as if pulled by some mischievous puppeteer. "I made a promise to you, Kat. And I wanted to keep that promise."

"Is that the only reason you came here tonight?" she asked. "A promise?"

The snow, already falling steadily, began to fall harder. Its heavy wetness clung to her hair and seeped into her clothes and skin.

"No, I came here for so much more than that." Mick slipped off the coat he was wearing and wrapped it around her shoulders. "I came for you."

His words slipped into that hollow space inside her, softening the rough edges. *He came for me.* Kat sucked in a shuddering breath, wanting to hold this moment tight, collect it like a shiny pebble and put it in her pocket to take out and touch whenever she liked.

"I was an asshole, Kat. I was a scared, jealous asshole. I was an asshole with low self-esteem issues and an asshole with a bit of an inferiority complex."

"Oh, shut up," she ordered. "Just shut up."

A goofy grin slanted across his face. "I think I've seen that movie. Is this where you tell me I had you at hello?"

"No. This is where I tell you to shut up. I don't want to hear you say 'asshole' again." Her lips quirked. "Also, you never said 'hello.'"

"Oh." Mick bent forward, touching his forehead to hers. "Well," he whispered. "Hi."

He was so close Kat had to dip her chin to meet his eyes.

"Hi," she whispered back.

Wrapped in his coat, with the snow swirling all around them, she felt like the world seemed to shrink to just the two of them.

"It's like we're in a snow globe," Mick said.

"A magic bubble," Kat agreed, her smile matching his.

"Kat, there's something else I didn't say. Something I've been wanting to say for a long time. Something I should have said before . . ." Mick trailed his lips over the line of her jaw, moving to the shell of her ear. "I love you."

"Oh . . ." Kat tried to say more, but she couldn't. Her heart swelled, the hollow filled to overflowing with a rush of love so tender and pure that it took her breath away. She looked up at him, knowing her heart was in her eyes but not caring, because she wanted to give it to him, wanted him to have it. "I love you too."

The grin he flashed her could have melted half of Chicago. Mick pulled her to him, wrapping an arm around her and kissing her softly. Once, twice. He brushed an ice-crusted curl from her cheek. "You want to get out of the snow?"

"Is it still snowing?" Kat murmured, gaze still locked on his. "I hadn't noticed."

Mick raised one frosty eyebrow. "Is that another line from one of your rom-coms?" he asked with a note of suspicion.

"Maybe." Kat grinned. Impishly. "Sort of."

"All right, then let's do this properly. What comes next?"

Kat thought for a moment. "Well, you already bumbled your way through an apology."

"Bumbled!" He coughed. "I don't recall apologizing."

"True, you just admitted you were an asshole," she teased. "Lucky for you, I happen to be irrationally attracted to assholes."

"Lucky me." He winked. "What comes after that?"

"You declare your love."

He kissed her brow. "Check."

"Then I declare my love for you."

He kissed her nose. "Check"

"And then . . ."

"And then what?" he urged.

"And then I suppose you should kiss me some more," Kat's mouth curved with anticipation. "On the lips."

"Ah," Mick said. Pulling her even closer, he wrapped his arms tight around her, and right before he pressed his lips to hers, he whispered, "Check."

He kissed her again and again. First soft and sweet, like snow-flakes on her tongue. Then deeper, longer, hotter. "Am I doing this right?"

"You know something?" Kat tilted her head back so she could gaze into his eyes. "As long as I'm with you, nothing could ever be wrong."

Mick's eyes lit up at her words, constellations twinkling in their depths. His smile contained an entire solar system. He bent his head to kiss her again, but Kat stopped him with a finger to his lips. "Actually, if this were really a rom-com, I'd be standing here in nothing but my panties and a shirt right now."

"In the snow?"

"Yep." Kat nodded. "Like in *Bridget Jones's Diary*."

His gaze shifted, tracing the lines of her body. "I wouldn't complain," he said in a horny whisper.

"Oh my god, you are such a weirdo." Kat gave him a playful slap.

"It's true." He reached up, trapping her palm against his cheek. "I am."

Kat shivered, enjoying the tingly scrape of his scruff against her skin. "Well, you're my weirdo," she said, pulling him down for another kiss.

Suddenly, light spilled across the parking lot and a burst of music floated overhead as a window in the reception hall was shoved opened. Andie, still sporting the jaunty little hat and veil, popped her head out of the window and yelled, "I TOLD YOU SO!" Then she blew Kat a kiss and disappeared back inside.

The window stayed open, music and laughter drifting down over them as the snow continued to fall.

"Did you want to go inside?" Mick asked.

Kat shook her head. She was warm and snug inside the coat Mick had given her, and the snow had slowed to a soft dusting that twinkled in the night air like fairy lights. "I kind of like it out here. Just the two of us in our snow globe."

"In that case," Mick took her hand, "may I have this dance?"

Kat laughed as he twirled her around. "Careful," she warned, even while loving every second, "I'm going to slip."

"Not a chance. I promise I won't let you fall." Mick pulled Kat in close and dipped her over his arm. "I've got you." A heartbeat later he lost his footing, sending them both tumbling to the ground.

"Ack, Mick!" Kat yelped as she landed on top of him. "Well, this is familiar," Kat said dryly.

"Yeah," Mick grunted. "Your ass is cutting off my oxygen. Only this time there are no dead bodies nearby."

Kat laughed. Shifting so he could breathe, she lifted her head and looked into his eyes. The deep brown gaze she'd come to trust. To love. She'd found him. Mick was her friend, her partner, her one. All those nights spent watching rom-coms with her friends, reading romances with Babcia, all the times she'd wished to have something like what was in those stories . . . Something like this. Right here. Right now.

"What are you thinking?" Mick asked.

She smiled, and in that moment, Kat's heart was so full it hurt. "I think I finally got my happy ending."

"Ending?" Mick's palms were warm on her cold cheeks as he pulled her face closer to his. "Princess, we're just getting started."

EPILOGUE

Kat

It was five minutes to five on Friday night when the chimes above the shop's entrance clanged dramatically. Laura strolled in, wearing one of the store's new T-shirts. Kat grinned. It had been almost nine months since the official rebranding launched, but she still felt a burst of pride every time she saw their logo.

Laura paused in the doorway to scowl at the array of metal bits swinging overhead. "Remind me, why did we think it was a good idea to dismantle Mr. Pokey and string up its corpse?"

"I like our little upcycled tribute to Allen." Kat followed Laura's gaze to the haphazard collection of pieces from the ancient coffee maker that had once haunted the back room. "Besides, it definitely beats the sounds that old dinosaur used to make."

"That's debatable," Laura grumbled.

"Hey," Ronnie said, popping their head out of the back room. "I don't hear you complaining whenever you fire up the new espresso machine." They eyeballed Laura's crochet bag. "Did you bring it?"

"Bring what?" Kat glanced between them suspiciously.

Ignoring Kat, Laura nodded and followed Ronnie into the back room.

"What are you two plotting?" Kat asked, scurrying after her mischievous business partners. Even if it wasn't almost closing time, thanks to Mr. Pokey's new life as a door chime, she wasn't worried about leaving the front of the store unattended. The second she entered the back room, Ronnie and Laura blew loudly on a pair of plastic party horns.

"Surprise!" Ronnie hollered as they held up JoJo. Nestled in her little donut bed, the hedgehog was sporting a crocheted birthday hat, complete with tasseled pom-pom.

"Happy Gotcha Day!" Laura cheered.

"Ah . . ." Kat hesitated, wrinkling her nose in confusion. She gazed at her spikey cuddle bug, contentedly munching on a slice of fruit. It was hard to believe JoJo had been hers for an entire year now . . . "Oh!" Understanding shot through her. "*Gotcha* day!"

Laura beamed and tooted her horn some more. "Exactly one year ago today, you became JoJo's adopted mama."

"And what a year it's been, huh?" Ronnie shook their head and set JoJo's donut on the break room table.

"That might be the understatement of the year," Kat agreed.

"Time for cake!" Laura announced, holding up a cake with a plastic hedgehog stuck on top. "I was going to have them make it in the shape of a hedgehog, but I thought eating that might be a tad grim. Have you seen the baby shower cakes that look like an actual baby?" Laura chuckled darkly. "That's some macabre shit."

"*Changing the subject*," Ronnie sang cheerfully as they lit the candle on top of the cake, "Kat, make a wish."

"But it's JoJo's special day," Kat protested.

"Gotcha Day is for both of you," Laura insisted.

"Besides," Ronnie added, "JoJo is very talented, but I doubt blowing out candles is in her skill set. Now hurry up and *make a wish*."

"Um, okay." Kat squeezed her eyes shut, but as she tried to focus on something to wish for, she realized she had everything she wanted. She'd dreamed of owning her own flower shop, and now she did; even better, she shared it with two amazing people she loved and respected. She'd feared she was losing her best friends, but now she cherished their time together more than ever. Over the past year, they'd faithfully kept up with monthly CCC nights, and having it only once a month made it that much more special. Best of all, there was Mick. Scruffy, messy, weird, and wonderful Mick.

Shit. Her eyes snapped open. *Mick!* "I gotta go," Kat declared.

"But what about the cake . . . ," Laura protested.

"I'm sorry, this is amazing and you're both so thoughtful, but I'm supposed to be at O'Sullivan's for a consultation."

"Fine," Laura grumbled. "Business before pleasure."

Ronnie snorted. "You know Kat's going to mix the two."

"It's a possibility," Kat admitted, matching Ronnie's teasing grin with one of her own.

"Then move over," Laura said, sliding in front of the cake. "I'm going to make this wish."

......

At O'Sullivan's, Kat found Joe waiting for her in the foyer. "Sorry I'm a little late . . ."

"Don't worry about it." He shrugged her off with a casual wave. "Mick's counseling session is running long anyway. As usual." He gave her a knowing smile, brown eyes warm and kind.

Over the months they'd been working together, Joe had become more than a business partner. More than a friend. In all the ways that mattered, Joe had become more of a brother to Kat than her own. He was family.

He'd stepped into the role so effortlessly that Kat wondered how she ever could have pictured more between them. It felt so strange now, the idea that Joe could be her Mr. Right. All the things she appreciated about him made him an excellent friend and business partner, but he was not the one for her.

A door opened down the hall and Kat's one-and-only appeared. She drank Mick in, parched soil soaking up fresh water. He had paired his usual faded T-shirt and jeans with a waistcoat, his compromise with Joe about dressing more professionally. Combined with his ever-present scruff and messy hair, the effect had a hot, disheveled-professor vibe Kat found irresistible. If they had been alone, she would have shown him exactly how irresistible.

Mick stepped aside, holding the door open for two elderly women who were chatting, laughing, and crying as they swapped stories about their husband like the best of friends.

"Looks like the session went well," Kat said under her breath to Joe.

"Quite a difference from the pair of widows your first time here," Joe chuckled, then composed his face and stepped forward to greet the women. "Ladies, if you follow me, we'll get started on the casket selection, and then Ms. Kowalski here will help you choose floral arrangements . . ." Joe paused and turned to Kat. "I'll see you in a few minutes?"

Kat nodded.

"Did you hear that?" Mick asked after the trio had moved on down the hall. "We have a few minutes." He clasped her fingers in his and tugged her toward the office.

The door clicked shut and he pressed her against it, lips soft on her neck. "I've missed you," he whispered, breath tickling the sensitive skin below her ear.

"I was in your bed this morning, weirdo," Kat reminded him.

"Mm-hmm," he kissed the grin tugging at the corner of her mouth, "and I've been thinking about getting you back in it all day."

Kat tilted her head to return the kiss but froze as loud smooching sounds erupted from across the room. She glanced past Mick to discover Seamus watching them from his cage. Kat giggled. "It seems we have an audience."

Mick sighed, muttering under his breath about cock-blocking cockatoos.

In response, Seamus resumed making loud, smacking kissy noises.

Kat snorted with laughter and soon Mick was laughing too. He leaned his forehead against hers, inhaling deeply, breathing her in like she was the most fragrant of blossoms. "God, I love you," he whispered.

"I love you too," she whispered back. They'd said the words to each other before—many times—but tonight something felt different. Kat slid her hands underneath Mick's vest and brushed her palms over his chest. His skin was warm and firm beneath the faded cotton. "Did you know this is the one-year anniversary of when we first met?"

"Actually, I did." Mick nodded. "Did you know on that very first night, I knew . . ." He paused, Adam's apple bobbing sharply as he swallowed.

"Knew what?" she pressed.

"I knew you were something special."

"Is that so?" Kat strained to keep her voice light and teasing while inside, her chest ached, heavy and tight, her ribcage a dam holding back a flood of emotion.

"It is," Mick insisted, eyes dark and intense. "And I know that what we have—you and I, together—is special." He wrapped his arms around her, pulling her against him in one of those hugs that made the entire world melt away.

Suddenly, like the petals of a rosebud unfurling and finding their light, Kat's heart bloomed. The weight in her chest shifted, and she sucked in a breath, realizing that *this* . . . this was the feeling her friends had told her about but couldn't describe. And now she understood why.

This moment of knowing, this moment of *right* . . . Kat couldn't possibly come up with the words to express the sureness that had settled deep into her bones. The certainty that she was exactly where she was supposed to be—with who she was supposed to be with. That night in the snow, she'd thought she loved Mick, believed he was her one, but now she knew. She lifted her gaze to his, the prick of tears stinging the corners of her eyes. *She knew.* She knew!

"Kat?" A crease formed between his brows as he studied her.

"Are you crying?" Mick brushed a tear away, his thumb a warm, rough tickle against her cheek. "What's wrong?"

"Nothing," Kat said, voice laced with still more unshed tears. "Nothing is wrong," she repeated, pulling him closer for a deep, lingering kiss, tasting the salt of those tears on her lips and his. But they were happy tears. Tears she'd hoped to cry for a very long time.

"Everything is exactly right."

ACKNOWLEDGMENTS

Too Wrong to Be Right is my fifth published novel. While this is not my first rodeo, it's certainly been the bumpiest. Life threw me off the horse many times during the course of writing this story, but I was able to get back on and keep going with the help of some wonderful people.

To my editor Jennie Conway. We didn't reach the end of this book together, but I appreciate the time and care (and patience!) you gave me and this story. I'm beyond grateful for starting my publishing journey with you. Warmest regards in the best ways.

To my new editor, Lisa Bonvissuto. Talk about diving into the deep end, huh? Thanks for encouraging me to keep swimming. Your bright energy and fresh perspective breathed new life into these pages, and I never would have stayed afloat throughout the process without you. How I continue to be so lucky with the talented people I'm teamed up with is a mystery, but I'm thankful for it and for you. You deserve all the cookies.

To my sweet, smart friends Lynne Hartzer and Erica O'Rourke, who gave generously of their time and skill as beta readers. Lynne, you're a brilliant editor with a sharp eye; thank you for the deft, kind care you take. Erica, your notes arrived in the eleventh hour, and your comments and insight on my story were exactly what I needed to push through. Again, I'm such a lucky bitch.

Special thanks to dear friend Christine Palmer, who sent surprise Grogu-themed goodies and nudged me with Monday-morning emails that said annoying stuff like "you have to write!" And thanks to the entire Palmer family, who, as the proud owners of three (yes, three) hedgehogs, provided a constant source of delightful hedgie content.

Blowing kisses to Rebelle Island and all the fabulous author buddies who share that special refuge. Special hugs to Alexis Daria. The book will be done when it's done, right? I hope you know how much those "babysitting" sessions we shared helped me get it done.

Shout out to my Reading Lushes group on FB, always there to share silly stuff, swap cocktail recipes, and help with things like names for a certain foulmouthed cockatoo (and an ex!).

To my husband and daughters. You are my heart and my home. Thanks for putting up with all the quirks of deadline mom, including that time I didn't change clothes for three days.

And finally, always, to my readers. Thank you for spending time with my characters. I hope this story provides an escape for a few hours. In these "interesting times" we live in, it's more important than ever to be good to yourselves. Embrace the things that bring you pleasure. Eat cookies. Read books. Buy flowers for people you care about. Buy yourself flowers. You fucking deserve it.

ABOUT THE AUTHOR

Heather Stumpf

USA Today bestselling author Melonie Johnson—aka #thewritinglush—enjoys sipping cocktails that start with the letter M. Declared a "writer to watch" by *Kirkus* and a "fizzy, engrossing new voice" by *Entertainment Weekly*, her smart, funny, contemporary romances include *Too Good to Be Real* and her award-winning Sometimes in Love debut series: *Getting Hot with the Scot*, *Smitten by the Brit*, and *Once Upon a Bad Boy*. She lives in Chicagoland with her husband and their two redheaded daughters. A former high school English and theater teacher, she now spends her days in her Star Wars office, dreaming up meet-cutes.